THE COMICS

AN ILLUSTRATED HISTORY OF COMIC STRIP ART

Hogan's Alley, R. F. Outcault, from the
colored supplement of The *World,* May 17, 1896.

THE COMICS

AN ILLUSTRATED HISTORY OF COMIC STRIP ART

by Jerry Robinson

G.P. PUTNAM'S SONS   **NEW YORK**

About the author

Jerry Robinson is the writer/cartoonist of *still life,* a daily panel of political and social satire syndicated by the Chicago Tribune-New York News Syndicate, and *Flubs & Fluffs,* a humor feature for the New York *News.* The victims of Robinson's irreverent wit are often the collectors of *still life* originals, among them, Henry Kissinger and Presidents Johnson and Nixon. *Flubs & Fluffs* is a visual parody of actual classroom incidents based on over a million reader contributions. Robinson has written several books and illustrated over thirty others. The most recent, a children's book, is *Professor Egghead's Best Riddles* (Simon & Schuster, 1973). He is a past President of the National Cartoonists Society and has won their coveted Reuben Award for the Best Syndicated Panel (*still life*), Best Special Feature (*Flubs & Fluffs*), and Best Comic Magazine Artist. Robinson is a Director of the American Association of Editorial Cartoonists. He was one of three artists selected to represent the United States at the Montreal Pavilion of Humor in 1965 and was honored three times at the Annual Humor Festival in Bordighera, Italy, receiving the prized Presidente Senato Medal in 1967. He is a Consulting Director of the Graham Gallery in New York where he produced *Cartoon & Comic Strip Art* in 1972, the first major exhibition of the cartoon arts at a private American gallery. He was instructor of graphic journalism at the School of Visual Arts for ten years, and currently lectures on *The Cartoon Arts* at the New School for Social Research. During the 1950's and 60's he made a number of N.C.S. tours to entertain the armed forces throughout Europe, Africa, and the Far East where he first noted the profound influence abroad of the American comic strip. While studying creative writing at Columbia University, Robinson started his cartoon career on Bob Kane's *Batman,* for which he helped create a number of characters, notably the arch-villain, The Joker. Born in Trenton, New Jersey, he now resides in New York City with his wife, a psychotherapist and former journalist and museum curator; and his thirteen-year-old son. A married daughter is a painter and graduate student in art history.

For Gro, Kristin and Jens

ACKNOWLEDGMENTS

My first acknowledgments are to those who urged me to write this book and gave valuable and continued assistance during the three years it has been in preparation: Walter Betkowski, editor of G. P. Putnam's Sons; Charles T. Kline, President of the Newspaper Comics Council; Arthur Laro, former President of the Chicago Tribune-New York News Syndicate; Toni Mendez of Toni Mendez Inc.; and my long-time friends and fellow cartoonists, Al Andriola, Lee Falk, and Howie Schneider.

So many others have contributed so much, I fear someone may be inadvertently omitted. If so, I hope their generosity will extend even to this.

I am especially grateful to my daughter, Kristin Robinson Murphy, graduate student in art history at the Institute of Fine Arts, New York University, for her long hours of expert research; and her husband, Serre Murphy, for his patient and invaluable editorial assistance. Special too, was the editorial contribution of Avonne Keller of the Comics Council who also answered innumerable requests with her usual diligence and charm, and Arthur Foulkes, who is responsible for the superb book design. The privilege of working with them made the experience of the book more rewarding.

Ernest McGee, a fine cartoonist of an earlier age, was an invaluable consultant. A.T. & T. must have profited as much as I from our long, long-distance conversations. He was most generous with his collection of early comic pages. Joe Willicombe of King Features Syndicate and Jim Logan, cartoonist-animator and collector, were unstinting of their time and knowledge. My thanks also to Steve Becker for his excellent book, *Comic Art in America*, and for his kind help and advice.

I am particularly indebted to Robert Graham and Georgia Riley of the Graham Gallery in New York for the use of the gallery's extensive collection; and Robert La Palme, Curator of the Pavilion of Humor, Montreal, Canada, for his personal assistance and use of the pavilion's collection. Jud Hurd, cartoonist and publisher of the excellent magazine, *Cartoonist Profiles;* and Jon Campbell, collector and student of the cartoon arts, were most generous and helpful. I am grateful as well to the Museum of Modern Art, the Brooklyn Museum, the New York Historical Society, the New York Public Library, and the Bettmann Archive Inc.

A special word of thanks to all my friends and colleagues in the National Cartoonists Society for their assistance, and in particular, President Bill Gallo, past Presidents Jack Tippit and Mort Walker, scribe Marge Devine, Sam Galy, McGowan Miller, David Pascal, and George Wolfe.

In this book I have used the work of many cartoonists now deceased. I hope this volume will help to perpetuate their memory and art. I am most grateful to many of their families for their kind assistance: Mrs. Dorothy Breger, Mrs. Dee Cox, Mrs. Rudolph Dirks, Mrs. Winifred Gray, Mrs. Reuben Goldberg, Mrs. Bert Green, Mrs. Vernon Greene, Mrs. Walt Kelley, the Winsor McCay family, Mrs. Emily Sokoloff, Mrs. Jesse Kahles Straut, Mrs. John Strieble, Mrs. Joan Crosby Tibbetts, Mrs. Caulton Waugh, Mrs. Marie Willard, and Mrs. Ida R. Zagat.

I am appreciative of the cartoonists who have given their time for personal interviews: Walter Berndt, Ernie Bushmiller, Gene Byrnes, Milton Caniff, Al Capp, Harry Devlin, John Dirks, Edwina Dumm, Bob Dunn, Jules Feiffer, Frank Fogarty, Paul Fung, Jr., Chester Gould, Harry Haenigsen, Harry Hershfield, the late Walt Kelly, "Tack" Knight, Russell Patterson, Fred Laswell, Al Smith, Otto Soglow, Morris Weiss, and especially to Mrs. Gretchen Swinnerton who was so helpful on behalf of her husband, Jimmy, one of the founding fathers of the comic strip.

My appreciation also to the artists who have personally made their work available: William F. Brown, Dik Browne, Mel Casson, Tony DiPreta, Irwin Hasen, Dick Hodgins, Jr., Burne Hogarth, Bill Holman, Allan Jaffee, Fred Johnson, Mell Lazarus, Dick Moores, John Cullen Murphy, Russell Myers, Frank Robbins, Hilda Terry, and Morrie Turner, as well as many previously mentioned.

Many others have been no less helpful: F. O. Alexander, Arthur "Bugs" Baer, Jr., Tex Blaisdell, Jean McCusker, Hy Eisman, Jim Ivy, Yasuhide Kobashi, Bob Naylor, Frank Reilly of Disney Productions, Lew Schwartz, Jim Sterenko, and Draper Hill, author of *Mr. Gillray, the Caricaturist.* Thanks are also due to the noted art collectors: Woody Gelman, Bill Hamilton, Jack Herbert, Richard Marshall, Abe Paskow, Phil Seuling, George Ward, and Art Wood.

Last but most important, I am grateful to the syndicates and publishers who gave permission to reprint their cartoons. Their complete cooperation made this book possible.

Contents

Preface

In this history I try to relate the newspaper comic strip to literary and artistic traditions; to indicate its relationship to other media, from the novel to the film, radio, and television; to suggest the social, political, and economic milieu from which it sprang; and to trace its origins, idiosyncratic development, and the impact on it of technology and syndication. While the focus is on the comic strip, the newspaper panel cartoon with which it is so intimately linked is also treated in some detail. The comic strip is an American invention, and while American cartoonists and their creations have dominated the art form, it has been adopted by virtually every country. Although this book is primarily a study of the American newspaper strip, some of the outstanding work from abroad is represented.

The unique blend of disciplines of the comic strip endows it with a visual-verbal experience of remarkable versatility. The comic strip performs one of literature's most important functions—to examine our mores, morals, and illusions. John Bainbridge called the comic strip the most significant body of literature in America. And it was Heywood Broun who credited the comics with constituting the proletarian novels of America.

The influence of the comic strip on American life has never been fully documented. More than 100,000,000 Americans read comic strips every day in some 1,700 newspapers. There are also more than 200,000,000 readers abroad in 42 languages and 102 countries. They experience the unique one-to-one relationship that the comics provide. Among the devotees of comics have been Presidents, poets, Supreme Court justices, novelists, and movie directors. They have included Franklin D. Roosevelt, Carl Sandburg, e. e. cummings, Oliver Wendell Holmes, John Steinbeck, and Charles Chaplin. Woodrow Wilson relaxed before Cabinet meetings by reading *Krazy Kat*. During the newspaper strike, Mayor La Guardia read the comics on radio to comics-starved New Yorkers. Conrad Aiken wrote: "I get fun out of the comics . . . I actually find myself dreaming about them and becoming part of their tapestry."

Cartoons not only reflect American life, but help mold it. William Bolitho described cartoons as the great and indigenous record of life in the United States. A renaissance of interest in the comic arts is indicated by courses of study in universities and museum exhibitions; among them the University of Brasília and the Sorbonne, the Metropolitan Museum of Art and the Louvre. The Graham Gallery in New York recently held the most comprehensive show of cartoon and comic strip art at a major private gallery.

Cartoons have set styles for whole eras in clothes, coiffure, food, and manners. Our language has been permeated with comic idioms, and some words have become so much a part of our speech that their origins have been forgotten: Hot dog!, jeep, baloney!, a Rube Goldberg contraption, and innumerable other terms. Our language has also been enriched by hundreds of onomatopoeic words, such as Zap!, Plop!, Pow!, and Voom! Foods popularized in the comics might make a gourmet shudder but not the average American: Wimpy's hamburgers, Dagwood's sandwiches, Harold Teen's sundaes, and Jiggs' corned beef and cabbage. Strips have been turned into Broadway shows, radio and TV series, movies, popular songs, books, records, and toys. And let's not forget the magnificent statue of Popeye erected by Crystal City, Texas, the "Spinach Capital of the World."

While I have screened thousands of strips in an attempt to convey the essence of each feature, at best only elements could be indicated. The comic strip is a living art form, in constant change, and the cartoonist, his creation, and the reader grow and evolve together in continuous interaction. The comic strip is meant to be experienced for a few seconds or minutes at daily or weekly intervals. This time element is an essential ingredient. The repetition and constant renewal provide a cumulative force of great power. A strip's rhythm is discernible only over many months or even years. Each episode is part of a larger work, a continuum without end. The examination of one strip is as inadequate to the appreciation of a comic strip as a "still" would be to the study of a film or as one painting to the understanding of an artist's lifework. With this limitation in mind, I hope this work will stimulate the reader to his own study of the comic strip in the context for which it is conceived, the daily and Sunday newspapers.

Cartoonists reflect the diversity of America, as do their creations. Many cartoonists have been immigrants or first-generation Americans. They come from coast to coast, North and South, city, farm, and village. They have been everything from engineers and journalists to circus barkers and preachers, salesmen and servicemen. While many were self-taught artists, a great number were serious art students and graduates of art academies and universities. Some lead typical suburban lives, and others have life-styles as lusty as their creations.

A last observation about the nature of that curious breed, the cartoonist. He is an artist with an acute sense of the ridiculous, a peculiar controlled lunacy that destroys social pretensions, sacred cows, and illusions; who is more sensitive to stupidity than most, with an instinctive feeling for universal human values and the ability to translate them into exciting narrative, humor and fantasy, with unique characters, loving and exasperating; and, most of all, he has an overwhelming compulsion to set it all down in pen and ink.

JERRY ROBINSON

New York, New York
1974

The daily page of comics of the New York *Evening Journal* from November 23, 1915.

A New Art Form

The transition into the twentieth century brought spectacular and profound changes to American society, changes that gave it vitality. It was the era of the Progressives and "Fighting Bob" La Follette; the bitter war against monopolies and trusts; Socialists, Suffragettes, and Society; Teddy Roosevelt; the Panama Canal; the Chautauqua; the *nouveau riche* and the American plutocracy; muckrakers, magnates, and Maxfield Parrish prints; the technological explosion; the wonder of the cranked telephone; the magic of electric light and the talking machine: with the fragile wax cylinder whirling, ". . . everyone works at our house but my ole man!"; Jack London, James J. Jeffries, and William Jennings Bryan; the horseless carriage giving way to the automobile; the miracle of moving pictures and the flight at Kitty Hawk. Above all, it was the era of European emigration of the Irish, Germans, Russians, Swedes, Italians, Catholics, and Jews—whose strange customs and accents were the delight of vaudeville comedians—all participating in the great, gorgeous, bubbling melting pot—the continuing American experiment.

This was the cultural stew that nourished a new American art form which proved to be of unprecedented vigor and longevity: the comic strip. William Laas in the *Saturday Review of Literature* observed: "The comic strip is one of the liveliest cultural offshoots of our slam-bang civilization." America and the comic strip were made for each other.

All the essential ingredients of the comic strip form were there, developing and evolving over centuries in many societies and cultures, waiting for the right combination of time, place, and cast. Two of the actors, Joseph Pulitzer and William Randolph Hearst, were the giants of the press, and their bitter rivalry proved to be the necessary catalyst for the creation of the comic strip.

The drama began in 1893, when Pulitzer bought a Hoe four-color rotary press in an attempt to print famous works of art for the Sunday supplement of his New York *World*. This effort was not successful, and the press was used instead to reproduce large drawings. Morrill Goddard, Sunday editor, strenuously advocated using the equipment for comic art. Pulitzer, already graphically oriented and with ample fortune to experiment, agreed. The best comics talents of the day were already contracted to *Judge*, *Puck*, and *Life*, so on the advice of *Puck*'s Roy L. McCardell, the inspired Goddard brought in R. F. Outcault.

Outcault, a graduate of McMicken University in Cincinnati, studied art in Paris and had a penchant for comic drawing. One of his earliest efforts was *The Origin of a New Species* in 1894. To burlesque current events, Outcault created *Down in Hogan's Alley*, the title adapted from the opening words of the song "Maggie Murphy's Home." The setting was the city slums, squalid tenements and backyards filled with dogs and cats, tough characters and various ragamuffins. One of the street urchins was a flap-eared, one-toothed, bald-headed kid, with an Oriental-like face and a quizzical yet knowing smile. He was dressed in a long, dirty nightshirt, which Outcault often used as a placard to comment on the cartoon itself. The last essential element, color, was still to fall into place, albeit accidentally.

While most of the problems of the color press had been solved by 1895, yellow ink did not dry properly and had a tendency to smudge. But as recounted by Don C. Seitz in his biography of Joseph Pulitzer:

> The pressman in charge, William J. Kelly, owed most of his experience with colors to printing block samples for George Mather's Sons, the ink makers. When his efforts were criticized, he replied that no one could print the wishy-washy color schemes that came to him in plate form; give him something solid and he would show results.

So Charles Saalberg, foreman of the color-press room, decided to experiment with a quick-drying tallow-yellow ink, turned to Outcault's page, and arbitrarily chose the urchin's nightshirt for the test area. That Sunday, a splash of pure, vivid yellow attracted every eye to Outcault's cartoon. The *Yellow Kid*, as he was soon known, was born and with him an indigenous American art form that is now read by more than 200,000,000 people every day, nearly 75 billion a year, making its authors and graphic artist the most widely read and seen in the world.

The historic debut of the *Yellow Kid* as the first comic strip has been previously dated by most authorities with *The Great Dog Show in M'Googan Avenue* on February 16, 1896. While it featured the *Yellow Kid*, it was not his first appearance, nor was it his first time in yellow, and it was not in the *Hogan's Alley* series, which Outcault reverted to thereafter. (During 1895, Outcault experimented with various locales, such as *Riley's Pond*, *Coney Island*, *Casey's Alley* and *Shantytown*, while shaping his basic concept and characters.) There were, however, several earlier *Hogan's Alley* cartoons with the *Yellow Kid* character. The first, on May 5, 1895, was *At the Circus in Hogan's Alley*, with the Kid seen in a blue nightshirt. This cartoon has the essential criteria to credit it with being the first comic strip. In addition to full color, it would be a *continuing series* with a *regular cast* (the Kid and gang), *title (Hogan's Alley), theme (life in the slums)*, and the *written word integrated into the drawing*. Later episodes gradually developed a profusion of messages on signs, posters, and the Kid's nightshirt, as well as *speech balloons*. Outcault also experimented with *sequential narrative*, instead of the one tableau, that was to become the characteristic structure of the comic strip with the *Katzenjammer Kids*. The next in the series was *The Day After "The Glorious Fourth" Down in Hogan's Alley* on July 7, 1895, with the Kid still in a blue nightshirt, followed by *The Merry Xmas Morning in Hogan's Alley* on December 15, 1895, with the Kid's nightshirt now a red polka dot. But on January 5, 1896, in *Golf—The Great Society Sport as Played in Hogan's Alley*, the Kid is first seen resplendent in the bright yellow that indelibly marked him for his readers as the *Yellow Kid*.

The *Yellow Kid* became the *World*'s star attraction. Incidentally, it also became the first commercial success of a comic strip character, comparable to the *Peanuts* phenomenon of today. The *Yellow Kid* soon appeared on buttons, cracker tins, cigarette packs, ladies' fans, and was even a character in a Broadway play.

The first of a historic series, *Hogan's Alley* by R. F. Outcault, May 5, 1895.

The battle for newspaper supremacy between Hearst and Pulitzer had begun the previous year when Hearst bought the failing New York *Morning Journal* from Albert Pulitzer, Joseph's brother, and began a series of raids on the staff of Pulitzer's *World*. The success of the *Yellow Kid* didn't escape the notice of Hearst. In his fight to win over the *World*'s readers, Hearst brought out the first issue of the *American Humorist* on October 18 of the same year, advertising:

NEW YORK JOURNAL'S COMIC WEEKLY—EIGHT FULL PAGES OF COLOR THAT MAKE THE KALEIDOSCOPE PALE WITH ENVY ... Bunco steerers may tempt your fancy with a "color supplement" that is black and tan—four pages of weak, wishy-washy color and four pages of desolate waste of black.

But the JOURNAL'S COLOR COMIC WEEKLY!
Ah! There's the diff!
EIGHT PAGES OF POLYCHROMATIC EFFULGENCE THAT MAKE THE RAINBOW LOOK LIKE A LEAD PIPE.
That's the sort of color comic weekly the people want: and they shall have it.

And have it they did, including no less than the *World*'s star, Outcault. Stephen Becker in *Comic Art in America* gives this account:

Hearst had bribed Outcault away from Pulitzer earlier in the year; Pulitzer had brought him back; Hearst upped the ante again, and Pulitzer had washed his hands of Outcault. Not, however, of the *Yellow Kid*, to which he still had a legal right. He hired George Luks, who later became a master American easel painter, to continue the Kid.

It was a time when, as Thomas Craven in *Cartoon Cavalcade* described it, ". . . artists were bought and sold like baseball players." William Murrell in *History of American Graphic Humor* described the ferocious struggle as ". . . a series of raids and counter-raids, injunctions and lawsuits by both Hearst and Pulitzer." Comics artists were in the enviable position of having Hearst and Pulitzer trying to outbid each other for their services. At one point, Hearst, in a raid that would have earned accolades from Captain Kidd, pirated the entire Sunday supplement staff of the *World*.

With two rival *Yellow Kids* appearing in the two rival papers, a new phrase in the American language and newspaper vernacular was born: "yellow journalism." The term came to symbolize the unscrupulous practices of the sensational press.

Paleolithic painting in the Altamira Cave, Spain.

Drawing of Egyptian God, Amon-Ra, with quadruple head.

Origin and Evolution

If we consider cartooning a means of pictorial communication, as well as an art, then surely it all must have begun in Paleolithic times with the scratches and simple, stylized drawings on cave walls, some of which may be thirty thousand years old. The grazing reindeer found at Font-de-Gaume, France, is a remarkable example. Far from primitive, it has a delicate line and excellent design. Undoubtedly the purposes of the earliest paintings were magical or religious, as well as to record and communicate. Prehistoric man and his children must also have found in them a measure of primitive visual delight. As James Parton in *Caricature and Other Comic Art* wrote: "Much as the ancients differed from ourselves in other particulars, they certainly laughed at one another just as we do, for precisely the same reasons, and employed every art, device, and implement of ridicule which is known to us." The caricature of man with potbelly and elongated nose, found at Tassili n'Ajjer in Africa, dating from 4000 B.C., must have enlivened the perilous days of those Stone Age people. Prehistoric man could draw thousands of years before man devised a system of writing. Visual communication needed no language or translator and was able to ignore the barriers of race and geography.

Egyptian, Greek and Roman Caricature

The Egyptians made extensive use of burlesque and caricature and were perhaps the first to picture animals to ridicule men and the first to satirize another picture in a cartoon. One Egyptian specimen shows a lion seated on a throne representing the king, receiving an offering of a goose and a fan from a fox, representing the high priest. On other papyri are found tigers carrying hoes, a hippopotamus washing its hands, and rats attacking a fortress defended by cats. The Egyptian artists and satirists imperishably recorded every detail of their social existence. Some examples of their satire were even executed in strip form.

Comic art and caricature also thrived amid the art of ancient Greece. Strangely, it was the Greek gods and goddesses that were most ridiculed. One pottery specimen shows a rude burlesque of one of Zeus' love adventures and a Hermes ludicrously gross and very unlike the agile messenger of the gods. The action friezes on Greek vases and buildings were pure narrative art. The fabled exploits of Hercules on the Parthenon can be considered the first picture story of the superhero.

The ancient Romans delighted in comic drawing. Even cartoon graffiti by Roman soldiers survive. Burlesque scenes of pygmies and dwarfs were a favorite subject of Roman artisans. Almost every house unearthed in Pompeii had some example. In common with many early peoples, the Romans had a childlike enjoyment of representing animals engaged in the labor and sport of humans. They frequently employed the device of placing animal heads on human figures.

Comic Art in the Middle Ages

Cartoon art and satire, religious and secular, continued throughout the Middle Ages. There were crude burlesque carvings on ecclesiastical architecture (those at the cathedral of Rheims were so obscene that later church authorities partly chiseled them away); oaken church stalls with comic carvings (a schoolmaster whipping the bare behind of a schoolboy, a monk caught making love to a nun, a wife beating her husband, monkeys wearing bishops' miters); painted panels with caricatures of the devil; richly illuminated manuscripts, the Books of Hours, the psalters and other church works, all ornamented with satiric or humorous drawings, some with caricatures of fantasy (hens with two bodies, one neck and two dog heads; and human heads, one a bearded man and one a woman, on animal bodies). The Bayeux Tapestry, an embroidered strip 230 feet long by 20 inches high, was a pictorial narration in color and legend of the Norman invasion of Harold's England by William the Conqueror; this monumental work has been called a remarkable precursor of the comic strip form.

As E. H. Gombrich in *The Cartoonist's Armoury* pointed out, the cartoonist ". . . makes it easier for us to treat abstractions as if they were tangible realities . . . [and] secures what language has prepared. The abstraction becomes an entity . . . [and] takes hold of our mind." It was the personification of abstract ideas that enabled man to comprehend such concepts as God, the Devil, death, the heavens and hell, good and evil, as well as the mythological world of Greece and Rome. This ability of the artist had much to do with the spread of Christianity and also the early belief in the ancient Olympians.

A section of the Bayeux Tapestry (William's army attacks the castle of Divan), a unique example of sequential narrative.

15

The Reformation and Puritan periods saw no diminution in the use of caricature. It was employed both in sympathy with, and in opposition to, reform. Caricature was encouraged and even sanctioned by the church. Martin Luther himself employed the art of satire, having a cartoon drawn for the title page of a pamphlet ridiculing a proposal of Pope Clement VII. He brought another cartoon from Rome, a parody of Sebastian Brant's *Ship of Fools*. It showed a ship filled with monks, friars, and priests, casting lines to the people in the sea while the Pope sat comfortably in the stern with his bishops and cardinals. Luther, as well as his enemies, made extensive use of caricature, executed with little, if any, restraint, making most political satires of today seem rather tame by comparison. For example, the Pope was shown in one with an ass' head. Another unique use of the cartoon was a Luther pamphlet of caricatures contrasting the humble Jesus with the pompous Papacy. A cartoon on one page depicting an incident in the life of Christ (Jesus washing the feet of His Disciples) was juxtaposed with a cartoon of the papal system (the Pope presenting his toe to be kissed).

Pictorial pamphlets and broadsides of caricatures were an essential part of the stock-in-trade of the booksellers who traveled from village to village. In many English examples can be seen the precursor of the "op-ed" page of varied editorial comment as in today's newspapers. The cartoonist depicted both sides of the argument in dialogue balloons streaming from the mouths of the principals. Sometimes the entire history of a controversy was reported in cartoon verse and prose.

Spayne and Rome Defeated by Samuel Ward was one of the most notable cartoon broadsheets published in the Puritan period. Ward, accused of reviving Spanish-English animosity, was imprisoned and persecuted for the work. It was engraved in Holland, which was then and for a century and a half after the printing house and type foundry of northern Europe. It is interesting to note that some of the Pilgrim fathers may have had a hand in its production. Some were engaged in the printing of such works, for distribution in England, while they were in Holland awaiting news of the *Mayflower*.

The reign of Charles I inspired a flood of cartoons as did the deliverance of the Puritan clergy in 1640. The careers of Archbishop Laud and the Earl of Strafford were satirized right up to their end on the scaffold. The Civil War, the Welsh (whose brogue was a source of comedy), Cromwell, the debauchery of the Cavaliers of Charles II—all were chronicled by the cartoonist.

With the accession of William and Mary, religion as a principal theme gave way to political and social concern. Queen Anne, the exploits of Marlborough, the conflicts of Whigs and Tories, Louis XIV and his vanities and mistresses, and new social and literary subjects engaged the attentions of the cartoonist, who ushered in a vibrant age of social satire.

The Rise of Social Satire

From the sixteenth century onward, numerous artists, most notably Francisco Goya and Honoré Daumier, took up graphic journalism in the form of prints and broadsheets. Goya's series of etchings, *Caprichos*, *Proverbios* and *Tauromaquia*, were social satire of the highest order, and his great *Desastres de la Guerra* is one of the most terrifying indictments of war ever created by an artist. Daumier, the master satirist of the bourgeoisie, was even imprisoned for six months for one of his political cartoons, *Gargantua*.

Three great English artists contributed to the art of social satire: William Hogarth, Thomas Rowlandson, and James Gillray. Hogarth won lasting recognition as a social satirist with his three magnificent series, *The Harlot's Progress*, *The Rake's Progress*, and *Marriage à la Mode*. Rowlandson's pictorial narrative in strip form, *The Loves of the Fox and the Badger*—or the

Honoré Daumier's *In the Theater*, "Robert, Shame On You. Let's Go."

16

Francisco Goya's etching from his epic series, *Disasters of War.*

Coalition Wedding (lampooning Charles James Fox and Lord North), published in 1784, utilized frames, captions, and balloons, and is certainly a prototype comic strip. Dr. Syntax in Rowlandson's *Tours of Dr. Syntax* was perhaps the first regular cartoon character. Fox was also Gillray's *bête noire.* Gillray depicted him with huge beetle brows, heavy jaws, and a swarthy complexion (strikingly analogous to Herblock's Joseph McCarthy in the 1950's). Draper Hill in *Mr. Gillray, the Caricaturist* credits Gillray with being the first master draftsman to take caricature as a primary occupation and shaping the simplicity of approach that is the essential feature of modern newspaper cartooning. Gillray produced nearly a thousand engravings of which his forty-odd satires of Napoleon Bonaparte made the most lasting impact, revealing the ludicrous aspects of the man with a comic fertility and scathing ridicule rarely equaled. Rowlandson and Gillray were particularly responsible for the increased use of balloons to indicate dialogue. The roots of modern cartooning can be traced to these satirical printmakers.

The first continuing cartoon character, *Dr. Syntax,* by Thomas Rowlandson, from *The Doctor's Dream.*

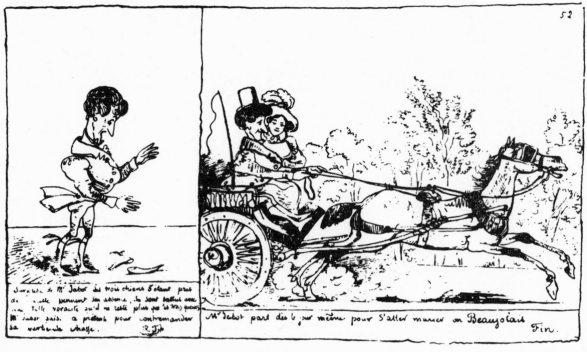

Rodolphe Töpffer's prototype comic strip, *Mr. Tarbot,* 1833.

— « Suivez-moi, dit le chien, vous aurez un sort égal au mien. Vous n'aurez qu'à flatter les gens de la maison, faire bonne garde. » A la pensée d'un tel bonheur, le loup pleure déjà de tendresse.

Excerpt from the nineteenth century *Image d'Epinal.*

Artistic Development

Numerous, varied factors were involved in the development of the comic strip form: the evolution of narrative art; the welding of story and picture; the technique of creating time illusion; the refinement of social satire; the impact of advancing technology; and the nature of man and his unique ability, alone among all the animals, to laugh at himself. The development was haphazard, often impelled by social, political, and economic forces, at times by individual genius, and, occasionally, by sheer chance.

The Picture Story and Time Concept

Rodolphe Töpffer is considered by some historians the inventor of the picture story, as he called it, and consequently the father of today's comics. Certainly he accurately gauged the power of the new genre, the blending of two storytelling devices:

> The drawings without their text, would have only a vague meaning; the text, without the drawings, would have no meaning at all. The combination of the two makes a kind of novel, all the more unique in that it is no more like a novel than it is like anything else.

Töpffer, a Swiss artist, educator, author, and teacher, devised the first of his picture stories in 1827 for his students. With the encouragement of Goethe, some were later published.

Töpffer described his picture stories as true "drama-in-pictures . . . with faces that are . . . alive: they talk, they laugh and cry . . . you have on paper a whole society with whom you can converse . . . if some of these partners are thrown together, a diverting scene can ensue; so you bring them together, add others, find the scene that went just before, devise the next; and there you are on the road to making a picture-story."

What Töpffer defined, of course, almost one hundred years before its realization, was today's continuity adventure strip. He may also be considered an ancestor of the cinema, the two art forms having a remarkable parallel development.

It is also worthwhile to note Rodolphe Töpffer's ability both to write *and* draw—a combination of talents that proved to be so important in the development of the comic strip. Indeed, the ability to conceive and execute in pictures and words is the essence of cartoon art. E. Wiese in *Enter the Comics* wrote: "With Töpffer's invention of the picture-story, the medium of graphics enlarged its resources: it appropriated from verbal language the property of developing in time, thus giving the visual arts a fourth dimension with a potential that was practically incalculable."

This concept of creating time by a chronological sequence of images proved to be the unique power of the comic strip as well as the film. One frame is essential to the next; each frame truly grows out of the one before and impels a further image as a result. The comics and their storytelling techniques had an effect on pioneer film makers. The cartoonist was always able to do his own editing and cutting to achieve the illusion of time and space—an art which remained for D. W. Griffith to introduce to the film. Griffith was also to revolutionize film technique with the introduction of the close-up, which the comic strip cartoonist had already developed as part of his bag of tricks. Contemporary film makers Orson Welles, Alain Resnais, and Federico Fellini credit the comic strip with influencing their work.

As Wiese points out, Töpffer completed the transition from illustration in the Hogarthian sense to the composition of an entire story in pictorial terms. The captions no longer carried the story, as in the *Image d'Epinal*, but became a subsidiary element. A new form took its place in the visual tradition.

Later artists contributed to the picture story genre, notably Wilhelm Busch and Gustave Doré. It was Busch who illustrated his own poems, one of which, *Max und Moritz*, was to be the inspiration for the *Katzenjammer Kids*. Doré, whose work has not been fully appreciated, was only in his early twenties when his epic series of 477 drawings in continuity form, *L'Histoire de la Sainte Russie*, was published in Paris. As George Perry and Alan Aldridge confirm in their *Penguin Books of Comics*: "Doré anticipated many of the techniques of the modern comic strip—the sudden plunging of action into silhouette, the use of speed lines to simulate movement, the juxtaposition of close-up and long-shot." His later series of illustrations of the Bible, the Crusades, and *Paradise Lost* are remarkable in their power, scope, and detail.

Technology

The introduction to Europe of printing in the fifteenth century made large-scale book publishing possible and began the evolution of the cartoon drawn for reproduction. Wood blocks or xylographs were first used in the primitive presses. One of the earliest specimens of a wood engraving is a cartoon depicting the endless conflict between good and evil in a frontispiece of *A Poor People's Bible*.

Johann Gutenberg's invention of movable type about 1436 enabled the woodcut to become integrated with the text, and the illustrated book became a new art form. Books were still only for the educated few. With the proliferation of printing in the sixteenth century came a form of mass communication, the broadsheets and public prints profusely illustrated with cartoon woodcuts. They informed the public of topics of the day, from crime and scandal to popular songs and politics. Speech balloons and labels in cartoons had made their appearance as early as the fourteenth century, and the frame technique appeared by 1600; both were basic elements of the comic strip. Newssheets were the forerunners of the modern newspaper, which evolved in the seventeenth century. The first in England was the *Weekly Newes* in 1622, and the *Gazette* made its debut in France in 1631. Thereafter the advances in printing technology in large measure dictated the technique and medium of the artist.

The later developments of copper engraving, etching, aquatint, and lithography in the eighteenth century again separated, for technical reasons, the illustration and text. The introduction of wood-block engraving resulted in the reintegration of the illustration, which had been relegated to the margin, with the text.

Direct chemical engraving onto zinc came about 1850 and line photoengraving in 1873. Color printing was achieved in the early 1700s, but it was not until chromolithography and the trichromatic process were perfected that color printing became widespread, ultimately leading to the color comics of today.

19

The first cartoon published in an American newspaper, "Unite or Die" by Benjamin Franklin in the *Pennsylvania Gazette,* May 9, 1754.

The Cartoon in America: 1754-1895

Benjamin Franklin was the first American cartoonist and the father of our humorous literature. As he observed: "Pieces of pleasantry and mirth have a secret charm in them to allay the heats and tumults of our spirits and to make man forget his restless resentments."

Franklin, along with Paul Revere, another early patriot of considerable and versatile artistic talents, drew cartoons of resistance to British tyranny. It was Franklin's drawing of a snake severed in as many pieces as there were colonies, with the motto "Unite or die!" that was the most effective symbol in urging the colonies to unite against the British. James Parton noted that Franklin's use of pictures whenever he desired to make a strong impact on the public mind was an inheritance from the period when few people could read.

Franklin was a writer and publisher. He conceived the federal postal system and became the first Postmaster General. In his varied career was born the association of cartooning with newspapers and magazines, which, incidentally, through the postal service enjoyed a new and growing audience.

As early as the administration of George Washington, cartoonists were commenting on and influencing public policy. Thomas Nast, still in his early twenties, gained his reputation as a cartoonist in *Harper's Weekly* during the Civil War. His later series, which destroyed the Tammany Ring and Boss Tweed, included the most powerful political cartoons ever executed. "Stop them damn pictures!" Tweed cried upon seeing Nast's latest attack. "I don't care so much what papers write about me. My constituents can't read. But, damn it, they can see pictures!" Nast turned down Tweed's offer of one-half million dollars to "study art in Europe" and continued his scathing ridicule. Ultimately, it was Tweed who fled to Europe, and in an ironic twist of fate, a Spanish official recognized Tweed from Nast's caricature in *Harper's Weekly* and Tweed was arrested and extradited. Tweed's baggage was found to contain a complete set of Nast's cartoons, except for the one which was to send him to jail. The symbols of the Republican elephant and Tammany Tiger and the American portrayal of Santa Claus were first drawn by Nast.

American political cartooning of the nineteenth century was for the most part confined to almanacs and satirical weeklies, such as *Leslie's Illustrated Weekly* and *Harper's Weekly*. The drawings were heavily embellished in the rococo style of the Gilded Age. The typical cartoon contained dozens of figures, complex backgrounds, employed extensive modeling and tone, and was loaded with detail. There was widespread use of satire with classical and Shakespearean allusions. The text was often integrated into the cartoon along with captions, labels, and balloon dialogue. The style was of European origin, as were most of the leading cartoonists of the day. Nast was

Bavarian; Joseph Keppler was Viennese; William Newman, who signed his work with the initial *N*, was British, as were the Gillam brothers.

While the first political cartoon for newspapers dated back to 1814 and occasional newspaper cartoons appeared throughout the nineteenth century, it wasn't until the 1870's that the New York *Daily Graphic* became the first newspaper to feature cartoons. Walt McDougall's "The Royal Feast of Belshazzar," printed on the front page of the New York *World* during the Presidential campaign of 1884, established the editorial cartoon as a regular feature in American newspapers. McDougall's cartoon, as well as the series *The Tattooed Man* by Bernard Gillam, was credited with defeating James Blaine and electing Grover Cleveland in one of the most bitterly contested of Presidential races. April 29, 1894, the Boston *Post* devoted its entire front page to the political cartoons of William (Norman) Richie. By 1906 there was a newspaper in every major American city, and the political cartoon proved an equally powerful force in local, state, and national politics.

Satirical journals and magazines of caricature began to flourish in the early nineteenth century and soon spread throughout western Europe. The cartoon began to divide into two distinct genres, the political and the humorous, and both were absorbed into the fabric of the new mass publications. *Charivari*, founded in Paris in 1838, established itself as the most influential journal of its time, publishing cartoons of the master satirist Daumier, André Gill, Decamps, Joseph Traviès, and others. *Punch*, originally subtitled the *London Charivari*, was founded in 1841, featuring the artistry of John Leech, John Tenniel, and George du Maurier. The year 1894 saw *Le Rire* published in Paris with cartoons by Toulouse-Lautrec, and *Yellow Book* in London with those of Max Beerbohm and Aubrey Beardsley. The German satiric tradition reached its zenith in 1896 with *Simplicissimus*, displaying the talent of Theodor Thomas Heine and of Olaf Gulbransson.

An English émigré, Frank Leslie, brought the graphic humor magazine to America in 1863 with *Budget of Fun, Jolly Joker, Comic Monthly*, and *Phunny Phellow. San Francisco Wasp, Punchinello*, and *Wild Oats* followed his lead. There proved to be a growing market for humorous literature and cartoons, nurturing writers like Artemus Ward, Josh Billings, John Phoenix, "Brick" Pomeroy, and Mark Twain; and cartoonists like Ed Jump, Dan Beard, Frank

"Let Us Pray" by Thomas Nast, 1871. Boss Tweed and fellow vultures waiting for the storm to blow over.

Bellow, Livingston Hopkins, and Frederick Opper. Comic lithography and portfolios were popular and widely published, notably those by Currier and Ives.

Joseph Keppler, a Viennese artist, came to America and founded *Puck* in 1877. It was *Puck, Judge* (1881), and *Life* (1883) that gave birth to a new age in American graphic and literary humor.

Frederic Hudson in his *History of Journalism*, published in 1873, wrote: "Our people don't want their wit on a separate dish. Wit cannot be measured off like tape, or kept on hand for a week, it would spoil in that time . . . no one can wait a week for a laugh; it must come in daily with our coffee." The humor in the some five hundred daily and weekly publications of the time was mostly in columns: *Sparks from the Telegraph, Flashes of Fun, Columns of Nuts, Sunbeams, Brevities, Twinklings*, and others. The more eye-catching visual humor, however, soon became dominant. Among the leading cartoonists were A. B. Frost, C. Jay Taylor, Palmer Cox (the *Brownies*), E. W. Kemble (*Blackberries*), T. S. Sullivant, Walt Kuhn, S. D. Ehrhart, Walt McDougall, James Montgomery Flagg (*Nervy Nat* in *Judge*) and perhaps the most admired and widely influential, Charles Dana Gibson. The cartoons were often illustratively drawn in a single panel with the joke captioned below. Their work, a mixture of accurate observation and a love of the ridiculous, elegant at times, crude and vulgar at others, secured the social satire cartoon as a fixture in American literature.

From the early 1880's to 1900 graphic humor was largely confined to the comic weeklies and monthlies. The popularity of comic prints by lithography houses waned. But, as we have already seen, in the space of a few years the history of American graphic humor underwent a radical change with the creation of the newspaper comic strip.

"Imaginative Animals" by A. B. Frost. *Life* Magazine, 1921.

"The Story of His Life" by Charles Dana Gibson. *The Gibson Book,* 1906.

"The Fake Blind Man," a prototype comic strip by F. M. Hutchins from *Puck* magazine, 1892.

by Milton Caniff

One day recently I drove past a house in which I had lived when I was ten—the site of my personal Ancient City where, years ago, I had built a metropolis along a dry gulch which edged the isolated dwelling in Redlands, California. My buildings were packing boxes of all sizes; the street vehicles and railway equipment were made from smaller cardboard containers, such as butter boxes. The nearby arroyos and canyons were choice hunting country, which my friends and I combed for used shotgun shells. The heavy caliber casings became men and the smaller gauges served as girls and women. The brass ends enabled the shells to stand upright.

Every activity in my city was fully manned and ready for whatever the plot line of the Saturday and Sunday story called for. My hero was a bold venturer named Tom Martin (a nonethnic label—editorial caution came early!). There I would act out the villains and the good guys and plot devices against the sinister elements.

Drawing *Steve Canyon* stirs up recollections of the city I built long ago. The full-time catalyst of my resident company is Steve Canyon himself. In time, he has taken unto himself a wife (following a goodly string of chicks in many parts of the world) and altered his life-style to conform to the accepted standards of home-delivered newspapers. When I move the focus to Poteet Canyon (Steve's onetime ward and kissin' cousin), another level of everyday life opens to the reader's eye. She is a newspaper reporter, a Libber, and a member of the singles' world so often in the news of the day. Leighton Olson (son of Steve's wife, Summer, by an earlier marriage) leads me in that turbulent area of the college set whose members work so hard at being identified by conformity.

After myriad devices to hold circulation in the competitive newspapers of the past, the hang-'em-on-the-cliff story cartoons are the only remains of the technique which sought to force the reader to come back the next day to learn what happened to the characters he has come to love or hate.

In a real sense we involve the reader as much as an audience participation show in the theater or on television. Our reader loyalty is less overt, but has a longer life expectancy. People never forget the first cartoon which broke through their consciousness.

My task is to combine the pleasures of yesterday with the expectations of tomorrow and serve it up as the ten-cent black-and-white special available today. On Sunday, of course, there is color—for a slightly higher price.

★ ★ ★

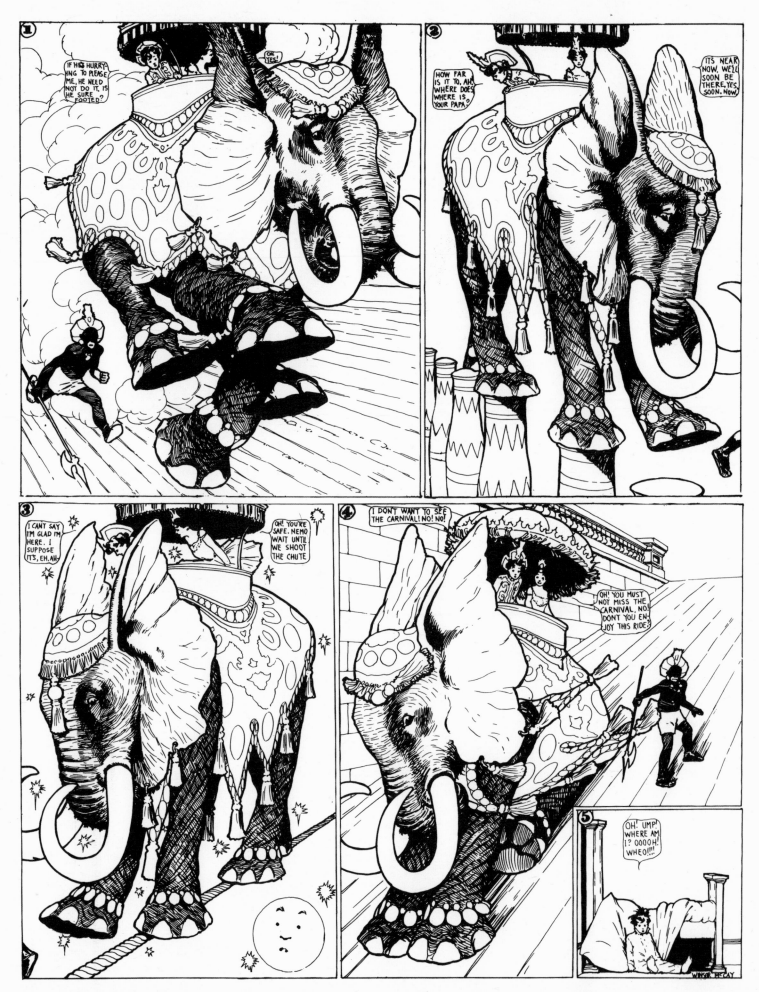

Winsor McCay's *Little Nemo in Slumberland. A* rare combination of artistry and imagination. 1906.
This print by permission of the McCay family.

The Formative Years: 1896-1910

Once the *Yellow Kid* proved that comics sold newspapers, the basic structure of the profession was born. The cartoonist found the mass audience on which his art thrives, and the publishers found the circulation builders they needed.

Hearst had visited Europe as a boy and brought back a collection of Wilhelm Busch's *Max und Moritz*, the illustrated adventures of two young pranksters. Either Hearst or his comics editor, Rudolph Block, suggested that a staff artist, Rudolph Dirks, then only twenty, develop a new strip based on the German work. The *Katzenjammer Kids* (German slang for "hangover"—literally, "the yowling of cats") was the result. The demoniac kids, Hans and Fritz, who tor-

mented Momma, der Captain, and der Inspector with their antics, made their debut on December 12, 1897. Dirks, like Outcault, employed a permanent cast of characters, and consistently used the frame sequence instead of one large panel. (Outcault had used frames in several sequences.) Dirks' characterizations were drawn in greater depth than before; stereotyped though they may have been, the principals were involved in the stories rather than merely participating in events. Dirks soon expanded the use of balloons. He found that the addition of the bizarre German dialect, for which he had a genius, greatly enhanced the humor. The balloon proved to be an invaluable device; it revealed the character's mind with the thought bal-

Max und Moritz by Wilhelm Busch, 1865.

loon, enabling the inanimate to speak, giving voice to offstage characters, and, most important, enhancing the illusion of immediacy. Balloon dialogue has become a standard fixture of almost all strips since that time. The evolution of the Sunday color comic strip was complete.

For sixty years, in fact, there have been two Hanses and two Fritzes committing their mayhem each week. In 1912, after a contractual dispute, Dirks left the *Journal* for the *World*. What followed was in large measure a replay of the 1896 charade: lawsuits, injunctions, appeals, and reversals. The *Journal* finally retained the rights to the title of the strip with the original characters. Dirks won the right to draw the same characters but under a different title. The case established an important precedent for the cartoonist: His characters, if not the title, are as much his own as his signature. The *Katzenjammer Kids* resumed with H. H. Knerr who previously drew the imitative *Die Fineheimer Twins* (with Uncle Louie, Jakey *und* Johann in place of the Captain and the Kids). Dirks retitled his version *Hans und Fritz*, later changed to the *Captain and the Kids* because of the anti-German sentiment engendered by World War I. Several unabashed imitations of the *Kids,* also in dialect, were to follow, such as *Dinklespiels* by George V. Hobart and Harry J. Westerman (with the kids, Louie and Rosie), and *Dem Boys* (Max and Chulus), which, with some discretion, was unsigned.

Captain and the Kids by Rudolph Dirks, 1938. After forty years of mischief, still going strong.
© United Feature Syndicate, Inc.

Rudolph Dirks' self-caricature with cast.

Dirks died in 1968. His son, John, a noted sculptor, graduate of Yale University, attended the Art Students League before assisting his father on the strip, which he has carried on alone since 1956. Knerr died in 1949. Joe Musial, a multitalented cartoonist, writer, and editor, who has ghosted such strips as *Popeye, Barney Google, Tillie the Toiler*, and *Pete the Tramp*, has drawn the *Katzenjammer Kids* since 1956.

There is much merit in the argument that Jimmy Swinnerton, rather than Outcault, was the real father of the comic strip. His *Little Bears* started in 1892, had a permanent cast of characters (although they were not always individually identifiable), and it appeared regularly. Swinnerton, however, did not consistently use either the frame sequence or balloon dialogue. Each page was generally a collection of individual thematic drawings of the amusing antics of the bears.

However, there is no question that Swinnerton, along with Outcault and Dirks, was one of the true pioneers of the comic strip form, no matter how students of the art may date its final crystallization.

At fourteen, Swinnerton enrolled in the San Francisco Art School and the same year started to work for Hearst's San Francisco *Examiner* at $10 a week. The *Little Bears* developed from his bear character that first appeared with the daily weather story in 1891. When Swinnerton moved to New York in 1899, the feature became *Little Bears and Tigers* (the tiger, after the New York Democratic symbol, the Tammany Tiger). During this fertile period he also created *Mount Ararat, Mr. Batch, Professor Noodle*, and *Sam Laughed*. In 1905 he started *Little Jimmy*, which ran for fifty-one years. However, he contracted tuberculosis and in 1903 was forced to move to Arizona, a place he liked so much "I forgot to die." That the climate restored his health is a master bit of understatement. Swinnerton had been living in retirement since 1965 until his death in August, 1974. *Little Jimmy* ran as a daily until 1937 and as a Sunday page, with *Mr. Jack* as its supplementary feature, until 1958, except for the years 1941–45. In 1938 he created *Bar None Ranch* and in 1941 *Rocky Mason, Government Agent.*

Swinnerton's love of the West and its Indian lore led to his creation of the *Canyon Kids*, a monthly page in line, wash, and color, which appeared in *Good*

Housekeeping magazine for forty-two years. He was also a fine easel painter, and his oils and watercolors of the desert, Indians, and Western landscapes are in numerous museums and collections.

Little Jimmy, in contrast with most newspaper art of the time, was drawn with a clean-cut line and quiet simplicity. The minute figures of Jimmy and the other children scampering among the towering adults, and set against the horizontal lines of the Western landscape, had a unique charm and evoked the mysterious stillness of the desert.

A montage of characters by Jimmy Swinnerton from a half century of creativity. Mr. & Mrs. Swinnerton appear in lower right.

Little Jimmy by Swinnerton with *Mr. Jack* as the top feature.
© 1926 International Features Service, Inc.

So rapidly did the comics become a fixture in newspapers that by December, 1900, the *World* ran a full-page tribute to the comics under the heading: GRAND CONGRESS OF A GALAXY OF WIT & HUMOR BY WAY OF CELEBRATION. In this montage of comics and portraits of their creators were the *Yellow Kid*, "the most popular humorous creation of the century," *The Fluffy Duff Sisters* and *The Silhouettes* by J. K. Bryans, *The Roly Polys* by Paul West, "one of the World's Greatest Successes," *Father Goose* by W. W. Denslow, and others. In the text announcing the increase of the Funny Side (the comics section) to eight pages, the *World* pointed with pride to:

> . . . the greatest comic creations of the last decade, the things that have made you laugh not only once, but watch for them week after week. In them, from the Brownies to the latest invention you see what you have laughed at for years. That the *Sunday World* has been responsible for many of them—in fact, the great majority—you will admit after you have looked at them. Under the able directorship of Hon. George W. Peck the Funny Side will doubtless furnish you with many more surprises.

Dutch artist Gustave Verbeck created *The Upside Downs* in 1903, a series of ingenious drawings that were read right side up and then continued upside down. In *The Terrors of the Tiny Tads* Verbeck conceived a world of unique wildlife such as the Hippopatamusket and the Eleganteeter.

Alphonse and Gaston by Frederick Opper.

Immigrant and racial themes were the basis for much of the humor at the turn of the century. It was the time of Lew Dockstader's black minstrels and the German dialect of Weber and Fields. The comic strips were not immune. In fact, quite the opposite.

Many of the first wave of strip cartoonists were themselves immigrants or first-generation Americans. Dirks was born in Germany. Frederick Burr Opper, son of an Austrian immigrant, created three notable strips: *Happy Hooligan* in 1899, *And Her Name Was Maud* and *Alphonse and Gaston* in 1905. Happy was a clownlike character with limitless good nature, the eternal fall guy. A pathetic and ludicrous figure, with a tin can for a hat, he was the butt of his own good intentions that unfailingly backfired. He proved to be a classic type in the comics, subsequently refined, with variations, in dozens of strips. Stylistically *Happy*

Opper's *Happy Hooligan* drawn seven years before his death in 1937 (excerpt).
© International Feature Service, Inc.

And Her Name Was Maud by Opper, 1906. Maud got a kick out of everything.

Hooligan was effective: He had a round head with an enormous upper lip; the backgrounds were simple; and the accent was on visual action. *Hooligan* ran for twenty-five years, and as the New York *Times* said, "He never lost his tin-can hat or his healthy vulgarity."

Maud was a mule, and the strip was an endless variation on a theme: Maud's revenge. A triphammer kick of Maud's hind legs blasted the victim clear out of the last panel. *Alphonse and Gaston*, however, had more lasting impact. The pair became the symbol of absurdly overdone courtesy. "After you, my dear Alphonse. . . . No, after you, my dear Gaston" became one of the first of innumerable phrases and words that the comics were to contribute to the American idiom. Another creation was *Howson Lotts*, one of the earliest satires on suburban life.

An artist of unusual talent and versatility, Opper was also a noted editorial cartoonist. Like most cartoonists of the day, Opper was a staff artist on a newspaper. He drew one, sometimes two or three, of his features every Sunday for the New York *American* and *Journal*. As Coulton Waugh describes it in *The*

Comics: "If Opper got an idea for one of his characters, he drew that for the next Sunday. Thus he juggled *Happy Hooligan*, *Maud*, and *Alphonse and Gaston*, often combining them, and sometimes, in a playful mood, introducing characters from other staff artists' work." Most cartoonists of this period created many features, tested and developed them, often to find them too limiting in theme or without wide appeal, or in some cases they simply tired of the strip and went on to a new inspiration. Along the way, one idea would jell and perhaps gain a wide following for a time. Even then, the feature might be dropped for another brainstorm. Newspaper space was available to try out new strips; there were often three or more competing papers in the large cities, and the investment to launch a new property was still modest. This fluid situation had much to do with the first burst of remarkable creativity in the new medium. While the later syndication of strips ensured tremendous readership and brought fortunes to their creators, it gradually restricted this freewheeling productivity of the early cartoonists.

Buster Brown with Tige by R. F. Outcault.

After interest in the *Yellow Kid* subsided, Outcault experimented with *Lil' Mose* and *Buddy Tucker*. In 1902 he created another strip that caught the public's imagination: *Buster Brown*. Buster's personality became the ideal for America's childhood. The model for Buster's talking bulldog, Tige, was Outcault's own dog. Soon it seemed that everyone's kid was called Buster, and his dog, Tige. *Buster Brown* became synonymous with the style of his collar, and a generation of boys was dressed in the Buster Brown outfit: sailorlike cap, huge white collar with large bow tie, long belted jacket, above-the-knee knickers, and button shoes. An inventive promoter, as well as an artist, Outcault set up a booth at the St. Louis Exposition in 1904 and sold the commercial rights to *Buster Brown*. Buster was used to advertise everything from children's shoes and hats to cigars and whiskey!

In what was a bizarre replay of his *Yellow Kid* experience, Outcault left Hearst's *American*. Hearst bought him back, this time from James Gordon Bennett's *Herald*. The result was that, just as there once were two *Yellow Kids*, in 1906 there were two *Buster Browns,* one in the *American* and one in the *Herald*. Buster's cartoon life ended in 1926. Outcault was sixty-five when he died in 1928.

An excerpt from an early *Buster Brown* Sunday page circa 1906. The aphorism in the last panel was standard.

32

Outcault's *Lil' Mose* was a sympathetic portrayal of the black for its time
and the first strip with a black as its principal character, from the New York *Herald,* 1901.

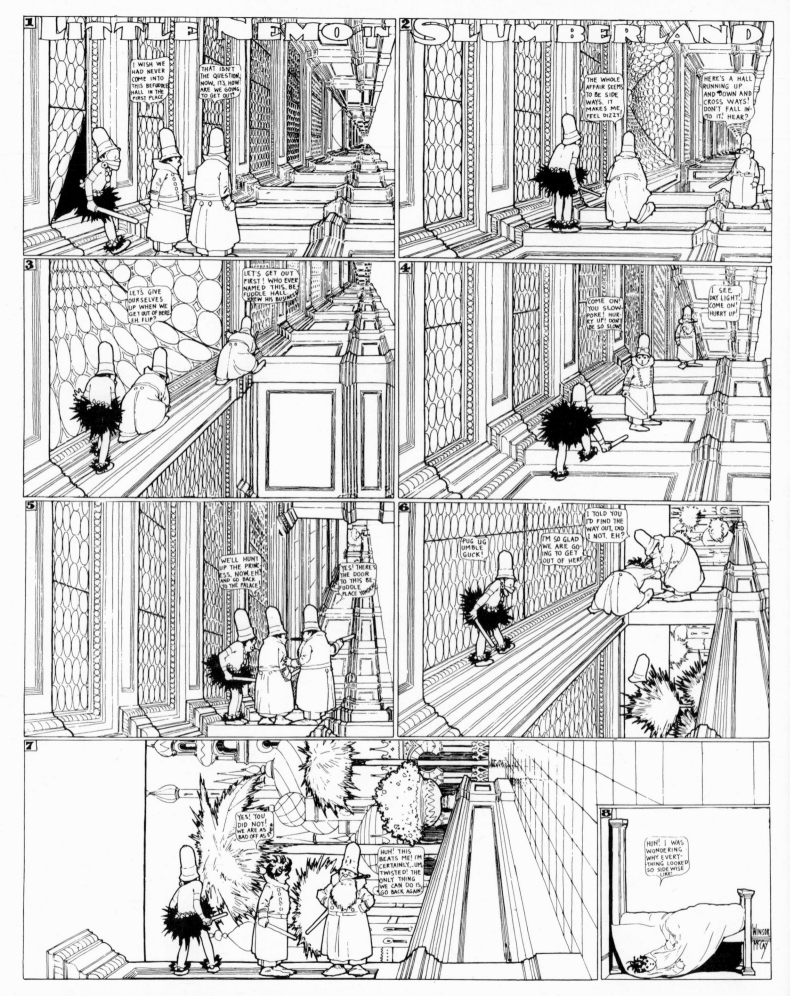

Little Nemo in Slumberland, 1908. A fine example of
Winsor McCay's artistic wizardry in spatial fantasy.
This print by permission of the McCay family.

A world of magic, dreams, and whimsy, enhanced by a superb craftsmanship that some think has not been equaled in the comics since, appeared in 1905: *Little Nemo in Slumberland* by Winsor McCay. Each of Nemo's weekly adventures was a story of the dream of a tousle-haired boy of about six that concluded with his waking up or falling out of bed (reminiscent of the back-to-reality ending of *Alice's Adventures in Wonderland*). His dream world was peopled by Flip, a green-faced clown in a plug hat and ermine-collared jacket; a cannibal; a certain Dr. Pill; and a vast array of giants, animals, space creatures, queens, princesses, and policemen. There were sky bombs, wild train and dirigible rides, exotic parades, bizarre circuses, and festivities of all kinds in Byzantine settings and rococo landscapes. In other words, just the dreams a small boy would like to have. McCay was a master of scale. His unique use of perspective transformed the two-dimensional picture plane into an illusion of vast size and space. A. Hyatt Mayor, of the Metropolitan Museum of Art in New York, pointed out that McCay's cities in some episodes were previsions of cities that were not to rise in actual steel for another half century. John Canaday, art critic for the New York *Times,* saw the pattern of McCay's drawings as pure *art nouveau* and the extreme fantasy as predating surrealism's formalization.

Dream of the Rarebit Fiend (excerpt), 1906, by Silas (Winsor McCay).

Dr. Pill on an urgent house call in a *Nemo* nightmare.
Excerpt. from a 1906 episode. This print by permission of the McCay family.

McCay's son Robert was Nemo's model. *Nemo* ran from 1905 to 1912 and from 1924 to 1927. In 1947 Robert revived the strip for a time, restoring many of the original drawings.

McCay experimented with a number of strips—*Little Sammy Sneeze, Dream of the Rarebit Fiend* under the pseudonym Silas, *Hungry Henriette, Tales of Jungle Imps,* and *Poor Jake*—before the inspiration of Nemo. In 1909 he created *Gertie the Dinosaur,* the first commercially successful animated cartoon. He did ten thousand separate drawings for Gertie! Thus McCay pioneered two new art forms, the comic strip and the animated film.

A post World War I political cartoon
by the versatile Winsor McCay.
This print by permission of the McCay family.

The comics quickly spread throughout the country, and by 1906 syndicates were already in competition. Hundreds of cartoonists were trying to satisfy an insatiable demand for the new funnies. Even small-town newspapers were running weekly comic supplements in full color—they also had circulations to build. There proved to be a reservoir of comics talent in the country. The first generation of comics artists, mostly self-taught, many of them political or magazine cartoonists, found the new medium a perfect vehicle for the lusty American humor. Some titles of early strips give a clue to their subjects: *Billy the Bellboy, Big Chief Simon, Mr. Grouch and His Wife, Alex the Cop, Little Ah Sid the Chinese Kid, Yanitor Yens Yenson, Lazy Lew, Sammy Small, Circus Solly.*

Gertie the Dinosaur, a still from McCay's pioneer animated film in 1909.

Charles Kahles, one of the most inventive of the pioneer cartoonists, created several Sunday features that constituted firsts in the rapidly expanding medium. The most important was *Our Hero's Hairbreadth Escapes* (1906), which became *Hairbreadth Harry, the Boy Hero* and, after a few years, simply *Hairbreadth Harry*. It marked a radical departure in comics structure. Instead of a distinct ending each week, usually a gag, some weeks a suspense situation was created for the following episode. The device extended the story potential. The cliffhanger, the final panel of impending danger, proved to be a valuable circulation builder and an essential technique in the modern adventure strip, as well as in the movie serial which it predated by several years.

The daily *Hairbreadth Harry*, begun in 1923, would end in such reader teasers as ". . . calm yourself—Yes! We've gotta suspend our suspense till tomorrow," ": . . . tomorrow may unscrew the inscrutable," and "Cheer up! Tomorrow we'll clear up this baffling mystery! Positively! Ab-so-lute-ly!" The full potential of the new form of story continuity was not to be realized until the advent of the adventure strip in the late 1920's.

Hairbreadth Harry was a burlesque of the dime novel and theater melodrama. Our Hero Harry rescued the Beautiful Belinda from her first buzz saw in 1907. Originally, Harry was much shorter than Belinda Blinks, the Beautiful Boiler Maker, but by 1916 Harry had grown into a mature movie hero type and they

Excerpt from *Billy Bounce*. *"Billy takes the Bunch to the World's Fair"*
by C. W. Kahles, 1904.

became true sweethearts. For thirty-three years he continued to save her from the clutches of that dastardly rogue, Relentless Rudolph. Rudolph became the prototype villain in top hat and tails, evilly curling his mustache and flashing his sparkling incisors. After Kahles' death, the feature was carried on for eight year by F. O. Alexander. Alexander later had a distinguished career as an editorial cartoonist for the Philadelphia *Bulletin* until his retirement in 1967.

Kahles also created the first police strip, *Clarence the Cop*, which ran from 1900 to 1909. Clarence was hardly a model of law enforcement; his bumbling kept getting him transferred to remote beats on Staten Island or the Gowanus Canal. ("Oi wonder what they sint me way at here fer?") *Sandy Highflyer*, another of his creations, ran from 1902 to 1903 and was the first in a long line of aviation strips. Sandy's flights, preceding

those of the Wright brothers, were in a flying motorboat suspended from a sausage-shaped balloon.

Born in Bavaria, Kahles was reared in New York and studied art at Pratt Institute and the Brooklyn Art School. His consuming ambition was to be a painter, but his first job at age sixteen as staff artist on the New York *Recorder* led to one of the most prolific careers in cartooning. His prodigious output included twenty strips between 1900 and 1916, in addition to cartoons for *Life* and *Judge*. At one time he did seven weekly strips simultaneously: *Billy Bounce*, *Clumsy Claude*, *The Teasers*, *Pretending Percy*, *Mr. Butt-In*, *Clarence the Cop*, and *The Yarns of Captain Fibb*. Billy Bounce, who was a precursor of the comic book *Super-boy*, wore an inflated rubber suit and bounced his way in and out of trouble.

Hairbreadth Harry in "Held by the Enemy" (excerpt).
C. W. Kahles' classic melodrama drawn shortly before his death in 1931.

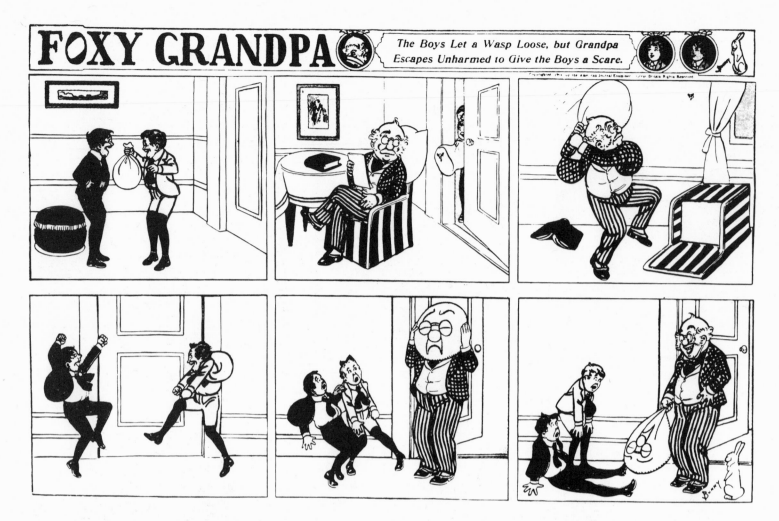

Foxy Grandpa by Charles (Bunny) Schultze, 1904 (excerpt). A twist to the
Katzenjammer Kids theme. Grandpa upstages the kids.

A great number of cartoonists and strips were
enormously popular in the period from 1900 to 1910.
Some were *Foxy Grandpa* by Charles "Bunny"
Schultze, *Wags, the Dog That Adopted a Man* by
William F. Marriner, *The Monkeyshines of Marseleen*
by Norman Jannett, *Latest News from Bugville* by Gus
Dirks and later Paul Branson, *Percy the Robot* and
Prince Errant by Cornell Greening, *Oliver's Adven-
tures* and *What Little Johnny Wanted—And—* by Gus
Mager, *Phyllis in Love* by Gene Carr, *Petey Dink* by
Charles Voight, *The Kid* by Follett, *Pups* by William
Steinigans, *The Naps of Polly Sleepyhead* by Peter
Newell, a precursor of the Keystone Kops, *Slim Jim*
(and the Grassville Force), by Raymond Ewer, *Simon
Simple* by Ed Carey, *Somebody's Stenog* by A. E.
Hayward, *Brainy Bowers* by R. W. Taylor, and *Lulu
and Leander* and *Old Opie Dilldock* by Frank M.
Howarth.

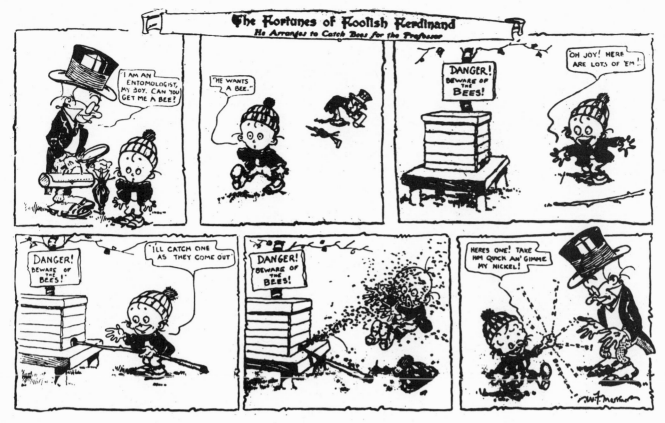

The Fortunes of Foolish Ferdinand by William F. Marriner, 1902.

Slim Jim in "Believe Us, It Was a Wet Day in Grassville" by Raymond Ewer, circa 1912.

Pa's Imported Son-in-Law (excerpt)
by Ed Carey, 1916, reflected
the worldwide popularity
of Charlie Chaplin.

Lulu and Leander by F. M. Howarth, 1906. With the text below, in the tradition of the nineteenth century *Image d'Epinal*.

Somebody's Stenog by A. E. Hayward. An archtypical strip of women's liberation.
© 1931 Public Ledger.

Lyonel Feininger was an Expressionist and Cubist painter of the first rank, whose prismatic canvases of land, sea, and city scenes hang in leading museums. Born in New York City in 1871, he studied art and music in Europe where he lived most of his life. He was also one of the continent's foremost cartoonists. Feininger the painter was always grateful to Feininger the cartoonist: "Far be it for me to underrate those important years as a comics draftsman. They were my only discipline." His career, along with Dirks and Luks, prominent painters of the Ashcan School, formed the early boundaries between the comics and the fine arts. In 1906 the Chicago *Tribune* started publishing two of his strips, *The Kin-der-Kids* and *Wee Willie Winkie's World*. Feininger had a gift for whimsical fantasy, and his cartoons were executed with a delicacy of line, form, and color. His characters were highly stylized, usually extremely short or elongated, and the settings were in the exaggerated perspective seen in many of his paintings.

Wee Willie Winkie's World drawn in Germany for the Chicago *Tribune* by Lyonel Feininger in 1906.
The form was Expressionist, the color often somber.

"Mr. A. Mutt Starts In To Play the Races" by Bud Fisher November 15, 1907.
The first daily newspaper comic strip.

Mutt is still the World War I doughboy in this 1919 *Mutt and Jeff* by Bud Fisher.

In 1929 Mutt trains for a big fight with Schmeling.

The *Mutt and Jeff entourage* by Al Smith.

In 1907 a twenty-two-year-old artist created an unlikely hero drawn from down-on-their-luck race-track types and set the comics on a new course. On the sports page of the San Francisco *Chronicle*, November 15, 1907, was a new cartoon in a new format, *Mr. A. Mutt Starts In to Play the Races*, by Bud Fisher. In a departure from the usual square or rectangular grouping, it ran in a horizontal strip across the page. It was published six days a week, in contrast to the sporadic appearance of earlier dailies. (A feature by Clare Briggs, *A. Piker Clerk*, ran for a short time in 1904 in the Chicago *Daily News*.) Thus it became the first successful daily comic strip.

A. Mutt, the harried race tout, was not to meet his pint-size, silk-hatted protégé for another six months when, in a moment of rare, kindly impulse, he rescued Jeff from an insane asylum. In 1908 there was excitement in the sporting world over the coming Jeffries-Johnson fight. Jeff was named for Jim Jeffries, and the strip became *Mutt and Jeff*.

In 1908 Fisher went over to Hearst's *Examiner*. His contract with the Wheeler Syndicate in 1915 brought him a $1,000-a-week guarantee plus eighty percent of the gross! Fisher had fortunately copyrighted his strip, the first cartoonist to do so, and a subsequent legal battle with Hearst left Fisher with all rights to the characters. He was one of the first cartoonists to hit the high income bracket before it was also a high tax bracket. In a few years Fisher was making $4,600 a week, not counting the income from vaudeville appearances and Mutt and Jeff toys and books. Not the least remarkable aspect of the strip is that it is still a popular feature, sixty-seven years later. With the exception of the first few years before the Sunday page began, it has appeared every day since 1907, in well over twenty-three thousand episodes. Even more remarkable, only two artists have been responsible for this astonishing body of work; the creator, Fisher, and, since his death in 1954, his former assistant, Al Smith. Smith started with Fisher in 1932 and was so good that he soon took over and ghosted the entire production. What successful long runs in the movies, theater, radio, or television can compare to that of *Mutt and Jeff* or the *Katzenjammer Kids*?

by Lee Falk

"Where do you get your ideas?" This perennial question seems to interest fellow artists and writers as well as readers. Even more interesting is the question: "Where did you get *the* idea?" Where and how did Charlie Schulz get the idea for *Peanuts*? Where did Outcault get the idea for *The Yellow Kid*? Where did I get the idea for *Mandrake the Magician* and for *The Phantom*?

All ideas must come from our experience and knowledge. Where else? Since I started Mandrake while I was still a student (University of Illinois) and the *Phantom* shortly thereafter, I believe that both ideas came from my early interests.

As a boy, I was fascinated by the great stage magicians of the time—Thurston, Blackstone, Cardini. I was equally intrigued by the great fictional detectives—Sherlock Holmes, Arsene Lupin, etc. I was also fascinated by the true tales of the great adventurers and explorers, from Marco Polo on. I suppose Mandrake is a synthesis of all these early interests—magician, detective, adventurer.

The gods and heroes of antiquity also thrilled me. Hercules; Ulysses; Perseus; Thor; the Arthurian heroes—Lancelot, Gawain; Roland; Siegfried; David; Samson; El Cid, and all the others of that mighty host. I was also intrigued by jungle tales—Tarzan, the *Jungle Books* of Kipling. From these heroes evolved my modern masked hero, the Phantom.

One of the things that has given me the most satisfaction in my work has been the worldwide acceptance of my stories. I am told the difficult-to-believe statistics of 100,000,000 readers a day in forty languages. This never had much meaning for me until I began to travel and meet these readers. Their diversity amazed me. Shoeshine boys in Naples, dock workers in Trinidad, shoe salesmen in Helsinki, clerks in Kerala, etc. How could all these people of such varied backgrounds, cultures and traditions relate to my backround out of Missouri, USA?

For example, I was once in Yucatan, exploring the amazing Mayan ruins of Chichén Itzá. This is far off the beaten track, even for other Mexicans. The guide and I were hacking our way through the jungle with machetes to inspect some overgrown ruins. A little Indian boy popped out of the bushes. He was wearing a loincloth, and had come from who-knows-where—since I'd seen no villages. He spoke neither Spanish nor English, only his native Yucatecan. He looked at me suspiciously—with dark alien eyes like some forest animal. I remember thinking I couldn't possibly communicate with this strange boy. The guide, who knew my work was published in the boy's language, talked to him. The boy stared at me, then suddenly pointed at me, smiled, and said "Mandrake."

One more little tale has always excited me. During World War II, the German occupation of Norway was rigid and harsh. The Germans controlled the Norwegian press and daily in their papers printed untrue propaganda that the United States was being destroyed, New York and Washington bombed, etc. But at the same time, *The Phantom* was being smuggled across the border from Sweden and being printed daily in Norwegian in these same papers. (We knew nothing about this until after the war.) The German occupying authorities paid no attention to this comic strip and did not know it was of American origin. But all the Norwegians knew where it came from. And while their controlled newspapers were telling them each day that the USA (and other Allies) was in ashes, *The Phantom* kept appearing—thus assuring readers that the USA was still going strong. My unimpeachable informant in this matter—a Norwegian newsman—tells me that it was one of the biggest jokes of the war there. And because of this, one of the passwords of the Norwegian underground in World War II was "Phantom."

★ ★ ★

by Vincent T. Hamlin

I don't know where Alley Oop came from, but I remember when and why.

It was back in the twenties, out in the southwestern Texas oilfields—dinosaur country. The fossilized skeletons of these Mesozoic monsters were popping up all over the place . . . and being a newspaperman, I felt the urge to tell the world about them. Pictorially, of course.

And so Dinny the dinosaur was born, a creature the like of which never existed. I gave him the body of a diplodocus with the spine plates of a stegosaurus and the head of a duck (swiped from a Blue Book cover painting by Herbert Morton Stoops). For purposes of acceptable animation, I gave him the running gear of a mammal rather than a reptile.

The comic strip began to take form with the advent of the dinosaur's master, who in the beginning was known as Oop, the Mighty. After a time the "Mighty" was discarded.

So what goes with Oop? Why, Alley, of course, the violent and often profane French *allez*, the "get-to-hell-outa-here!" so well-worn by millions of us of the AEF.

That's how we got Alley Oop, a big, brutal-looking sort of a not-too-bright prehistoric caveman.

Alley Oop certainly wasn't tailored to the architectural specifications of the artist who, although athletically oriented and venturesome, stood a scant five feet six and weighed a full fifty pounds less than his creation.

I found it expedient to keep my hero's intelligence quotient somewhat inferior to my own limited mental machinery. I never could understand how a comic artist could live with a character inherently smarter than he was.

But even this precaution has failed many times to keep Alley Oop from taking over the course of events in my pen and ink world.

As impossible as is the overall concept of Alley Oop, paleontologically speaking, everything in its story line must be four-square, flat-footedly logical.

So how to explain the love affair of a man and a huge, toothy monster like Dinny? I found the answer in Aesop's "Androcles and the Lion" . . . and took it as my own. But I didn't steal Ooola, King Guz, or Queen Umpateedle. They appeared as needed along with rhyme-talking Foozy, the Grand Wizer and all the rest of Oop's companions.

We were off and running. However, you've no idea how fast a daily and Sunday feature can devour material, especially in a world as limited as my ancient Land of Moo. So in about five years we expanded our stage with a time machine to give us the whole of history in which to perform—Egypt, Greece, Rome, the Arabian "Knights," the Vikings, the Indians of our own West, even the moon.

But there are a few historical areas we find it advisable to avoid—the American Revolution and the War Between the States, to name a couple. Actually, I do this comic for my own amusement, but if in its pursuit, I judge the subject to be distasteful, physically or historically, to groups or nationalities, I go elsewhere for my material.

Even the low-keyed incongruity-type comedy we employ, can sometimes be sharp and cruel, and it's not my wish to offend. Neither do I feel called upon to make a forum of the comic page.

A gracious God gave me the tools I use. I strive to be worthy of His gift.

★ ★ ★

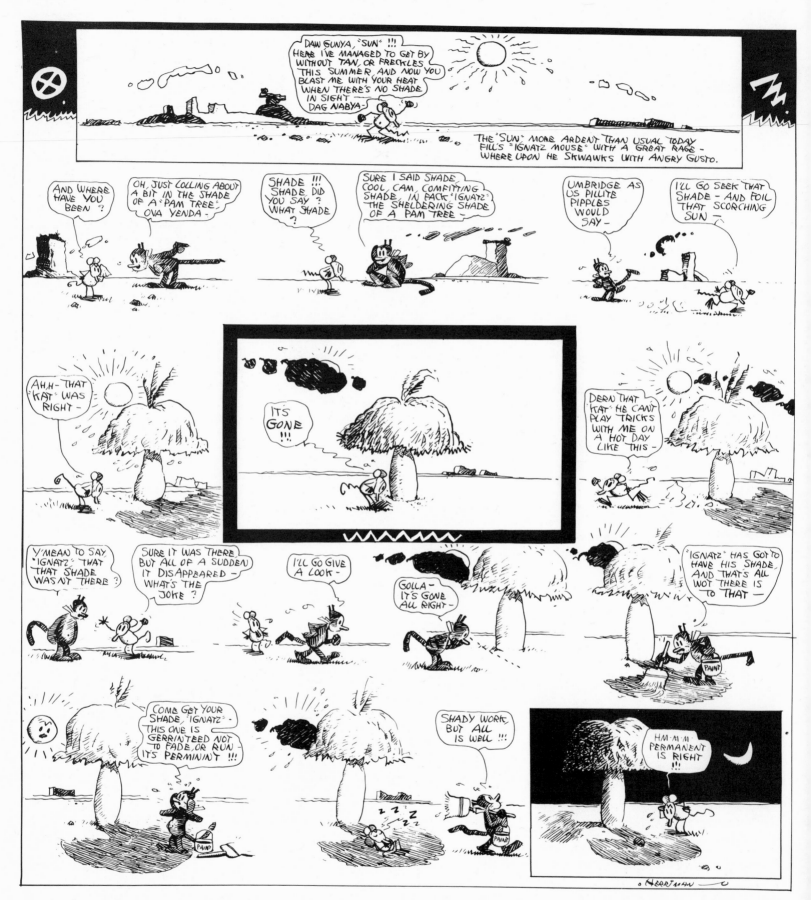

A superb example of George Herriman's classic *Krazy Kat*, September 24, 1922.
© King Features Syndicate, Inc.

The Golden Age: 1910-1919

In 1910 the nation was singing "I Love My Wife But, Oh, You Kid," "Heaven Will Protect the Working Girl" and "Come, Josephine, in My Flying Machine." It was also the year Congress passed the Mann Act, Woodrow Wilson resigned from Princeton University to enter politics, and Halley's comet reappeared. The Gibson Girl was the acme of womanhood. Glenn Curtis won the New York *World*'s $10,000 prize for the first continuous flight from Albany to New York. Nearly every woman carried a sunshade and the right length for sweaters was to the knee. Anna Pavlova made her American debut on Broadway, the John Philip Sousa Band toured the world, and the big hits were the *Ziegfeld*

Follies and Marie Dressler. Mark Twain died. The twenty-first depression since 1790 lasted one year. Just published were *Hopalong Cassidy* by Clarence Mulford and Charles William Eliot's 50-volume Harvard Classics. Henry Ford II began the mass production of the Model T. The beat was ragtime and the turkey trot the dance rage. Ty Cobb batted .377, William Howard Taft was the twenty-seventh President, and the population was 93,402,151.

The year 1910 was also the beginning of the golden age of the comics. They developed new audiences and continued to reflect the changing society in America, aided by an increasing flow of new comic geniuses to interpret it.

Copyright, 1915, by Newspaper Feature Service, Inc. Great Britain rights reserved

H. A. McGill's *The Hall Room Boys*, 1915.

Almost all strips now followed Fisher's lead, and six daily strips plus a Sunday page became the norm. The Sunday page had been aimed primarily at the kids; now the dailies began to attract new readers, the adult commuters. This resulted in themes aimed at a more mature audience. The year 1910 saw the birth of two new strips by H. A. McGill, *The Hall Room Boys* and *Hazel the Heartbreaker*, which reflected the new pattern in comics readership. Percy and Ferdie, the indigent pretenders to social eminence, who were boarding house roomers in *The Hall Room Boys*, struggled to finance their careers. *Hazel the Heartbreaker* was plotting her future by trying to catch a man of means. (McGill also created *Cinderella Peggy*.) In 1914 *Pa's Son-in-Law* by C. H. Wellington was another strip with a theme intended for mature readers.

Harry Hershfield's *Abie Kabibble*.

The year 1910 also saw the start of Harry Hershfield's *Desperate Desmond*, suggested by Arthur Brisbane, the great editor of the *Journal*, to compete with Kahles' popular *Hairbreadth Harry*. Gomatz, a cannibal chief and Desmond's man Friday, would occasionally and inexplicably voice Yiddish phrases. This led to Hershfield's creation of his classic strip *Abie the Agent* in 1914. Abie Kabibble was a middle-class businessman and paterfamilias, a role with which more and more Americans could identify. Although minorities had been fair game for satire in the past, a cast of Jewish characters using dialect was a touchy endeavor. That Hershfield was able to make their qualities and traits universal is a tribute to his skill, gentle wit, and humanity.

Abie was a thoroughly human character. He could be quarrelsome and petty (as in an argument with a waiter about an overcharge: "It's not the principle either, it's the ten cents") as well as generous (he delighted in buying his wife, Reba, some "fency little gifts"). Abie met the complexities of the cutthroat business world with a mixture of shrewdness and naïveté. A devoted family man, he could alternately be gay, angry, tyrannical, and unselfish. Brisbane was undoubtedly right when he credited *Abie* with being the first of the really adult comics in America.

Desperate Desmond (excerpt) by Harry Hershfield. Desmond's desperate attack on Rosamond is foiled again in this 1912 melodrama.

Hershfield was born in 1885 in Cedar Rapids, Iowa, two weeks after his immigrant parents arrived from Odessa. He created his first strip, *Homeless Hector*, for the Chicago *News* when he was not yet fifteen years old. Hector was a stray pup who popularized the expression "I gotta get located!" and the strip was a dog's-eye view of the world, mostly feet. In 1902 the belltower in the Piazza San Marco in Venice collapsed. For a cover story featuring other imperiled structures, young Hershfield retouched what he took to be an off-angle photograph of a tower. The first edition of the morning paper showed the Tower of Pisa miraculously straightened. As Hershfield recalls,

"I was given two weeks to complete my education." He also made line drawings from photographs and covered breaking stories with on-the-spot sketches, including the famous Iroquois Hotel fire in 1903. At the time, most staff artists did both cartoons and illustrations and their efforts were considered "fillers."

Hershfield once asked Brisbane if he considered a cartoonist a newspaperman. "Would you call a barnacle a ship?" was the reply. Brisbane, however, aware of cartoonists' ability to attract readers, once cut off their signatures in order to reduce their personal following and thereby their salary demands. Hershfield took the issue directly to Hearst, who not

Hershfield's *Abie the Agent* in 1930. Refined from his early lush style (see page 10) but with Abie's world of business chicanery intact. © King Features Syndicate, Inc.

אויב׳ שוין יא נעהמען א הייטען מאן, וויל
זי ער זאל כאטש בראנגען א סך אינשורענס.

Gimple Beinish the Matchmaker by Samuel Zagat, 1917. (Read right to left)
"This experienced widow warns Gimple that any man she marries must carry ten thousand dollars insurance. Her former husbands left her only one thousand apiece."

only restored the signatures but ordered bylines as well. This credit has become standard practice since.

Although still one of the country's best-known cartoonists, Hershfield ended his cartooning career in 1932 in a contract dispute with Hearst. (*Abie* became *Meyer the Buyer* for its final year in the *Tribune*.) His remarkable career as a humorist took new directions. He has been a columnist (*If I'm Wrong, Sue Me!*), radio commentator (*One Man's Opinion*), performer (for seventeen years a regular panelist of *Can You Top This?*), and head of animation for Warner Brothers studio. At eighty-nine, Mr. New York, a title officially bestowed on him by Mayor Robert Wagner, is one of America's finest masters of ceremonies and raconteurs. After seventy-five years as a newspaperman Hershfield remains philosophic: "The only change is now when I go out with a girl, I won't take yes for an answer."

The ethnic press produced its own comic strips. As early as 1912 Samuel Zagat created *Gimple Beinish the*

Matchmaker for the New York Yiddish daily *Warheit*. Gimple, a little bearded man in top hat and frock coat, had one ambition: to lead all single males and females into a blissful life of matrimony. The comic strip ran until 1919 when Zagat, an artist of great force, became the editorial cartoonist and illustrator for the *Jewish Daily Forward* until he died in 1964. Walter Krawiec, the editorial cartoonist since World War I for the *Polish Daily News* in Chicago, created the feature *From Our Window*, of intimate scenes of urban life. Krawiec is a master draftsman and portrait artist. The first French strip in the Americas, *Toinon* by Alberic Bourgeois, appeared in Montreal's *La Presse* in 1905. Other pioneer cartoonists who created features for the French Canadian readers were Louis Wain and Raoul Barré, around 1910, and J. A. Boisvert in the 1920's, both also in *La Presse*, and Arthur LeMay *(Timothé)* in the 1920's for *La Patrie*.

J. A. Boisvert's *Benoni*, 1922, from *La Presse*, Montreal.

Gilbert Seldes, author of *The Seven Lively Arts*,
called *Krazy Kat* the most amusing, fantastic, and
satisfactory work of art produced in America. It was a
strip of pure fantasy; the lush language was insane
poetry. The outrageous love-hate tragic-farce took
place on a surrealistic stage of sparse Western landscape: abstract cathedrallike mountains and
mysterious vegetation, ever-changing and evolving,
disappearing or suddenly springing from the void.
Coconino County's basic characters were a cat (Krazy
Kat), a mouse (Ignatz), and a cop (Offissa B. Pupp),
and the basic props: a brick (from Kelly's Exclusive
Brick Yard) and a jail. Ignatz was a mouse with a
mission: to "Krease that Kat's bean with a brick."

Krazy Kat by George Herriman. An essay in matter over mind.
© 1936 King Features Syndicate, Inc.

Offissa Pupp, Krazy's unrequited lover, regularly tossed Ignatz behind bars, despite the fact that to Krazy Kat each brick from the "li'l ainjil" was a missile of love. It could have been the eternal triangle except for Ignatz, the anarchist and cynic.

George Herriman created this classic comic in 1911, and it died with him in 1944. *Krazy Kat* never gained a large syndicated list of newspapers. Its appeal was apparently too intellectual. Among the *Kat*'s avid collectors were the poet e. e. cummings and Woodrow Wilson, who refused to miss a single episode.

Herriman, born in New Orleans, was the son of a Greek baker. His first strip was *Lariat Pete* in 1903. Other features from his seemingly inexhaustible fund of zany ideas were *Major Ozone, the Fresh Air Fiend; Baron Bean; Bernie Burns; Rosy Posy Mama's Girl; The Dingbat Family; Stumble Inn;* and *The Family Upstairs*, from which *Krazy Kat* was an offshoot.

Baron Bean, an early Herriman burlesque (excerpt).

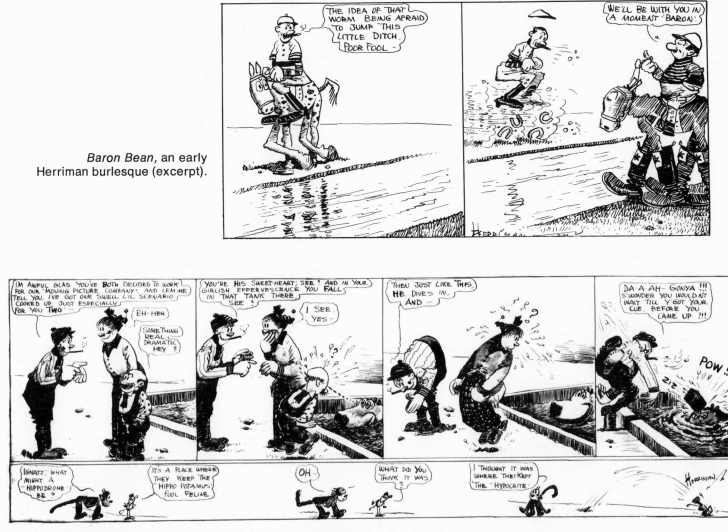

Krazy Kat's inauspicious birth beneath "the floor" of *The Dingbat Family,* 1910.

A Chinese duck establishes *Krazy*'s raison d'être, by Herriman. © 1935 King Features Syndicate, Inc.

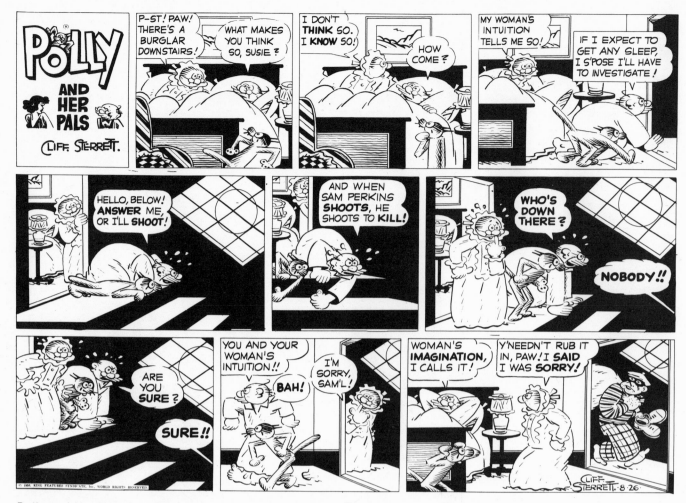

Polly and Her Pals. Note Sterrett's use of abstract design. (For the embryonic *Polly* of 1915, see page 10.) © 1956 King Features Syndicate, Inc.

Paw and the Rite of Spring.
© 1935 King Features Syndicate, Inc.

In 1912, a time when the suffragette movement was lobbying for women's independence, a strip about an independent woman began: *Positive Polly* by Cliff Sterrett. Polly was the first heroine to be the central character in her own strip. The name was soon changed to *Polly and Her Pals*. After Sterrett's first strips (*For This We Have Daughters, When a Man's Married,* and *Before and After*) he cited his problems with censorship: "... we couldn't show a girl's leg above the top of her shoe. Furthermore, a comic strip kiss was unheard of, and all the action had to take place and be completed before nine o'clock." Polly was a girl of high spirits, a tall beauty with curly hair, snub nose, and, as the rising hemlines were to reveal, gorgeous legs. She was of the first generation of women who bobbed their hair and even used lipstick. Towering over her Maw and Paw, she handled them and her innumerable suitors in the forty-six years of the strip with equanimity. Sterrett's art developed into a delicate balance of flat black and white, contrasted with rhythmic patterns and textures, and an abstract quality in form and line.

George McManus was one of the most prolific and talented of the early masters of the comics. *The Newlyweds*, begun in 1904, was the first family strip. It established a recurring theme in the comics: the crisis in the household of a young couple; the pretty and capable wife and the good-hearted but bumbling husband, a theme Chic Young's *Blondie* was to refine to near perfection. Baby Snookums in *The Newlyweds* became the best-known child in America. *Rosie's Beau* was the forerunner of *Bringing Up Father*, created in 1913, which set the pattern for the domestic war between the sexes. Among those comic strips to follow the basic theme were *The Bungle Family, The Gumps, Moon Mullins, Mr. and Mrs.* and the more recent version, *Andy Capp*. Family situation comedy became a staple in the comics as it would on television fifty years later. Jiggs, in *Bringing Up Father*, is the Irish immigrant worker who has made good but yearns only for a night out with his old cronies at Dinty Moore's—playing pool, cards, and relishing his favorite dish: corned beef and cabbage. Maggie, his parvenu wife, is the epitome of the aggressive, domineering, and ambitious social climber. It was a time when the expanding American economy ab-sorbed waves of immigrants and enriched many of them, and McManus drew upon this social phenomenon in characterizing Maggie and Jiggs.

Panhandle Pete; O, It's Great to Be Married; Let George Do It; Nibsy the Newsboy in Funny Fairyland; Cheerful Charley; and *Their Only Child* were among other McManus creations. McManus employed a delicate line, carefully spotted solid blacks, and tasteful use of white space, balanced with finely de-tailed backgrounds: rococo lamps, ornate staircases, vases, rugs, etc. He also paid lavish attention to Mag-gie's and her daughter Rosie's clothes. McManus was in the mainstream of *art nouveau;* his work was reminiscent of Aubrey Beardsley. The effect of his style was so elegant that the reader could actually sense Jiggs' dis-comfort in his opulent surroundings.

When McManus died in 1954, Vernon Greene, a veteran cartoonist, who previously worked on *Polly and Her Pals* and did *The Shadow* from 1938 to 1942, drew *Bringing Up Father* until his own death in 1965. William Kavanagh now writes the script, and Frank Fletcher (Sunday) and Hamlet Campana (daily) do the illustration.

George McManus' mystery of line and his parvenu theme already evident in this early *Bringing Up Father,* circa 1915.

Bringing Up Father. Note McManus' *art nouveau* interiors and zany byplay in panel three.
© 1949 King Features Syndicate, Inc.

Rosie's Beau. A Sunday feature created by McManus in 1913 became a subfeature to *Bringing Up Father* in the 1920's and was replaced by *Snookums* in 1945.

Spare Ribs and Gravy, circa 1905. One of McManus' early creations.

One of the most remarkable careers in American cartooning began one day in 1904 when a young engineer, a graduate of the University of California, quit designing sewers for the city of San Francisco and talked himself into a job on the San Francisco *Chronicle.* Reuben Lucius Goldberg began as a sports cartoonist. In fact, sports cartooning was the entrée to the comic strip for many cartoonists, among whom were "Tad" Dorgan, Frederick Opper, and Robert Ripley. In 1907, now in New York, Rube Goldberg created the first of the series *Foolish Questions* for the *Evening Mail.* (Foolish Question No. 807: Spectator asks battered man beside smashed auto, "Have an accident?" Answer, "No, thanks, just had one.") By 1916 his creations included *The Candy Kid, Lunatics I Have Met, Soup and Fish, I'm the Guy, They All Look Good When You're Far Away,* and *The Weekly Meeting of the Tuesday Ladies' Club.* That year the newly organized McNaught Syndicate took on Goldberg's *Boob McNutt.* Boob, a helpless clown with red hair

Foolish Questions (No. 2719) created by Rube Goldberg in 1908.

Rube Goldbergs' *Boob McNutt* (with Mike and Ike). Miss Jenks attempts a Pygmalion-like transformation of Boob. © 1934 King Features Syndicate, Inc.

and huge pumpkin figure, continued his zany misadventures until 1933. *Lala Palooza; Phoney Films; Mike and Ike, They Look Alike;* and *Life's Little Jokes* were other Goldberg inspirations. But his most enduring gifts to posterity are the inventions of Professor Lucifer Gorgonzola Butts, which he described as "a bewhiskered child of my brain, but a subconscious offspring of my engineering career." Butts' inventions were Goldberg's one-man war against modern gadgetry and the tyranny of machines. Wildly complex and ingenious contraptions full of zany coincidences to accomplish ludicrously simple ends, his inventions made him the satirist of the machine age. *How to Protect Yourself Against Slippery Scatter Rug,* created in 1951, required Margaret Truman, a sack of wheat, Jawaharlal Nehru, a movie camera, Esther Williams, Ambassador William O'Dwyer's hat, a Mexican hot tamale, an Iranian oil hound, a bone, and Roy Campanella's glove, all wondrously synchronized to catch you as you slip on the rug. A "Rube

Goldberg" contraption has become part of the American vocabulary. Goldberg was a social satirist in the tradition of Daumier and Hogarth. Author, essayist, poet, playwright, Pulitzer prizewinning editorial cartoonist, unforgettable phrasemaker ("No matter how thin you slice it, it's still baloney"), founder and first president of the National Cartoonist Society and winner in 1967 of its highest award, "The Reuben," named for him, Goldberg, at eighty, embarked on a new and successful career as a sculptor. He died in 1970.

Two early Goldberg creations. *Life's Little Jokes* (above) and *Soup and Fish* (below), circa 1920.

"Rube Goldberg Views the News for His Latest Invention." Goldberg's celebrated *Inventions* began in 1914 and ran intermittently for fifty years. © 1951 King Features Syndicate, Inc.

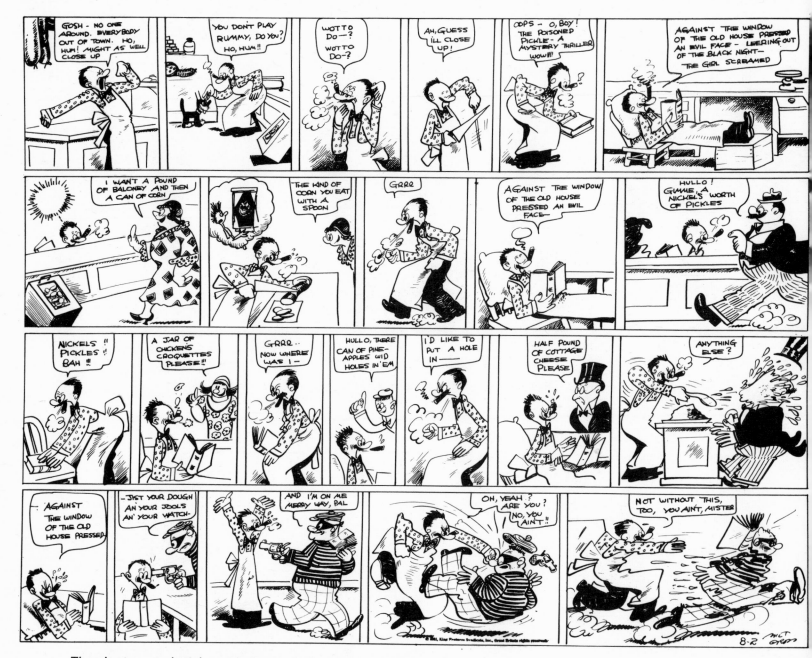

There's never a minute's rest in *Dave's Delicatessen* by Milt Gross.
© 1931 King Features Syndicate, Inc.

Count Screwloose

An excerpt from *Count Screwloose* by Gross. Once again the Count escapes from Nuttycrest to a world seemingly far less sane.

Another rare comic genius, with a flair for the absurd and bizarre and with an extravagant language of his own (in the tradition of Goldberg and Herriman), was Milt Gross, born in 1895 in the Bronx, New York. His first strip was *Henry Peck, A Happy Married Man*, for the New York *Evening Journal* in 1917. He is best remembered for *Banana Oil, Count Screwloose from Toulouse* (the Count escapes from the madhouse only to find the outside world even crazier and slips back into the asylum), *Looy Dot Dope, Dave's Delicatessen*, and *Grossly Xaggerated* in which *That's My Pop!* and *Could I Write a Book!* appeared. Gross was an engaging writer; his illustrated books *Nize Baby* and *Hiawatta with No Odder Poems* were classics in dialect humor. President Calvin Coolidge and Chief Justice Oliver Wendell Holmes were among his enthusiastic readers. Other titles were *Dunt Esk, De Night in de Front from Chreestmas, Famous Fimmales Witt Odder Ewents from Heestory*, and the innovative *He Done Her Wrong*, a wordless pictorial novel. Gross' comedic talents also led him to Hollywood, where he produced his own animated features, wrote screenplays based on *Nize Baby*, and worked on the film *The Circus* for Charlie Chaplin.

"That's My Pop!" a Gross-spawned shibboleth from *Grossly Xaggerated*. © 1937 King Features Syndicate, Inc.

The world of children has been one of the most enduring themes in the comics. It dominated the first wave of strips with the *Yellow Kid*, the *Katzenjammer Kids, Buster Brown*, and *Little Nemo*. None of them, however, captured the essence of small-town American childhood during the first decades of the century in the tradition of Tom Sawyer and Huck Finn. The *Yellow Kid* was more of an observer of the street life in the slums swirling around him. Hans and Fritz retained the flavor of their European origins. Buster was far too mannered and citified, and little was revealed about Nemo except for his dream world. One of the first attempts to depict the authentic American childhood, the neighborhood kid and his gang, their concerns, games, humor, and even cruelty was by Fontaine Fox.

The Toonerville Trolley That Meets All Trains, the official title of Fontaine Fox's classic panel, circa 1930. © Fontaine Fox

Toonerville Folks by Fontaine Fox. The skipper jumps the track to a wrong conclusion in this 1931 Sunday page. © Fontaine Fox

Fox, born in Louisville, Kentucky, in 1884, studied at the University of Indiana and started his cartooning career with the Louisville *Herald*. His father's reaction to Fontaine's first published cartoon, "All I have to say is it's a mighty queer way to make a living," has been echoed by many a cartoonist's family since. In 1908 Fox started a series of daily cartoons about kids for the Chicago *Evening Post*. It was a time when the brilliant John McCutcheon of the Chicago *Tribune* was the only daily cartoonist dealing with the subject.

It was in *Toonerville Folks*, begun in 1913 as a daily panel and later to include a Sunday page, that Fox found the perfect vehicle for his unique talents. The inspiration came on a visit to Charles Voight (creator of *Betty*) in Pelham, New York, where the rattletrap streetcar was skippered by a wistful old codger with an Airedale beard who knew every passenger by name and enlivened the ride with local chitchat. When Fox asked directions, the skipper stopped the trolley and climbed a knoll to point out the Voight house. The incident recalled to mind an early series of drawings in

Louisville on the indifferent trolley service, and the conception of his classic strip crystallized.

Fox drew upon memories of his boyhood when he created the Toonerville family. Each had a specific identity, and the strip was the first to deal with such diverse personalities. The skipper and the trolley added passengers to the cast at every stop, including such droll characters as: Mickey "Himself" McGuire, the Powerful Katrinka, the Terrible Tempered Mr. Bang, Aunt Eppie Hogg, Suitcase Simpson, and the gang of Little Scorpions. Fox was scrupulous in keeping their behavior in character. "I own their bodies, but I do not own their souls," he once wrote. Derby-wearing Mickey McGuire became so identified as the impish tough guy that the young child actor Joe Yule, Jr. took the character's name. Fox had to go to court to establish his copyright to the character. Yule then became Mickey Rooney.

The rickety, swaying Toonerville Trolley became synonymous with dilapidated public transportation everywhere. By 1950 this classic symbol of leisurely small-town life was rapidly disappearing. For a short time Fox brought the Toonerville Bus into service. But in 1955, after forty-two years of service, the Toonerville Trolley, with its stovepipe mast, took its last run when Fox retired.

Fox's lively, animated style was drawn with a nervous speed that gave it an identity as unique as his signature. His marvelously cursive and dashing line imparted a vitality that contrasted with his low-key, droll humor. He employed a high eye level in the drawings that gave a unique perspective to the Toonerville community; this innovation enabled him to chronicle a wide reaction to any situation.

Reg'lar Fellers by Gene Byrnes. Fashion has changed more than the kids.
© 1933 Gene Byrnes

The focus on the adventure of kid gangs began during World War I with *Reg'lar Fellers* by Gene Byrnes and *Freckles and His Friends* by Merrill Blosser, forerunners of Hal Roach's famous *Our Gang* comedies, the first of which was produced in 1922.

Reg'lar Fellers started as a panel adjunct to Byrnes' cartoon, *It's a Great Life If You Don't Weaken!* which became a favorite expression for the doughboys. By 1917 *Reg'lar Fellers* appeared in strip form, and it ran daily and Sunday until 1950. Jimmy Dugan, Puddin' Head Duffy and his kid brother Pinhead, and the rest of the gang explored their world with bubbling enthusiasm and never-flagging energy, whether leaping over backyard fences; investigating the junkyard, quarry, farm, circus, or candy store; building their clubhouse; warring with wooden swords; playing ball or tricks; or the myriad of other things a gang of kids does when there's nothing else to do.

Byrnes drew with the simple directness of good storytelling. The backgrounds and occasionally the figure were carefully constructed to set the scene but often were not carried to the frame which gave a light, airy effect to the strip, as in a vignette.

Byrnes, born in New York City in 1889, has continued a busy professional career after the end of the run of *Reg'lar Fellers*, publishing numerous cartoon books and art instruction courses, until his death in 1974.

The kid gang theme continued in the notable but more restrained strips of Al Carter's *Our Friend Mush*, Fera's *Just Boy*, and *On Our Block* by Tom McNamara.

Byrnes invokes the spirit of the neighborhood gang of a bygone era in this rousing
Sunday page. © 1927 New York Tribune, Inc.

Barney Google by Billy DeBeck (excerpt). © 1932 King Features Syndicate, Inc.

A Momentous Year: 1919

Syndication

After World War I, and continuing through the 1920's, came a period of crystallization in the comics. King Features, the first of the major comics syndicates, was founded in 1914. Syndication became big business. Each major syndicate developed its line of comics to compete in all the strip categories: family, kids, animals, girls, adventure, and slapstick.

The newspaper syndicate in America dates back to 1768, when a revolutionary tract, *Journal of Occurrences*, published by some Boston patriots was syndicated to a number of cities in the colonies. Occasional syndication of individual items by various papers continued until 1865. That year Ansel Nash Kellogg, publisher of a Wisconsin weekly, founded a syndicate in Chicago and was soon selling articles and advertising to fourteen hundred clients. By the 1880's syndication was flourishing. Stereotype plates that could be used directly on the presses, eliminating resetting and re-engraving, were now carrying news, gossip columns, features, and fiction to papers throughout the country. (Today, instead of costly metal plates, client papers are sent lightweight matrices from which they do their own plating or coated proofs for photo offset presses.) S. S. McClure syndicated Rudyard Kipling, Robert Louis Stevenson, and Arthur Conan Doyle, among others. The comics inevitably followed. When the readers of every small-town and country paper could enjoy the Sunday comics as did the readers of the major newspapers in New York, Philadelphia, Chicago, and San Francisco, where most of them originated, the comics became a truly American institution.

The national audience forced the cartoonist to take a new approach to his strip. Fontaine Fox described this change: "In drawing for many scattered newspapers, instead of one published in the city in which I lived, I had to alter the type of work I had been doing. I realized the need of identifying myself in the minds of my following with a series of characters, so as to make each cartoon's appeal as sure in San Francisco as in New York."

The tempo of American life changed drastically after World War I and so did the comics. In 1919 Knute Rockne was head football coach at Notre Dame. Commercial aviation and airmail had just begun. Speakeasies were in, and so were the gigolo and bobbed hair. *Seventeen* was a hit on Broadway, and Charlie Chaplin was filming *The Kid*. Skirts were six inches off the ground. Jack Dempsey knocked out Jess Willard. *Gasoline Alley* by Frank King, *Barney Google* by Billy DeBeck, *Harold Teen* by Carl Ed, and *Thimble Theatre* by Elzie Segar made their debuts.

Thanksgiving Day 1921 in *Gasoline Alley* by Frank King. Walt Wallet shows baby Skeezix his first turkey. © 1921 The Chicago Tribune.

February 14, 1921—The foundling.

Walt selects a name.

1926—First day in school.

1931—Skeezix's first love.

1937—And first shave.

1941—The proposal.

1942—Skeezix's twenty-first birthday. © The Chicago Tribune.

Skeezix's wartime wedding, June 28, 1944. © The Chicago Tribune.

Gasoline Alley started as a panel of neighborhood automobile enthusiasts gathering in backyard alleys. Tinkering with the family car on Sunday morning was the passionate hobby of millions of men. However, on Valentine's Day in 1921, a foundling was left on Walt Wallet's doorstep and changed the course of the strip. It also marked a unique departure from comic dogma: that comic characters are ageless. Skeezix, as the baby was called, started growing up, and the rest of the cast aged as well. Skeezix went to grade school, fought in World War II, was married and raised a family and is today a grandfather. Meanwhile, Walt, a bachelor, married Phyllis Blossom, and eventually Corky and Judy were added to the family group. The Wallets aged day by day and year by year at the same pace as their readers. It is the only strip that grew up along with three generations of Americans. Frank King, born in 1883, continued the strip until his semiretirement in 1959. He died in 1969. His assistants, Bill Perry (Sunday) and Dick Moores (daily), have continued since. Perry has continued in the King tradition, while Moores has evolved the daily into a new area of contemporary rural folklore of unique charm.

A 1972 cast portrait of *Gasoline Alley* by Dick Moores. Skeezix is fifty-one!
© 1972 The Chicago Tribune

Barney Google, the born loser with great difficulty in adjusting to life, must have struck a responsive chord in millions of World War I veterans. Barney was short, with a potato-shaped nose, a wisp of mustache, and huge saucer eyes, which Billy Rose immortalized in the hit song "Barney Google with the Goo-Goo-Googly Eyes." A convention of the time, which has in many instances persisted in the modern era, was for the artist to have a smaller supplementary strip, commonly known as the top, that ran above (or below) the main strip on his Sunday page. Billy DeBeck's top for *Google; Parlor, Bedroom & Sink,* is worthy of note. It starred Bunky, a ridiculous baby with a bulbous nose, who, when beset by the evil Fagin, would let out a heart-rending cry, "Youse is a Viper!" Billy DeBeck had a great knack for creating sounds and phrases that were quickly picked up: "the heebie-jeebies," "osky-wow-wow," "taitched in the haid," "shifless skonk," and "jughaid." Spark Plug, Barney's horse, was added

to the cast in 1922, and Snuffy Smith and a company of hillbilly "revenooer" haters in 1934. Snuffy was eventually to take over star billing. DeBeck's characters were drawn with great verve. No matter how absurd they appeared, as in his ridiculous rendition of Sparky, they somehow came to life. DeBeck's loose pen technique ran from bold, thick, and thin strokes to delicate flecks that gave the whole a rich tonal quality.

Upon DeBeck's death in 1942, the strip was left to Fred Lasswell, who had started assisting DeBeck when only seventeen. In 1947 the National Cartoonists Society established its award for the "cartoonist of the year," known as the Billy DeBeck Award. (It became the Reuben Award in 1952.) DeBeck would have been delighted that the winner in 1963 was his talented protégé, Fred Lasswell, for *Barney Google and Snuffy Smith.*

Barney Google by Billy DeBeck. Spark Plug's track record was questionable.
© 1932 King Features Syndicate, Inc.

Barney Google and Snuffy Smith by Fred Lesswell. Snuffy is now the featured character.
© 1947 King Features Syndicate, Inc.

Billy DeBeck's *Barney Google and Spark Plug.* © 1925 King Features Syndicate, Inc.

Carl Ed's *Harold Teen*
© The Chicago Tribune.

Pop Jenks' Sugar Bowl was the hangout for the "razzmatazz" adolescents of the twenties in Carl Ed's *Harold Teen*. Ed's influence on the teen-agers of the time was demonstrated by his popularizing such expressions as "shebas" (girls), "sheiks" (boys), "Yowsah!" "Yeh, man, he's the nertz!" "pantywaist," and "Fan mah brow!" Sugar Bowl ice-cream emporiums throughout the country were so besieged by demands for the Gedunk Sundae that Ed had to oblige by inventing its recipe.

Harold was inept and clownish and unable to cope with the local girls, especially his steady, Lillums, whom he found "hard to dope." Harold also contributed to setting teen-age fashion with enormous bell-bottom pants, autographed sweatshirts, and yellow slicker raincoats. In 1928 *Harold Teen* was adapted for the movies, starring Arthur Lake (later to play Dagwood in the *Blondie* movies) and again in 1935, starring Hal LeRoy. Carl Ed, born in Moline, Illinois, in 1891, died in 1959 and the strip with him. The heyday of the drugstore cowboy was over.

Harold Teen by Carl Ed. The news of Harold's exploit reaches the Sugar Bowl. © 1932 The Chicago Tribune.

In 1919 another event occurred which was to have profound impact on the course of American comics. Captain Joseph Patterson, co-publisher of the Chicago *Tribune*, with his cousin, Colonel Robert McCormick, shifted his operations to New York and started the *Daily News*. He also tried a new experiment in American journalism, a tabloid. No other publisher, with the possible exception of Hearst, played as vital a role in the development of the comics. The first issue of the *Daily News* carried only one strip, which Patterson himself had conceived and named

The Gumps by Sidney Smith. Finances were a constant source of worry.
© 1935 News Syndicate Co., Inc.

The Gumps. He switched Sidney Smith, who had been doing *Old Doc Yak*, to the new strip. It was a phenomenal success, and within five years Smith signed the first million-dollar contract in the business: $100,000 a year for ten years.

Andy Gump was a chinless, optimistic failure, who, when hopelessly involved in some difficulty, would in desperation call for his wife with what became a familiar cry: *"Oh, Min!"* When the family lives reached a crisis, as when billionaire Uncle Bim came perilously close to being trapped into marrying the grasping Widow Zander, some papers even printed the strip on front-page extras. Smith was perhaps the

first to allow one of his main characters to die, Mary Gold, the fiancée of an inventor friend of the Gumps. He even depicted the details of the crime. Another episode which created a sensation was when Andy entered the 1924 Presidential campaign.

In 1935 a new contract was offered, $150,000 a year for five years. In what must have been an ironic twist of fate that would be rejected as too melodramatic for a comic strip, Smith signed the contract and was driving home when tragedy struck. Within an hour Smith was dead at fifty-eight, the victim of an automobile accident. Gus Edson continued *The Gumps* until 1959, when he teamed up with Irwin Hasen to create *Dondi*.

The Gumps in 1952 by Smith's successor, Gus Edson. Andy became a perennial Presidential candidate. © News Syndicate Co., Inc.

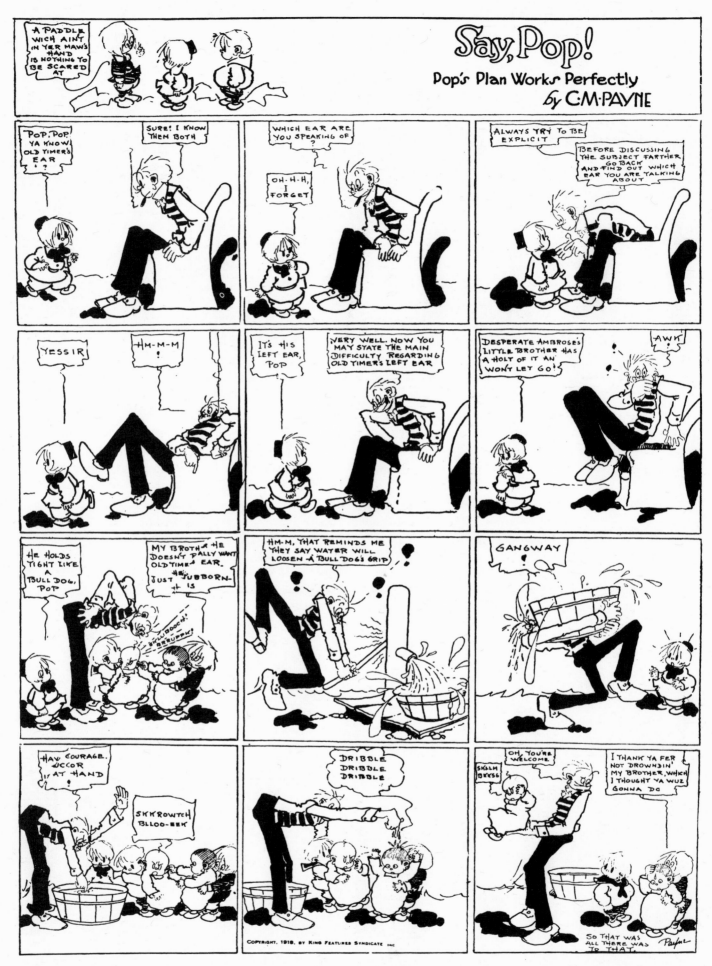

Say, Pop! by Charles M. Payne, 1918. (also titled *Nippy's Pop* and *S'matter Pop?*).
An early stylist with great élan.

Lady Bountiful by Gene Carr. Her beneficence usually went unappreciated. © King Features Syndicate, Inc.

The Radio Bug in "If 8:15 isn't a good hour, what is?" by the great editorial cartoonist, Walt McDougall.

The comic sections grew throughout the decade, demanding a continuing flow of new features. Many of them indicated the new preoccupations and fads of the day, from the automobile, camera, and suffragette movement, to the Florida land boom. Russ Westover experimented with *Looie and His Tin Lizzie, Snapshot Bill,* and *The Demon Demonstrator,* about a frenetic door-to-door salesman. The great editorial cartoonist, Walt McDougall, did two offbeat strips, *The Radio Bug* and *Hank: and His Animal Friends,* about a retired Uncle Sam type living in a Florida resort boardinghouse. Gene Carr, who did *Nobody Works Like Father* in 1906, created *Lady Bountiful, Little Darling,* and *Poor Mr. W.,* about the trials of the husband of a suffragette. Alfred Frugh created *Hem & Haw,* a comic team in the vaudeville tradition, drawn in an economic style that was later refined in his famed *New Yorker* caricatures. Charles Payne, one of the early individual stylists, did *Nippy's Pop,* later renamed *S'matter Pop? Mr. Twee Deedle* by John D. Druelle was one of several early pages without balloons but with accompanying text. Two early pioneers in animated films made important contributions: John Bray's *Mr. O. U. Absentmind,* and Pat Sullivan's *Old Pop Perkins, Obliging Oliver,* and later, *Felix the Cat.*

by Johnny Hart

A little-known fact is that the "comic strip" is one of three art forms that our infant nation has offered to the world. The second, I am told, is "jazz." The third escapes me, although I suspect that it is "rebellion."

As far back as I care to remember, I drew funny pictures, which got me in or out of trouble depending on the circumstances. A certain amount of prominence and popularity resulted, which, I guess, is what I was after all the time.

My formal education ended abruptly when I graduated from Union-Endicott High School. School was different in those days; they taught softly but carried a big strap. Nowadays you can bad-mouth the teachers. In my day you resorted to placing reptiles in their drawers, which was pretty risky because sometimes they were wearing them.

Soon after I had reached the age of nineteen, a young cartoonist named Brant Parker became a prime influence in my life. In one quick evening we met, became great friends, and began a relationship which would one day culminate in a joint effort called *The Wizard of Id.* Brant imparted to me, with remarkable insight and perception, the essence of all that he had absorbed from the practical application and study of his craft.

To this point in my life I had never really considered cartooning as a *profession,* but in the years to follow, it became a driving force, seemingly etched in my subconscious from that first meeting with Brant Parker.

My application for enrollment in the fraternity of comic heroes arrived in April, 1954, on a small farm in Georgia, when my wife, Bobby, came screaming from the mailbox with a sale from the *Saturday Evening Post.* We danced and sang and gorged ourselves on a chocolate cake which Bobby's mother whomped up for the occasion. Many magazine sales followed, but not with the frequency which is essential to sustain life. Two years in an art department with General Electric returned Bobby and me to a more substantial diet.

I continued my submissions to the magazines, utilizing those quiet hours when normal people slumber. Caveman gags, for reasons which I still cannot explain, were an obsession of mine in those days, although I must reluctantly confess that I have not sold a caveman gag to a magazine to this date.

During my two years with GE, I began to read with astonishment a comic strip called *Peanuts* by Charles M. Schulz. His sense of humor and my own seemed remarkably similar, which inspired me to attempt a comic strip, "I shall repair to my domicile this evening and create a nationally famous comic strip." I announced to my cronies. "Why don't you make it a caveman strip?" said one wag. "You can't seem to sell them anywhere else!"

So I did.

B.C. was rejected by five major syndicates before it was accepted. Two years after *B.C.* began, I created *The Wizard of Id,* which lay dormant for several years thereafter. I mentioned it to Brant Parker and asked him if he would be willing to take on the job of illustrating it. To my delight he consented. Brant and I threw the *Wizard* together during three wild days and nights in a small, dank New York hotel room, taping the finished drawings to the walls as we completed them. When the walls were filled, we called the syndicate and asked them if they would like to see a new strip. They said they would. The men from the syndicate arrived earlier than we had anticipated, finding Brant barefoot and shirtless and me in my shorts shaving off a three-day beard. Ignoring us, they edged their way around the walls and scrutinized our efforts, scuffing away an occasional beer bottle as they went.

When they had finished, they seated themselves about the room amidst the rubble and eyed us carefully. "We think you're disgusting, but the strip is great," they said. "We'll take it!"

Ideas are commonplace. We all have them. What to do with them is another thing. I had trouble for many years trying to come up with them because I needed them for my work. Then one day it occurred to me that it is impossible to run out of ideas . . . and . . . I . . . *GAD* . . . .

★ ★ ★

by Harry Hershfield

A wonderful thing about living in the past is that you can't be dispossessed.

I was born October 13, 1885, twenty years after Lincoln was shot. Thomas Nast was drawing for *Harper's* then. My God, what a giant. I worshiped his draftsmanship.

When I was thirteen I went to the Frank Holme School of Illustration in Chicago and I sold little single-column cartoons to the Chicago *Daily News*. Fifty cents apiece they paid for them. I remember some of them: a Chinese guy writing–"A Yellow Journalist"; a fat guy bowing before a king–"A Broad Subject." Fifty cents!

Frank Holme recommended me to the Chicago *Daily News* and they took me on. I was fourteen and a half years old and I did everything . . . illustrations, retouch, gags.

We had a staff of eighteen artists and everybody stayed around for emergencies. "Draw me a bum walking down the street," the editor would shout and we'd give him a bum.

We had a big staff of illustrators and cartoonists–H. T. Webster, Will Johnstone. . . . John T. McCutcheon was one of our teachers. They used to send us out to cover the courts and the morgue. I covered the Iroquois theater fire and I saved the life of Eddie Foy, Jr.

Well, eventually I knew I had to get to New York, and to get to New York I had to get the eye of William Randolph Hearst. I got a job with the San Francisco *Chronicle* doing sports cartoons, and Hearst, who owned the opposition paper, saw them and said, "We've got to have him in New York."

Tad–T. A. Dorgan–was the great sports cartoonist for Hearst's *Journal* in New York so I started a comic strip named *Desperate Desmond*.

That ran to 1914 when I started *Abie Kabibble*. That ran thirty years and it might still be running if I hadn't had a contract fight and quit. Stupid cartoonist!

Oh, the money! It was marvelous. You know what I got paid my first year? One thousand dollars a week. Tad made $2,000. Hearst didn't care about the money; all he cared about was beating Pulitzer. He knew cartoons sold his papers.

The *News* wanted to hire me away from the *Journal* and King Features for a lot more money, but they needed the title "Abie Kabibble" as well as the character. You know William Howard Taft, as the head of the Supreme Court, had held that the artist could take his character with him, but the title of his feature belonged to the original employer. So I was out at the *News* and out at King Features. I sued the *Journal*. And to show you what a wonderful man Mr. Hearst was—he paid me all the time I was suing him—$7,000.

The comic artists in those days lived like . . . well . . . they lived like *comic* artists. Drinking, gambling . . . I remember one time Brisbane stuck his head in the art department when Tad had started up a crap game. "What's going on here?" he growled. "Double Dome," said Tad—they always called Brisbane Double Dome. "There's a quarter open. Want to come in?"

Tad thought he was a fighter. "Can you box?" he said to me one time. He didn't know I'd been a boxer. (I can still box, but I can't take it anymore.) He had only one good hand, you know. He feinted with his stump and I knocked him cold. Square on the jaw. Cold. He never troubled me again.

The comics have changed a lot since we drew them for New York or Chicago, you know. Now the work is syndicated all over the country and you have to draw six weeks in advance. We drew day to day, and when you were sick, you just weren't in the paper.

They're mostly illustrators today, beautiful illustrators. I drew in the era of big feet and big hands. They don't draw like that anymore.

The cartoonists in the early days didn't have large staffs doing their lettering and inking and backgrounds. They only got together in the saloons. They didn't have any organization. Cartoonists, like actors, were not regarded as socially acceptable.

I'm proud to have been a comic artist. Everything that I have ever been has been because I was a comic artist. I made all my money by comic art. That is what I want to be known by . . . comic art.

★ ★ ★

Skippy by Percy Crosby. Smoking is dangerous to your health.
© 1931 Percy L. Crosby.

Girls, Family and Kids: 1920-1929

The Roaring Twenties. Harding, Coolidge, and Hoover. Prohibition, bootlegging, and gangsters. Will Rogers, Mary Pickford, and Rudolph Valentino. "Yes, Sir, That's My Baby." Sinclair Lewis' *Main Street*, F. Scott Fitzgerald's *This Side of Paradise*, and Theodore Dreiser's *An American Tragedy*. Bobby Jones, Red Grange, and Babe Ruth. The Charleston, black bottom, and lindy hop. Women won the vote, started smoking in the street, and "Heaven will protect the working girl!" And in the comics it was girls, families, and kids.

Captain Patterson set about to develop a group of new comics for the *News*. He proved to have an amazing astuteness and unerring instinct for selecting the right artist for the right feature and choosing the subjects and titles that would appeal to the mass audience he was building for the *News*. To comply with the requests from newspapers throughout the country for permission to carry *The Gumps*, the Chicago Tribune-New York News Syndicate was founded. By 1924, in addition to *Gasoline Alley* and *Harold Teen*, other important strips had made their appearance: *Winnie Winkle, Smitty, Moon Mullins*, and *Little Orphan Annie*. They reflected Patterson's predilection for strips of basic adventure and realism saturated with pathos. Hearst, the other great developer of strips, favored fantasy, burlesque, and humor.

Winnie Winkle the Breadwinner . . . and always in fashion. 1921 (left)—1922 (center)—1927 (right). © The Chicago Tribune.

1933. © The Chicago Tribune.

Winnie Winkle the Breadwinner was one of the earliest strips of the working girl. *Somebody's Stenog* by A. E. Hayward in 1906 must receive credit for being the first. But Hayward's creation never achieved the national impact of *Winnie Winkle (the Breadwinner* was dropped in later years). *Winnie* started as a gag-a-day but soon switched to continuity. Branner always clad Winnie in the latest fashion, and her career and romances were avidly followed by her real-life counterparts. Winnie married, and later her husband joined the Army in 1941 and disappeared, making her the first widow heroine in the comics. While Winnie continued her adventures in the daily, her kid brother, Perry, appropriated the Sunday page in the thirties and forties. Perry, Denny Dimwit, and the rest of his Rinkeydinks gang constituted one of the liveliest of the kid gang strips.

Winnie, Perry and the Rinkydinks from a 1922 Sunday page. © The Chicago Tribune.

Martin Branner's life had all the ingredients of a classic 1930's MGM musical. In the heyday of vaudeville, the Keith and Proctor circuits, Weber and Fields, George M. Cohan, and Lillian Russell, young Branner was an assistant to a team of vaudeville producers. He had some talent as a hoofer and one day was given the job of working up a dance act for fifteen-year-old Edith Fabrini. The eighteen-year-old Branner fell instantly in love. They soon married, against the wishes of their families (another film musical must), who even tried to annul the marriage, although in those days parental consent wasn't required. The youngsters formed a new dance act, and again in movie tradition, they faced years of adversity, at times playing twenty shows a day, painting scenery, living out of trunks, and enduring stretches of "at liberty" in abject poverty. At one time the theater burned down with all their clothes, costumes, and money. The act, however, finally began to click, and by 1914, now billed as Martin & Fabrini Continental Dance Act, they played the Palace and were making $400 a week. Then came their exciting break—"a triumphant tour of Europe was booked"—abruptly canceled by World War I. Branner enlisted. After the Armistice the act resumed, but now Branner had another dream, one nurtured since high school: to be a cartoonist. Between acts he spent every spare minute backstage drawing and developing strips. He finally sold his first, *Louie the Lawyer,* in 1919, followed by *Pete and Pinto*. In the finale of the hypothetical musical, the budding cartoonist would be signed to a contract create a sensational new strip, winning fame and fortune. And so Branner did with *Winnie Winkle,* which opened in the New York *Daily News* in September, 1920.

Branner died in 1970 and Max Von Bibber, his assistant since 1938, continued the strip.

The Winkle family faces a heavy decision in this unique strip from 1926. © The Chicago Tribune. з.

Louie the Lawyer displays his courtroom wizardry in Branner's first feature, 1919.

The debut of *Smitty* by Walter Berndt, November 29, 1922. © The Chicago Tribune.

Smitty's precocious kid brother Herbie in "Elementary, dear Watson." © 1953 The Chicago Tribune.

Berndt's *Smitty*, the demon office boy, in "Safety First," 1948. © The Chicago Tribune.

Walter Berndt's *Smitty* recounted the trials and tribulations of a typical American office boy of the day. Smitty started life in knickers at thirteen, the minimum working age in 1922. He grew over the years to about twenty-three and married Ginny, the office receptionist. Kid brother Herbie, originally a precocious tyke of four, dropped his lisp and matured to eight years—and long pants. In a classic early continuity Herbie lost his dog, which wound up in the pound with five days to live. Berndt milked the story to its fullest. The suspense grew each day as the countdown went to the wire. The *News* was flooded with calls and even money orders to bail out the doomed mutt. It required a news story and a Berndt drawing of the dog climbing out of an inkwell to remind the readers that the dog was not real. Berndt learned to evoke such reader response from the legendary Captain Patterson, as this letter to him dated November 3, 1923, reveals:

DEAR MR. BERNDT:

I believe it would be proper to try an experiment. That is, put a little pathos in the *Smitty* strip. This came to me: Suppose Smitty is unjustly suspected of stealing. Things disappear from the office, which he doesn't take, but the boss, very much against his wish, is convinced of this thievery and that Smitty is light-fingered. So, reluctantly, he fires Smitty who goes home in disgrace and everybody points the finger of scorn at him. Eventually, of course, he is exonerated and all is well.

I believe that you could get some Jackie Coogan appeal by this method.

Sincerely yours,
J. M. PATTERSON

Berndt, a native New Yorker, was himself an office boy for the New York *Journal*, where he met the great cartoonists Milt Gross, Harry Hershfield, and "Tad" Dorgan and set his sights on a cartooning career. His first break came in 1915 when he earned $10 for doing a half page of sports cartoons on Dorgan's day off. A *Journal* custom of the day was that only cartoonists were privileged to go jacketless and wear hats and vests in the office. Berndt, aged seventeen, finally achieved that distinction when Gross left to do *Dave's Delicatessen* and he took over the panel *Then the Fun Began*.

Berndt once explained in *Cartoonist Profiles* how he had sustained *Smitty* for so long: "Well, maybe it's because I've never grown up . . . for instance, when I draw Herbie kicking a can I get just as much of a kick as if I were doing it myself. Drawing was really never work for me . . . it seems to involve native enthusiasm—when I start to draw, I'm off in a cloud of dust with my characters—I'm practically walking down the street with them myself." For fifty-two years the warmhearted adventures of Smitty; Mr. Bailey, his boss; and Herbie reflected the genial nature of their creator, until his retirement in 1974.

Moon Mullins in an elegant animation of the indelicate Willie. Frank Willard often drew upon his own roustabout background. © 1930 The Chicago Tribune.

Lord Plushbottom, Moon Mullins, Uncle Willie and Kayo.
© 1947 The Chicago Tribune.

Frank Willard, a self-acknowledged lowbrow, created an entire ménage of low-life types in *Moon Mullins* in 1923. Raucous, googly-eyed, roughneck Moon originally was simply a bum; at least he was never seen doing an honest day's work. Moon loves girls and is a devotee of pool halls and of making a fast buck. His kid brother, Kayo, is a pint-size Moon (even to the derby hat) who sleeps in a dresser drawer. The rest of the frowzy household are Uncle Willie, a sloppy, unshaven ex-tramp, usually attired in an undershirt; Mamie, his huge blimplike wife; and the down-at-the-heels phony social pretenders Lord and Lady Plushbottom (the former Emmy Schultz). Enough social gaffes are committed to keep an Emily Post busy full time. A Canadian premier once complained that Moon was setting a bad example for the youth, although in debate he admitted reading it

himself, but only because he was past the age when it would do him any harm. Willard's rough, bold style was perfectly suited to the lowbrow humor that attracted readers of all brows.

Willard, born in Anna, Illinois, in 1893, was expelled from school, reduced in rank three times from sergeant to private in the Army, and was an operator of a floating hamburger stand at county fairs before turning to cartooning, thinking at last he had found an easy touch. However, the unrelenting deadlines of the daily and Sunday strip proved to be his lifelong nemesis. Willard died in 1958, and Ferd Johnson, his assistant for thirty years, has continued the strip. Johnson has made some concessions to time: Moon is now a taxi driver and has exchanged his derby for a hat, Willie is slightly less unkempt, Mamie somewhat slimmer, and Emmy is even a bit less homely.

Willard's *Moon Mullins.* Kayo's dresser drawer bunk was standard.
© 1956 News Syndicate Co., Inc.

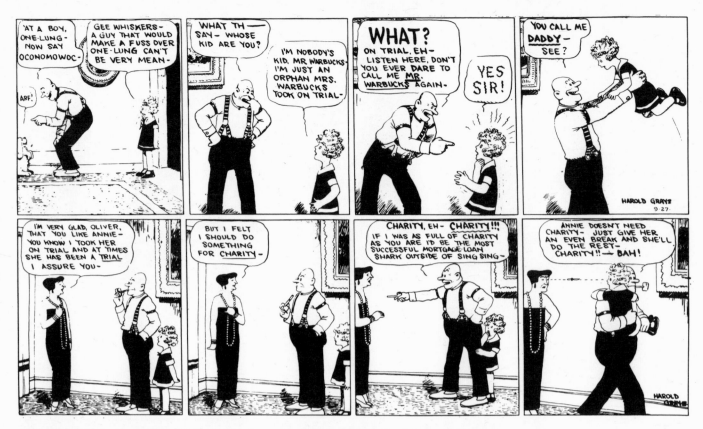

Little Orphan Annie by Harold Gray. Annie meets Daddy Warbucks for the first time. The relationship and the Warbucks philosophy are quickly established. © 1924 The Chicago Tribune.

Two curiously blank eyes stared out at the world for the first time on August 5, 1924. They were the eyes of a fuzzy-haired tyke of eleven in a red dress, who has not aged a day (or changed her dress) in almost fifty years. The lyrics of one of the most frequently heard songs on radio in the thirties described her:

Who's that little chatterbox?
The one with pretty auburn locks?
Who do you see?
It's LITTLE ORPHAN ANNIE. . .
Bright eyes, cheeks a rosy glow,
There's a store of healthiness handy.
Mite-size, always on the go.
And if you want to know—"Arf!" says Sandy. . . .

Annie has made her way through years of constant peril—kidnapping, murder, and Tong wars—despite her lack of pupils, a device that enables readers to supply their own proper expressions. As Coulton Waugh points out, it recalls the work of Daumier, who often drew a face in a white blur but with such skillful accents that its meaning was marvelously clear. Annie's constant companion is a remarkable dog named Sandy, also without pupils, whose basic response to all situations is either "Arf" or "Arf! Arf!" Annie's favorite expression is "Leapin' lizards."

Annie has a foster father, Daddy Warbucks, also pupilless, a benevolent munitions tycoon. This is perhaps the only time a war profiteer has been elevated to hero status in literature. The diamond-studded Warbucks has in his employ two resourceful and mysterious men, an Oriental giant, Punjab, and the sinister Asp. Annie is always losing and being reunited with Daddy Warbucks, and her constant heart-rending quest to find him creates a pathos comparable to that in Pinocchio's search for Geppetto. *Little Orphan Annie* is an unabashed tearjerker. On one unhappy separation from Warbucks, Annie confided to her doll, "I'm just borrowed to work here—and Miss Asthma is getting paid for taking care of me just the same, and keeping the money for herself." Another anguished search, this time for Sandy, provoked an urgent telegram: "PLEASE DO ALL YOU CAN TO HELP ANNIE FIND SANDY STOP WE ARE ALL INTERESTED [signed] HENRY FORD." Annie is constantly at the mercy of the adult world—a world that towers over the little orphan and points up her vulnerability.

Little Orphan Annie is essentially a morality play about the good and evil in the world, at least as seen by its author, Harold Gray. Gray was the first to break the unwritten law against injecting politics into a strip. A

Republican conservative, he never made a secret of his personal philosophy. It was basic laissez-faire, rugged individualism, and the traditional pioneering virtues of piety, hard work, and courage. "A publisher once told me that Annie should be on the editorial page," he said. "I told him that some of the funniest stuff I ever read was in the editorials so why not put them in the comics pages? . . . Liberals and intellectuals are guys who don't do their homework, they don't know history." Gray believed in "skinning your own skunks and not asking the government to help." Annie first took on a detectable conservative coloration in the 1930's, revealing Gray's antipathy to gas rationing, income tax, labor, Communism, left-wingers, and welfare (one character's name was Mrs. Bleeding Heart).

Other cartoonists have since dealt with political satire, notably Al Capp (Li'l Abner) and Walt Kelly (Pogo). It is interesting to note that the Daily Worker had its own advocate in Lefty Louie.

Harold Gray was born in Kenchee, Illinois, in 1894 and was graduated from Purdue University. He originally planned to make the strip's central character.a boy, but Captain Patterson prevailed: "Put skirts on the kid and call her Little Orphan Annie."

The appeal of the homeless waif to millions of compassionate readers is undeniable. A cliff-hanging predicament once caused thousands of phone calls, telegrams, and letters from outraged fans when the Chicago Tribune inadvertently left out one day's episode. A front-page apology ran the next day.

A fugitive Annie with Sandy on the road in 1932. . . . full of pluck and ingenuity.
© The Chicago Tribune 1932,

Annie and Daddy Warbucks, the tycoon.
© 1967 News Syndicate Co., Inc.

Gray died in 1968, a millionaire in the mold of his creation, Daddy Warbucks. Annie was continued by the veteran cartoonist Philip "Tex" Blaisdell. Blaisdell, like Gray and innumerable other cartoonists, learned his craft as a cartoonist's assistant. Known as a master background artist, he practiced his specialty for more than thirty years on dozens of strips, among them On Stage, Dondi, and The Heart of Juliet Jones. Despite the efforts of Blaisdell and brief experiments with new writers and artists, by 1974 Annie fell on hard times. Her dwindling popularity forced the Chicago Tribune-N.Y. News Syndicate to a novel experiment that could have profound implications for the future. On April 22 the original Little Orphan Annie of Harold Gray began its nostalgic revival with an episode first seen thirty-eight years ago in the depression year of 1936.

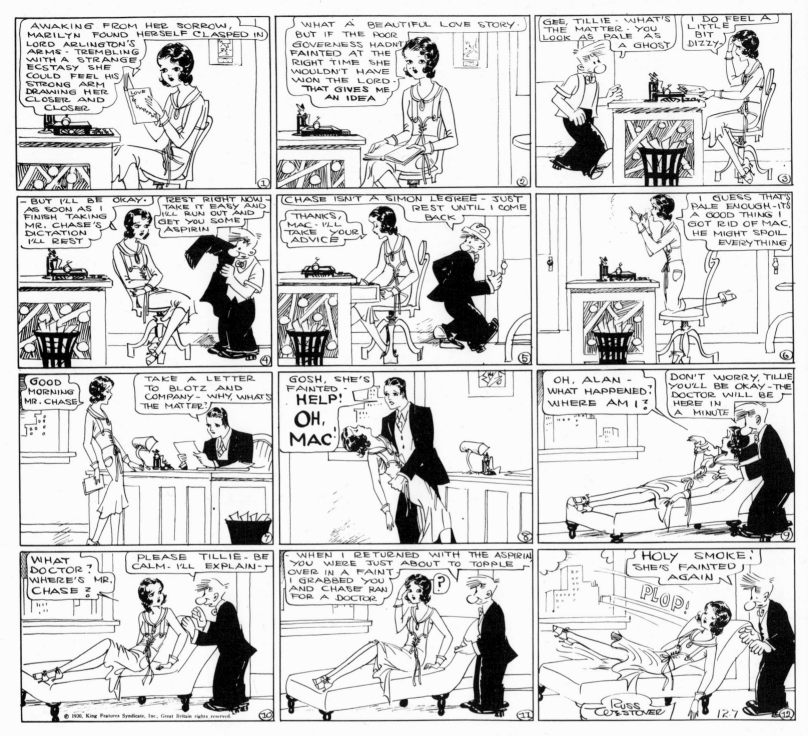

Tillie the Toiler by Russ Westover. Mac, the loyal suitor, is always there even when not needed. © 1930 King Features Syndicate, Inc.

In 1921, a year after *Winnie Winkle*, another working girl with an alliterative title appeared: *Tillie the Toiler,* by Russ Westover. Tillie was a tall, curly-haired secretary with Clara Bow lips. The focus was on her problems with men, office intrigue, and her off-and-on-again courtship with Mac, her pint-size suitor. Westover's early work displayed an unusual virtuosity with the pen and he drew the lithe figure of Tillie with great delicacy. Born in Los Angeles, he studied at the Mark Hopkins Institute of Art in San Francisco and was an experienced newspaper artist before creating his popular "steno" (with *Van Swaggers* as its top). Westover retired in the early 1950's and died in 1966. Bob Gustafson, who now draws the *Beetle Bailey* comic book, continued *Tillie* until the end of its run in 1959.

Paul Robinson's *Etta Kett* began in 1925, as the name might imply, giving etiquette hints for the younger set. However, the Emily Post approach was soon discarded, and Etta, surrounded by a bevy of beaus, started on a long career as the girl most seniors wanted as their prom date. Robinson, born a farmer's son in Kenton, Ohio, started as a professional artist at the Bray Studios, where he contributed to one of the early colored animated films. This training shows in his precise thick and thin line and sparkling black patterns. The image of Etta in the rumble seat of a "flier" crowded with rah-rah collegians identified the thirties and forties for millions. Etta remains the glowing raven-haired charmer forty-eight years after her debut.

Etta Kett by Paul Robinson. Etta in full glory: a date, convertible and a surfeit of suitors.
© 1934 King Features Syndicate, Inc.

Tom Sawyer and Huck Finn.
by Clare "Dwig" Dwiggins, 1919.

generation of kids in *Nipper*. The humor and adventure of youngsters were ideal subjects for the pictorial narrative. In addition to *Reg'lar Fellers, Smitty,* Charles Payne's *S'matter Pop?,* Walter Hoban's *Jerry on the Job, Smitty, Little Orphan Annie,* and *Little Folks* were Ad Carter's *Just Kids* (1921), Doc Winner's *Elmer* (1926), Wally Bishop's *Muggs and Skeeter* (1927), R. M. Brinkerhoff's *Little Mary Mixup* (1927), Ernest McGee's *Hardhead Harry* (1928), Darrell McClure's *Little Annie Rooney* (1927), and Bert Green's *Kids* (1928). *Muggs and Skeeter* and *Little Orphan Annie* are hardy survivors of that era.

Muggs and Skeeter by Wally Bishop. © 1947 King Features Syndicate, Inc.

Kids have always provided raw material for cartoonists, and the twenties were no exception. The literary tradition of *Tom Sawyer* and *Huckleberry Finn, Tom Swift, The Rover Boys,* and *Penrod and Sam* was continued in the comics. Indeed, Mark Twain's classic *Tom Sawyer* and *Huckleberry Finn* were adopted to the comics by the noted illustrator Clare "Dwig" Dwiggins, who also depicted the escapades of a later

Bert Green's *Kids.* 1928 © The Chicago Tribune

Tippie by Edwina (Edwina Dumm). Tippie's enthusiasm is contagious.
© 1941 The George Matthews Adams Service, Inc.

One of the most delightful strips about a boy was *Cap Stubbs and Tippie* (the Sunday page was titled simply *Tippie*). It was written and drawn with warm insight into the relationship of a boy, his grandmother, and his dog. The creator is Edwina Dumm, one of the few women strip cartoonists. Edwina, as she signed her work, born in Upper Sandusky, Ohio, started her art career with the Landon Correspondence Course, and later studied at the Art Students League under Frederick Gruger and George Bridgman.

Tippie was one of the most engaging dogs in comics, marvelously expressive and frisky. Three of Edwina's own dogs, over the years, served as models. Tippie, in fact, can be seen to get furrier in the course of the strip, as were her later models. Grandma Bailey, the eternal fussbudget, never stops worrying over Cap, alternately warning, scolding, or admonishing him, but with an ill-concealed tenderness that has made her one of the comics' unforgettable characters.

Tippie also became a weekly feature, beautifully rendered in wash, in *Life* magazine and the London *Tatler,* changed only to the extent that the dog answered to the name of Sinbad. Harpo Marx, seeing one of Edwina's drawings, enthusiastically described it to Alexander Woollcott. It resulted in her illustrating Woollcott's book *Two Gentlemen and a Lady.* For many years, in addition to writing and drawing *Tippie,* she illustrated a panel feature of verse, *Alex the Great.* In 1967, after almost fifty years, Edwina retired from the pressures of the daily strip, but she hasn't entirely abandoned *Tippie.* Much of her time is now devoted to painting exquisite watercolor portraits of dogs.

Little Annie Rooney by Darrell McClure. A finely illustrated episode. Note the changing vantage points for dramatization. © 1951 King Features Syndicate, Inc.

"Tack" Knight's *Little Folks* in "A local situation." © 1931 The Chicago Tribune.

One kid strip became a classic of the genre: *Skippy*, created by Percy Crosby in 1923. Skippy was one of the most personable kids—even to his costume: an amorphous, checked hat, white collar and huge bow tie, jacket, short pants, and eternally drooping socks. Crosby was an accomplished painter and illustrator, and his expert draftsmanship underlined his wonderfully fluid penstrokes. His loose style had a flair and vigor and an indefinable charm.

Crosby was born in Brooklyn, New York, in 1891 and studied at both the Art Students League and Pratt Institute. His paintings, watercolors, and lithographs have been widely exhibited in leading museums and galleries here and abroad. While turning out *Skippy* daily and Sunday, he somehow found time to write more than a dozen books and innumerable articles and pamphlets on humor, politics, and philosophy.

Skippy, with his hat perched at a rakish angle and a touch of casual elegance in dress, sauntering along, hands in pockets or swishing a stick, or lolling on a stoop or curb, made an indelible impression. The humor had an endearing quality of whimsy and a degree of sophistication not found in his predecessors. Skippy was maturely philosophic and yet boyishly mischievous. He could be cocky, exuberant, lazy, and inquisitive. Charles Dana Gibson once appraised Skippy: "He deserves to be placed with Kim, Huck Finn and Penrod in the gallery of real boys." A successful motion picture version of *Skippy* starring Jackie Cooper appeared in 1931.

Crosby died tragically in 1964, his last sixteen years spent in a mental institution. Even there, his artistic drive never left him; he sketched incessantly, often drawing his fellow patients.

Benjamin Thackston "Tack" Knight, Gene Byrnes' assistant for a number of years on *Reg'lar Fellers*, created another charming kid strip, *Little Folks*, in 1929. It featured sailor-hatted Baxter, Horace, Mary Bright, and Kitty Carr (inspired by his daughter), all remarkably precocious, drawn in a crisp, easy linear style with well-placed decorative blacks. Born in Dillsboro, North Carolina, in 1895, Knight has had a varied career as a newspaperman, commercial artist, animator with Walt Disney and Fleischer Studios, and author of several books on cartooning.

Percy Crosby's *Skippy*.
The boy chauvinist plans ahead.
Circa 1929. © Percy L. Crosby.

95

Mr. and Mrs. by Clare Briggs. This time Joe and Vi's squabble is over child and punishment.
© 1926 New York Tribune, Inc.

Charles A. Voight's masterful pen technique in an unusual one-panel strip of *Petey*.
© 1929 New York Tribune.

The twenties also saw a variety of unique and diverse comic geniuses with enormous technical virtuosity and with a flair for rich and exuberant humor. Some of them created several popular features, in panel format as well as strips, such as Thomas Aloysius "Tad" Dorgan (*Indoor and Outdoor Sports*, panels; *Judge Rummy's Court, For Better or Worse*, strips), Clare Briggs (*When a Feller Needs a Friend, The Guiltiest Feeling*, panels; *Mr. and Mrs.*, strip), J. R. Williams (*Out Our Way*, panel; *The Willetts*, strip), H. T. Webster (*Life's Darkest Moment, Bridge*, panels; *The Timid Soul*, strip), Gene Ahern (*Our Boarding House*, panel; *Room and Board*, panel and strip; *The Squirrel Cage*, strip), and George Clark (*Side Glances, The Neighbors*, panels; *The Ripples*, strip).

The tradition of the emancipated woman started by *Polly and Her Pals* continued with *Winnie Winkle* and *Tillie the Toiler* and was followed in *Fritzi Ritz* by Larry Whittington in 1922 and later by Ernie Bushmiller, *Boots and Her Buddies* by Edgar Martin in 1924, *Etta Kett* by Paul Robinson and *Flapper Fanny* by Gladys Parker in 1925, *Dumb Dora* by Chic Young in 1926

Dumb Dora by Paul Fung. © 1932 King Features Syndicate, Inc.

Fritzi Ritz by Ernie Bushmiller. © 1956 United Feature Syndicate, Inc.

Ella Cinders by Charlie Plumb and Bill Conselman. © 1929 Metropolitan Newspaper Service.

Paul Fung's *Gus and Gussie*.
© 1929 King Features Syndicate, Inc.

and later by Paul Fung, *Ella Cinders* by Charles Plumb and Bill Conselman in 1927 and later by Fred Fox and Roger Armstrong, *Betty* by Russ Westover and later by Charles Voight, *The Kid Sister* by Lyman Young in 1927, and *Dixie Dugan* by J. P. McEvoy and John H. Striebel in 1929 as well as Violet in *Freddie the Sheik* by Jack Callahan and *Dolly of the Follies* by Chet Garde. All but *Winnie Winkle* and *Etta Kett* have gone.

The comics, as did films, continued to reflect the changing tastes in the ideal of American beauty in the 1920's. The films saw the successive popularity of such types as the Vamp (Gloria Swanson), the It Girl (Clara Bow), the Girl Next Door (Janet Gaynor), the Flapper (Joan Crawford), the Classic Beauty (Dolores Costello), the Exotic (Greta Garbo), and the French Doll (Claudette Colbert). In the comics the classic beauty was seen in *Betty*. Charles Voight employed an exquisite pen style in defining the visual delights of the

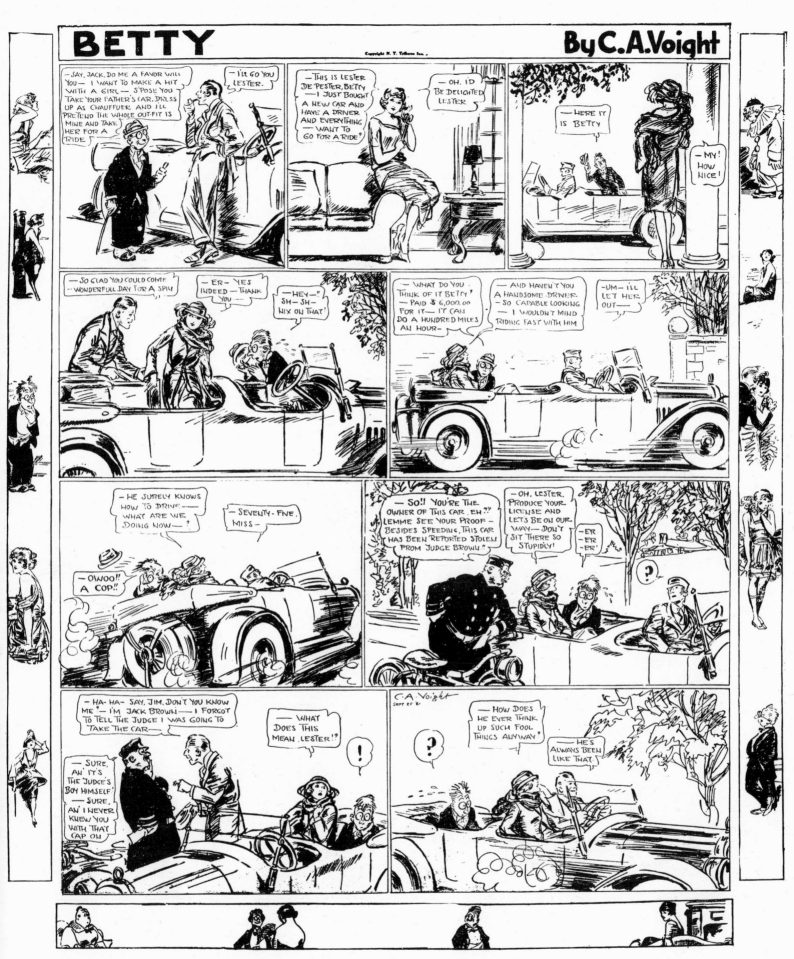

Betty by Charles Voight. Lester de Pester's pretense leads to the inevitable denouement.
© 1921 New York Tribune, Inc.

long-legged, cool sophisticate in the extreme fashion of the day, including beach wear that revealed areas not previously shown on the comic pages. The vogue for the French doll look was seen in *Betty Boop*. Tillie (of *Tillie the Toiler*) and Winnie Winkle were the girl next door. Toots (in *Toots and Casper*) evoked the image of the saucy flapper. Dixie Dugan was a unique type. She exuded an indefinable charm and mystery, enhanced by jet-black hair and almond-shaped eyes. There was a subtleness in her portrayal that is not often seen in the cliché idealizations of the American beauty in the comics. The pretty girl was usually distinguishable by her dress or color of hair, and dimensional characterizations were seen only in older women and men.

McEvoy and Striebel, boyhood friends and graduates of Notre Dame, were both successful before their collaboration on *Dixie Dugan*; McEvoy as a newspaper columnist and screenwriter and Striebel as a commercial artist and illustrator. Their first joint effort was *The Potters,* a Sunday feature. In the 1920's Striebel also did an imaginative feature, *Pantomime,* and a daily panel, *Kids*. McEvoy's serial story, titled *Showgirl,* first published in *Liberty* magazine and illustrated by Striebel, became the basis for *Dixie Dugan*. It began as *Showgirl,* but the name was soon changed when the snappy chorine theme was dropped for a warm, domestic approach. Striebel beautifully adapted his illustrative style to the comic idiom. His figures of the thirties conveyed the nuances of movement and expression. His gestures were fluid and natural, and he avoided stiff or hackneyed poses.

Show Girl (original title of *Dixie Dugan*) by J. P. McEvoy and John Striebel.
"Dixie Wins the First Down." © 1929 McNaught Syndicate, Inc.

Toots and Casper by Jimmy Murphy (excerpt). *It's Papa Who Pays!* was its top feature.
© 1933 King Features Syndicate, Inc.

Striebel's *Dixie Dugan* in a superb example of a tight sequential narrative.
© McNaught Syndicate, Inc.

The family strip had its own population explosion. *Roger Bean* by Chic Jackson, one of the first comic families to age, had started back in 1913, *Pa's Son-in-Law* by C. H. Wellington followed in 1914, and *Doings of the Duffs* by Walter Allman appeared in 1915. *Toots and Casper* by Jimmy Murphy and *The Bungle Family* by Harry Tuthill began in 1918. Others joining the growing comic strip community in the twenties were *The Nebbs* by Sol Hess and W. A. Carlson in 1923; *For*

Better or Worse by "Tad" Dorgan, and *The Man in the Brown Derby* by H. T. Webster in 1923; *The Timid Soul*, also by Webster, and *Mr. and Mrs.* by Clare Briggs in 1924. All have since been replaced by later generations of comics families.

The slapstick tradition was continued by such strips as *Casey the Cop* by H. M. Talburt, *The Doo Dads* by Arch Dale, and *Cicero Sapp* by Fred Locher.

Dimples by Grace G. Drayton, 1914. The origin of the Campbell Soup Kids is apparent.

"Blue-Ribbon Winners," a typically elaborate rendition by Nell Brinkley, 1915.

The female contribution to newspaper comics has been more than merely decorative. A small, yet significant minority, women artists and writers, have created a wide range of features. One of the earliest was Grace Drayton who originated the roly-poly children of the Campbell soup advertisements. Born in Philadelphia, the daughter of an art publisher, her first syndicated series was *Toodles and Pussy Pumpkins*. Her "funny babies," as she called her creatures, became a popular vogue in *Dolly Dimples* and *The Pussycat Princess*. She worked at top speed with never-failing zest and was both author and illustrator of numerous books and magazine articles. Others include: Rose O'Neill (*The Kewpies*), Ruth Carroll (*The Pussycat Princess*), Nell Brinkley (*Nell Brinkley's Cartoon*), Virginia Clark (*Oh, Diana*), Fanny Y. Cory (*Little Miss Muffit, Sonnysayings*), Martha Orr (*Apple Mary*), Dale Connor (*Mary Worth*), Mabel Odin Burvik (*Dickie Dare*), Gladys Parker (*Mopsy*), Ethel Hays (*Flapper Fanny*), Hilda Terry (*Teena*), Tarpe Mills (*Miss Fury*), Marty Links (*Bobby Sox*), Linda Walker (with husband, Jerry, on *Susie Q. Smith*), Marge Henderson (*Little Lulu*), Dale Messick (*Brenda Starr*), Elsie Hix (*Strange as It Seems*), Kate Oscan (*Tizzy*), Kim Grove (*Love Is . . .*), Kate Murtah (*Annie & Fanny*), and Mary Gauerke (*The Alumnae*).

The Timid Soul by H. T. Webster. A typical display of Caspar Milquetoast's pusillanimity.
© 1932 New York Tribune, Inc.

by Alfred Andriola

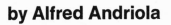

. . . And on Sunday, there were the funnies in full color! In our house they may even have been called the jokes at that point; I'm fairly sure one of my sisters must have said, "Did you see the jokes today?"

It was the Sunday ritual: the comics were passed from hand to hand, and then, when everyone had read them, they would come back to me and I would carefully cut out those I liked best and keep them in envelopes, piled on a chair in my room.

I would open the color pages of the New York *Herald Tribune* with great anticipation. The sight of *Little Nemo in Slumberland* in those magnificent muted tints was cause for great awe and excitement. To be able to draw like that, to write those vivid and exciting adventures, to create such a phantasmagoric setting—what a remarkable man, what a remarkable world! I never tired of Nemo's wild, wild dreams. Weren't mine comparable—didn't I aspire to drawing and writing, when no one I knew had ever done such bizarre things?

A full page of *Betty* was tantamount to going to a Philip Barry play years later: so this was how smart, chic, rich people lived—always in evening clothes at country clubs, or in bathing suits on beaches. I looked forward anxiously to Lester de Pester's weekly humiliation by the crusty *haute monde,* and even by Betty herself, that cool, beautiful carnivore, that everlastingly posing she-bitch, that female castrater of small men (Lester *and* me), whose only flaw was that we adored her!

And the New York *American*—filled with strange, absurd characters like Boob McNutt, Happy Hooligan, Barney Google, Abie the Agent, and Maggie and Jiggs. Yes, even Maggie and Jiggs. Where had I ever seen an Irish millionaire who always wore spats and a top hat and whose hellion of a wife threw rolling pins at him because he wanted to eat corned beef and cabbage? Not at our house!

And talking animals! Of course in today's comics we expect mice, dogs, birds, inanimate objects, and even precocious children to speak more intelligently than prophets and philosophers—but in those faraway years there was only the topsy-turvy world of *Krazy Kat,* who was masochistically in love with Ignatz Mouse and was stubbornly protected by Offissa Pup. This was all contrary to nature, but nature itself was perverse and hieroglyphic in Krazy's quixotic, mad, sweet world.

And there was also the wonderful world of the New York *News* comics: *Harold Teen,* all fun and the latest fads—not to be taken *seriously* like *Winnie Winkle* and her many romances, which always fell apart at the altar. And *Moon Mullins* and his raffish relatives—not like anybody I knew, but wildly funny and just as believable to me as my very proper grandmother, with her solemn piety and her vinegar-soaked headache bands. And *Gasoline Alley,* the strip which really started me to cutting out sequences and saving them: How could you physically *throw away* the strip that showed Walt discovering a foundling on his doorstep? And the next day? And all the months after that, during the long court case between Uncle Walt and Madame Octave? (Was she or wasn't she Skeezix's mother?)

Those peaceful summer years of my life in Rutherford, New Jersey, passed all too quickly—not then, not when you're eight and ten and fourteen years old—but certainly in nostalgic retrospect. Soon I was carrying a large black portfolio around New York City, trying to make somebody—anybody!—understand that I had people in my head who wanted to get out—and they had to get out if only for the sake of my own sanity. I wanted to write about these people and draw them, but no one would listen or understand.

Over the years that followed there were many encouraging rewards and of course a number of disappointments: the time McNaught Syndicate wanted me to sign a ten-year contract to do *Charlie Chan* and that seemed like a lifetime to me, so we compromised on five; the day a syndicate head, looking at my samples, suggested that I change my name, because an Italian by-line would not help sales (this, after Mussolini started making the sounds of a jackal abroad); the time that *It's Me, Dilly!* (which I personally loved and enjoyed doing) was discontinued; and the night that I won the Reuben Award for *Kerry Drake.* But the day I remember most passionately was when I received a letter that opened the door to the heart and soul of this whirligig world of comics. It was in response to a letter I had written, early in 1935, which started out like this:

"Dear Milton Caniff:

"I have read 'Terry and the Pirates' since it started last October and I want to tell you . . ."

★ ★ ★

by Charles Schulz

One of the most remarkable qualities of comic art is its potential for flexibility. The really amazing thing is that we do not see more of it on the comic page today.

When people talk about "putting meaning" into comic strips, too often they mean *political* meaning or refer to crime. In the first case, it seems to me that the meaning is directed into too narrow an area; in the second, it deals with something which plays a relatively minor role in the lives of most people.

It is surprising, therefore, that so many cartoonists working in such a marvelously flexible medium have not dealt more closely with the real essential aspects of life such as love, friendship, and day-to-day difficulties of simply living and getting along with other people.

Comic strip language is notoriously simple, and, of course, this is understandable when one considers the small space to which we are confined in the newspaper. As strips have been reduced in size, due to newsprint shortage and other such difficulties, dialogue has been reduced and real conversations have all but disappeared.

Lack of space, however, is not the only reason for this. I believe that a more important reason is simply a lack of desire and imagination. One of the most delightful aspects of life is conversation. Talking with a new friend, discovering new ideas, and learning about each other can be one of the great experiences of life.

Good writers know this and make use of it in other media. I have been trying to introduce this into the *Peanuts* strip for the past several years because I feel it is an area that has not been well cultivated.

All of us seem to like to remember things and to talk about important happenings from earlier days, but these are hard to illustrate and put into a peculiar medium such as the comic strip.

It is easy enough to criticize political leaders in cartoons and to make statements about the plight of mankind as it stumbles on from day to day, but it is more difficult to talk about something like love in a positive way. It is even more difficult to show people trying to understand their own feelings and making an effort to put these feelings into words.

It is the varieties of relationships within the human condition that interest me. The little boy and girl talking about a subject that is really way beyond them, and the little boy somehow sensing that a father has told him something very profound, and the other little kids in the neighborhood, each with his own desires and feelings, all make for an intriguing set of mysteries to pursue.

This, of course, requires more than one thought. All too often we cartoonists are willing to settle for the easy gag in order to stay on top of our schedules. Syndicate deadlines are a terrible burden to bear, and it is very tempting to let them rule our profession. I am convinced, however, that it is worth falling behind on the deadline a little bit now and then to pursue the second, third, and sometimes fourth thought on a subject in order to say something more meaningful.

Anytime we discuss trying to say something new and of relative importance in a comic strip, we come across another difficulty. The very nature of our profession sets us apart from such free artists as novelists, painters, and classical composers. Ours is a commercial trade and our product has to be sold to newspaper editors who wish to use it to help market their publications.

Initially, our product is taken out to the various newspaper editors by someone who is probably the most unsung hero of all—the syndicate salesman. Whenever I am experimenting in my work and whenever I am searching for a new way to say something, I always think of the salesman who has worked sometimes for years to try to market my strip and of the anxiety he must feel when he wonders if I am going to keep up the standard that he has promised the subscribing editor. I feel a great deal of responsibility toward this salesman and I feel a similar responsibility toward the newspaper editor who has purchased the strip and is using it in his comic section.

The space given to me each day is not literally mine, and, therefore, I have to use it carefully, but I think with the cooperation of all concerned, the comic strip can say more than we probably have been saying in the past. There are gentle things to talk about and there are emotions that can be discussed and laughed at and cried about and I think we can do these things if we pursue them hard enough.

by Mort Walker

My father liked to laugh, and my fondest childhood memory is of seeing him doubled up in his chair after reading *Moon Mullins* on a Sunday morning. His face was red and tears streamed from his eyes. He was obviously enjoying himself. If he didn't choke.

That was over forty years ago, but I can still remember the cartoon that produced this paroxysm. Uncle Willie had brought home a pig he'd won in a poker game. The pig got loose and Willie and Moon (three sheets to the wind) tumbled around the yard trying to catch it, only succeeding in tearing up Mamie's garden, knocking down the clothesline and breaking the fence. As Mamie runs out, the pig escapes through the broken fence with all three in pursuit. Of course, Mamie is not interested in catching the pig as much as she is in grabbing Willie and Moon. The last panel shows Lord Plushbottom describing the scene from the window. "Now they've passed the pig," he exclaims.

It was probably at that moment I decided to become a cartoonist. I wanted to bring laughter and joy into the home every day the way Frank Willard had done. The joy of laughing is almost as strong a desire as the joy of making someone else laugh.

In Kansas City where I grew up, the Main Public Library had a huge newspaper room containing editions from over a hundred cities. I hung out there reading every comic published in this country. The librarian saved the old papers for me, and I clipped my favorite strips and stored them in our attic. That experience gave me a broad overview of the comic business and some ideas about it that you may or may not agree with.

For instance, I don't think the comic strip product has changed much since its inception seventy-five years ago. The number of panels has been reduced, and there is more economy of space and less dialogue and fewer ink lines. But the basic ingredients have endured. The main theme of all the strips is the humanity of man and the universality of his problems. Success isn't funny; failure is. Authority is something to be put down by ridicule. Physical mayhem (if it's happening to someone else) is hilarious. Seeing our comics' characters suffer and fail and resist authority helps ease our own failures and frustrations.

You can see some of these elements at work in my *Beetle Bailey* and you can see the link between Beetle, Sad Sack, Private Breger, Bruce Bairnsfather's cartoons of World War I, and so on back as far as they have had civilians drafted into the military who fail to adjust to regimentation.

We all have our ancestors in the comics as well as in life. Many of the themes are far too familiar, but it's the way the artist embellishes the theme that gives his strip distinction and energy.

My wife worries that people will think everything that happens in *Hi and Lois* happened in our house. All of it doesn't, but plenty of it does. Whenever I remember to do it, I carry a note pad around to jot down observations and humorous incidents around the house. If I'm observant and the kids do their part, I can often arrive at the studio Monday morning with my week's *Hi and Lois* ideas prewritten. If I forget my notepad, I bring back notes written on the back of golf scorecards, match covers, even on the edge of dollar bills.

Hi and Lois is a very realistic strip in that it reflects true happenings in the home. Beetle gets a little more ridiculous in that the characters can fall off cliffs with impunity and stomp each other to smithereens with complete recuperation by the next day. The events are still only exaggerations of reality though, and I stretch the reader's credulity only so far. I wanted another outlet for the flights of fantasy that kept popping in my mind, so *Boner's Ark* was born with talking animals and boundless opportunities for satire to round out my sphere of creativity. Now, with the three strips, I can use just about any type of humor that occurs to me.

The themes, like underground springs, keep new artists supplied with the juices of comic life. I'm sure someone will come along with another strip about a kid's special world done in his own special way and have another hit. And someone will make another million by drawing a father who is likable but whose efforts are laughable. And I'm sure there will be many more "way-out" fantasies involving creatures who make satirical comments on the current scene.

I may do some of them myself.

Tarzan by Hal Foster. A masterful page of Foster's narrative techniques from the epic series that ushered in the era of the adventure strip. © 1936 United Feature Syndicate, Inc.

The Vintage Years: 1929-1939

For millions of Americans the 1930's were mostly a decade of despair. The crash of 1929 brought the Roaring Twenties to a shuddering stop. Thirty billion dollars were lost in the stock market, 2,300 banks failed, and twenty-five percent of America's work force was unemployed.

If you were lucky, you could make $30 a season picking peas, $435 a year as a textile worker, or $1,227 as a teacher (if you were paid). Steaks cost twenty-five cents and men's suits with a vest and two pairs of pants were a "Thrifty $12.50." President Herbert Hoover promised a chicken in every pot and two cars in every garage, and predicted that prosperity was just around the corner. He was wrong.

It was the Great Depression. The American dream had become a nightmare. A time of breadlines and soup kitchens, apples being sold on street corners, "Brother, Can You Spare a Dime?" and *Tobacco Road*; the luckless and homeless roaming the country, fleeing from dust bowls, floods and foreclosure.

The 1930's were dominated by Franklin Delano Roosevelt. While FDR's fireside chats inspired the majority of dispirited Americans, for many he was the object of intense hatred. He dramatized the nation's schizophrenia. The Empire State Building, the tallest building in the world, opened on Fifth Avenue while ruined financiers were jumping from windows on Wall Street. Thousands took luxury liners to Europe at a time when tens of thousands were being dispossessed.

It was also a time of fads, follies, and fancies; the wacky, witless, and inane: marathon dancers and rocking chair derbies, flagpole sitters, and goldfish swallowers. There were other diversions: mah-jongg, contract bridge, crossword puzzles, bingo, Monopoly, and miniature golf.

The comics reflected society's contradictions and its need for escape with the development of two disparate forms—adventure strips and comedy strips.

The Adventure Strip

Americans needed new heroes and heroines to divert them—Charles Lindbergh, Babe Ruth, Commander Richard E. Byrd, J. Edgar Hoover, and Amelia Earhart. Motion pictures, the dream factories for 100,000,000 Americans a week, supplied the romantic heroes and heroines: Fredric March, Clark Gable and Richard Dix, Joan Crawford, Jean Harlow and Greta Garbo. In the comic strips of the thirties, the adventure strip, a new genre, provided the action hero.

Wash Tubbs by Roy Crane, a major contributor to the development of the continuity strip. © 1927 NEA Service, Inc.

One of the earliest and most influential contributors to the development of the adventure strip was Roy Crane. Crane created *Wash Tubbs* in 1924, about the humorous escapades of a pint-size, bespectacled opportunist. In February, 1929, Crane added a new character, Captain Easy, and the strip chronicled the rollicking adventures of the two footloose soldiers of fortune.

The era of the adventure strip really began, however, with the introduction of two epochal strips: *Tarzan* and *Buck Rogers*, which, incidentally, made their debuts on the same day—January 7, 1929.

Tarzan reflected a nostalgic longing for the simpler times of the past when man could come to grips with his environment and exercise control over his destiny. Tarzan was the hero with the Charles Atlas physique, pitting his strength and guile against the forces of nature, wild beasts, and evil men. *Buck Rogers* was man's dream of the future, of solutions to social ills and injustices, and of escape to other planets, where

man employed technology to survive and to combat the evil creatures of other worlds.

The adventure strip demanded new techniques of the cartoonist in order to heighten suspense and drama and create a greater illusion of reality. The disciplines of the illustrator were required: expert draftsmanship; a thorough knowledge of anatomy; the mastering of composition, perspective, light, and shade; and accurate research for authenticity in all details.

The first *Tarzan* strips were adapted from *Tarzan of the Apes* by Edgar Rice Burroughs, published in 1914. (Elmo Lincoln starred in the first of the *Tarzan* films in 1918.) A successful young illustrator, Harold Foster, was selected to do the drawing for the first experimental series of sixty installments. Foster, born in Canada, was a professional boxer, gold prospector, fur trapper and guide before turning to art. He studied at the Art Institute of Chicago, the National Academy of Design, and the Chicago Academy of Fine Arts. As he himself once admitted in *Cartoonist Profiles:* "I was no darn good at a lot of things but I was always good at drawing."

In Burne Hogarth's *Tarzan* intricate composition and dynamic figures created a kinetic tension.
© 1949 United Feature Syndicate, Inc.

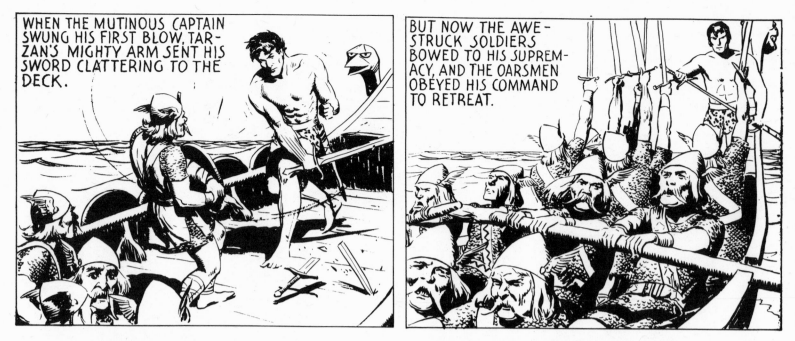

WHEN THE MUTINOUS CAPTAIN SWUNG HIS FIRST BLOW, TARZAN'S MIGHTY ARM SENT HIS SWORD CLATTERING TO THE DECK.

BUT NOW THE AWE-STRUCK SOLDIERS BOWED TO HIS SUPREMACY, AND THE OARSMEN OBEYED HIS COMMAND TO RETREAT.

A Viking episode in *Tarzan* presaged Foster's creation of *Prince Valiant* two years later (excerpt). © 1935 United Feature Syndicate, Inc.

After the first episode, Rex Maxon took over the daily strip as well as the Sunday page (added March 15, 1931). Unable to continue both, Maxon relinquished the Sunday page to Foster six months later. In 1937 Foster relinquished *Tarzan* to create *Prince Valiant*. Burne Hogarth continued *Tarzan*, except for two years, until 1950. Hogarth, a teacher of art history and a student of the old masters, especially the baroque, added his own style to the strip. His command of classic composition and dynamic movement of form and line, and his unique vision and interpretation of nature, are admired by students of the comic arts. A number of cartoonists drew Tarzan for various periods over the years. Since 1968 the strip has been drawn by Russ Manning, who had previously drawn *Tarzan* for the comic magazines.

While some experts consider Foster's magnificent art on *Tarzan* to be the apogee of his work, *Prince Valiant* established him as one of the masters of the illustrative strip. For thirty-five years, each Sunday's episode has been a visual *tour de force:* stunning panoramic scenes of medieval battlefields and castles, tournament spectacles, and vast seascapes. His recreation of the Middle Ages and the derring-do of King Arthur and the Knights of the Round Table is storytelling at its best. Foster does not neglect charac-

....A WORLD OF CONTRASTS; SONS OF THE ICY NORTHLANDS ROW A VIKING SHIP THROUGH A STEAMING, FEVER-HAUNTED JUNGLE. HIDEOUS DRAGONS SQUIRM ON SLIMY MUDBANKS. BEAUTY AND HORROR EVERYWHERE!

HAL FOSTER

NEXT WEEK- The Giant.

A stunning jungle panorama from Hal Foster's *Prince Valiant*. © 1944 King Features Syndicate, Inc.

Prince Valiant by Hal Foster. The exacting draftsmanship and authenticity are evident.
© 1967 King Features Syndicate, Inc.

terization; his script is rich in personal drama. He is unsparing in his devotion to detail and authenticity: in architecture, heraldry, clothing, arms, interiors, ships, and the customs and life-style of the time. An excellent example of his fidelity in re-creating the period is *The Medieval Castle,* which was the "top" for *Prince Valiant* in 1944–45.

In *Prince Valiant,* as well as *Tarzan,* he eschewed balloons in favor of printed narrative beneath the drawings. This enhanced the romantic realism and permitted greater freedom in the composition without intruding on the picture plane or disturbing the aesthetics. Alex Raymond (*Flash Gordon*) was also to employ this device in the tradition of the French nineteenth-century *Image d'Epinal.*

In September, 1971, Foster partially retired. John Cullen Murphy, an expert draftsman, took over the illustration while continuing his own strip, *Big Ben Bolt.* Foster still writes the *Prince Valiant* continuity as well as creates the color scheme.

IN DELIRIUM VAL LIVES AGAIN THE CROWDED, ZESTFUL DAYS OF HIS SERVICE UNDER KING ARTHUR, WHEN HE RODE AT ADVENTURE TO FAR, STRANGE PLACES; AGAIN HE SEES THE GREAT SEA CROCODILE, BALDON'S STUPID, CRUEL FROWN; BOLD THAGNAR AND HIS MIGHTY EXECUTIONER, THE GREAT KING AND MERRY GAWAIN, BEAUTIFUL, EVIL MORGAN LE FEY AND THE OGRE OF SINSTAR WOOD AND AGAIN HE FOUGHT PRINCE ARN WHILE THE NOON SUN SLID DOWN THE WESTERN SKY,— IRON TRISTRAM'S CHARGE, COURTEOUS LAUNCELOT AND WISE MERLIN; HIS MOTHER'S STILL FACE AND EVER HOVERING NEAR; GENTLE ILENE.

NEXT WEEK— *THE GREAT PLAN*

Prince Valiant's dramatis personnae as of 1938.
© King Features Syndicate, Inc.

LIFTING HIS CLEAR VOICE IN A WILD, HAUNTING MELODY, HE SINGS OF HIS HOME IN THE LONELY MARSHES WHERE THE SEA-WIND FOREVER WHISPERS AN ANCIENT SONG AMONG THE SWAYING REEDS. THE FIERCE SEA-ROVERS RELAX AND DREAM OF THEIR LITTLE HOMES BESIDE THE RESTLESS SEA.

The romantic realism of Foster's *Prince Valiant.*
© 1938 King Features Syndicate, Inc.

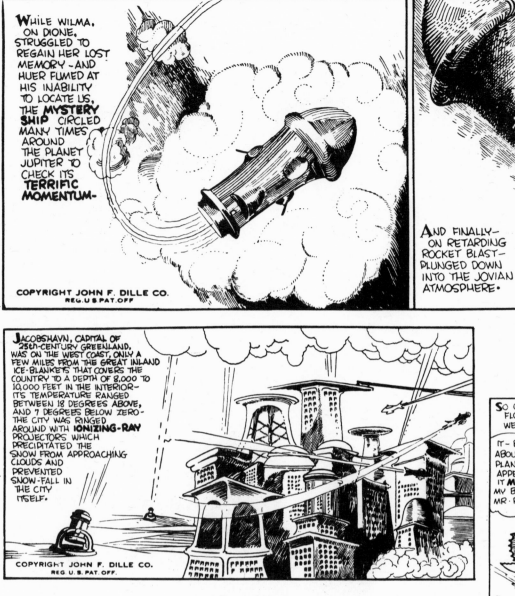

Previsions in *Buck Rogers* by Richard Calkins: (above left to right) orbiting spaceship, retarding rocket, ionizing ray and sky cycle. © 1932 John F. Dille Co.

Jules Verne is acknowledged to be the father of modern science fiction, furthered by H. G. Wells in the late nineteenth century, and by the 1920's the new literary form had become a staple of the pulp magazines.

John F. Dille, head of the National Newspaper Service, saw the potential of science fiction for an exciting strip. New technology was giving a degree of plausibility to the most outlandish speculations about the future, and this made science fiction an even more intriguing idea. Dille's notion crystallized when he read "Armageddon 2419," a short story by Philip Nowlan, in the August, 1928, issue of *Amazing Stories*. He teamed Nowlan with his creative staff artist, Richard Calkins, a World War I Army pilot, and the first science-fiction strip resulted.

Many of the fantastic developments foreseen in *Buck Rogers* have since been realized. In the first sequence alone there were rocket guns and explosive bullets, "jumping belts," "hovercrafts," radar-equipped robots, television-controlled rockets, and the first landing on the moon. In a 1939 sequence, six years before Hiroshima, *Buck Rogers* even described the atom bomb. Ray Bradbury, in his introduction to

Twenty-fifth-century intrigue. Kayla and Killer Kane plot while Buck, near death, floats in space. © 1931 John F. Dille Co.

The Collected Works of Buck Rogers in the 25th Century, analyzed the strip:

> . . . it was not so much how the episodes were drawn but what was *happening* in them that made the strip such a success. The enemy of every boy is gravity, and here in the first few days of *Buck Rogers* that incredible stuff inertron plucks us off our feet and hurls us through the sky, free at last. And free not only to jump over dogs, rivers, and skyscrapers, but to challenge the stars.
>
> Yes, earlier in the 20th Century other cartoonists had shown the inter-planetary wanderings of such characters as *Little Nemo*. But all that was fantasy. *Buck Rogers*, now, was the coming reality, fantasy with a vengeance. . . .

Buck and Wilma cling with magnetic grapplers to a derelict space ship. © 1931 John F. Dille Co.

Calkins drew *Buck Rogers* until his death in 1962. Rick Yager, his assistant, continued the strip until its demise in 1967, apparently a victim of advancing technology and the realization of too many of its predictions.

New Forms in Humor

As America gained its equilibrium in the thirties, it also regained its sense of humor. Tin Pan Alley responded with "Smile, Darn You Smile," "I Found a Million Dollar Baby in the Five and Ten Cent Store," and "Who's Afraid of the Big Bad Wolf?" Comedians dominated the airwaves. From 7 to 7:15 P.M., Monday through Friday, 30,000,000 Americans, including the President of the United States, tuned in *Amos 'n' Andy,* which was later to inspire Sidney Smith to create *The Gumps.* Radio belonged to a different comic each night: Eddie Cantor, Burns and Allen, Fibber McGee and Molly, Will Rogers, Edgar Bergen and Charlie McCarthy, Jack Benny and others. Radio and movies provided the sound and pictures of the twentieth century. But millions could not afford the price of a movie, and radio could still reach only the 10 percent of American families with electricity. Thanks to Rural Free Delivery, rural Americans got their newspapers (along with the Sears, Roebuck catalog), and with them, the comics. In the 1930's, in addition to the adventure strips, a new wave of creativity brought unique and diverse styles of humor to the comics.

Popeye's first appearance in Elzie Segar's
Thimble Theatre, 1929. © King Features Syndicate, Inc.

February 17, 1929, ten days after the debut of *Buck Rogers* and *Tarzan,* another character of great strength and charisma made his appearance. Considering his later worldwide fame, it was rather inauspicious. A one-eyed, banana-nosed sailor smoking a corncob pipe was asked: "Hey there! Are you a sailor?" "'Ja think I'm a cowboy?" was the reply. His name was Popeye, one of Elzie Segar's inspired creations who joined the raffish cast of *Thimble Theatre* (Olive Oyl, her boyfriend, Ham Gravy, and Olive's nasty brother, Castor Oyl), which had started ten years earlier in Hearst's *Evening Journal.*

One of Segar's first cartoon jobs was drawing *Charlie Chaplin's Comic Capers,* a strip that was passed along to a number of artists. During the twenties Segar also did a family strip, *5:15,* later retitled *Sappo,* which became the "top" of *Thimble Theatre* in 1924. While Segar's rich comic talent was evident throughout the twenties, it was not until Popeye arrived on *Thimble Theatre's* stage that the strip reached thematic maturity. Popeye gradually became the featured performer and finally took over star billing in 1932.

Popeye is a comics forerunner of *Superman*: He dives out of planes and lands safely on his ample chin; impervious to bullets, he calmly coughs them up if shot in the chest; knocks out gorillas, human and otherwise; and lifts houses and most anything else. But he himself is more modest about his attributes: "I yam what I yam an' tha's all I yam!" Popeye represents the triumph of beneficent violence as a solution employed only after extreme and villainous provocation. One of Popeye's earliest displays of prowess was when he got rid of Olive's boyfriend Ham in a "fisk fight" and took Olive as his own "Sweet Patootie." Popeye, to be generous, is not very handsome. Olive, in fact, once remarked, "I'd hate to go through life with a thing like that on my neck." Olive, herself a most ungenerously endowed female, is a notable exception to comic strip heroines. But perverse destiny has united them, along with Popeye's "adoptik infink" Swee'pea.

Segar's stories were rambling and strung out. They are a further development of the potential of the continuity strip first seen in *Hairbreadth Harry*. He laced his plots with suspense and a full measure of zany characters: Geezil, Roughhouse, the Sea Hag, Poop Deck Pappy, Eugene the Jeep, Alice the Goon, and the incomparable con man and moocher, J. Wellington Wimpy.

One night, June 20, 1931, to be exact, Popeye took Olive to dinner at Café de Roughhouse. It was at the café that Wimpy's addiction to hamburgers was first evidenced. His passion for them was so strong that he once lost a $20,000 bet with Popeye when he couldn't hold one for ten minutes without eating it (he lasted nine minutes and fifty seconds).

Spinach is the source of Popeye's strength. He gorges himself on the leaf by the barrel, especially when faced with an emergency need of muscle. For some unexplainable reason, Popeye's biceps, large as

Thimble Theatre

A pre-Popeye *Thimble Theatre* by Segar. © 1926 King Features Syndicate, Inc.

Popeye delivers a typical coup de grâce, by Segar. Circa 1935. © King Features Syndicate, Inc.

watermelons, have seemingly slipped to his forearms, leaving his upper arms as thin as pipestems. This anatomical phenomenon only increases the illusion of his power.

Segar, born in Chester, Illinois, was only forty-four when he died in 1938, but his creation was already a solid success, appearing in hundreds of newspapers, on radio, in Max Fleischer animated films, and in countless products.

Bud Sagendorf, Segar's assistant, was still in high school when he met Popeye's creator in 1931, and he lived with him until Segar's death. Except for a period when the strip was drawn by Bill Zaboly, Sagendorf has since been responsible for Segar's classic burlesque.

Minute Movies by Ed Wheelan began in 1922. Although its title is reminiscent of *Thimble Theatre,* the concept was quite different. In pseudomovie form, starting with "Ed Wheelan Presents," the audience was offered comedies, travelogs, newsreels, and miniature versions of such literary works as *Hamlet, Treasure Island,* and *Ivanhoe.*

American heritage in humor dating back to Ben Franklin was of the "cracker barrel" variety. This was gradually shed in the early years of the comic strips, and until 1930 much of the humor was based on the distinction of the "highbrow" and "lowbrow" as in *Boob McNutt* and *Mutt and Jeff.* They were not exactly solid-citizen types but were the "little men" similar to Charlie Chaplin's tramp and the ineffectual underdogs that were later found in the works of Ring Lardner, James Thurber, and Robert Benchley. *Maggie and Jiggs, Polly and Her Pals,* and *Abie the Agent* were essentially lowbrow characters who had already fought their way to middlebrow status and who were striving for highbrow acceptance. A new strip which was about to make its appearance created a new middlebrow white-collar hero, who has achieved a shaky, if not solid, respectability without highbrow aspirations, reaffirmed the basic solidarity of the family, home, mother, and all the Judeo-Christian ethic.

Minute Movies by Ed Wheelan. Circa 1928. © Geroge Matthew Adams Service, Inc.

Blondie by Chic Young. The newlywed Dagwood has much to learn. © 1934 King Features Syndicate, Inc.

Humor in Suburbia

Blondie by Murat "Chic" Young began life on September 15, 1930, as the vivacious and exceedingly cute but bold fiancée of Dagwood Bumstead, heir to his billionaire father, who objected to their marriage. They finally made it to the altar on February 12, 1933, but were cut off without a penny from the Bumstead fortune. The strip then settled into its well-known pattern. Dagwood goes to work in an average job (boring), with an average boss (grumpy and vexed), lives in an average suburb (overrun with door-to-door salesmen), rears an average family (Baby Dumpling in 1934 and Cookie in 1941—both smarter than their father), has an assortment of average neighbors (nasty and nastier), with an average number of marital spats (daily), and lives a more or less happy life. The only unaverage part of Dagwood's life is his beautiful and resourceful wife, Blondie. George Dangerfield in *Harper's Bazaar* saw *Blondie* as "... a fine, old-fashioned picture of modern domesticity with all the colors, except those of disillusion and boredom. It's Utopia in the suburbs, a consolation to the married, and to those who are not married, a means of imagining themselves married for two minutes a day."

Blondie, as contrasted with preceding family strips, takes on the more frantic pace of "modern" life. Dagwood still retains traces of his "little man" heritage. While he is not a patriarch and master, he is at least the wobbly man of the house. Blondie, while not exactly the liberated woman in today's terms, has at least progressed past the subservience of Polly's mother and Phyllis Blossom of *Gasoline Alley*. She is the typical wife to whom her husband says he owes everything he has done or achieved. In Dagwood's case it's true.

The concept of American family life depicted in *Blondie* has since been perpetuated in the movie and TV family situation comedy. *Blondie* has been successfully translated into all media. Consider some of the basic dogma: Dagwood is inept and bungling but a well-meaning husband and father. Blondie is the patient and understanding wife. Dagwood is not handsome but endearing and loves Blondie no matter how provoked. Blondie is attractive but no siren and loves Dagwood no matter what he does. Dagwood is the hardworking breadwinner, albeit underpaid. Blondie manages the finances carefully except for ex-

Blondie in 1932. Dagwood's marriage the following year increased his stature. © King Features Syndicate, Inc.

Dagwood's irrepressible appetite creates a neighbood crisis in this typically frenetic *Blondie* Sunday page. Chic Young constructs his humor with unerring precision.
© 1965 King Features Syndicate, Inc.

pensive lapses of impulse buying. Dagwood is exploited unmercifully by kids, mailmen, boss Dithers, Herb Woodley, and other neighbors. Blondie is adored by everyone.... In short, everything is enshrined as it should be in comic-strip middlebrow suburbia. As Max Shulman, the author of *Rally Round the Flag, Boys!*, pointed out, "Humor is something people can read, or say, or see. ... 'I know somebody just like that,' but never anything that could make them say 'that's me!'" The Bumsteads have become everyone's next-door neighbor. When Blondie's baby was expected, 400,000 people wrote in, suggesting names!

Blondie is reputed to be the most widely syndicated strip. Throughout the world the Bumsteads are the quintessential American family. After all is said, however, the essential ingredient of *Blondie*'s success is simple: It's funny. The quality and consistency of its gags have rarely been equaled. The humor is alternately warm, outlandish, slapstick, and sentimental.

Young drew *Blondie* with meticulous care. His storytelling techniques gave the illusion of witnessing a stage play. Whole episodes were often drawn from a fixed position, and the scenes proceeded logically with an easy flow.

Chic Young's most enduring contribution to American culture, however, may turn out to be the Dagwood sandwich, an incomparable, mind-boggling concoction that makes today's hero (or submarine sandwich) a mere tasty canapé.

Chic Young died in March, 1973. *Blondie* is continued by his veteran staff, his son, Dean, and Jim Raymond, who has done most of the drawing in recent years.

For Blondie love is a liverwurst sandwich. © 1968 King Features Syndicate, Inc.

The Sports Strip

Another phenomenon starting in the Roaring Twenties and continuing through the thirties was the spectacular rise and popularity of spectator sports. Baseball was America's most popular pastime and the New York Yankees the most feared team. Professional football was still in its infancy, but millions with their raccoon coats and hip flasks filled college football stadiums throughout the country. Sports, like the movies and the comics, had its golden age, and this was it. Each sport seemed to produce a towering figure that dominated the era. Baseball had Babe Ruth; golf, Bobby Jones; football, Red Grange; tennis, Bill Tilden, and boxing, Jack Dempsey. The comics would seem to be the perfect medium for a sports adventure story, yet no strip had emerged with an athlete as its central figure. In 1930, however, Ham Fisher, after years of trying to sell a boxing strip, launched *Joe Palooka*.

Ham Fisher was a staff cartoonist for the Wilkes-Barre *Herald*. The idea for *Joe Palooka* came one day after an interview with a gentle, childlike boxer. The irony of a mild-tempered man engaged in a brutal profession struck Fisher as the theme on which to base a new strip. In 1927 Fisher came to New York with

© McNaught Syndicate, Inc.

Joe Palooka by Ham Fisher. Like his real-life counterpart, heavyweight champion Joe Louis, Palooka fought while in service. © 1944 McNaught Syndicate, Inc.

carfare and $2.50, but *Palooka* was turned down by syndicate after syndicate. Landing a job at the New York *Daily News*, Fisher continued the rounds of the syndicates without success. His opportunity came when he got a job as a salesman for McNaught Syndicate and General Manager Charles McAdam promised, in time, to give *Joe Palooka* a tryout. Fisher demonstrated his sales ability with *Dixie Dugan*, which, after a promising start, had gained few subscribers. Fisher's sales trip set a record by signing up thirty papers in thirty days. He felt he could do the same with *Palooka*, but by this time the syndicate was more interested in keeping a star salesman than adding any promising property. When McAdam went on

vacation, Fisher, on a gamble, took *Palooka* on the road and in three weeks sold twenty papers. The first sports adventure strip was launched. *Palooka* became one of comics' greatest successes and Fisher's start a part of the profession's lore.

As Coulton Waugh describes Fisher: "He tried college for two weeks, spending, he says, most of his time in night clubs. Ham was a racy young man with a touch of sawdust in him; he had the instinctive feel of the boxing and wrestling world, a sharp nose for the various smells of politics, an earthy guy, Ham." Perhaps it was these qualities that enabled Fisher to weave his tale of adventure, suspense, romance, and humor about the seamy fight racket. Joe makes his

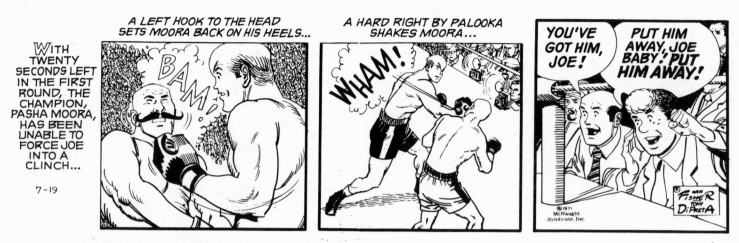

Joe Palooka by Tony DiPreta. After thirty-four years, Joe is still battling for the championship. © 1971 McNaught Syndicate, Inc.

simple, unsophisticated, and humble way through the crime world and the fight game—the training camps, the seconds, trainers, handlers, and hangers-on—the big fight hoopla, the crowds, the ring, the weighing in, and the smashing, bruising fights.

Palooka found a vast audience of sports buffs of all ages, but the strip was also the classic confrontation of good versus evil, the virtuous and innocent versus the corrupt and the corrupters. Joe Palooka was a young heavyweight champion, simple, big-hearted, incorruptible, with a perfect physique and a dynamic left cross.

The name is well contrived. "Palooka," prizefight slang for a third-rate boxer, also gives a sense of immigrant origins and, with the common name Joe, gives the image of an average pug whom everyone can root for. Despite Palooka's prowess, his name implied that

somehow he could be taken and was always susceptible to winding up as the patsy for those with less ability but more guile.

The other characters are typecast: his brash fight manager, Knobby Walsh ("OK, Knobby, I'll do jus' like ya say, thank . . . ya!"); devoted friends, Jerry Leemy and the mute Little Max; and his best girl, the beautiful sweet Anne Howe, who in time was to become Mrs. Palooka.

Paradoxically, Ham Fisher, a complicated man with an outgoing personality, created a character of sublime innocence. Fisher committed suicide in 1956. Since October, 1959, the strip has been in the able hands of artist Tony Di Preta. Joe Palooka, now happily married and the father of two, Joannie and Buddy (Joe, Jr.), is still the heavyweight boxing champion of the world. Palooka is not as naïve as he once was, but

Curly Kayoe by Sam Leff. © 1944 United Feature Syndicate, Inc.

Ozark Ike by Ray Gotto. © 1949 King Features Syndicate, Inc.

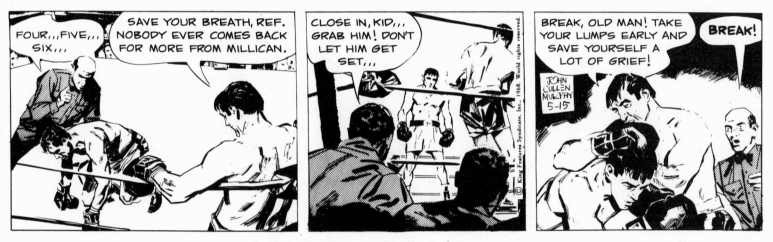

Big Ben Bolt by John Cullen Murphy. © 1968 King Features Syndicate, Inc.

as Di Preta observes, "He's still almost too good for today. He really needs a vice or two to make him more human."

Despite the success of *Palooka*, no rash of sports strips followed, as often happens in syndication. In the 1940's *Joe Jinx*, a strip created by Sam Leff before 1920 and continued by Vic Forsythe, turned to boxing when Jinx became a fight manager, and subsequently the strip was renamed *Curley Kayoe*. Another boxing strip, *Ned Brandt* by B. W. DePew, appeared in 1947, Ray Gotto's *Ozark Ike*, a hillbilly baseball player, had a period of popularity in the forties and fifties. *Big Ben Bolt*, a beautifully delineated boxing strip, started in the 1950's and was executed by one of comics' best illustrators, John Cullen Murphy. Bolt, however, is not a palooka but a college-educated fighter who handles himself with great competence in or out of the ring.

Aviation Strips

It was inevitable that the public's preoccupation with the exploits of the new aviator heroes would inspire aviation adventure strips. The heroics of the aces of World War I still fired the imagination of the public. Lindbergh's dramatic solo flight across the Atlantic was only a few years in the past, and he, Richard E. Byrd, Amelia Earhart, Wiley Post, and dozens of others continued to make headlines with daring flights around the world. It seemed as if every day would bring new records in speed, distance, altitude, or endurance by aircraft of every kind. Among the first of the aviator adventure strips were *Tailspin Tommy* by Hal Forrest (1929); *Scorchy Smith* by John Terry (1930); and Eddie Rickenbacker's *Ace Drum-*

125

Smilin' Jack by Zack Mosley with a vertical twist for dramatics. © 1959 News Syndicate Co., Inc.

Barney Baxter by Frank Miller, a virtuoso of pen techniques. © 1942 King Features Syndicate, Inc.

Tim Tyler's Luck by Lyman Young. An early adventure strip by Chic Young's brother. © 1942 King Features Syndicate, Inc.

mond, drawn by Clayton Knight (1935); *Smilin' Jack* by Zack Mosley (1933); and *Barney Baxter* by Frank Miller (1936). Following *Buck Rogers* into space were *Brick Bradford* by William Ritt and Clarence Gray (1933) and *Flash Gordon* by Alex Raymond (1934). In the wake of *Tarzan's* success came a number of jungle and exploration strips, including Raymond's *Jungle Jim* (1934) and Frank "Bring 'Em Back Alive" Buck's *Ted Towers* (1934). Lyman Young's *Tim Tyler's Luck,* which started as a routine kid strip in 1928, added a Sunday page in 1931 and developed into a full-fledged adventure strip.

In 1932 Roy Crane's strip *Wash Tubbs* was retitled *Captain Easy,* reflecting the complete change that the strip had taken from its inception. Crane exerted a great influence on his contemporaries, many of whom consider him one of the finest artists and storytellers the medium has produced. His constant striving for new pictorial effects led him to experiment with the Benday, a mechanical method of achieving halftone. He became its master. He used it with exquisite taste to accent his beautifully composed black-and-white drawings, giving them an amazing range of depth, tone, and texture. Crane remains a step away from the purely illustrative strip; his figures and characterizations are a unique blend of the comic and illustrative styles. In 1943 Crane created a new vehicle for his talents, *Buz Sawyer*. Leslie Turner, his longtime friend and associate, took over *Captain Easy*. After a brilliant career Turner retired in 1970 and was succeeded by his art assistant, Bill Crooks, and writer Jim Lawrence. Crane has continued his superlative work in the adventures of the naval aviator Sawyer.

Captain Easy by Roy Crane, a master storyteller.
© 1940 NEA Inc.

Roy Crane's *Buz Sawyer*. Crane's bold black and white style accented by Benday.
© 1947 King Features Syndicate, Inc.

A striking one-panel *Buz Sawyer* by Crane. © 1964 King Features Syndicate, Inc.

Captain Easy. A fine specimen of Leslie Turner's continuity. © 1968 NEA, Inc.

127

Chester Gould's first daily strip of *Dick Tracy*, October 12, 1931. Tracy proposed to
Tess the next day but they were not wed until 1949. © 1931 News Syndicate Co., Inc.

The Crime Strip

Gangsterism during the Prohibition Era reached its savage nadir with the St. Valentine's Day massacre of 1929. The thirties saw a new crime wave—Al Capone, John Dillinger, Machine Gun Kelly, Pretty Boy Floyd, Legs Diamond, Ma Barker's Gang, Bonnie and Clyde—and the new folk heroes of law enforcement, J. Edgar Hoover and his G-men. The films glamorized the deadly game of cops and robbers in Paul Muni's *Scarface*, Edward G. Robinson's *Little Caesar*, and Jimmy Cagney's *Public Enemy. The Last Mile* was a hit on Broadway.

The time was ripe for a crime strip, and on October 4, 1931, *Dick Tracy*, the first serious police strip, made its appearance.

Tracy's creator, Chester Gould, born in Pawnee, Oklahoma, in 1900, was a graduate of Northwestern University and a staff artist on a number of Chicago papers. He submitted his creation to Captain Patterson of the New York *Daily News* under the title *Plainclothes Tracy*. Patterson, with his unerring instinct, renamed it *Dick Tracy*.

The adventures of the razor-jawed, hawk-nosed Tracy; his girlfriend, Tess Trueheart (also named by Patterson); assistant, Pat Patton; and his protégé, Junior, took only a few months to become a roaring success. Among its millions of readers was J. Edgar Hoover, one of the inspirations for the strip. The first week set Tracy's pattern. Tess' father, Jeremiah Trueheart, was brutally shot—the first time anyone had been gunned down in the funnies.

While *Tarzan* and *Buck Rogers* were adaptations of existing works of fiction, *Tracy* was the first modern adventure strip created for the medium. While the former are in the school of romantic realism, as is *Prince Valiant*, Gould introduced a new, hard-hitting type of realism dealing with contemporary themes. It marked a radical and historic departure: The comics became a misnomer; the comics were no longer just funny.

Tracy is in a line of fictional sleuths starting with Edgar Allan Poe's C. Auguste Dupin and Sir Arthur Conan Doyle's Sherlock Holmes (both of whom Gould admired), and the hard-boiled detective action story pioneered by Dashiell Hammett and Erle Stanley Gardner in *Black Mask*, a pulp magazine of the twenties.

Ellery Queen in his introduction to *The Celebrated Cases of Dick Tracy* cites Tracy as the world's first procedural detective in fiction: "... Dick Tracy's methods have been mental as well as muscular, deductive as well as dynamic ... he is a proficient craftsman of true-life police techniques. [And these] ... have included the newest procedures known to science...."

Gould's invention: a two-way wrist TV
(sequel to the two-way wrist radio).
© The Chicago Tribune.

DICK TRACY

Tracy's modern crime detection brings to bay the notorious Flyface.
© 1960 The Chicago Tribune.

It has been the succession of bizarre villains in *Dick Tracy* that has caught the public's imagination. No real-life gangster could match their chilling menace. In naming his characters after their looks, traits, or vices, Gould followed an old literary device. Gould's Grotesque Gallery includes Pruneface, Flattop, The Blank, The Rodent, Itchy, Measles, The Brow, The Midget, Flyface, Mumbles, B-B Eyes, and The Mole.

It is worthwhile to view Gould's work in the tradition of the grotesque in literature dating back to the horrific masks of Greek comedy. Victor Hugo, Ben Jonson, and Edgar Allan Poe, among others, have elevated the grotesque, the bizarre, and the ugly to art. Among the best Gould examples are the hideous duo

Another Gould innovation: the first closed-circuit TV lineup in 1953.
© The Chicago Tribune.

A gallery of Gould grotesques:
(clockwise from bottom) B.O. Plenty, Flattop,
Pruneface, Mrs. Pruneface, the Brow.
© The Chicago Tribune.

of B. O. Plenty and Gravel Gertie. The tradition was continued in the horror films of the twenties and thirties with *Dracula, Frankenstein, The Phantom of the Opera, Dr. Jekyll and Mr. Hyde*, and *King Kong*.

Gould's style of drawing is like a blueprint. The figures are stiff and angular. Everything is in stark contrast, as if caught in a searchlight. Tracy always stands out in flat black. He meticulously details the ingenious devices of the villain and the methodology of crime detection. Labels are freely used to make everything crystal clear.

Tracy was the first to depict rampant violence. The crooks never escaped by pleading the Fifth Amendment, but wound up riddled with bullets, or met a more gruesome end. It is not surprising that Gould has his critics in this day of parental concern about the extensive portrayal of violence in the entertainment media. Gould remains unconvinced: "If I were a kid, the thing I would fear the most would be ending up with a bullet whirling through my head. We need more graphic portrayals of where the road of crime leads."

Dick Tracy appears in more than 600 domestic and

Secret Agent X-9 by Alex Raymond.
© 1934 King Features Syndicate, Inc.

50 foreign newspapers. Movies, radio shows, books, games, and toys (including the famous two-way wrist radio and Sparkle Plenty dolls) have made Gould a millionaire. Contrary to the teaching of Tracy, Gould has proved that crime does pay.

Other police and detective strips soon followed. In addition to Sax Rohmer's *Fu Manchu* (1931) were *Radio Patrol* (originally titled *Pinkerton Jr.*) by Eddie Sullivan and Charlie Schmidt (1933); *Don Winslow of the Navy*, essentially a police-spy strip, by Frank Martinek and Leon Beroth (1934); Alex Raymond's *Secret Agent X-9* (1934); Lank Leonard's *Mickey Finn* (1936), continued since Leonard's death in 1970 by his assistant and veteran cartoonist-writer, Morris Weiss (*Joe Jinks*, *Joe Palooka*); and Alfred Andriola's *Charlie Chan* (1938).

Mickey Finn by Lank Leonard. Circa 1944. © McNaught Syndicate, Inc.

New Directions in Humor

Prehistoric man had to wait until August 7, 1933, before the twentieth century discovered what an incredible creature he was. V. T. Hamlin's *Alley Oop* and his girlfriend, Oola, have had some remarkable adventures during the forty-one years since Alley's encounter with a lovable and playful dinosaur, Dinny (who bawls like a baby when Alley, mistaking his intentions as less than honorable, cracks him over the head). Not the least astonishing thing about *Alley Oop* is that, according to all paleontologists, dinosaurs had died out by the end of the Cretaceous period, roughly 75,000,000 years before man appeared. But of course Alley is no ordinary man, primitive or otherwise.

Hamlin, born in Perry, Iowa, in 1900, served in France in World War I, studied journalism at the University of Missouri, and started a career as a reporter and photographer before turning to cartooning. Hamlin's interest in prehistoric life was actually stimulated by a geologist while he was working for an oil company in Texas.

After six years of Alley's romping in the early Stone Age in the Kingdom of Moo, ruled by King Guzzle and various heretofore-extinct reptiles, Hamlin decided to have Alley vault a few more ages of man. On April 5, 1939, Alley and Oola were about to be captured by King Guzzle's minions when they disappeared before the astonished eyes of the king. The last box carried a cryptic note: "You must now say good-

© NEA, Inc.

bye to Moo, if you would follow Alley Oop in this strangest of many strange adventures." The disappearance was due to the incredible time machine of the twentieth-century scientist Dr. Wonmug. The good doctor was embarked on a scientific experiment to bridge the void of time. When the machine ran a mite too long, Alley and Oola were miraculously plucked from the past and materialized in the twen-

Two strips from the first weeks of V. T. Hamlin's *Alley Oop*. © 1933 NEA Service, Inc.

132

tieth century. Hamlin's ingenious device has been used to enable the displaced cavemen to roam throughout the ages, from the present to ancient Egypt, Rome, the Middle Ages, back to the Stone Age, and back again. By this time the pàradox of the dinosaur was submerged in such a time fantasy that Dr. Wonmug himself was forced to conclude, "Well, behold the unheard of!"

Alley's gigantic forearms and calves, puny upper arms and thighs, like those of his fellow cavemen, are in the Popeye tradition. The stylistic quirk seems to convey a feeling of primitive power.

Hamlin's forte is action. In Alley and Dinny's first encounter the entire range of the cartoonist's art was superbly employed in creating the illusion of movement: a shot of Alley clinging for dear life to the neck of the wildly fleeing Dinny, wonderfully articulated, captures the fluid motion of weight in space, which seems to want to leap off the page.

Oola, by the way, doesn't show her prehistoric age at all. While her cavewomen contemporaries reflect their evolutionary stage of development, Oola could have been a recent contestant for Miss America. So far, she is the only gal Alley has ever carried off to his cave.

Hamlin retired in 1971 and his assistant, Dave Graue, continues the strip.

The Pantomime Strip

The thirties also saw a number of humor strips that were, like *Krazy Kat*, singularly unique personal comic visions. *The Little King* by Otto Soglow is one of them. Soglow's character first appeared in a series of drawings in *The New Yorker*. Syndicated by King Features in 1933 under the title *The Ambassador*, it became *The Little King* the following year.

Otto Soglow's pantomime classic *The Little King*. © 1956 King Features Syndicate, Inc.

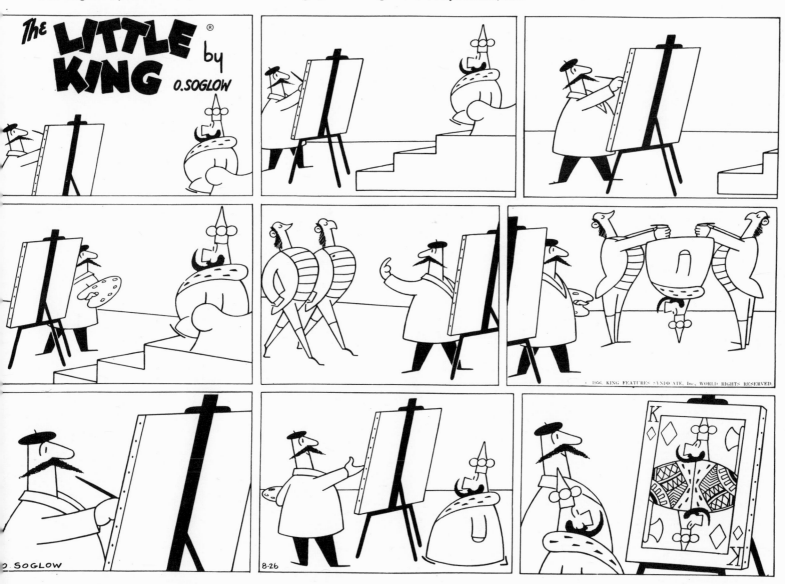

In one of the few strips employing the ancient art of pantomime, the silent mythical King is as eloquent as William Jennings Bryan, proving that a Soglow picture is worth a thousand words. The King is a quixotic figure, most of whose troubles come from attempting to be too democratic. Soglow is a rare comic genius with an ingenuous and delightful wit.

Soglow's drawings have a rhythmic flow and are executed with a pure economy of line and precise spotting of black. A performer as well as a cartoonist, he is a man of instinctive comic talent and has a classic countenance reminiscent of Buster Keaton. He studied at the Art Students League in New York and found his first job by consulting the telephone book and jotting down the names of all the publications. As Soglow described it, "I took a handful of drawings and started to call on six publishing houses. I started at the Battery and worked my way uptown from there. The following day I started from the street I left off the previous day." Soglow reached Thirty-fourth Street before he landed a job for a publisher of cheap pulp magazines. "I received seven dollars for my first

published drawing," he recalled. "From then on I decided to become a cartoonist."

One classic Soglow sequence that typifies his gentle humor has the democratic Little King waking up in his royal bedroom, walking through the magnificent marble halls, down the grand staircase of the palace, and as the huge oak drawbridge opens, the King saunters out to take in the morning milk. Soglow's humor is gentle, civilized, and sophisticated but uncomplicated. If any humor can be said to be based on man's humanity to man, it's Soglow's.

Another long-running pantomime feature also born in the magazines made the transition to the comic strip the year following *The Little King*. *Henry* had been appearing since 1932 in the *Saturday Evening Post*. A German pictorial magazine reprinted a page of *Henry* under the title *Henry, der Amerikanischer Lausbub*. William Randolph Hearst, on one of his European trips in 1935 and with his keen eye for new cartoon talent, noticed it. It took one wire back to New York and *Henry* was a new strip with King Features Syndicate.

Henry drawn a year before Carl Anderson's death at age eighty-three.
© 1947 King Features Syndicate, Inc.

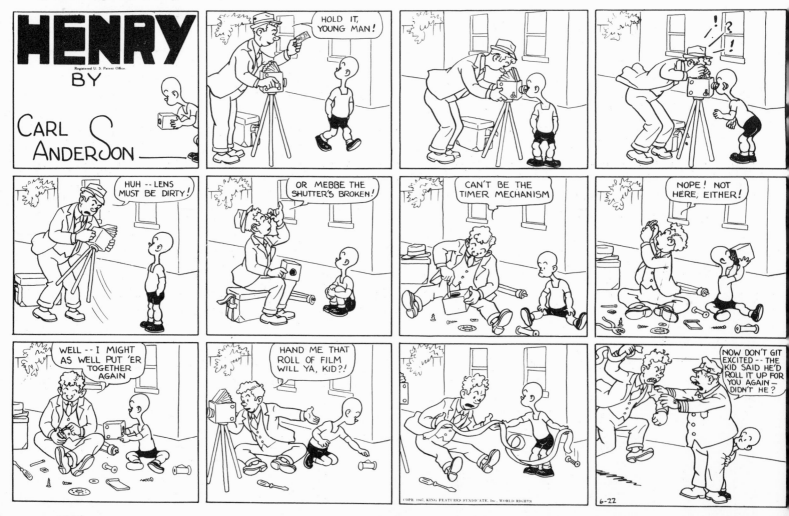

Ferd'nand by Mik (Dahl Mikkelsen). © 1963 United Feature Syndicate, Inc.

Benny by J. Carver Pusey. © 1937 United Feature Syndicate, Inc.

Louie by Harry Hanan. © 1971 New York News, Inc.

Henry's creator, Carl Anderson, was hardly new, however, and reached his greatest fame at probably the most advanced age of any cartoonist. He was past seventy when Henry made his newspaper debut. Anderson was born in Madison, Wisconsin, in 1865, and had been a contributor to *Judge*, the old *Life*, and *Collier's*, and was a staff cartoonist for many newspapers for more than forty years. *Henry* is another strip noted for its economy of line, even extending to Henry's perfectly hairless head. He is also expressionless, and the strip depends on the gags and the unexpected twists to Henry's dilemmas. Anderson died in 1948, and *Henry*'s mentors are now John Liney (daily) and Don Trachte (Sunday).

The pantomime strip is a specialized and demanding form. There have been relatively few over the years able to maintain its exacting requirements, but those that have survived for any period of time have had an exceptional quality. *Benny* in 1931 was a Chaplinesque figure in a huge drooping overcoat drawn by J. Carver Pusey. Another was *Silent Sam* in 1934 by Jacobson. Two more of great skill appeared in the forties: Mik's (Dahl Mikkelsen) *Ferd'nand* and Harry Hanan's *Louie*. Others that followed are *Little Sport* (1949), *Little Eva* (1954), and *Boy and Girl* (1955), all by the talented, transplanted Englishman John Rouson, and Irving Phillips' *The Strange World of Mr. Mum* (1958).

A superb example of Alex Raymond's artistry. One of the few *Flash Gordons* rendered in pen.
© 1935 King Features Syndicate, Inc.

Jungle Jim, Raymond's top for *Flash Gordon.* The last fashion panel was a feature of a number of strips at the time. © 1934 King Features Syndicate, Inc.

The Vintage Year: 1934

If the 1930's were the Vintage Years of Comics, then 1934 must be considered the finest year. The year saw the birth of Alex Raymond's *Flash Gordon, Jungle Jim,* and *Secret Agent X-9*; Milton Caniff's *Terry and the Pirates*; Lee Falk's *Mandrake the Magician*; and Al Capp's *Li'l Abner.*

Alex Raymond was one of the most brilliant creators of illustrative fantasy. He started as an assistant to Russ Westover (*Tillie the Toiler*), Chic Young (*Blondie*), and Chic's brother, Lyman Young (*Tim Tyler's Luck*). When King Features was looking for a strip to

combat *Buck Rogers*, Raymond came up with the answer: *Flash Gordon,* a Sunday page. Raymond also created the top for *Flash, Jungle Jim* (for three months in 1935 it was drawn as a full page), and illustrated Dashiell Hammett's *Secret Agent X-9,* a daily strip. All three started in January, 1934, but a year and a half later the pressure was too much even for the prolific twenty-five-year-old, and Raymond gave up *X-9.* Al Williamson, a brilliant artist in the Raymond tradition, now draws *X-9,* which has been retitled *Secret Agent Corrigan.*

Al Williamson's *Secret Agent Corrigan.* © 1972 King Features Syndicate, Inc.

Raymond's characters in *Flash Gordon* were mostly one-dimensional: Flash is a blond, lithe, handsome hero; Dale is Flash's strikingly beautiful companion; and the supporting cast are suitably crafty tyrants and gorgeous, seductive femmes fatales. Federico Fellini, the famous director, who started his career as a cartoonist, describes the strip's impact on him in *The Steranko History of Comics*:

> *Flash Gordon* . . . appeared instantly as a model of a hero insuperable, a real hero, even if his achievements were in remote and fantastic worlds. I had a profound affection for *Flash Gordon* and his creator, along with those of my age group. When I think of it, it seems as though he actually existed. At times in my films, I seek to find the color and verve of *Flash Gordon* and his world.

What made *Flash Gordon* a classic strip was Raymond's artistry and the rich imagination he brought to his conceptions of the future. His early work on *Jungle Jim* and *Flash Gordon* was executed in a fluid, dry-brush technique. The later period, with the exception of a few pages rendered in pen, was characterized by sleek, brilliantly polished brushwork.

Raymond's strip career was interrupted during World War II. After seeing action as an officer and combat artist in the Pacific theater, he returned with an idea for a new strip, *Rip Kirby*. Kirby is a former American officer turned detective and criminologist, a new kind of detective hero: not the typical hard-hitting private eye but a sophisticated intellectual, who even wears glasses! Raymond continued to develop his extraordinary talents until his sudden and tragic

Alex Raymond adopted a flat decorative style for the debonair detective, *Rip Kirby*.
© 1950 King Features Syndicate, Inc.

Flash Gordon by Dan Barry (excerpt). © 1971 King Features Syndicate, Inc.

John Prentice's *Rip Kirby.* © 1958 King Features Syndicate, Inc.

death in an automobile accident in 1956. John Prentice, an exceptional artist and an admirer of Raymond, and writer Fred Dickenson have continued *Rip Kirby*. *Flash Gordon* is continued in the Raymond style by a fine craftsman from the comic magazines, Dan Barry.

A Classic Style Evolves

Milton Caniff, son of a printer, was graduated from Ohio State University as a fine arts major in 1930. After a number of staff newspaper jobs, he was recruited by the Associated Press in New York, where his first assignment was to illustrate *Puffy the Pig*, followed by his first features, *The Gay Thirties* and *Dickie Dare*. A number of artists played important roles in Caniff's artistic development: John T. McCutcheon, Roy Crane, and Russell Patterson. The most profound influence was exerted by his close friend and associate, Noel Sickles.

Sickles had taken over *Scorchy Smith* in 1934 and pioneered the sparkling black-and-white style which brought the art of chiaroscuro to the comics and which influenced generations of cartoonists. An expert draftsman, Sickles at times employed Benday with superb effect. *Scorchy*, an aviation hero patterned

The Gay Thirties by Milton Caniff circa 1932. © AP

Noel Sickles pioneered the black-and-white style in *Scorchy Smith.* © 1936 AP

after Charles Lindbergh, never achieved great popularity, but it established the black-and-white school of comic art. Sickles left *Scorchy* and the comics in 1936 to become one of America's finest illustrators.

Captain Patterson of the New York *Daily News*, needing an adventure strip to fill out his line of comics, invited Caniff to submit an idea. Once again Patterson played a vital role in the development of one of his strips: suggesting locales, characters, and changing the name of Caniff's submission from *Tommy Tucker* to *Terry and the Pirates*.

Caniff's *Terry and the Pirates*
Pat and Terry in their first year, 1934.
© News Syndicate Co., Inc.

In *Terry and the Pirates* all the storytelling techniques of the adventure strip fused and a classic style emerged. Caniff developed and integrated the narrative and its visual expression into a uniform aesthetic balance. His graphic style gradually evolved from the pen technique employed on *Dickie Dare* to the brilliant use of the brush as employed by Sickles. In his visual conceptions he utilized film-making techniques: long, medium, and angle shots; close-ups; cross cuts; and establishing shots to set the scene or introduce characters. Incidentally, in 1916 Caniff was a child actor in early two-reelers shot in California. The comic strip and the film both tell a story in a visual linear progressive series of pictures. Caniff typifies the adventure strip cartoonist who performs the film functions of the producer, screenwriter, casting director, costume and set designer, cinematographer, lighting director, special effects man, actor and film editor. Cartoonists would probably add that meeting a deadline seven days a week qualifies him as a stunt man as well.

Some critics maintain that Caniff's plots are occasionally too intricate and top-heavy in dialogue, but to Caniff it is purposeful: "That's the way I keep the reader involved and interested; he has got to stay with it every day and I've got him hooked."

The death of Raven Sherman in the arms of her sweetheart, Dude Hennick. A poignant sequence from Caniff's *Terry and the Pirates* evoked thousands of telegrams of condolence. © 1941 News Syndicate Co., Inc.

Terry and the Pirates. Terry earns his Air Force wings. An Air Force colonel was the model for Flip Corkin.
© 1943 News Syndicate Co., Inc.

GI's enjoyed the exposure not seen in the family newspapers in Caniff's World War II *Male Call.* © 1945 Milton Caniff.

During World War II Caniff created a special strip, *Male Call,* for the two thousand service newspapers. The erotic adventures of Miss Lace, the voluptuous and sexy heroine, together with George Baker's *Sad Sack,* Leonard Sansone's *The Wolf,* and Bill Mauldin's *Up Front,* made life in service a bit more bearable for millions of American GI's.

In 1947 Caniff again made comics history, becoming the first cartoonist to abandon a successful strip to create another. Not owning the copyright on *Terry,* he signed with Field Enterprises, where he retained ownership of his new creation, *Steve Canyon.* Caniff's reputation was such that 125 newspapers signed up for the strip sight-unseen. *Steve Canyon* made its much heralded appearance on January 13, 1947.

Canyon, a former captain in the Air Transport Command during the war, opened offices as a freelance troubleshooter. He is intelligent, urbane, a man's man *and* a ladies' man, ready for an intriguing assignment anywhere, no matter what the risk.

Caniff continues his mastery of the visual-verbal experience in *Steve Canyon.*
© 1963 Field Enterprises, Inc.

Steve Canyon by Milton Caniff. The last panel is the reader bait for the next adventure.
© 1963 Field Enterprises, Inc.

Canyon's high adventures are worldwide: to Nirvana, Canada, to fly a secret bomber; to rescue a Communist prisoner in China; to track missiles in the South Atlantic. Canyon, today a middle-aged colonel, has always been identified with the Air Force, and the strip has consequently come under occasional fire as being too militaristic. Caniff sees Canyon as a professional doing his job and says he is careful not to have Canyon take sides in determining U.S. policy. Wherever he goes, there's sure to be another luscious temptress in Caniff's Dragon Lady tradition: Copper Calhoun, financier; Princess Sun Flower; Miss Mizzou from Missouri; Savannah Gay, actress; Cheetah, pert Oriental; Herself Muldoon, underworld queen; Doe Redwood, an aviatrix; and Madam Lynx, spy.

Caniff has been called the Rembrandt of the comic strips by his biographer, John Paul Thomas. But perhaps the ultimate accolade was when the name of Squirrel Gulch, Colorado, was changed to Steve Canyon.

George Wunder, a native New Yorker, was Caniff's successor on *Terry and the Pirates*. Wunder served in World War II in the Army Air Corps and Intelligence on charting expeditions throughout Europe. He was also stationed in Oran and Casablanca and took part in missions to India, Pakistan, Iran, and numerous other strategic territories. His extensive experience proved to be invaluable when he took over the wide-ranging adventures of *Terry*. Wunder, a left-handed artist (as is Caniff), is a meticulous craftsman. His training as a map maker is evident in his tightly controlled line and elaborately detailed rendering.

It is perhaps curious that as the Bamboo Curtain to China was opening and the war in Vietnam closing, both events heralding a new era in America's relations with the Far East, a strip based on the once-popular myths of the mysterious, romantic Orient, *Terry and the Pirates*, also came to an end. After thirty-eight years, *Terry* completed his last adventure on February 25, 1973. At its peak *Terry* appeared in more than 300 newspapers with more than 30,000,000 readers. Also grounded in 1973, after forty years, was another flying adventurer, *Smilin' Jack* by Zack Mosley. The time of the Chinese "Big Stoop," the Dragon Lady, Hot Shot Charley, and the fly-by-the-seat-of-his-pants pilot in the open cockpit, with blazing scarf streaming in the sky, is over.

From the last week of *Terry and the Pirates* by George Wunder, 1973.
© News Syndicate Co., Inc.

Mandrake the Magician by Lee Falk and Phil Davis. The master illusionist at work.
© 1959 King Features Syndicate, Inc.

A New Medium for Writers

The greater preoccupation with story and plot in the adventure strip began to attract the talents of creative writers. The modern continuity strip required a well-structured plot; drama, suspense, and comic relief; and crisp dialogue full of rich imagery and up-to-the-minute idiom and slang.

One of the finest and most successful of this new core of writers has been Lee Falk. Falk was a student of the University of Illinois when he took his spring vacation to go to New York and sold King Features the archetype of magical strips, *Mandrake the Magician*. Mandrake, a dapper figure with pencil-thin mustache, looking much like his creator, dressed in opera cape, top hat, and tails, is the amalgam of the great stage magicians: Cardini, Thurston, and Houdini. Mandrake, a gentleman adventurer and amateur detective, is constantly accompanied by Lothar, a man of Herculean strength who was the first major black character in an adventure strip. Phil Davis, the original artist, drew *Mandrake* until his death in 1964. Fred Fredericks, a talented young cartoonist, has since continued the collaboration.

In 1936 Falk created another strip and another first in the comics: *The Phantom*, the first costumed superhero. An innovative story device is the basis of his supposed immortality. The Phantom, also known as The Ghost Who Walks, is the last in a line of masked crusaders for justice that has passed from father to son since the sixteenth century. Falk teamed with cartoonist Ray Moore on *The Phantom*. Wilson McCoy took over in 1941, and Sy Barry has continued the strip since McCoy's death in 1961.

The Phantom by Lee Falk and Ray Moore. The prototype costume hero.
© 1936 King Features Syndicate, Inc.

Mandrake in a space fantasy from 1958. © King Features Syndicate, Inc.

Two epic characters originated in the comic magazines: (left) *Batman* by Bob Kane and (below) *Superman* by Jerry Siegel and Joe Shuster.

Lee Falk's *Phantom*. Wilson McCoy established a surreal mood.

Mandrake and *The Phantom* are widely syndicated abroad and admired by connoisseurs of American strips in Europe and South America. Falk is also a playwright, theatrical producer, and director. His theatrical experience is reflected in his dramatic and expertly plotted suspense stories.

Other notable characters of the costumed genre are two that first appeared in the comics magazines: *Superman* by Jerry Siegel and Joe Shuster in 1938 and *Batman* by Bob Kane in 1939. *Superman* and *Batman*, both sensational successes in magazines, also became newspaper strips in the early 1940's.

Satire in the Hills

A social satire in the tradition of Jonathan Swift and Mark Twain came to the comics in 1934—*Li'l Abner* by Al Capp.

Born Alfred George Caplin in New Haven, Connecticut, in 1909, Capp studied at the Academy of Fine Arts at the Boston Museum School before going to New York to fulfill his dreams of glory. Capp recalls the inspiration for his career in cartooning: "I heard Bud Fisher [*Mutt and Jeff*] got $3,000 a week and was constantly marrying French countesses. I decided that

145

Li'l Abner by Al Capp. Daisy Mae still pursued Abner without success in 1949.
© United Feature Syndicate, Inc.

was for me." Having landed a job with the Associated Press, he was assigned the feature *Colonel Gilfeather*, previously drawn by Dick Dorgan, brother of the famed "Tad" Dorgan. When an editor wrote the syndicate six months later saying that the new version was "by far the worst cartoon in the country," Capp quit. His replacement, incidentally, was another young staffer whose work Capp describes as "so superior to mine that I shudder to think of it." His name was Milton Caniff.

After further art training in Boston, Capp again attempted to break into the New York art world . . . with little success. A chance encounter in 1933 that had all the improbability of a comic strip fantasy provided Capp with his break. A flashy, expensively dressed stranger with an expensive-looking girl in an expensive limousine pulled up next to Capp. Seeing the portfolio of cartoons tucked under Capp's arm, he offered him $10 to help finish a Sunday page. It was Ham Fisher. It is not an infrequent emergency for a comic strip cartoonist to be in desperate need of help to meet a deadline, and Fisher's colorful life-style made him emergency-prone. Capp became Fisher's full-time assistant on *Joe Palooka* until he left to do *Li'l Abner*. Although Capp was later to credit Fisher with having a great influence on his work, a bitter feud developed, punctuated by charges, countercharges, and lawsuits that lasted until Fisher's death.

Li'l Abner, like most strips, went through a shakedown period. A strip grows and develops as its creator refines his art and brings his concept into focus. The process often takes years, and at times a new direction or character is required before a strip takes off. (*Beetle Bailey* and *Peanuts* are recent examples.) It was a few years before Capp developed the basic graphic quality for *Li'l Abner*. In 1936 the heads were still small, and Mammy Yokum was still a foot taller than she "grew" to be. The bold, thin and thick flexible pen line was just emerging.

Li'l Abner's humor has its roots in the rural tall tales that go back to Davy Crockett and Paul Bunyan. The rustic and hillbilly vernacular and dialect humor are a Southern tradition dating from the early 1800's. "*All* comedy is based on man's delight in man's inhumanity to man," says Capp.

Abner, like Palooka, generously endowed physically but a simpleton of abject stupidity, is never debased by evil forces trying to exploit him, remains naïve and incorruptible and a fountainhead of human goodness. He is the vehicle through which Capp exposes all folly.

Abner was fearful of marital entrapment, and Daisy Mae was the eternally pursuing female, fruitlessly seeking love. But in March, 1952, took place a social event of such magnitude that *Life* magazine featured it as a cover story: the long-deferred nuptials (their courtship lasted seventeen years) of Daisy Mae Scragg and Li'l Abner of Dogpatch. Marryin' Sam, of course, performed the $1.35 ceremony. A Marryin' Sam ceremony is a thing of unsurpassed beauty.

Over the years Capp has created an extraordinary collection of grotesques, rivaled only by those of Chester Gould. It is Gould's *Dick Tracy* that Capp parodies with the strip within a strip, *Fearless Fosdick*, "the ideel of every red-blooded American boy." Fosdick is a fiendish blunderer whose stupidity is exceeded only by Abner himself. Fosdick, a detective, usually winds up an investigation riddled with bullets and as perforated as a slice of Swiss cheese. Consider some of the other bizarre citizens of Dogpatch: General Bullmoose (What's good for General Bullmoose is good for the U.S.A.), Evil-Eye Fleegle,

Evil-Eye Fleegle. © 1967 News Syndicate, Inc.

J. Roaringham Fatback.
© 1969 News Syndicate Co., Inc.

Fearless Fosdick. © 1956
United Feature Syndicate, Inc.

Hairless Joe, Senator Jack S. Phogbound, Joe Btfsplk (Dogpatch's version of the Yiddish schlemiel), Henry Cabbage Cod, Sir Cecil Cesspool, Adam Lazonga, and J. Roaringham Fatback, the hog tycoon, who once jacked up Onnecessary Mountain just to keep its shadow from falling on his breakfast egg. The women, by contrast, are usually courageous, supremely endowed, and often quite pungent: Moonbeam McSwine, Stupefyin' Jones, Appasionata von Climax,

The Shmoos. © 1968 News Syndicate Co., Inc.

Moonbeam McSwine. © 1967 News Syndicate Co., Inc.

Tobacco Rhoda. © 1965 News Syndicate Co., Inc.

and Tobacco Rhoda, who combines the love techniques of the Boston Strangler and a walrus in heat. Some of Capp's humor *has* been criticized as being too "barnyard."

An annual Dogpatch event in November has become an institution, Sadie Hawkins Day—a day when all the unmarried gals chase all the unmarried guys and "if they ketch them the guys by law must marry the gals, and no two ways about it!" It proved to be one of the most successful gambits in comics history. Soon hundreds of schools and 350 colleges were staging mock Sadie Hawkins days.

Other fertile inventions of Capp include: Kickapoo Joy Juice, brewed in Big Barnsmell's Skonk Works, the fumes of which have been known to be lethal; West Po'k Chop Railroad, built by Stubborn P. Tolliver, which goes up the impossible grade of Onnecessary Mountain and never reaches the other side; and Lower Slobbovia, ruled by King Nogoodnick, whose subjects are eternally adrift in snow up to their noses.

Capp is at his allegorical best in the epics of the Shmoos and, later, the Kigmies. Shmoos are the world's most amiable creatures, supplying all man's needs: They lay bottled grade-A milk and packaged fresh eggs; when broiled, they taste like sirloin steak and, when fried, like chicken. As in a fertility myth gone berserk, the Shmoos reproduced so prodigiously they threatened to wreck the economy. Kigmies are also amiable creatures and the epitome of masochism. Kigmies love to be kicked and thereby release all human aggression, threatening to bring peace to the world. Shmoos and Kigmies are obviously a menace to the establishment.

Sadie Hawkin's Day. © 1949 United Feature Syndicate, Inc.

Lonesome Polecat

Marryin' Sam

Pappy

Mammy

Wolf Gal

Hairless Joe

It was such outrageous postulations and Rabelaisian wit that first endeared *Li'l Abner* to the intellectual and academic liberals. John Steinbeck called Capp the best satirist since Laurence Sterne: "Capp has taken our customs, our dreams, our habits and thoughts, our social structure, our economics, and examined them gently like amusing bugs." In recent years Capp's work and speeches have reflected his subjective political views. Critics claim his scathing satire is often directed at targets of personal pique: individuals (Joan Baez became Joanie Phoanie), college students (especially the Ivy Leaguers, activists and longhairs), demonstrators (particularly war protesters and draft card burners), and the welfare state. Accused of going from the left to the far right, Capp retorts: "It's the political spectrum that has shifted, not Al Capp ... they left me, I didn't leave them." In any event, his most memorable satire remains that of the universal foibles of the human condition—pomposity, lust, greed, power, and intolerance.

Fred Harman, cowboy and rancher, gives *Red Ryder* (with Little Beaver) an authentic western flavor. © 1953 McNaught Syndicate, Inc.

The Western Strip

"Straight shooters always win!" Straining at their radios, millions of American youngsters thrilled to hear this battle cry from their hero, Tom Mix. The western was a Hollywood staple. It was inevitable that the thirties were also to see a western trend in the comics: Zane Grey's *King of the Royal Mounted* (1935) illustrated by Jim Gary, *Bronc Peeler* (1935) and *Red Ryder* (1938) by Fred Harman, *Big Chief Wahoo* (initially titled *The Great Gusto)* (1936) by Elmer Woggon, and *The Lone Ranger* (1939), adapted from the radio show by Fran Stricker and illustrated by Charles Flanders. Also in the 1930's were Harry O'Neill's *Bronco Bill*, Garrett Price's *White Boy*, Joe Leffingwell's *Little Joe*, and Vic Forsythe's *Way Out West*.

Bronco Bill by Harry O'Neill (excerpt). Basic western ingredients: secret gold shipment and an outlaw ambush. © 1942 United Feature Syndicate, Inc.

Burlesque

Few men have risen to nobler heights of pure foolishness than Bill Holman. As if born with fun house mirrors for corneas, everything Holman sees has a zany twist. He is a master nut in the tradition of Gross and Goldberg. Holman, at age sixteen, tended a dime-store popcorn machine in his hometown of Crawfordsville, Indiana, where he was born in 1903. He abandoned his early ambition to become a fireman to study cartooning under Carl Ed (*Harold Teen*) at the Chicago Academy of Fine Arts.

Bill Holman's *Smokey Stover.* Pure unadulterated zaniness. © 1944 News Syndicate Co., Inc.

Holman started his career at the Chicago *Tribune* for $6 a week, where his new cronies were Harold Gray (*Little Orphan Annie*) and Garrett Price (later of *New Yorker* magazine fame). He moved to Cleveland to draw his first strip, *Billsville Birds*. Here he met two cartoonists who became lifelong friends—a fellow in a fur collar, J. R. Williams (*Out Our Way*), and a tall skinny blond with whom he was to swipe gags from the local vaudeville house, Chic Young (*Blondie*). At twenty-one Holman felt ready for the big time in New York. His first strip was *G. Whizz, Jr.* for the *Herald Tribune*. The Tribune Syndicate office in the twenties

was a colorful rallying place. The great Winsor McCay (*Little Nemo*), smoke curling from under his straw hat, presided over an India ink court of cartoonists, assorted actors, publicists, writers, and odd characters who dropped in at all hours. W. C. Fields taught Holman to juggle. Will Rogers often dropped by. Also on view were three other great cartoonists: Charles Voight (*Betty*), Clare Briggs (*Mr. and Mrs.*), and Frank Fogarty, an artist of great versatility who drew *Clarence*, written by Weare Holbrook, for twenty years (1929–49) and *Mr. and Mrs.* (created by Briggs) from 1935 until his retirement from the comics in

Clarence by Frank Fogarty and Weare Holbrook (excerpt). © 1948 New York Herald Tribune.

"Sometimes I get the impression they're
undressing us in their minds!"

"What'll you have—tuna fish and sand,
salami and sand or liverwurst and sand?"

"Well, I see what he sees in her!"

"Baiting Suit Time" by Reamer Keller.
© 1971 New York News, Inc.

1949. Since then Fogarty has revived the art of hand-illuminated manuscripts. His work rivals the best of the Middle Ages, and to receive a scroll executed by the eighty-two-year-old master is considered recognition of the highest order.

Holman was one of the most prolific contributors to national magazines before creating *Smokey Stover*, the frenetic fireman, in 1935. Holman is an outrageous punster and wordsmith. Among the latter are his "Foo," "Notary Sojac" and "1506 nix-nix." Although there are numerous theories, no one, including Holman, probably knows for sure what they mean. Holman himself looks and acts like a cross between W. C. Fields, P. T. Barnum, and Groucho Marx. His foibles are legendary in the profession. Many refer to his parsimonious resemblance to Jack Benny, others to his compulsive generosity. Both are probably true. Holman's outgoing nature is restrained by his conservative Midwestern rearing and early days of financial insecurity. He says of his peers, "They are a pixie bunch of notary sojacs, which stamps them as tops on my fire ladder."

Two other prolific creators of slapstick humor are George Swanson and Reamer Keller. Swanson's *Salesman Sam* ran from 1920 to 1927, and later strips included *High Pressure Pete*, *Officer 6⅞*, *Elza Poppin* (adapted from the Olsen and Johnson show), and *Dad's Family*, which Hearst himself renamed *The Flop Family* in the 1940's. Keller, a leading magazine cartoonist with a marvelously fluid brushline, created *Kennesaw*, featuring a wild assortment of hillbillies, and later a Sunday page of changing thematic humor.

The Flop Family by George Swanson. © 1965 King Features Syndicate, Inc.

Raeburn Van Buren brings the discipline of the illustrator to *Abbie an' Slats*.
© 1945 United Feature Syndicate, Inc.

Raeburn Van Buren, one of the country's leading magazine illustrators, joined the comic strip fraternity in 1937 with *Abbie an' Slats*. Al Capp, upon seeing Van Buren's deft pen and ink illustrations, decided he would make a great comic strip cartoonist. Capp wrote the first *Abbie an' Slats* scripts and talked Van Buren into taking over the strip. Born in Pueblo, Colorado, in 1891, Van Buren studied at the Art Students League, served in World War I, and had illustrated more than 400 *Saturday Evening Post* stories before embarking on his new career.

The seacoast town of Crabtree Corners was the setting for the adventures of Slats; his girl, Becky Groggins; her father, Bathless; and the homely spinster, Aunt Abbie. Van Buren describes them as a part of his own family: "I've tried to draw them so they will be as real to other people as they are to me, and from the beginning I've tried to give each individual panel the same artistic quality that I formerly gave to magazine illustration.... As my early training taught me,

newspaper printing requires simple, clean line drawing. But good newspaper art can have accent and grades of balance of composition." Van Buren supplied all these in good measure for almost thirty-five years, until his retirement in 1971.

Animal Strips

Some of the new strips reflected the continuing appeal of tried and true themes. Anthropomorphic animal strips have been a favorite vehicle ever since Jimmy Swinnerton's *Little Bears and Tigers* and Harrison Cady's *Peter Rabbit*. Others were a duck, *Johnny Quack* by C. Twelvetrees; of course the dog *Tige* in *Buster Brown*; and the cat, mouse, and dog in *Krazy Kat*.

A new mouse, duck, cat, and dog joined the growing comics menagerie. Two, already famous in the animated films, were the inspired creations of Walt

Felix the Cat by Pat Sullivan. A fine example of the animator's style. © 1932 King Features Syndicate, Inc.

Clifford McBride's *Napoleon.*
© Times-Mirror Syndicate.

Disney: *Mickey Mouse* in 1931 and *Donald Duck* in 1938. *Felix the Cat* was originated by Pat Sullivan in 1931 and later continued by Otto Mesmer. The dog was *Napoleon* in *Napoleon and Uncle Elby* by Clifford McBride in 1932. Napoleon, a huge Irish wolfhound and one of the most expressive and human dogs in the comics, was brought to life by McBride with a marvelous pen technique of great style and dash. McBride died in 1952 and Roger Armstrong continued with great fidelity until the strip ended in 1961. George Scarbo's *Comic Zoo* was an encyclopedia of whimsical wildlife.

A number of other humor strips joined the expanding family of comics in the thirties. Some have survived and others have not. There has always been a

Oaky Doaks by Ralph Fuller. Circa 1940. © AP Features.

certain rate of attrition, even among old favorites. Tastes change, the original artist dies and a suitable successor is not found, and other features are dropped to make room for promising new ideas. The latter has become more and more common in recent years as newspaper space and budgets have shrunk.

Some notable strips that were born in the thirties but have since expired were *Sweeney & Son* (and its "top" *Jinglets*), a strip of great warmth and gentle humor drawn by Al Posen, a warm and gentle cartoonist; *Oaky Doaks*, a witty parody of the Middle Ages and King Arthur's court by Ralph Fuller; and, by contrast, the world of the twentieth-century racetrack in *Joe and Asbestos* by Ken Kling; *Tuffy* by the noted *New Yorker* cartoonist Sid Hoff; and C. D. Russell's classic hobo, *Pete the Tramp*, which first ap-

peared in *Judge*. *Doc Sykes* by Ving Fuller was the first burlesque of the new era of psychiatry, and Gus (Watso) Mager contributed a delightful spoof on crime detection and the Sherlock Holmes-type hero with *Hawkshaw the Detective*. A strip adaptation of Max Fleischer's *Betty Boop* ran for several years. Pop Momand's *Keeping Up with the Joneses* and Rea Irvin's *The Smythes* focused on the classic neighborhood game of one-upmanship. *Big Sister*, created by Leslie Forgrave in 1930 was continued by Bob Naylor from 1954 until the strip's demise in 1972.

And so the thirties and the Golden Decade of Comics drew to a close. It saw the introduction of the adventure strip, the start of a new realism, and a continuation of the tradition of humor. But still new trends and a greater realism were in store.

Pete the Tramp by C. D. Russell. © 1956 King Features Syndicate, Inc.

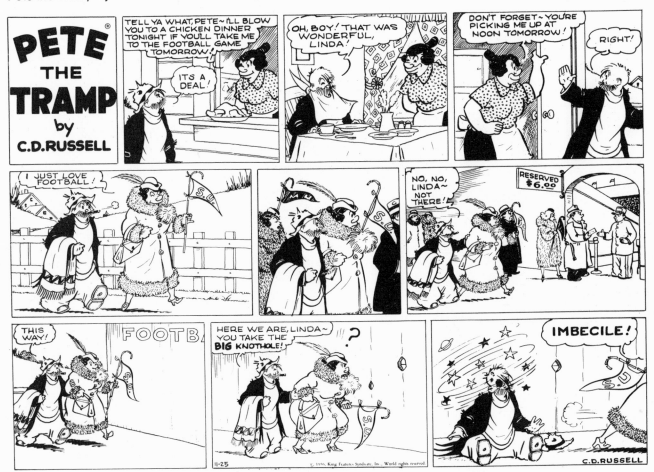

Doc Syke by Ving Fuller. Circa 1940. © McNaught Syndicate, Inc.

Hawkshaw the Detective by Watso (Gus Mager). Circa 1944. © United Feature Syndicate, Inc.

The Smythes (excerpt) by the noted *New Yorker* cartoonist Rea Irvin © 1932 New York Tribune Co.

Keeping Up with the Joneses by Pop Momand (excerpt). © 1932 Associated Newspapers.

America was enjoying a growing prosperity. And while there were threatening signs and ominous rumblings abroad, we were still at peace. Harry Haenigsen's *Our Bill*, a lighthearted teen-age strip, started in 1939. But perhaps the most significant, and the last strip of note to be launched in the thirties, was one reflecting the pioneering spirit and simple virtues. As the radio show, from which it was adapted, intoned: "Return with us now to those thrilling days of yesteryear! From out of the past come the thundering hoofbeats of the great horse Silver! The Lone Ranger rides again!"

The Lone Ranger by Charles Flanders and Paul Newman. © 1968 King Features Syndicate, Inc.

by Chic Young

I get frightened when I think about it, but I've drawn a comic strip for the newspapers every day including Sundays and holidays since 1921. Previous to that I went through the business of being born in Chicago in 1901 and exposed to education in the public schools of St. Louis.

My first attempt at drawing was art in its most primitive form—making "hopscotch" panels on the pavement with white school chalk for the little girls of the neighborhood. That paid off only in gracious smiles and "thank you's" from the little girls.

I soon found out, however, that if you worked humorous little ideas into similar panels it was called a comic strip and that the newspapers, bless their little hearts, paid you money for it. In spite of all the mean things they say about money, I've always found it pleasant stuff to have on hand, so I turned professional comic strip artist.

My first comic strip was distributed by the Newspaper Enterprise Association and must've been a honey because it lasted only six months. The comic strip *Dumb Dora* which I drew during the 1920's fared better and appeared in more than four hundred newspapers. I gave my all to this strip until 1930, when, at the depth of the Depression, I created the strip *Blondie.* Originally, Blondie was single and simply another "pretty girl" strip. But it really took off when she married that scamp, Dagwood Bumstead. The marriage was a complete success, and now, forty years later, the two continue to perform in blissful togetherness in seventeen languages all over the world.

In Latin countries, Blondie becomes "Pepita" and Dagwood is "Lorenzo." In France, Dagwood is "Emile" and in Sweden he is "Dagobert." I think the popularity of *Blondie* is due to the fact that it deals mostly with eating, sleeping, and the business of raising children—three projects that almost everybody is involved in at one time or the other. As everybody has a "boss," too, the world over, I threw in "Mr. Dithers" for good measure.

Here are answers to questions most often asked me and a few "don't's" for aspiring young comic artists. What are the problems of drawing a daily comic strip? Of course the biggest problem is drawing an entertaining strip every day. When I break this down into little specific problems, I find that the "restrictions" and "don't do's" give me the most trouble. A comic strip of national circulation must fit into a certain groove to entertain the greatest number of people and offend no one.

A few "don't do's": a comic strip should not lend itself to propaganda, its sole purpose being the amusement of the reader. Politics, religion, and racial subjects should be avoided for obvious reasons.

The comic strip is a medium that goes right into the home, and its contents should be of the most wholesome nature, this, in spite of the license now given to other forms of entertainment.

I think reference to liquor should be avoided—the characters in *Blondie* do not even use cigarettes. Divorce, infirmities of the body, sickness, and other such unpleasant subjects do not lend themselves to satisfactory humor for comic strips and should not be used.

The material should not be localized. Remember, when it's snowing in New York people are swimming in Florida, California, South America, and Australia. Jokes about the United States are meaningless in Europe. If your strip is translated into foreign languages the text should be such that it will not lose its meaning in translation. It is up to the careful comic artist to see that he offends no one, hurts no group, and that his strip is all in good, clean fun. All in all, drawing a comic strip is very interesting, in a dull, monotonous sort of way!

★ ★ ★

A Cavalcade of Color

The following thirty-two pages represent a cavalcade, in color, of seventy-five years of comic strip art. The date given for each page is that of publication and not that of the strip's creation.

1. 1896 HOGAN'S ALLEY—Richard F. Outcault
2. 1897 THE LITTLE NIPPERS' KIND KIDS' COLONY—George B. Luks
3. 1898 (top) THE FIRST GOLF PLAYER SEEN AT M'MANUS'S FENCE—Jimmy Swinnerton
    (bottom) THE KATZENJAMMER KIDS—Rudolph Dirks
4. 1899 WHEN THE HORSES HAD THE LAUGH ON THE AUTOMOBILE—T. S. Sullivant
5. 1907 BUSTER BROWN—Richard F. Outcault
6. 1907 THE KATZENJAMMER KIDS—Rudolph Dirks
7. 1908 LITTLE JOHNNY AND THE TEDDY BEARS—Bray and Constance Johnson
8. 1914 (top) MR. HUBBY—William Stenigans
    (bottom) THE NEWLYWEDS—George McManus
9. 1915 THE ORIGINAL KATZENJAMMER KIDS—Harold H. Knerr © King Features Syndicate, Inc.
10. 1919 BRINGING UP FATHER—George McManus © King Features Syndicate, Inc.
11. 1923 HAPPY HOOLIGAN—Frederic Opper © International Feature Service, Inc.
12. 1923 BARNEY GOOGLE—Billy DeBeck © King Features Syndicate, Inc.
13. 1923 POLLY—Cliff Sterrett © Newspaper Feature Service, Inc.
14. 1924 LITTLE NEMO IN SLUMBERLAND—Winsor McCay© McCay Features
15. 1924 MR. AND MRS.—Clare Briggs © New York Tribune, Inc.
16. (top) THE MODEL—H. T. Webster
    (bottom) 1928 THE MAN IN THE BROWN DERBY—H. T. Webster © New York World
17. 1929 (top) BOOTS AND HER BUDDIES—Edgar Martin © Newspaper Enterprise Association
    (bottom) OUR BOARDING HOUSE—Gene Ahern © Newspaper Enterprise Association
18. 1931 THE GUMPS—Sidney Smith © The Chicago Tribune
19. 1933 (top) MOM 'N POP—Wood Cowan © Newspaper Enterprise Association
    (bottom) FRECKLES AND HIS FRIENDS—Merrill Blosser © Newspaper Enterprise Association
20. 1936 ALLEY OOP—V. T. Hamlin © Newspaper Enterprise Association
21. 1936 KRAZY KAT—George Herriman © King Features Syndicate, Inc.
22. 1936 JOE PALOOKA—Ham Fisher © McNaught Syndicate, Inc.
23. 1938 TERRY AND THE PIRATES—Milton Caniff © Chicago Tribune-New York News Syndicate, Inc.
24. 1938 THE TIMID SOUL—H. T. Webster © New York Tribune, Inc. and courtsey of Mrs. H. T. Webster
25. 1938 BUCK ROGERS—Dick Calkins © John F. Dille Co.
26. 1939 (top) BLONDIE—Chic Young © King Features Syndicate, Inc.
    (bottom) CHARLIE CHAN—Alfred Andriola © McNaught Syndicate, Inc.
27. 1939 LI'L ABNER—Al Capp © United Feature Syndicate, Inc.
28. 1942 DICK TRACY—Chester Gould © The Chicago Tribune
29. 1945 (top) MANDRAKE THE MAGICIAN—Lee Falk and Phil Davis © King Features Syndicate, Inc.
    (bottom) BRICK BRADFORD - William Ritt and Clarence Gray © King Features Syndicate, Inc.
30. 1946 LITTLE ORPHAN ANNIE—Harold Gray © News Syndicate
    1947 MUTT AND JEFF—Bud Fisher © Aedita S. de Beaumont
31. 1949 PRINCE VALIANT—Harold R. Foster © King Features Syndicate, Inc.
32. 1965 WIZARD OF ID—Brant Parker and Johnny Hart © Publishers Newspaper Syndicate
    1971 PEANUTS—Charles Schulz © United Feature Syndicate, Inc.

THE AMATEUR DIME MUSEUM IN HOGAN'S ALLEY.

THE LITTLE NIPPERS' KIND KIDS' COLONY—A COURT-ROOM SCENE.

THE TRAGEDY OF THE OVER-CONFIDENT FROG—A TALE OF A LONG REACH.

1. Frog—Ah! I'm out of reach of that fellow. I'll just sing my little song: 2. "Just tell him that you—   3. —saw me—   4. —and he will do the rest!"

WHEN THE HORSES HAD THE LAUGH ON THE AUTOMOBILE.

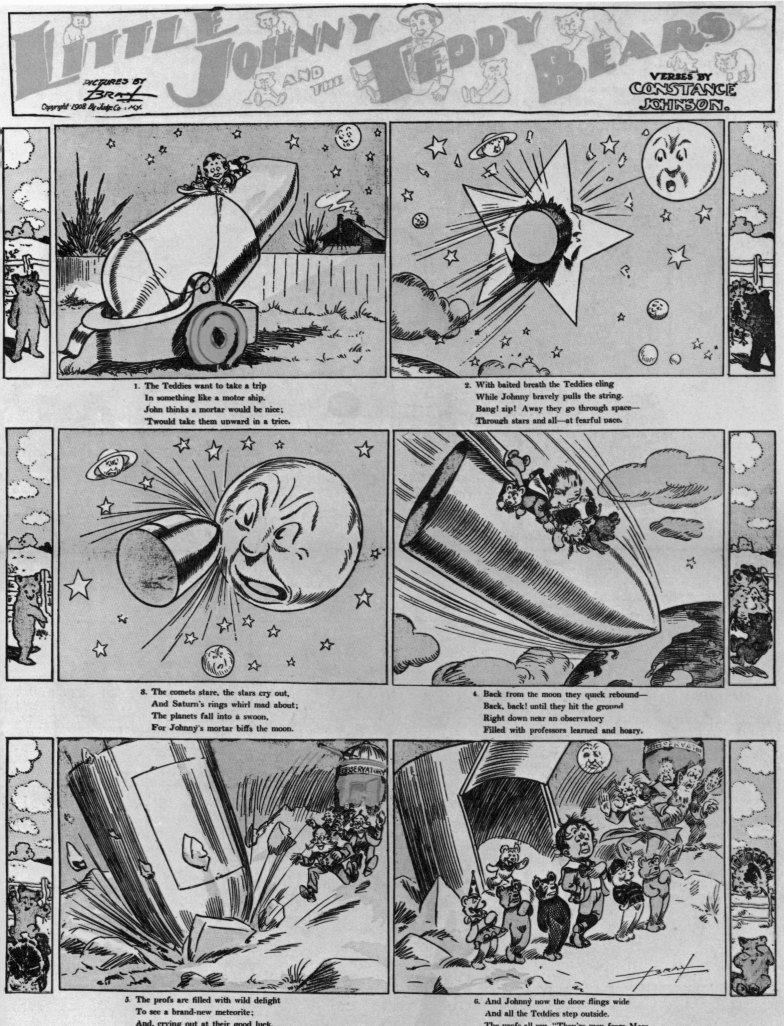

LITTLE JOHNNY AND THE TEDDY BEARS

PICTURES BY BRAY

VERSES BY CONSTANCE JOHNSON.

1. The Teddies want to take a trip
   In something like a motor ship.
   John thinks a mortar would be nice;
   'Twould take them upward in a trice.

2. With baited breath the Teddies cling
   While Johnny bravely pulls the string.
   Bang! zip! Away they go through space—
   Through stars and all—at fearful pace.

3. The comets stare, the stars cry out,
   And Saturn's rings whirl mad about;
   The planets fall into a swoon,
   For Johnny's mortar biffs the moon.

4. Back from the moon they quick rebound—
   Back, back! until they hit the ground
   Right down near an observatory
   Filled with professors learned and hoary.

5. The profs are filled with wild delight
   To see a brand-new meteorite;
   And, crying out at their good luck,
   They rush to where the mortar struck.

6. And Johnny now the door flings wide
   And all the Teddies step outside.
   The profs all cry, "They're men from Mars,
   Bringing a message from the stars!"

Polly--Pa's "Evidence" Makes a Quick Get-Away.

Happy Hooligan

Barney Google
Registered U. S. Patent Office

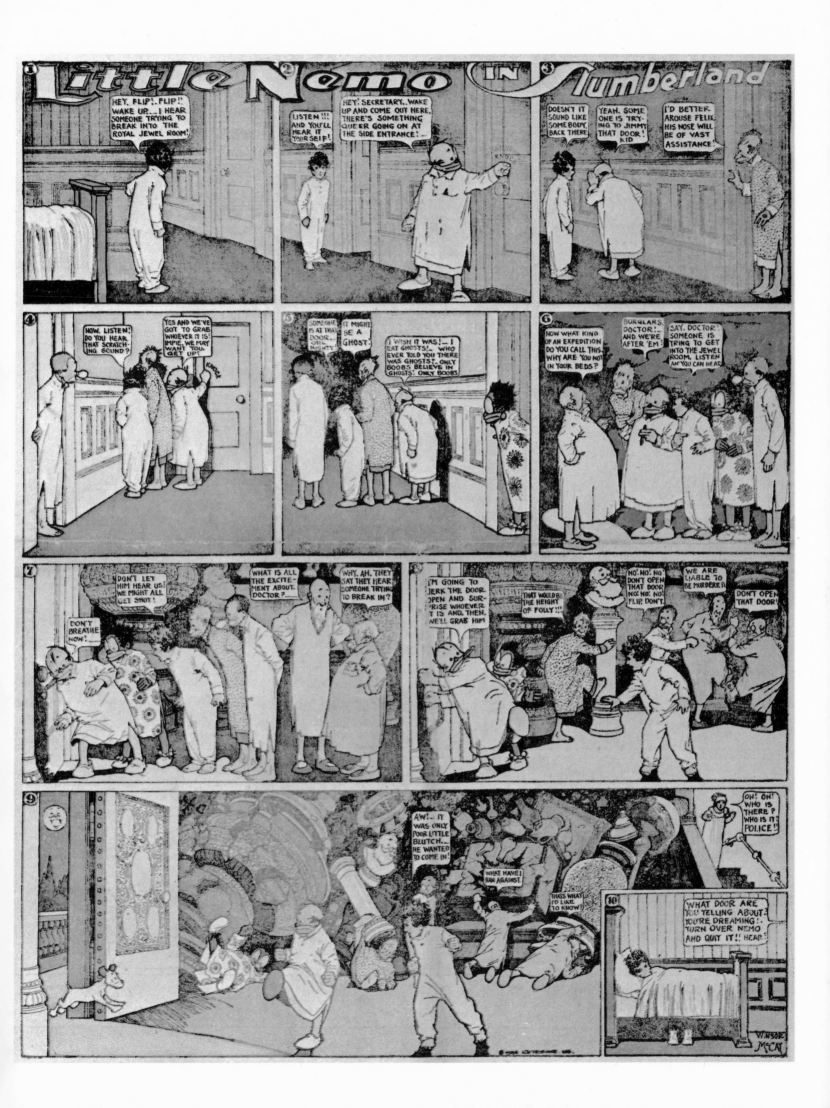

THE MAN IN THE BROWN DERBY

By H. T. Webster

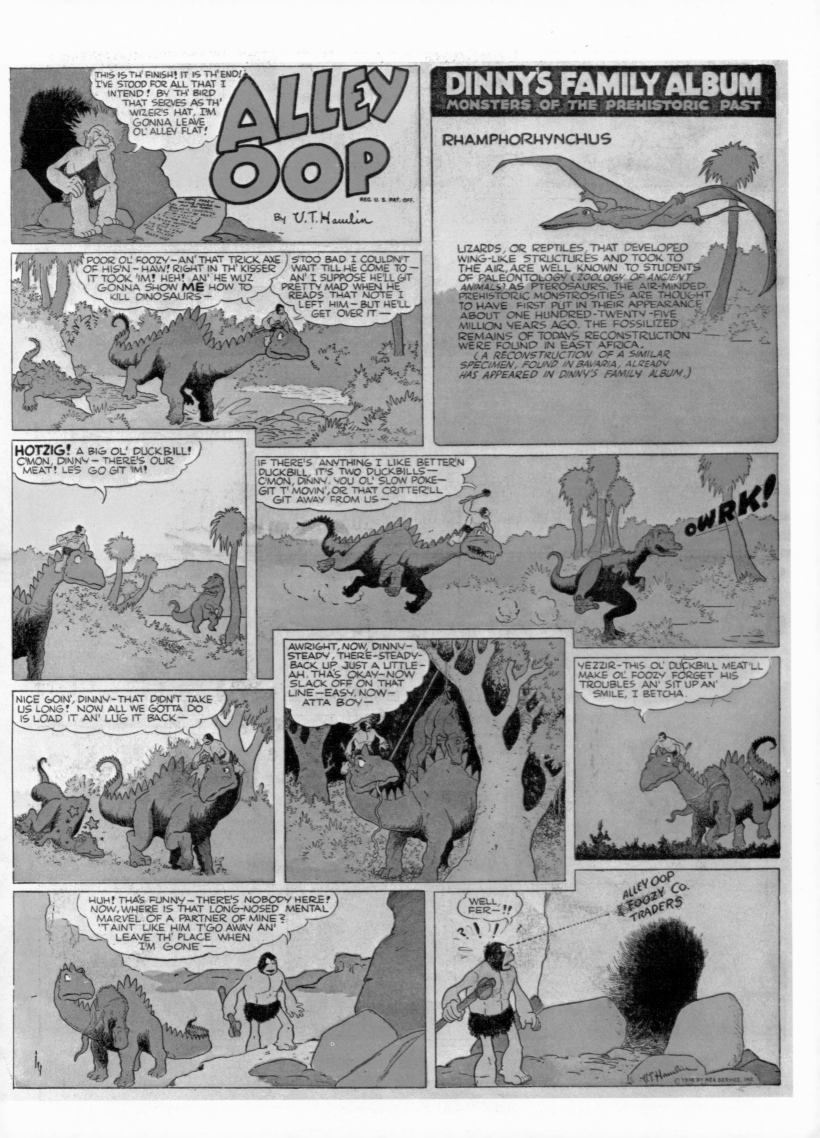

Prince Valiant
IN THE DAYS OF KING ARTHUR
BY HAROLD R FOSTER

Synopsis: DOWN FROM THEIR MISTY HILLS COME THE PICTS TO CROWD THROUGH THE OPENING IN THE GREAT WALL INTO BRITAIN. BUT WITHIN THE MILECASTLE ARE PRINCE VALIANT, AND HIS KNIGHTS, AND EACH PICT IS DISARMED AS HE PASSES THROUGH!

THE PICTS WHO HAD BREACHED THE WALL EARLIER SWEEP SOUTHWARD UNCHECKED, LAYING WASTE THE LAND. BUT THE COUNTRYSIDE DOES NOT PROVIDE ENOUGH FOOD FOR SUCH AN ARMY AND NO SUPPLIES COME UP FROM THE REAR!

INSTEAD GREAT NUMBERS OF THEIR COMRADES ARRIVE UNARMED AND STARVING TO TELL OF PRINCE VALIANT CALMLY STANDING OVER BOTH THEIR SUPPLIES AND THEIR MEANS OF RETREAT!

AHEAD LIES THE CITY OF YORK, A RICH PRIZE, THEIRS FOR THE TAKING. NOT ONCE HAVE THEY THOUGHT OF RETURNING UNTIL THEY LEARN THE WAY IS BLOCKED. THEN ALL EYES TURN TOWARD THEIR NORTHERN HILLS!

"GENTLEMEN," SMILES VAL, MOUNTING HIS STEED, "YOU WANTED SOME FIGHTING. IN A FEW DAYS THERE SHOULD BE PLENTY!" AND HE RIDES AWAY ALONG THE WALL.

HE WISELY CHOOSES TO RIDE ON THE ENEMY SIDE OF "THE WALL," KNOWING THAT EVERY PICT HEREABOUT HAS JOINED THE INVASION.

AT A POINT SOME DISTANCE FROM THE BREAK-THROUGH THE SENTINELS ON THE WALL ARE SURPRISED TO SEE ONE OF KING ARTHUR'S KNIGHTS RIDE UP FROM THE NORTH AND DEMAND ADMITTANCE!

TO THE CAPTAIN OF THE GUARDS VAL SAYS: "SEND SWIFT MESSENGERS ALONG THE WALL TO TELL EVERY MOUNTED MAN TO MEET HERE!"

WITHIN A FEW DAYS VAL IS LEADING THE POOREST-LOOKING TROOP HE HAS EVER SEEN AGAINST THE INVADING HORDES OF FIERCE HILLMEN!

NEXT WEEK - The Raiders.

by Mell Lazarus

I like to compare doing each daily strip to producing a play. Let's use *Momma* as an example. First, I write the gag, or script, in finished form, even as a play would be written before the production process could begin. And it is, I hope, a playlet which will note something about the human condition of which the audience may have been aware of but had never themselves articulated. Then, I cast my script from the feature's regular repertory company as well as from a pool of extras—specially created characters—when necessary. Momma herself might star, possibly supported by her unmarried son, Francis, and a cute new girl in the role of Nubile College Freshman. I then put on director's boots and block my people through the little play. I determine with what expressions or emphasis they will deliver their lines and how and where they will stand or move. *A little more chagrin, Francis. Momma, you betray too much hurt. Sybil, stand a little this way so we can see your, uh, figure.* Meanwhile, as set designer, I am also providing backgrounds and props to establish locale and atmosphere. *The corner of a table. Vase of flowers. Picture of late husband.* Finally, everything rehearsed to my pleasure, I, the cartoonist-producer-playwright-director-set designer, freeze the play, so to speak, by inking the drawing. And, on its proper release date, my play opens.

Now, imagine having three hundred and sixty-five plays open every year for the better part of one's lifetime! Plays which either work or don't, please or anger, are hits or flops. Granted, the audience tolerance level is higher where fifteen seconds of comic strip reading is concerned, as opposed to an evening of theater, but only *somewhat* higher. Because if I produce more flops than hits, they'll stop coming to my four-column theater. Or worse yet, my whole company could be evicted by the landlord.

"Three hundred and sixty-five plays a year" reminds me that there is no Hot Stove League in comic stripping. No off-season. Unlike the other big series-medium, TV, comic strip artists produce day in and day out. Which thought suggests that since *Miss Peach* began, fifteen years ago, I have drawn more than 5,500 strips. Assuming an average of four characters per strip, that's 22,000 characters. They have spoken a total of a quarter-million words. They've been equipped with 44,000 feet, 220,000 fingers (although not necessarily in equal distribution, the way I draw) and, on those characters which are blessed with individually distinguishable hairs, 308,000 individually distinguishable hairs. And, moreover, counting only Kamp Kelly summer sequences, I have drawn the astounding number of 480,000 blades of grass!

The matter of writing and drawing two comic strips has revealed some things about myself which, like most things about myself, are very interesting to me. For one thing, I find I need the same number of working hours to do *Miss Peach* and *Momma* as I formerly needed for *Miss Peach* alone.

For another, I find my social orbit has widened. By this I mean there have always been certain social areas which provided much of my *Miss Peach* source material. Certain sophisticated cultural levels (the ones I've dwelt upon and been bewildered by for years) which provide enough Tartuffery in a single evening to give Marcia and Ira cynical things to say for a whole week.

But then along came *Momma*, which now sends me off, on alternate Tuesdays and Thursdays, in a totally different sociocultural direction—namely, back to the bosom of Mother. Anybody's mother. And I'm not ashamed to say that because *Momma* actually does reflect my long-time interest in my own mother, whose psychology had become more and more fascinating to me as I moved further and further from her direct influence. I now find she is an intelligent, interesting, and lovable lady. In other words, I visit my mother more frequently these days, and that's a nice thing. Even if it is for commercial purposes.

Oh, yet another interesting thing which doing two strips has revealed about me is that I have a split personality.

★ ★ ★

Terry and the Pirates by Milton Caniff. © 1942 News Syndicate Co., Inc.

The Comics Go To War: 1940-1949

In September, 1939, Adolf Hitler invaded Poland and World War II began. While a strong isolationist bloc resisted America's growing involvement, the country's sympathies were clearly with the Western Alliance against the Axis powers . . . and so were the comic strips'.

Terry and the Pirates was already involved on the side of the Chinese, fighting the Japanese invasion. *Barney Baxter* joined the British Royal Air Force. *Vic Jordan*, a new strip drawn by Elmer Wexler, launched in the new New York daily *P.M.*, was fighting with the French underground. America was slowly awakening to the dangers of a Hitler victory, but the war was still remote and America felt secure.

The New York World's Fair opened in 1939 with sixty nations participating. Germany was not represented. *The Grapes of Wrath* by John Steinbeck, *Peace, It's Wonderful* by William Saroyan, and *The Nazarene* by Sholem Asch were best sellers. Marian Anderson, noted black contralto, was barred by the Daughters of the American Revolution from giving a concert in their Constitution Hall. *Life with Father* broke all existing box office records on Broadway; it was not to close until 1947, two years after the war. In 1940 America sang Johnny Mercer's "Fools Rush In" while Germany invaded Denmark and Norway. Belgium, Luxembourg, the Netherlands, and France were overrun by Nazi panzers and the British retreat-

ed from Dunkirk. An antiaircraft gun appeared on a two-cent stamp. The big movies in 1940 were *Gone with the Wind*, Charlie Chaplin's *The Great Dictator*, Walt Disney's *Fantasia*, and *Ninotchka* with Greta Garbo. The big bands were in full swing. Roosevelt became the first President to be elected for a third term. New films in 1941 were *Citizen Kane*, *The Man Who Came to Dinner*, and *How Green Was My Valley*. While the war sometimes intruded on our entertainment (the play *Watch on the Rhine*, the film *Sergeant York*, and William Shirer's book *Berlin Diary*), America was still singing "Chattanooga Choo-Choo," "Jersey Bounce," and "You Are My Sunshine." We were basically optimistic, and so were the comics.

In 1941 *It's a Girl's Life*, a delightful strip about teen-agers, made its debut. It was retitled *Teena* the following year. Its artist, Hilda Terry, was discovered by Cleveland Amory, then cartoon editor of the *Saturday Evening Post*, where the characters first appeared. Terry's husband is the noted painter and cartoonist Gregory D'Alessio, creator of the panel *These Women*. A pixielike Mexican character, *Gordo*, reminiscent of the famous comedian Cantinflas, also appeared in 1941, imaginatively drawn by Gus Arriola.

Teena by Hilda Terry. © 1959 King Features Syndicate, Inc.

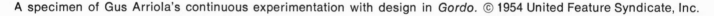

A specimen of Gus Arriola's continuous experimentation with design in *Gordo*. © 1954 United Feature Syndicate, Inc.

The exigency of war interrupts *Joe Palooka*'s romantic idyll. © 1943 McNaught Syndicate, Inc.

After Pearl Harbor America plunged into sudden all-out war and so did the comics. Joe Palooka refused a commission and was to fight through the entire war as a buck private. Terry became a flight officer with the Air Force, and Pat Ryan a lieutenant in Naval Intelligence. Captain Easy was his counterpart in Air Intelligence. Freckles left his friends to join the Air Corps. Buz Sawyer was a Navy pilot (and, after the war, reenlisted at the request of the United States government). *Gordo* was continued by S/Sgt. Gus Arriola. Even Little Mary Mix-Up contributed to the war effort and helped capture some Nazi spies. Tillie the Toiler joined the WAC's. Smilin' Jack flew in the Air Force while his creator, Zack Mosley, flew anti-submarine patrol.

Flash Gordon's Alex Raymond joined the Marines. Bert Christman (who had taken over *Scorchy Smith* from Noel Sickles) joined Chennault's Flying Tigers. He was flying a P-38 Tomahawk over Burma in 1942 when he was shot down by the Japanese and machine-gunned to death while parachuting to the ground. Frank Robbins later drew *Scorchy* and took

Frank Robbins' *Scorchy Smith* on the Russian front. © 1941 AP.

Ella Cinders by Charlie Plumb. The Nazi symbol spins into the British insignia! © 1943 United Feature Syndicate Co., Inc.

Private Breger by Dave Breger. © 1943 King Features Syndicate, Inc.

"C'mon! You don't have to register NŌW!"

him to the Russian front, the first time the Red Army was sympathetically shown in the popular arts. In 1942 a new war strip appeared, *Captain Yank* of the Marine Corps by Frank Tinsley. *Navy Bob Steele* by Wilson Starbuck and William King also joined up. Jungle Jim fought the Japanese in Burma while Tarzan prevented the Nazis from setting up a secret base in Africa.

American strips were still being translated and published in occupied Europe. Mussolini finally banned all American comic strips except one—his favorite, *Mickey Mouse*. Mickey was apparently not considered a serious threat to the Fascist ideology. A fitting climax to the comics' war effort came when *Das Schwarz*, a Nazi propaganda organ, branded Superman a Jew.

With the drain on America's manpower, women were needed to supplement the nation's work force. They became everything from riveters to cabdrivers. Their new roles gave a new impetus to women's liberation. The women breadwinners who bought the daily newspapers became a new audience; and their counterparts appeared in the comics. Career girls made an auspicious start with *Brenda Starr*, a newspaperwoman, in 1940. Brenda's creator, appropriately enough, is female, Dale Messick. Mobility and glamor made the theme appealing as a strip. Brenda was the first of three attractive additions to the city room. *Debbie Dean*, another chic newspaper career girl, was created in 1942 by Bert Whitman, a versatile cartoonist who formerly drew *The Green Hornet* and in

Dale Messick's *Brenda Starr* proves a tough reporter can be beautiful (excerpt).
© 1972 The Chicago Tribune.

recent years has turned to editorial cartooning. The third was *Jane Arden* by Monte Barrett. Another female heroine was *Claire Voyant* by Jack Sparling. Claire appeared in 1943, picked up at sea by a lifeboat, a victim of amnesia, destined to go through the war without knowing who she was. Sparling previously drew *Hap Hopper*, a strip about the experiences of a Washington correspondent, the writing credited to the columnist Drew Pearson and Robert Allen. The trend of the career girl climaxed in 1944 with a superheroine, *Wonder Woman*, a comic book transplant.

A Time of Transition

The transition from wartime to peacetime was best exemplified by a new strip by the veteran cartoonist Coulton Waugh. In 1945 Waugh, who had taken over *Dickie Dare* from Milton Caniff, launched *Hank*, which concerned the adjustment of a returning one-legged veteran. The attempt to deal with serious and downbeat postwar themes was ambitious. (He also experimented with structural elements, such as white lettering in black balloons.) Unfortunately eye trouble forced Waugh to abandon the strip, but he did not forsake the profession. His book *The Comics*, published in 1947, was a most valuable contribution to comics literature.

A number of cartoonists returned from the war to resume their careers, some with characters created in service for *Stars and Stripes* and other military newspapers: Len Sansone's *The Wolf*, Bill Mauldin's *Up*

"Haven't I seen you—somewhere—before?"

Leonard Sansone's *The Wolf* and Milton Caniff's *Miss Lace* teamed up in this rare World War II panel.
© 1943 Leonard Sansone and Milton Caniff.

Up Front by Bill Mauldin.
© 1944 United Feature Syndicate, Inc.

Hank by Coulton Waugh.
© 1945 The Newspaper PM, Inc.

"Yer lucky. Yer learnin' a trade."

George Baker's *Sad Sack*
© 1946 George Baker.

Front, and Dick Wingert's *Hubert*. Dave Breger had been doing *Private Breger* but changed it to *G.I. Joe* for *Yank* magazine in 1942, thereby coining possibly the most widely used term in World War II. The cycle was complete when the artist *and* his character were discharged and the strip became known as *Mr. Breger*. Another service-born strip was George Baker's *Sad Sack*, about the plight of a little private who was a study of frustration in fatigues. The classic Army fall guy continued as a pathetic civilian in 1946.

Ernie Bushmiller makes typical inventive use of a prop in *Nancy*. © 1946 United Feature Syndicate, Inc.

Kid strips were not completely ignored. Loy Byrnes' *Spunkie* made its debut in 1940. So did an obstreperous little girl with black prickly hair named Nancy, created by Ernie Bushmiller in *Fritzi Ritz*. Like Snuffy Smith (*Barney Google*) and Popeye (*Thimble Theatre*), Nancy was a peripheral character who succeeded to stardom, and in 1940 the strip was renamed *Nancy*.

Bushmiller's gags are mostly visual, with a minimum of dialogue. *Nancy* remains unaffected by today's trend toward sophisticated kid strips.

Bushmiller, born in the Bronx, New York, a high school dropout and student at the National Academy of Design, started as a copyboy for the New York *World*. His break came when Larry Whittington, who created *Fritzi* in 1922, left to launch *Maisie the Model* in 1925 and Bushmiller fell heir to the strip. When the *World* folded, it left its reigning cartoonists stranded for work space. Milt Gross, H. T. Webster, Dow Walling, Harry Haenigsen and Bushmiller, dependent on one another's repartee, decided to share a one-room studio on the forty-fourth floor of the Chrysler Building—undoubtedly one of the greatest concentrations of cartoon talent of the day. In 1930 Bushmiller spent a year in Hollywood creating gags for Harold Lloyd's *Movie Crazy*. Now living in Connecticut, he is approaching his fiftieth year as a cartoonist with undiminished enthusiasm.

Effective use of the wide-angle panel in *Nancy*.
© 1946 United Feature Syndicate, Inc.

168

Alfred Andriola employs cross-cutting to keep three simultaneous story elements moving to a climax in *Kerry Drake*. © 1974 Field Enterprises, Inc.

Two disciples of the Sickles-Caniff school, Alfred Andriola and Frank Robbins, left their strips for new creations in the 1940's.

Andriola, a native New Yorker, studied journalism at Columbia University and art at Cooper Union. In 1935 he became an assistant on *Terry and the Pirates*, a happy result of a fan letter he sent to Milton Caniff. His association with Caniff and Noel Sickles, who was then doing *Scorchy Smith*, was a decisive influence. Andriola developed quickly under their tutelage and

in 1938 launched his first strip, *Charlie Chan*, an adaptation of the fictional detective. In 1942 he took over *Dan Dunn* and launched *Kerry Drake* a year ater.

Andriola gradually developed his own style, a blend of black-and-white illustration and caricature that permits realism but is not photographic. Backgrounds and props are authentic and carefully delineated. Fashion and decor, as well as the expert use of Benday, are employed to provide color, tone, and contrast with the flat blacks.

Another Andriola device in *Kerry Drake*, the "flash-ahead" shows impending action in graphic rather than narrative terms. © 1973 Field Enterprises, Inc.

For the first ten years Kerry Drake was an assistant district attorney, but as a result of the death of his fiancée at the hands of the villains of the episode, Bulldozer and his wife, Trinket, he decided to go into active police work. The white-haired sleuth has brought to justice such flamboyant villains as No Face, Dr. Zero, Bottleneck, Stitches, Yoyo, Kid Gloves, and DDT. In the last fifteen years *Kerry* has developed a new approach to the classic crime detective theme, with the emphasis on the characters' emotional development. As Andriola put it: "I have stressed the human issue, how crime affects the people involved, rather than spelling out crime for crime's sake. . . . Now my characters look and act much more like everyday people. Their names are more likely to be Dooley, Jim, Vanessa, Vince, or Judy. The emphasis is where the heart is . . . in a comic strip a touch of evil goes a long way."

In 1958 Kerry married Mindy, an attractive widow of a policeman killed on duty. Apart from his crime-fighting career, Kerry's proudest accomplishment occurred in September, 1967. Mindy gave birth to quadruplets, making Kerry the first father of a multiple birth in the comics!

Frank Robbins, born in Boston, took over *Scorchy Smith* in 1939. Robbins, too, gradually added his own touch to the basic Sickles-Caniff style. His compositions became almost pure sparkling patterns of black and white. He developed a mastery of dramatic lighting and cast shadows, where figures bleed into black and the backgrounds become a series of contrasting planes. Robbins left *Scorchy* for the creation, in

A dramatic counterpoint from Frank Robbins' *Johnny Hazard.* © 1969 King Features Syndicate, Inc.

1944, of the adventures of an Air Force flying officer, *Johnny Hazard.* In his first episode, Hazard escaped from a Nazi prison camp by stealing a bomber. Recently Hazard has become an agent with a supernatural organization, WING, a group fighting for justice and democracy. Mr. Alpha, head of WING, speeds Hazard from one hair-raising adventure to another by means of a special atomic-powered delta-wing plane.

Robbins studied at the National Academy of Design and is a serious painter of note. His works have been exhibited at the Corcoran Gallery and the Metropolitan and Whitney museums.

A sample of the brilliant black-and-white brush-work in *Johnny Hazard* by Frank Robbins. © 1969 King Features Syndicate, Inc.

Allegory and Fantasy

Every decade has somehow seen the rise of one or more rare comic geniuses in the mold of Outcault and Herriman. The forties were no exception.

One of the most delightful comic zoos is the collection of wildlife assembled by Walt Kelly in *Pogo*, a mixture of hilarious slapstick, brilliant satire, and subtle humor, involving a seemingly endless cast of Kelly-created creatures. Pogo, "a possum by trade," is the warmhearted and naïve star performer. Featured players include: the raffish Albert the Alligator; Deacon Mushrat; a prideful hound, Beauregard Bugleboy; a turtle and reformed pirate captain, Churchy La Femme; Howland Owl, a nearsighted sorcerer; a fox, Seminole Sam; Wiley Catt; Mole MacCarony; Snavely the snake; Boll Weevil, a gloomy realist; Porkypine; a frog, Moonshine Sonata; a skunk, Ma'm'selle Hepzibah; and innumerable bit players who Kelly thought must work in other strips on their days off.

Walt Kelly was born in Philadelphia in 1913 and reared in Bridgeport, Connecticut. In 1935 he set out by bus with a borrowed stake for the Disney Studios in California. He landed a job and for six years worked on such films as *Snow White*, *Fantasia*, and *Pinocchio*, learning the techniques of the craft that were to influence his later work. Kelly first put the ingredients together for *Pogo* in a series of animal stories for the comic magazines built around a little black boy named Bumbazine. In the tradition of A. A. Milne's Christopher Robin in *Winnie the Pooh*, Bumbazine talked with the animals. Bumbazine, however, soon disappeared, and Kelly's characters have been verbose but other than human ever since. Albert the Alligator and Pogo had appeared from time to time in comic book stories and became the basis of the strip. Kelly recalled the process: "After a hit-or-miss exis-

Pogo's penchant for rhyme knows no depth. © 1972 Walt Kelly.

Churchy La Femme and Beauregard Bugleboy
in a typical Walt Kelly soufflé. © 1971 Walt Kelly.

tence for a few years, the feature was pounded into shape as a comic strip, and I have kept busy ever since trying to learn to draw, spell and master a few fast moves on the feet."

In 1949 Kelly was hired as a political cartoonist, art director, and comic strip editor for a new newspaper, the New York *Star*. In the latter capacity, Kelly the editor promptly hired Walt Kelly, cartoonist, to do the comic strip *Pogo*. The *Star* folded in less than a year. *Pogo* was signed by Hall Syndicate and started national syndication in May of the same year.

Kelly's art is as enchanting as his stories. Every character and detail of Okefenokee Swamp is pampered and caressed with pen strokes of infinite variety to convey contour and texture, giving the strip a rich quality. The calligraphy is an essential part of the art. Two characters have lettering styles of their own that suggest each personality and tone of voice. Deacon Mushrat speaks in pious Old English, and P. T. Bridgeport, who bears a striking resemblance to P. T. Barnum, in circus poster type.

A Kelly favorite: the *Pogo* Christmas panel for 1953. © Walt Kelly.

Kelly was unique in his use of gobbledygook verse. Nonsense poems, such as "Deck Us All with Boston Charlie" in 1948, have become classics:

Deck us all with Boston Charlie,
Walla walla, Wash, an' Kalamazoo!
Nora's freezin' on the trolley,
Swaller dollar cauliflower alleygaroo! . . .

In 1952 *Pogo* added a new dimension—political allegory. As Kelly remembered it: "After all, it is pretty hard to walk past an unguarded gold mine and remain empty-handed.'' A new character, Simple J. Malarkey, a snarling, jowly dog, who bore a startling resemblance to Senator Joseph McCarthy, appeared. Along with Dwight Eisenhower and Adlai Stevenson, Pogo ran for President in 1952. He was a reluctant candidate who never had the nerve to say yes or no. But Pogo was the Presidential choice of millions of college students. Satirizing Presidential candidates has become a *Pogo* tradition. In 1964 Richard Nixon, Nelson Rockefeller, and George Romney were portrayed as windup dolls (Romney ran backward). President Lyndon Johnson appeared in the form of a nearsighted Texas longhorn with a bulbous nose. Nixon has also appeared as a spider. A hyena looked suspiciously like Vice President Spiro Agnew. Whereas Capp (*Li'l Abner*) uses a machete, Kelly prefers to tickle his opponent into submission. Kelly's scathing and rarely disguised political satire has caused some newspapers to complain or drop the offending episodes. Kelly, however, drew substitute

strips for nervous editors, "full of cute little bunny rabbits," to be used in place of the censored material.

In recent years *Pogo* has been victimized by the reduction of the size of the strips for the sake of economy. In many papers sizes have shrunk from six to four columns. *Pogo*'s rich and often lengthy dialogue when reduced in size becomes more difficult to read and the spirit of the strip is diminished. Sunday pages have also been cut in size, and both the illustrative art, as in *Prince Valiant*, and the "comic" art of *Pogo* suffer. It is doubtful that the *Yellow Kid* and *Little Nemo* would have made the impact they did if they had been restricted to today's sizes.

Since Walt Kelly's death in October, 1973, *Pogo* has been carried on by his wife, Selby, who writes and draws the Sunday page, while his son, Stephen, draws the daily strips, and Don Morgan writes the script.

Kelly's political caricatures: (clockwise) Joseph P. McCarthy (Simple J. Malarkey) with Deacon Muskrat; Spiro T. Agnew with the Deacon; Nelson Rockefeller, George Romney, and Lyndon B. Johnson with P. T. Bridgeport and Pogo; Richard M. Nixon with Bridgeport and Pogo. © Walt Kelly.

Crockett Johnson's ethereal *Barnaby,* circa 1948. © Crockett Johnson.

"Cushlamochree!" was a favorite expression of a fat, pixielike, fast-talking, middle-aged, egocentric, greedy, arrogant, winged leprechaun named O'Malley who ambled into the comics pages of the short-lived New York daily *P.M.* in 1942. The strip was *Barnaby.* It quickly captured a coterie of intellectual fans, including Dorothy Parker, who hailed *Barnaby* as a major addition to American arts and letters. Contrary to expectations, *Barnaby* proved to have a wide appeal to kids as well.

O'Malley, the fairy godfather of a small boy named Barnaby, was invisible to all except the boy, his dog Gorgon, and of course the reader. O'Malley was a rather bumbling and ineffectual fairy (his cigar doubled as a magic wand) who had difficulty in pulling off even the smallest demonstration of his supernatural power. He did, however, conjure up Gorgon as a Christmas present for Barnaby to give to his father. Even this bit of magic was dispelled when a news item appeared: "Doubtless imbued with too much Christian spirit, someone broke into the ASPCA shelter last night and freed all of its 216 canine inmates and 93 cats. Authorities are puzzled."

O'Malley's solution for the paper shortage was to eliminate comic strips! He uniquely concluded that since 96 percent of newspaper readers follow the comics, it wouldn't be worthwhile to print the rest of the paper without them.

Barnaby's pace was leisurely, the characters moved on and off as in a miniature play, "stage-right" and "stage-left." The story was told as if filmed from a fixed position; the picture plane was flat, without angle shots or close-ups. The focus was on the dialogue and characterization. The balloons were an innovation; rather than the conventional hand-lettered cartoon style the dialogue was set in type which accentuated the storybook quality of the strip and became part of its aesthetics, as did the use of varied lettering styles in *Pogo.*

Barnaby's creator, Crockett Johnson (David Johnson Leisk), tired of the grind of a daily strip and retired *Barnaby* in 1952. For two years it was by-lined by Jack Morley and Ted Ferro. Johnson has since authored numerous successful children's books.

The Soap Opera

One of the most dramatic transformations of a character brought still another genre to the comic strip in the forties.

The thirties and forties saw the rise of the soap opera on radio. The "soaps," named for the program's sponsors, were daytime serials directed toward the nation's housewives: *Mary Noble, Backstage Wife, Ma Perkins,* and *The Romance of Helen Trent* ("The real-life drama of Helen Trent who, when life mocks her, breaks her hopes, dashes her on the rocks of despair, fights back bravely . . . to prove . . . that because a woman is thirty-five or more, romance in life need not be over . . ."). *Mary Worth* was to become the first comic strip soap opera.

The soap opera in the comic strip and on radio reflected the change in public tastes. Real problems were dealt with, romanticized to be sure, but nevertheless with a greater degree of sophistication and depth than before. The literary form has continued its popuarity in the comic strip, although it faded from radio, only to reemerge on television in the sixties.

Mary Worth began life in 1932 as a dowdy busybody known as *Apple Mary. Apple Mary* was created by Martha Orr, niece of the political cartoonist Carey Orr. After seven years Miss Orr relinquished the strip to her young assistant, Dale Conner. Allen Saunders took over as writer, and they used the pseudonym Dale Allen. The first step in the strip's metamorphosis was to change the name to *Mary*

Mary Worth's Family by Dale Allen (Dale Conner and Allen Saunders). © 1941 Publishers Syndicate, Inc.

Worth's Family in 1940. (It became *Mary Worth* in 1944.) Saunders began to remold the maudlin tear-jerker and remove Mary from the lower-class neighborhood where she performed her self-sacrificing good deeds. A radical revision came in 1942 with Ken Ernst as illustrator.

Ernst gave the strip a new sleek and sophisticated look. Mary became a modern grandmother type, coiffured and dressed in the latest mode. Ernst applies expert draftsmanship with lavish attention to fashion and decor and a wide range of illustrative techniques in the storytelling. His characters are varied and distinct, even the innumerable attractive females, which is not always an easy task.

Saunders' scripts deal with contemporary themes previously avoided: alcoholism, infidelty, and emo-

tional problems of every description, particularly of young women. Mary, the gentle white-haired widow, became an itinerant mender of broken hearts, confidante and counselor to young and old (resisting a suitor or two of her own along the way), leaving a trail of problems solved, happier people—and faithful readers.

Allen Saunders, born in Lebanon, Indiana, Phi Beta Kappa, former professor of romance languages and newspaper drama critic, believes the comic strip is a valid narrative art form that can be entertaining and teach its readers something about themselves as well. "If the great American novel is ever written," Saunders observed, "it may be a picture and textbook."

Saunders has proved to be a comics "doctor." An

Mary Worth by Ken Ernst and Allen Saunders. Mary's counsel is not always detached.
© 1959 Publishers Syndicate, Inc.

175

Rex Morgan, M.D. (excerpt) by Marvin Bradley and Frank Edgington.
© 1971 Field Enterprises, Inc.

earlier comic strip "patient" was *Chief Wahoo* originated by Elmer Woggon. Saunders replaced the "ailing" Chief with a supporting character and, together with cartoonist William Overgard, transformed it into *Steve Roper*, a successful modern adventure, since retitled *Steve Roper & Mike Nomad.* Saunders is one of the growing number of professional writers, following Lee Falk (*The Phantom* and *Mandrake the Magician),* who have found the comic strip a serious medium of literary expression. Another is Elliott Caplin (brother of Al Capp), a noted author of books and plays, who is dedicated to the comics form. He has been story consultant for a number of strips, among them: *Abbie an' Slats, Heart of Juliet Jones, Big Benbolt,* and *Little Orphan Annie.*

Harold Anderson, as president of Publishers (now Publishers-Hall) Syndicate, pioneered the use of scientific public opinion polls to chart the reaction to existing strips and to gauge the audience for prospective strips. The polls showed there was a public for realistic adventure strips about conventional professions. The first result was *Rex Morgan, M.D.* This strip also reflects a trend toward packaging a team of experts to produce comic strips. Dr. Nicholas Dallis, a psychiatrist and former head of the Toledo Mental Hygiene Center, draws upon his years of medical experience in writing the script. The team of Marvin Bradley and Frank Edgington do the art. Dallis, continuing the formula, teamed with cartoonists Dan Heilman, in 1952 to produce *Judge Parker,* and Alex Kotsky, on *Apartment 3G* in 1962. Heilman died in 1966, and Harold LeDoux continues *Parker.* The success of *Rex Morgan* and *Judge Parker* in the comics was to be duplicated in the doctor and lawyer dramatizations on television in the sixties and seventies.

Steve Roper (excerpt) by William Overgard and Allen Saunders.
© 1966 Publishers Newspaper Syndicate.

Judge Parker's decisions are not all on the bench, by Harold LeDoux, circa 1970.
© Publishers-Hall Syndicate, Inc.

A new teen-age culture emerged in the thirties and forties. It was the heyday of the Big Bands: Artie Shaw, Benny Goodman, and the Dorsey brothers. The girls swooned to Frank Sinatra's "This Love of Mine," and the boys worried about the draft while incessantly playing the pinball machine at the corner drugstore. *Our Bill* in 1939 was the first to attempt to capture the world of the bobby-soxer and bring a fresh ambiance to the genre of the teen-age strip.

Harry Haenigsen, *Our Bill*'s creator, was born in New York City in 1900. Spurning a career in engineering, as did Rube Goldberg, Haenigsen gave up a scholarship at Rutgers University for a job in animation at the Bray Studios. Soon after, he joined the art department of the New York *World* for $7 a week. At night he studied at the Art Students League. It was a time, as Haenigsen recalls, that artists were barred from drawing in the courtroom, and H. T. Smith miraculously drew vivid scenes of the trials with cutdown pencils on small blocks of paper secreted in his pocket.

Haenigsen's first strip in 1922 was *Simeon Batts,* about a radio ham who constructed sets out of kitchen utensils. He then developed a panel takeoff on the news which ran from 1925 until the *World* folded in 1931 and which he continued in the New York *Journal* under the title of *News and Views* until 1937. During this time, Haenigsen also became a noted illustrator of magazines, books, and advertising. For years his elegantly designed drawings were identified with *Collier's* magazine.

Our Bill (excerpt) by Harry Haenigsen. Pop finds the younger generation does have more fun.
© 1941 New York Tribune, Inc.

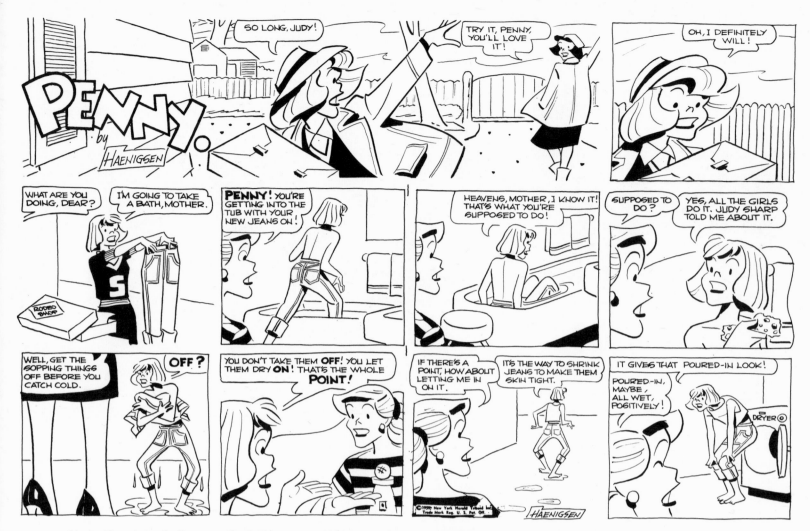

Harry Haenigsen's *Penny* reflected teen-age fads and foibles. © 1959 New York Tribune, Inc.

After a period as a story editor for the Max Fleischer Studios, he created *Our Bill,* a Sunday page, which ran until 1966. Although *Our Bill* remained his personal favorite, *Penny* was his most popular and widely syndicated feature. *Penny,* introduced in 1943, was a teen-ager of blithe spirit. The strip was frequently punctuated by warm sequences with droll dialogue between Penny and her exasperated but sympathetic father. Haenigsen captured Penny's pert manner and supple but awkward gyrations in precise line punctuated by a few discriminating blacks. Expert use was

also made of selective focus, close-ups, and long shots, not usually seen in strips of its genre. Since ending *Penny* in 1970, Haenigsen has lived an active semiretirement at his Bucks County, Pennsylvania, home.

Four other popular teen-age strips also appeared during this period: Hilda Terry's piquant *Teena* (1941), Dudley Fisher's *Myrtle* (1942), which enjoyed wide popularity until Fisher's retirement in 1970; Bob Montana's classic *Archie* (1946), which originated in the comic books; and Hal Rasmussen's *Aggie* (1946), later continued by Roy Fox.

Bob Montana's resourceful *Archie.* © 1958 King Features Syndicate, Inc.

The forties also saw other notable additions to the staple comic strip categories. Some have survived the changes in American society; many have not. They all reflect in some measure the varied attempts to capture a segment of the comic's readership.

Family strips have been the most enduring, and many have thrived: Carl Grubert's *The Berrys* (1942), George Swanson's *The Flop Family* (1944), Buford Tune's *Dotty* (1944), and Al Vermeer's *Priscilla's Pop* (1947). Charles Kuhn's *Grandma* (1947) ran for twenty years until the artist's retirement.

There were fall guy strips by two leading magazine cartoonists: Eric Ericson's *Herkimer Fuddle* and Jay Irving's amiable but befuddled cop, *Pottsy* (originally *Willie Doodle)*, which ran until Irving's death in 1970.

Charles Kuhn's *Grandma*.
© 1965 King Features Syndicate, Inc.

Willie Doodle. Jay Irving's trademark was the bumbling well-meaning cop. © 1946 New York Tribune, Inc.

Adventure strips were the most vulnerable and few have survived until the present day: Burne Hogarth's *Drago* (1945), Ray Bailey's *Bruce Gentry* (1945), Michael O'Malley and Dean Miller's *Vic Flint* (1946), and Kreigh Collins' *Kevin the Bold* (1949) have all succumbed to shifting popular tastes. One, however, that has had continued success since 1946 is a unique feature of adventure that combines wildlife lore, natural history, and all manner of outdoor living, *Mark Trail* by Ed Dodd, who previously did a humor panel, *Back Home.*

Ed Dodd's *Mark Trail* on the trail.
© 1968 Publishers-Hall Syndicate, Inc.

by Leonard Starr

In our home we took only one paper, the New York *Daily News,* all we could afford even at two cents daily and five cents Sunday, for this was the Depression. Sunday was the highlight of the week, but I don't think I could have told it from any other except for the colored comic sections spread across the newsstands. I devoured the *News'* comics of course. But it was not enough.

Alas, even I could not make them last much beyond noon. I somehow discovered that the janitor of our building, a lovely German man, got the *Journal-American* and *Mirror,* and yes, he would save the comic sections for me and so the rest of the day became a period of clock watching, waiting until he could decently be expected to have finished the funnies himself, usually around five o'clock.

I would then go down two flights of stairs, collect my prizes, carry them back to our flat, my heart thumping with expectation and spread them out on the floor, the only area available to me that could accommodate the full-size standard size of the *Journal-American.*

Then, starting from the back page, I would very slowly turn those marvelous gaudy sheets, savoring every panel.

First the *Mirror,* it holding the lesser attractions for me, and when I finished with *Joe Palooka* on the front page I would reverently pull the *Journal-American* over on top of it.

The Katzenjammer Kids on the end page here. I was never much attracted to the humor strips, probably because the drawings never incited me to imitation. I would go through every strip very carefully nonetheless, mostly as a delaying action, deliciously holding myself back from the inside front page.

Flash Gordon. Approaching it, I now carefully kept my eyes on the linoleum above the page lest I inadvertently glance at the last panel as I opened on to it. First *Jungle Jim,* four tall panels across the top, no big deal for me even though it was also drawn by Alex Raymond. But I took my time over it because directly beneath, in a double space between the borders, I could see that fabulous name, set in simple Roman type, no pop lettering, no whirling planets. They weren't necessary.

My family was directly affected by the Depression. My father was out of work, savings were dwindling, and there were no harbingers of better times coming. I'm sure there was desperation all around me, but I was somehow unaware of that part of it. I can recall only that those years were totally gray. I know that the sun never once shone in all that time. Only on the planet Mongo was there any color; only there could be found any vitality, any life.

Today perhaps, the cartoonists of my generation, circa 1925, would be drawn to film or television, but perhaps not. What the comics had, and have, was and is an intimacy, a direct contact with their creators. The photograph involves a mechanical and chemical agent, but only human hands could put those drawings there, each unmistakably unique.

Milton Caniff was to lure me away from the marvels of Mongo with the more veristic adventures of *Terry and the Pirates.* Milton's impact was totally different from that of Alex Raymond, which was totally different from Hal Foster's and so forth. But the great thing about the comic strip was its accessibility to us as a means of expression. It needed no vast broadcasting networks or mammoth movie studios to enable us to try out our first fledgling extravaganzas. A breadboard, a sheet of paper, a bottle of India ink, and we were in business.

So now the comic strip has been doing its thing for seventy-five years, and I've been in business adding my bit for thirty of those years. How do I feel about it at this point? Well, it's a relentless, time-consuming job that requires tremendous self-discipline, but apparently among those components that go to make up a cartoonist is a degree of infantilism that leaves no room for self-discipline, so that most of us are always behind schedule, giving us the feeling that our lives are spent running in front of a train.

And times have changed, the troubles of today making the past seem pastoral by comparison. Against all this can we offer more than a moment's surcease? Maybe not, but if we can arrest someone's life for just that moment, say the equivalent of the restful pause afforded by the semicolon before they go on with the main business of their lives, then all right. That'll be fine.

by Hal Foster

In Gilbert and Sullivan's *Pinafore* a bright lad becomes Ruler of the Queen's Navy through his efficiency in polishing up the handle of the big front door. In 1957 I achieved the National Cartoonist Society's Reuben through ladies' underwear.

I had been fired from an office job under the flimsy excuse that I thought more of duck hunting than business! Who doesn't? So I gathered up my scribbles and applied for a job with a firm illustrating a mail-order catalog. Hired, and now a professional artist at last! Under my ardent brush the catalog blossomed with dainty white wear. I believe I had the honor of illustrating the last lace-trimmed panties equipped with a tailboard.

Rumors of a gold strike east of Lake Winnipeg aroused my avarice. Two friends of equal mentality but less experience were deluded into becoming partners. What fun! Portaging our outfit over rapids and falls, across rocky ridges and slogging through endless muskeg in a cloud of mosquitoes. Our triumphant return was somewhat deflated by learning our claims were worthless. My companions were not too dismayed. They were thankful that I had brought them back alive, barely.

A plateau had been reached, wider fields were a necessity for further development and Chicago looked like that field. I talked things over with my wife. She had become used to my ways, without becoming punchy, paid up my premiums and told me how much money there was at hand. Not enough for train fare and hotel rooms, so I induced a more affluent friend of mine to join me. We packed a few utensils in a blanket, tied them to the handlebars of our bicycles and took the cheap way to Chicago, pedaling a thousand miles over gravel roads, and were robbed the day we arrived.

After that I became a very good second-rate illustrator.

Then came the panic of 1929 and the Depression that followed, no work, no pay. It was at this hungry period that *Tarzan of the Apes* was offered me, and lo! I had become a cartoonist.

Very few can do their best work unless they can put something of themselves into it, and I wanted to direct the actions of my own hero. So the *Prince Valiant* idea was conceived. But it took nearly a year of research work before he could be dressed and armed correctly to take his place in the world, circa A.D. 500.

★ ★ ★

by Walt Kelly

The question of how anybody gets into any line of work is always fascinatingly dull and the answers are even more vapid or, perhaps, mysterious. How did a left-handed dentist wind up as one of the more beguiling and crafty baseball managers? Why did a sewer designer choose to become an inventor of weird machinery, a crazy cartoonist, and a fine writer to boot? How did a boy who was horrendous at primary scholastics finally arrived at the theory that $E = MC^2$?

At the Disney studio, in the early thirties, you'd ask an erstwhile gas station functionary, who was then busily drawing with both hands, how he had arrived and his answer was "I lived near the studio and I owned a pencil."

It was the conjecture of George Kerr, a turn-of-the-century great, that no cartoonist ever developed without the help of that great American tool, the hand-rolled cigar. That, he contended, was why there were so few lady cartoonists. "Ladies," said George, "don't look very good scooping low into a gutter to retrieve a butt."

With the possible exceptions of Milt Caniff, Sparky Schulz, Irma Selz and maybe a hundred other misfits, all cartoonists come equipped (from birth) with a conestoga or, at the very least, a cheek full of cut plug.

It is this ability to fetch and twirl a cigar that gives the youngster a facility with pen or brush which starts the subject on a life of magnificent flash. The early encounter with the cigar gives the young manipulator a sense of freedom and a kind of courage. A courage born of ignorance, perhaps, as when he feels infinitely secure as he smokes one of his father's cigars in his mother's bathroom.

Not knowing what one is doing, plus a solid grasp of freedom, can spell disaster for anybody. The cartoonist somehow weathers this. He is not bright enough to know he's in trouble, but, being a free man, he would not give much of a damn if he knew.

It was a surprise to hear Rube Goldberg say at one time, "All you young guys draw with a single line. When I was coming up, they made us use a line with little hairs on it. How do you get away with a single line?" Part of the answer was that animation cartoons had produced a line with no hairs. Other things had contributed, but by 1940 the line was generally simple and clear.

Rube never took strict orders from anyone, but he was a gentleman, and if some jackass wanted hairy lines, Rube didn't see it as a hurdle—he put hairs on his line. *Number One:* The cartoonist should be a gentle (two words) man.

Number Two: The cartoonist should be modest. One time on a train speeding at about four miles an hour between Boston and New York, a gent named Caniff remarked, ". . . and this fellow screamed in a voice that could only be heard by a tall dog." Since then Milt has attributed the classy phrase to many others, but the origin was on a slow train to Manhattan. Modesty is a fine, manly virtue.

Number Three: There is the matter of courage. Herblock has over the past three decades displayed courage on many occasions. But he has never won a Pulitzer Prize for courage; his prizes came from cartoons that were safe, against the common enemy as established by the establishment. But, despite the opinions of the Pulitzer committees, courage is indispensable.

Thus the cartoonist becomes and stays a cartoonist because of the freedom, the quiet, the peace of mind spawned out of the fearless knowledge that he doesn't know what he's doing. It's a good life.

★ ★ ★

Sophistication and Realism: 1950-1970's

The modern era of the comics started with the Korean War and has continued with the war in Vietnam. The population grew from 150,000,000 to 211,000,000. In 1950 Joe Louis, in his comeback attempt, was defeated by Ezzard Charles, and in 1971 Muhammad Ali failed in his try against Joe Frazier. The fifties saw the first march for civil rights and the sixties the first walk on the moon.

A national preoccupation with flying saucers and quiz show scandals switched to pot, psychedelics and pollution. 3-D movies, hula hoops, and chlorophyll gave way to pop art, graffiti, and fluoride. The fifties' Beat Generation, as portrayed in Jack Kerouac's *On the Road*, was replaced at the end of the sixties by the Age of Aquarius, as celebrated in *Hair*. The two decades brought new words, letters, names, and meanings: H-bombs, U-2's, and B-52's, Malcolm X and U Thant, NATO and SEATO, TV, VW, and LSD, Beatles, Sputnik, Kon-Tiki, Yippie, Twiggy, and Kukla, Fran, and Ollie. And the modern era was to see a host of new comic strips that were also to add names and idioms to our culture.

The New Humor

Since 1950 there has been a renaissance of humor strips following the era of illustrative adventure. Humor strips could be read quickly in the accelerated rhythm of contemporary life and did not require the day-to-day commitment of story strips. The modern period has also seen the development of a new brand of realism and greater sophistication and social awareness in both genres. The basic techniques and

185

Mort Walker's *Beetle Bailey* was "Joe College" in his first year.
© 1950 King Features Syndicate, Inc.

innovations of the comic strip form were established in the first half century, and the modern strip has seen the refinement of the existing structure. Stylistically, the humor strips have tended toward greater simplicity, at times a childlike drawing with a highly developed iconography. This is combined with mature humor and sophisticated dialogue, rich in social and philosophical implications, in the tradition of *Krazy Kat*. The anti heroes of the new humor strips seemed to symbolize man's impotence in his modern, complex society.

Two cartoonists, Mort Walker and Charles Schulz, have had parallel careers in many respects. In 1950 both launched strips that were to set patterns of humor for the modern era. Both were born in 1922, served in World War II, and began their careers as magazine cartoonists. And both of their strips, after rather inauspicious beginnings, developed into two of the most successful in comic strip history.

Mort Walker's *Beetle Bailey* is a satire of the military in the tradition of Bruce Bairnsfather's *Ole Bill* of World War I and Bill Maudlin's *Willie and Joe* of

Walker employs the silhouette and close-up in his *Beetle Bailey* Sunday page.
© 1968 King Features Syndicate, Inc.

Beetle faces up to the inevitable.
© 1965 King Features Syndicate, Inc.

of complaints from its GI fans soon forced the top brass to order it restored. The episode parallels General George Patton's attempt to censor Mauldin's irreverent dogfaces, Willie and Joe. *Beetle Bailey*'s private war with the Army still continues. When Sergeant Snorkle recently heard a strange sound and asked what that crumbling noise could be, the captain replied, "Army discipline."

Born Addison Morton Walker in Eldorado, Kansas, he drew his first strip, *Lime Juicers*, at fifteen for the Kansas City *Journal*. By age sixteen more than three hundred of his magazine cartoons had been published, and at eighteen Walker was chief designer for Hallmark Greeting Cards. Walker's preparation for *Beetle* (although he didn't know it at the time) began when he was drafted in 1943 and served as an infantry rifleman and later as an intelligence officer in Italy. After graduating from the University of Missouri, he moved to New York, and by 1949 he became a best-selling magazine cartoonist.

Walker lives a suburban Connecticut life with his wife and seven children. This background, in fact, provided the inspiration for the creation of *Hi and Lois* in 1954, with his collaborator Dik Browne. Browne, a native New Yorker, one of the leading advertising cartoonists (the creator of Chiquita Banana and redesigner of the Campbell Soup Kids), skillfully composes *Hi and Lois* in a clean, crisp style. While Walker has the reputation of being one of the most organized in the profession and looks like a prosperous Wall Street broker, Browne is more in the school of the late journalist Heywood Broun, who had the reputation of looking like an unmade bed. His fellow cartoonists claim Browne looks like an unmade Heywood Broun.

Hi and Lois actually first appeared in *Beetle Bailey*. Beetle, on furlough, visited his sister, Lois, and her husband, Hi. Their family now consists of fourteen-year-old Chip, twins Dot and Ditto, eight, and Baby Trixie, who doesn't speak but has an amazing thought vocabulary ("I love my daddy! He makes me laugh! I love my mommy. She's soft and cuddly. The others I haven't worked into my life-style yet."), and a pony-sized dog, Dawg..As Browne put it, "The whole thrust of the strip is recognition and identification. So many letters I receive start with, 'You must have been peeking in our windows!'" The phenomenal growth of modern suburbia provides a wide audience for this warm, genial view of the many small tribulations of an average young family.

World War II. The strip combines the comedic elements of slapstick, wildly preposterous involvements, and a healthy irreverence for authority. Beetle does his classical GI goldbricking at Camp Swampy, where the harried private's tormentors include: Sergeant Orville Snorkle, Beetle's gluttonous taskmaster; Cookie, the company's slovenly chef; Plato, the resident intellectual; Cosmo, the ranking wheeler-dealer and con artist; Lieutenant Fuzz, a fatuous toady; Killer, the self-styled Lothario; Lieutenant Flap, a cool character in goatee and Afro; and General Halftrack, the camp's misanthropic and ineffectual commanding officer.

Beetle started as a college student in pork-pie hat, a character that Walker developed in his magazine cartoons. The strip was revamped when Beetle was drafted during the Korean War. Beetle's transition mirrored the plight of millions of young Americans, and the strip found itself an enthusiastic audience in the process. In 1954 the Tokyo edition of *Stars and Stripes* dropped Beetle as being too flippant and encouraging a lack of respect for ranking officers. A tide

The kids find a loophole in *Hi and Lois*, by Mort Walker and Dik Browne.
© 1971 King Features Syndicate, Inc.

In 1961 Walker collaborated with Jerry Dumas, who also contributes to the writing of *Beetle* and *Hi and Lois* in the experimental avant-garde *Sam's Strip*. Its surreal humor, much of it a satire on other strips, was a favorite of cartoonists, but it proved to be too limited in appeal.

Walker's need for further expression and growth found its fulfillment in 1968 with *Boner's Ark*, which he signs Addison. The ark is a delightful animal zoo which provides a seagoing platform for still another facet of Walker's humor. Walker sees the strips as a chronicle of his life: *Beetle Bailey*, his Army days; *Hi and Lois*, his family life; and *Boner's Ark*, how he feels about today's mores and attitudes.

Joining *Boner's Ark* in the category of animal strips is Roger Bollen's *Animal Crackers*. Set in an African game reserve, it features Lyle, a slightly incompetent King of Beasts, a renegade gnu, and a member of a minority group, a dodo.

Family life has proved to be a continuing source of humor. The varied pressures of modern society on the family unit have inspired a wide range of comedic interpretations, from the rich burlesque of *The Smith Family* by George Smith, to the more gentle whimsy and petty traumas of *The Ryatts* by Jack Elrod; from the antics of the elderly in *Mrs. Fitz* by Frank Roberge and *Eb & Flo* by Paul Sellers, to the tart give-and-take of *The Little Woman* by Don Tobin and *The Better Half* created by Bob Barnes and continued since his death by his wife, Ruth.

Unlike prior children's strips Charles Schulz's *Peanuts* creates a society only of children, which is a microcosm of the adult world. Most of the humor derives from the precocious youngsters giving voice to mature philosophical and psychological observations.

The fifties and sixties were a time of rising interest in psychology. Everyone fancied himself a psychiatrist, and psychological terms became a part of the common

Mutiny on *Boner's Ark,* by Addison (Mort Walker).
© 1972 King Features Syndicate, Inc.

vocabulary: inferiority complex, identity crisis, anxiety-prone, neurosis, psychosis, the id and ego. *Peanuts* reflected this national preoccupation with one's own mental processes and emotional states. The strip developed a dedicated cult for its esoteric meanings and theological implications, which even inspired Robert Short's book, *The Gospel According to Peanuts.*

Schulz, the son of a St. Paul, Minnesota, barber, began his career with a correspondence course at the Art Instruction School in Minneapolis. After serving as a staff sergeant in Italy, he sold his first cartoon, a weekly panel, *Li'l Folks,* to the St. Paul *Pioneer Press.* Unduly encouraged, Schulz demanded that the editor run the feature daily and he succeeded in getting himself fired. After selling occasional cartoons to the *Saturday Evening Post,* Schulz submitted a strip based on the *Li'l Folks* panel to the United Feature Syndicate. The syndicate, over Schulz's reservations, renamed it, and in October, 1950, *Peanuts* appeared in

One of the earliest *Peanuts* strips by Charles Schulz.
© 1951 United Feature Syndicate, Inc.

Much ado about nothing with Charlie Brown and Linus. © 1968 United Feature Syndicate, Inc.

eight daily newspapers. However, it took more than five years for the elements of the strip to coalesce successfully.

Charlie Brown, the central character, developed from a slightly flippant wise guy to his present state of wishy-washy frustration. Along the way he acquired the zigzag-design shirt, gradually assumed his distinctive shape, or lack of it, and developed a seething mass of neuroses. Schulz's style, originally rather stiff and heavy, also evolved into a marvelously fluid, expressive, and deceptively simple line.

The magnificent *Peanuts* repertory company was assembled, each with a fully developed set of hang-ups. Charlie's tormentor, Lucy, an overemancipated, often hysterical girl, scorns the weaknesses of her many inferiors and is master of verbal karate. "I believe in ME! I'm my OWN cause!" she once cried in her gentle, spine-chilling fashion. Her one vulnerability is her wild but unrequited passion for

Snoopy as the melancholy World War I flying ace.
© 1968 United Feature Syndicate, Inc.

Schroeder, a pianist and music scholar. Schroeder's heart, however, belongs to Beethoven. Linus, a security blanket addict, realizing the inevitable day of parting, faces the future with resolve: "I've been thinking seriously of having it made over into a sportcoat." The annual celebration of the Great Pumpkin started with Linus' confusion between Christmas and Halloween. Linus once observed that no problem is so big or so complicated it cannot be run away from. Snoopy, perhaps the only dog with all the phobias of man, is given to flights of spectacular fantasy. The Walter Mitty of canines, Snoopy can be alternately a World War I ace, cursing the Red Baron as he executes incredible maneuvers in his Sopwith Camel, and Joe Cool, the big man on campus, hanging around the student union eyeing chicks. He also has moments of philosophic serenity. "I wonder why some of us were born dogs while others were born people," he once mused. "Is it just pure chance, or what is it? Somehow, the whole thing doesn't seem very fair—why should I have been the lucky one?" Most of the time, however, the hedonistic Snoopy can be found in his favorite position, flat on his back waiting to be fed atop his doghouse (lavishly furnished with a Wyeth, a Van Gogh, and a pool table—which Schulz carefully leaves to the reader's imagination).

As in most successful strips, Schulz has developed a unique world, complex, yet depicted with simplicity. The humor is not dependent on the gags, but evolves from the development of personality, as when Charlie, after losing another ball game, wails in frustration, "How can we lose when we're so sincere?" or when the imperious Lucy demands, "I don't want any downs—I just want ups and ups and ups." Schulz himself says, "I want to remind adults of the pressures children are always being put under." He draws upon his own boyhood anxieties and frustrations, from triumphantly flunking algebra, Latin, English, and physics and leading his baseball team to a 40–0 defeat,

to seeing his best cartoons for the graduation annual rejected. *Peanuts'* dreams of fulfillment are Schulz's dreams—and they have been realized. Today the *Peanuts* empire grosses $150,000,000 annually from movies, the theater, television, books, and various products which bear the *Peanuts* trademark. If *Peanuts* has not brought security to Linus, it has to Schulz. He lives on a twenty-eight-acre estate north of San Francisco, replete with artificial waterfall, tennis court, riding stables, park, baseball diamond, swimming pool, four-hole golf course, and a menagerie of animals. As Charlie Brown might say, "Good grief!"

Schulz, however, still writes, draws, and letters the strip himself. "I've thought of it—hiring someone to help. Sometimes I think it would be nice. But then, what would be the point? I don't do this for the money. . . . The things I like to do best are drawing cartoons and hitting golf balls. Now if I hire someone to do my work for me, what fun would I get? It'd be like getting someone to hit the golf balls for me."

Although Walt Disney never created original features for the medium of the comic strip, he exerted a significant influence on its style and direction on several levels. Many comic strip artists, such as Walt Kelly and Hank Ketcham, were Disney trained. The Disney animation style became part of the popular graphic imagery with the first Mickey Mouse film in 1928. And a number of Disney characters became successful comic strip adaptations.

None of the cartoonists of the Disney strips was permitted to sign his work. All carried the imprimatur of Walt Disney. The theory was that other names on *Mickey Mouse, Donald Duck,* or other strips would disturb the public, because the readers assumed that somehow Disney himself drew, wrote, and directed all the myriad enterprises of the Disney empire. The strips carried his signature until his death on December 15, 1966.

From the first year of *Mickey Mouse* drawn by Ub Iwerks. © 1930 Walter E. Disney.

The first episodes of *Mickey Mouse*, launched January 3, 1930, were written and drawn by Disney and Ub Iwerks, one of the earliest Disney animators. Since May of that year Floyd Gottfredson has drawn the daily strip, and Manuel Gonzales has drawn the Sunday page since 1938. For more than thirty-five years *Mickey* was written by Roy Williams; Del Connell is the current writer. *Donald Duck*, which started in 1938, had been the long-time collaboration between Bob Karp, writer and Al Taliaferro, artist. Frank Grundeen is now the cartoonist.

Uncle Remus, begun in 1945, has had a number of cartoonists, including Dick Moores, who now does the daily *Gasoline Alley*. Jack Boyd writes the *Remus*

Walt Disney's *Donald Duck* in an atypical pantomime. © 1959 Walt Disney Productions.

An authentically drawn animal series under the Disney imprimatur. © 1965 Walt Disney Productions.

scripts, and John Ushler has been the artist since 1963. Ushler also draws *The Treasury of Classic Tales,* which originated in 1952 and is written by Frank Reilly. *True Life Adventures,* created in 1955, is written by Dick Huemer, another pioneer in animated films, and illustrated, since its inception, by George Wheeler. *Scamp,* a spin-off from the film *Lady and the Tramp,* started in 1955. Bill Berg does the script and Manuel Gonzales and Mike Arens the art.

On March 12, 1951, a family car was stopped by a motorcycle cop. A four-year-old tyke leaned out of the window and shouted, "You didn't catch us. We ran outta gas!" It was the debut of *Dennis the Menace,* created by Hank Ketcham, who describes Dennis as ". . . curiosity, energy and rugged individualism all mixed in—and up—together." *Dennis* is firmly grounded in psychological knowledge of the behavior of youngsters; Ketcham's own four-year-old son was both namesake and inspiration for *Dennis.* Ketcham caricatures himself and his wife as Dennis' harried parents, Henry and Alice Mitchell.

Everyone has learned to expect disaster from Dennis, as when he greets his father, "I thought I'd come and meet you, Dad, so I could tell you *my* side of the story." His side is wisely left to the reader's imagination. Adults are perpetually exasperated. He conceals delight in his mayhem in a mask of innocence. Dennis' menace is in reality a child's cry for attention. As Ketcham points out, "He's sensitive. He likes security. When he needs help, he wants his parents right there." Once Dennis was seen shouting at an echoing cliff, for his parents' edification: "YOU'RE A GOOD BOY, DENNIS!"

Ketcham, a native of Seattle, left the University of Washington, after a year, for a job at the Walter Lantz animation studio. He later joined the Disney studio, where he worked on such films as *Pinocchio* and *Fantasia.* Ketcham also served four years in the U.S. Navy, where he designed posters and cartoon shorts. He now lives and works in Geneva, Switzerland.

Ketcham's style reveals his training in animation. His thick and thin pen strokes are crisp and precise. The panels are carefully composed with a highly developed iconography in the figures and background.

"WHAT TIME IS THE NEXT STAGECOACH, PARDNER?"

Examples of Ketcham's use of design in two panels of *Dennis the Menace*.
© 1964 The Hall Syndicate, Inc.

In 1970 Ketcham drew upon his naval experience in creating *Half-Hitch*. The pint-sized sailor is the problem child of the U.S. Navy. To the consternation of the frustrated old salts, Captain Carrick and Chief Grommet, Half-Hitch shoots garbage out of torpedo tubes and stores his laundry in the five-inch guns. Zawiki, his brawny buddy, Seaman Fluke, a seagoing hillbilly, and Poopsy, a talking sea gull, are other permanent members of the crew. Dick Hodgins, Jr., a versatile artist and editorial cartoonist, is Ketcham's assistant on *Half-Hitch*.

"YOU 'FRAID OF MICE?"

Half-Hitch by Hank Ketcham. The white silhouette is effective.
© 1970 King Features Syndicate, Inc.

Two delineators of American women adapt their highly stylized concepts to the comics: (except above) *Merely Margy* by John Held, Jr. © 1930 King Features Syndicate, Inc.; (below) *Mamie* by Russell Patterson. © 1954 United Feature Syndicate, Inc.

Russell Patterson and John Held, Jr., two artists with remarkable parallel careers, graphically defined the Roaring Twenties and left the images that have become synonymous with that age of innocence. The Patterson and Held girls set the fashion and fads for the generation of the flapper. Some of Patterson's symbols became synonymous with the jazz age: the raccoon coat and galoshes, and innovations such as women's pants and evening pajamas. Both also adapted their concepts of the American woman to the comic strip. Held's angular, vacuous, and languorous girl, drawn with his delicate line but rather stiff style became *Oh! Margy!*, a panel, which developed into *Merely Margy* (with *Joe Prep* as the top) in the 1930's. Another of Held's newspaper creations was *Rah! Rah! Rosalie*. Born in Salt Lake City in 1889, his only art training was with Mahonri Young, the well-known sculptor and grandson of Brigham Young. Held sold his first cartoon to the original *Life* in 1904. His portrayal of the flapper was seen in all the leading magazines of the 1920's. He turned to sculpture in 1939 and was later artist in residence at Harvard University. Held died in 1958.

Patterson's *Mamie*, also a Sunday feature, started in 1951 and came to an untimely end in 1956. But while it ran, it displayed the beautiful, long-stemmed Patterson girl in an elegant, sparkling style. As versatile as a Renaissance artist, Russell Patterson, born in Omaha, Nebraska, in 1894, set standards of excellence as an architectural designer, decorator, illustrator, painter, and cartoonist. Patterson has never retired; he still paints with youthful enthusiasm and is working on his latest exhibition and a book about his life and work.

Two other strips featuring the comic adventures of beautiful but completely different types of women were both also relatively short-lived. *Long Sam* (1954), written by Al Capp and drawn by Bob Lubbers (who later illustrated *Robin Malone),* was a luscious hillbilly, whereas *Dilly* (1958) by Alfred James (Alfred Andriola of *Kerry Drake*) and Mel Casson (the creator of *Angel*) was a glamorous urban bachelor girl.

A number of America's greatest illustrators have found the comic strip form a challenge for new expression. At the turn of the century James Montgomery Flagg drew *Nervy Nat*, which appeared weekly in *Judge* magazine. It chronicled the adventures of an expatriate American bum in Paris. Wallace Morgan, a contemporary of Flagg's, illustrated *Fluffy Ruffles*, verses of an idealized young heroine of the day. A. B. Frost, though he never did a regular feature, frequently experimented with sequential narrative in *Harper's* and *Life*. John Sloan, a leading illustrator and a member of the Ashcan School of American painters, as was his friend George Luks (*Katzenjammer Kids*), also did a weekly cartoon puzzle page for the Philadelphia *Press* from 1894 to 1909. It was a time when artists moved freely between the established forms of artistic expression—painting and illustrating—and the burgeoning medium of the cartoon and comic strip, without the artificial distinctions and snobbery that later developed.

Other outstanding illustrators made notable contributions to the comics idiom, including John Striebel (*Dixie Dugan*), Frank Godwin (*Rusty Riley*), and Austin Briggs (*Flash Gordon*). In the 1950's Harry Devlin, a versatile artist and brilliant illustrator of children's books, did a charming child strip, *Raggmopp*. Unfortunately it was short-lived, but it was stylishly drawn with a tasteful use of white space.

Briggs had been Raymond's assistant on *Flash Gordon* since 1936 before succeeding Charles Flanders and Nicholas Afonski on *Secret Agent X-9* in 1938. Briggs, a superb draftsman, was selected to illustrate

Flash Gordon by the noted illustrator Austin Briggs.
© 1947 King Features Syndicate, Inc.

ZARKOV WELCOMES THEM WITH TEARS IN HIS EYES: "BY TAO, I'D BEGUN TO BELIEVE THE RUMORS THAT KANG WAS BACK, AFTER KILLING YOU IN AN ATOM BLAST!"

"KANG'S ALIVE," FLASH ADMITS, "KEEP MY RETURN SECRET. GO ON ACTING AS PRESIDENT--I'LL HUNT KANG UNDER COVER. ANY TIPS ON HIS ACTIVITIES?" ZARKOV THINKS: "WE CAUGHT A GIRL SPY IN THE ATOM LABORATORY."

ZARKOV ARRANGES TO HAVE FLASH IN DISGUISE, ARRESTED AND PUT IN THE CELL NEXT TO THE GIRL SPY, SULTRA. FLASH IS STARTLED BY HER INTENSE, SULLEN BEAUTY---

NEXT WEEK: JAILBREAK. 6-8

the new *Flash Gordon* daily strip in 1940 and also did the Sunday page from 1944 to 1948. His work, although less polished than Raymond's, was solidly constructed, and he contributed fine narrative techniques to the space adventure. Briggs was followed by Emanuel "Mac" Raboy, who drew the daily until 1957 and the Sunday page until his death in 1967. Briggs, like Sickles, became one of America's finest illustrators after his comic strip career and in 1969 was voted into the Society of Illustrators Hall of Fame.

Children have been a popular theme since the *Yellow Kid* and the *Katzenjammer Kids*, whose comparative vulgarity, with the humor derived from pranks often involving mayhem and violence, has gradually been refined by such strips as *Reg'lar Fellers, Skippy*, and *Nancy*. Even Hank Ketcham's *Dennis the Menace* softened the Katzenjammer monster into a lovable rascal, whose pranks are more exasperating than dangerous. More recently, strips have seen a trend toward even greater sophistication, as seen in *Peanuts* and Mell Lazarus' *Miss Peach*. Other notable lighthearted kid strips in the modern era have been Marge Henderson's *Little Lulu*, Howard Sparber's *Timmy*, Dave Gerard's *Will-Yum*, Robert "Rupe" Baldwin's *Freddy*, Jack Mendelsohn's *Jacky's Diary*, Dick Cavalli's *Winthrop*, and Bud Blake's *Tiger*.

Little Nemo was the precursor of the children's adventure strip. *Johnny-Round-the-World* by William Lavarre King and an adaptation of Burt Standish's *Frank Merriwell* were to follow. Nemo's fantasy gave way to the melodrama of *Little Orphan Annie* and *Little Annie Rooney*. The tradition was continued in the modern era with the adventures of another waif, made homeless in World War II, *Dondi*.

Gus Edson and Irwin Hasen created *Dondi* in 1955.

Winthrop by Dick Cavalli. © 1972 NEA, Inc.

Bud Blake adroitly uses bold contours and patterns of black in *Tiger*. © 1965 King Features Syndicate, Inc.

Dondi by Gus Edson and Irwin Hasen. The angle accents the dark at the top of the stairs.
© 1959 The Chicago Tribune.

Edson was still doing *The Gumps* (which he took over after Sidney Smith's death), but the strip's waning career came to an end, after forty years, in 1957. Thereafter Edson devoted himself to the writing of *Dondi* until his death in 1966. Edson and Hasen first met on a National Cartoonists Society tour to entertain at U.S. Army camps in Germany. Their observations of war-torn Europe and the adoption by U.S. servicemen of war orphans inspired the concept of *Dondi*. Hasen's style is a skillful blend of realism and caricature. He accentuates the strip's pathos and sentiment with adroit use of such devices as low angles, silhouettes, dramatic long shots, and extreme close-ups.

Hasen studied at the National Academy of Design and the Art Students League before starting his career as a sports cartoonist. Drafted in World War II, he was editor-cartoonist for the Fort Dix *Gazette*. He sharpened his skills in the postwar comic magazines, drawing such characters as *Wonder Woman* and the *Green Lantern* and illustrating the *Goldbergs*, a strip based on Gertrude Berg's long-running radio show.

"I don't mind that my parents forbid me to go out tonight, Taffy! Lots of famous people have had unhappy childhoods!"

Emmy Lou by Marty Links
© 1973 United Feature Syndicate, Inc.

The touch of the skilled illustrator is manifest in Frank Godwin's *Rusty Riley*. © 1949 King Features Syndicate, Inc.

197

Dick's Adventures in pseudo-history by Neil O'Keeffe and Max Trell.
© 1947 King Features Syndicate, Inc.

"LET'S GO UPWIND FROM THEM, SO THEY CAN SMELL OUR PEANUT BUTTER SANDWICHES."

Ponytail by Lee Holley.
© 1961 King Features Syndicate, Inc.

Other child adventure strips in the modern era have been Bill Dyer's *Adventures of Patsy*, Max Trell and Neil O'Keefe's *Dick's Adventures in Dreamland*, and Frank Godwin's *Rusty Riley*.

Archie, started in the forties, has continued its popularity, and new strips have recorded the changing life-style of today's teen-agers as did *Harold Teen* in the twenties and thirties: *The Jackson Twins* by Dick Brooks, *Emmy Lou* by Marty Links, *Gil Thorp* and *Teen-Wise!* by Jack Berrill, *Seventeen* by Bernard Lansky, and *Ponytail* by Lee Holley.

Science Fiction

The modern technological explosion profoundly affected American life. The cold war spurred development in the science of rocket propulsion. The age-old dream of space exploration was not as fantastic as it once seemed. At the time of *Buck Rogers'* inception, such speculation was still in the realm of science fiction; while some prophesied that man would surely visit the moon, Mars, and beyond, it would certainly not be realized in *their* lifetime. The time certainly seemed propitious for another cycle of space adventure strips. They were not long in coming—*Tom Corbett, Space Cadet* by Ray Bailey; *Sky Masters* by Jack Kirby and Wallace Wood with writer Dick Wood; *Chris Welkin—Planeteer* by Russ Winterbotham and Art Samson; *Twin Earths* by Al McWilliams and Oscar Lebeck; and *Beyond Mars* by Lee Elias—all appeared in the 1950's. The acceleration of scientific achievement made the distinction between science and fiction smaller each day. This theme was explored in *Jet Scott* by Sheldon Stark and Jerry Robinson, which dealt with the projection of scientific achievement known to be currently technologically possible. Scott, the hero, was not a ray-blasting space ranger but a scientific investigator for the Pentagon.

Inexplicably, the renaissance was short-lived, proving that producing a successful strip, including one in science fiction, is an inexact science. Despite the best of expert knowledge and experience, launching a

198

Jet Scott by Sheldon Stark and Jerry Robinson. © 1955 The New York Tribune, Inc.
Problems in space. Life was soon to echo the comics . . .

comic strip is as risky an endeavor as producing a Broadway play. It is estimated that in the seventy-five years since the *Yellow Kid*, 10,000 strips have been launched—all with great expectations—and it is probable that only about one in every hundred was more than moderately successful.

The interest in science fiction faded, as did most of the science fiction strips. There was a backlash against the preoccupation with science to the neglect of the arts. Perhaps the sudden proliferation of science strips saturated the market to the detriment of all. In any event, the relapse was slightly premature. The last episode of *Jet Scott*, in September, 1957, for example, had a pilot in an experimental plane trapped in orbit around the earth. A week later, Nikita Khrushchev announced the Russian Sputnik was in orbit. It provoked a national traumatic uproar. America was once again absorbed in science and space achievement (too late, however, for the space strips), proving that timing is an essential ingredient in the birth or death of a strip. At least America was still first in space with *Flash Gordon* and *Buck Rogers*, who continued their interplanetary exploits. *Drift Marlo* by Tom Cooke and Phil Evans tried for another resurrection in the sixties. On July 8, 1967, even the granddaddy of them all, *Buck Rogers*, made his last space trip. *Flash Gordon* remains to refute the theory that science has brought an end to science fiction in the comic strips, although it is interesting to note that the genre has continued to flourish in films, popular literature, and comic books.

. . . and the comics echo life in *Drift Marlo* by Tom Cooke and Phil Evans.
© 1972 Cooke and Evans.

Many different professions lend themselves to the excitement of an adventure strip. Perhaps the unlikeliest is the ministry, the calling of *David Crane* (1956). Craig Flessel, a pioneer of the comic magazine, illustrated the strip with an expert sureness and flair. The world of journalism is the backdrop for *Jeff Cobb* (1954) by Pete Hoffman. Winslow Mortimer took over as illustrator in 1972. A U.S. Marine Corps major was the hero in Don Sherman's *Dan Flagg* (1963). *Captain Kate* (1967), the commander of an armed schooner, was created by the husband-and-wife team of Gerald and Hale Skelly and the skipper of a modern nuclear sub was *Thorn McBride,* in tales of international underwater intrigue by Kenneth Simms and Frank Giacoia. It may be a prophetic note that only the profession of journalism survived.

Catfish by Rog Bollen and Gary Peterman.
© 1974 New York News, Inc.

The Western

A new cycle of the classic western was generated by the TV series *Davy Crockett* in 1954. Fess Parker portrayed Davy on Walt Disney's *Disneyland* and created a hundred-million-dollar market for coonskin caps (it became *de rigueur* for every kid to have one, and the price of coonskin soared to eight dollars a pound), and Crockett records, lunch boxes, shirts, guitars, and bathing suits. In less than a year, however, the Crockett craze ran its course and millions of products were left unsold, but the new western vogue had just begun. "The King of the Wild Frontier" continued his adventures in the comic strip *Davy Crockett* by Jim McArdle. A new roundup of horse operas on TV followed: *Cheyenne; Gunsmoke; Have Gun, Will Travel; Wagon Train; Maverick,* as well as the earlier ones, *The Lone Ranger* and *Hopalong Cassidy.* It is notable that the first feature film, *The Great Train Robbery* by D. W. Griffith, was a western; two early strips, Swinnerton's *Little Bears* and *Little Jimmy,* were set in the West. The western has been an enduring and successful theme in both media ever since—at least until its decline in the comic strips in the sixties.

There seemed to be an inexhaustible appetite for tales of the West, cowboys and Indians, and the endless variations of the basic horse opera plot. *Hopalong Cassidy* was adapted to the strips by Dan Spiegel. Also corralled for the comics were movie cowboy heroes as in *Roy Rogers* (by Al McKimson) and *Gene Autry* (Bert Laws). Other strips based on western folk heroes joined the stampede: *The Chisholm Kid* (Carl Pfeufer), *Buffalo Bill* (Fred Meagher), *The Cisco Kid* (José Luis Salinas), and *Bat Masterson* (Herron and Nostrand). New strips and folk heroes were also created: *Casey Ruggles* and *Lance* (Warren Tufts), *Bronc Saddler* (Dell and Herb Rayburn), *Laredo Crockett* (Bob Schoenke), and *Straight Arrow* (Ray Gardner, Joe Certa, and John Belfi).

The western comic strip, however, has proved less durable than its counterpart in film and television. By the end of the 1960's almost all had been gunned down. While the practice of adaptations from film and TV has become more common over the years, the comic strip has usually dwindled with the fortunes of the original property. Even *The Lone Ranger,*

The Cisco Kid, by the gifted Argentinian artist José Luis Salinas.
© 1951 King Features Syndicate, Inc.

Common horse sense in *Redeye* by Gordon Bess.
© 1967 King Features Syndicate, Inc.

originally adapted from the radio show in 1929, finally bit the dust in 1971. The survivors are not the traditional western adventures but, perhaps appropriately, spoofs of westerns: *Rick O'Shay* by Stan Lynde, *Redeye* by Gordon Bess, *Catfish* by Rog Bollen and Gary Peterman, and *Tumbleweeds* by Tom K. Ryan. While *Redeye*, *Catfish* and *Tumbleweeds* are broad burlesques of the western, authentic western backgrounds are re-created in *Rick O'Shay*. Lynde, born in Billings, Montana, and reared on his father's ranch near the Crow Indian Reservation, knows the West firsthand, and accurate depictions of horses, costumes, and Indian lore are contrasted with a lighthearted satire on the classic western clichés.

Adaptations

The impact of television in the fifties caused a general decline in newspaper advertising revenue. Throughout the country, one hundred and sixty dailies folded. By the late 1960's New York City was reduced from seven major newspapers to three. This seemed to accelerate the practice of adapting strips from other media in an attempt to attract new readership. Most such transplants seemed, however, to lose some essential ingredient in the translation. Some theorized that newspapers should develop their own features and that further to popularize TV and film properties would be self-defeating. It was also argued that future success of the press depends on its providing feature material not available elsewhere. TV and the films, on the other hand, have shown no reluctance in adapting comic strips—and have done so with success.

There has been a tradition of fictional doctors since the original film series *Dr. Kildare*, starring Lew Ayres and Lionel Barrymore. It was continued in the soap operas of the forties and, aided by the advances of modern medicine, made a major renaissance on TV in the fifties and sixties with shows like *Medic*, *Dr. Kildare*, *Ben Casey*, and *Marcus Welby*. Two appeared in the comics: *Ben Casey* by Neal Adams and *Dr. Kildare* by Ken Bald.

Many animated cartoons in films and on TV were developed into strips: Additions to Walt Disney creations and Warner Brothers' *Bugs Bunny* were Hanna and Barbera's *The Flintstones* and *Yogi Bear*,

Stan Lynde's *Rick O'Shay* demonstrates the fast, *short* draw.
© 1958 The Chicago Tribune.

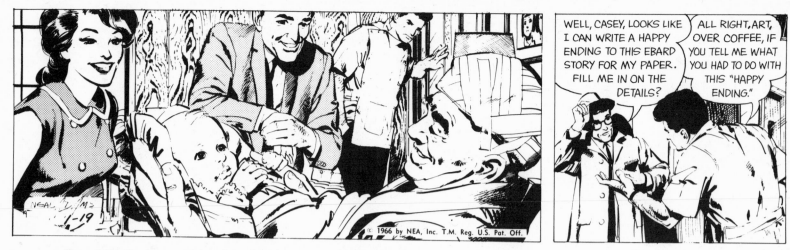

Two skillfully drawn adaptations (above) *Ben Casey* by Neal Adams. © 1966 NEA, Inc.
(below) *Dr. Kildare* by Ken Bald. © 1965 King Features Syndicate, Inc.

Jay Ward's *Bullwinkle*, drawn by Al Kilgore, Walter Lantz's *Woody Woodpecker*, and TV's *Howdy Doody*.

Popular detective fiction was also a favorite source: Leslie Charteris' *The Saint*, written by Charteris himself and illustrated by John Spranger; Erle Stanley Gardner's *Perry Mason*, drawn by Charles Lofgren; Ian Fleming's *James Bond*, drawn by John McLusky; and Sir Arthur Conan Doyle's *Sherlock Holmes*, drawn by Frank Giacoia. Strip adaptations were also made of Rex Stout's *Nero Wolfe* and Mickey Spillane's *Mike*

Hammer. A TV soap opera was the inspiration for *Dark Shadows* by Ken (K. Bruce) Bald. A special Christmas feature, *Rudolph the Red Nosed Reindeer*, adapted from the poem by Robert L. May, was drawn by Rube Grossman. *I Love Lucy* by Robert (Lawrence) Oksner (who also did *Soozi*) in the 1950's, *Laugh In* by Roy Doty, and *Sesame Street* by Cliff Roberts in the seventies, are other comic strip spin-offs from popular television programs.

Sherlock Holmes continues to baffle Watson with his deductive powers, by E. Meiser and Frank Giacoia. © 1954 New York Herald Tribune, Inc.

202

Searching for answers in *Feiffer* by Jules Feiffer. © 1971 Jules Feiffer.

Humor must be considered as part of the art of the cartoon and as inseparable as is consideration of color in a painting. While the psychology of humor has been explored by scientists and philosophers and the mechanics of humor identified and categorized (such as juxtaposition, reversal, surprise, and hostility), the mystery of humor and laughter remains. As E. B. White observed, "Humor can be dissected as a fly can, but the thing dies in the process and the innards are discouraging to any but the pure scientific mind." The comic strip has proved to be an amazingly versatile and expressive form for a dazzling range of visual and verbal humor, from the subtle shadings of fantasy and nonsense, burlesque and slapstick, to satire and parody, and to the sophisticated, elusive, and slyly ambiguous.

Jules Feiffer's dramatizations of man groping hopelessly in psychological turmoil and neurotic anguish, with social and sexual hang-ups, have enlarged the scope of the comics since 1956, when his cartoon,

Nixon, the song and dance man, by Jules Feiffer. © 1972 Jules Feiffer.

Sick Sick Sick, first appeared in the New York weekly *The Village Voice*. Feiffer has a Thurberlike simplicity in his subtle portraits and attempts to deal with emotions in other than cliché graphic terms in a new balance of visual and verbal elements. The words themselves float without balloons, and the images flow without restrictions of the frame in an abstract void. In his later work Feiffer has developed his own form of sardonic political satire with psychological insight, and in 1960 his was the first radical cartoon to be syndicated nationally. In the tradition of polemicist Art Young and his anti-World War I cartoons, Feiffer began to attack the Vietnam War and Presidents Johnson and Nixon and succeeded in breaking the strictures of many newspapers that published them in opposition to their own editorial positions.

Feiffer, born in New York City, attended Pratt Institute, served in the Army, and toiled in the vineyards of the comic books (as assistant to Will Eisner on *The Spirit*) prior to creation of his own feature, now titled simply *Feiffer*. His extensive use of dialogue created a new form of literary cartoon. His often toneless monologues and seemingly repetitious drawings (but with subtle variations) weave a languid spell of alienation that seems to stretch time into smaller-than-life fragments.

Feiffer has expanded his basic themes of anarchy, alienation, and impotence to other media. His credits include the books *Harry, The Rat with Women; Passionella and Other Stories;* and *The Great Comic Book Heroes;* the plays *Little Murders* and *The White House Murder Case;* and the films *Carnal Knowledge* and *Little Murders*.

In *Miss Peach* the Kelly School has an enrollment of dangerously mature moppets and singularly bewildered faculty. Miss Peach presides over a class of neurotic, nasty, and competitive students, including Marcia, a "dedicated bitch"; Ira, a pathological sissy and class coward; and Arthur, whose outward stupidity is a cover for his basic lack of intelligence. At times they seem overly concerned about their careers and future marital states. Lester, not one of the most independent creatures, once proposed to Francine, "I'd work and slave for you, and climb mountains for you, and swim oceans for you, and fight the world for you, as ferociously and devotedly as my mother will permit." Ira once observed, ". . . to get a good job these days, you need a high school diploma, a college degree, a Master's and a Ph.D." to which Arthur added, "Either that, or you have to be a very sweet person."

Two contrasting creations from the facile pen of Mell Lazarus: (above) *Miss Peach*. © 1964 Publishers Syndicate (below) *Momma*. © 1971 Field Enterprises, Inc.

Mell Lazarus, born in Brooklyn, was an art director and free-lance magazine cartoonist before creating *Miss Peach* in 1957. He has published a novel, *The Boss Is Crazy Too*. In 1970 Lazarus created *Momma* in the tradition of the fabled "Jewish mother," the "momism" of Philip Wylie's *A Generation of Vipers* and, more recently, Philip Roth's *Portnoy's Complaint*. As Lazarus himself admits, "*Momma* was the result of my own growing interest in my mother's psychology—now that I'm out of her grasp." Momma lives alone in a big house, hoping that her birds will return to the nest, the birds being son Thomas, forty-two and married; son Francis, twenty-two; and daughter Mary Lou, eighteen. Momma is the universal mother: She can't understand why any boy who has a mother would need a wife.

In Johnny Hart's *B.C.* one can discover the stunning lack of progress between the Neanderthal and nuclear ages. Hart's zestful style is achieved by seemingly intuitive and spontaneous pen strokes but is done with conscious precision; he is never satisfied until everything is refined to its ultimate simplicity. *The Wizard of Id*, written by Hart and brilliantly drawn by his long-time friend, Brant Parker, is a medieval fantasy about a diminutive despotic and perfidious king and his court of endearing but corruptible characters.

(The size of comic strip kings is in inverse ratio to their position: *The Little King* and *King Aroo* also found the anomoly appealing.) Seen in *The Wizard of Id* in addition to the king, a tyrant's tyrant, are Rodney (a crafty coward), an alcoholic jester, and the Wizard himself, a conjurer of erratic distinction. It was the Wizard who once discovered the jester stoned in the basement. "Your continual stupor is explainable . . . the *answer* is in the stars. What sign were you born under?" "Gunther's Bar and Grill" was the reply. When the king was informed that the peasants were revolting, he could only agree. At another difficult time in an election year the royal bank was almost broke and the army was tired of fighting, but Rodney let his worried sire know the *people* were *behind* him. The king was not consoled: "That's what really worries me."

B.C. starting in 1958, and *The Wizard of Id* in 1964, provided historical stages for Hart's rich collection of comic characters in a parody of twentieth-century society. As Hart himself explains, "I look at man today as not too far removed from man when he wore a skin. He does the same silly stupid things he probably did at the dawn of history, except now he is fitted out in a pin-stripe suit. He's a little more sophisticated because he knows how to cover up his . . . stupidity."

Johnny Hart finds humor in repose or in action in *B.C.* © 1966-1968 Publishers-Hall Syndicate, Inc.

205

Uneasy lies the head that wears the crown in *The Wizard of Id*
by Brant Parker and Johnny Hart. © 1968 Publishers-Hall Syndicate, Inc.

Hart, born in 1931, son of an Endicott, New York, fireman, was inspired by the success of *Peanuts* to turn to a cartoon career. After serving in the Air Force, where he did cartoons for the Pacific *Stars and Stripes*, he had sporadic success as a free-lance magazine cartoonist.

B.C. and *The Wizard of Id* are in the mainstream of today's off-beat, irreverent, topical, and low-key humor that has wide appeal for school and college audiences. The existentialist anteater of *B.C.* has been adopted as a mascot by the University of California at Irvine and the school cheer is "Zot!"—the Hart onomatopoeia for the anteater's tongue in action. The hairy Grog, retarded even for a Neanderthal, another favorite *B.C.* character, has even spawned his own fan clubs. Along with the gullible B.C., others in the prehistoric cast include Wiley, the one-legged poet; Clumsy Carp, the accident-prone sportsman; and Tor, the original Don Juan (and inventor of the comb). One entrepreneur, Peter, runs a publishing company. Clumsy Carp once submitted a new work, *The Compleat Angler*. "Another fishing book, I suppose," says Peter. "No," answered Carp, "it's about a shyster from Philadelphia."

Eek & Meek, Howie Schneider's anthropomorphic mice. © 1971 NEA, Inc.

Eek and Meek are erudite, lyrical, and involved mice; their loves, hates, and fears are human. When Eek sticks up Meek and is asked if he has a gun or any other weapon, he replies, "Heavens to Betsy, no! We're trying to cut down on the violence this year." They are politically aware mice as well. Eek is found by his dentist to be suffering from politician's mouth —a large credibility gap between his upper and lower teeth. On another occasion Meek described the people of the world as followers and leaders. He decided he was one of the leading followers.

Howie Schneider, *Eek & Meek*'s creator, is a native New Yorker. After Army service he started a small advertising agency, sold cartoons to all the major magazines, and published two cartoon books before deciding to try comic strips. As Schneider noted, his first four strip attempts were his education. The fifth was *Eek & Meek* in 1965, and the mice proved to be the perfect foils for his unique talents.

Nothing is better reflected in the comics than the changing American mythology of the relationship between the sexes, courtship, and marriage. From the time of *Bringing Up Father* (1913) a necessity for comic strip marital bliss has been a dominant, abrasive wife and the fearful, henpecked husband. This was the prevailing theme for over 40 years, exemplified by *the Timid Soul* and *the Gumps*. The humor was founded in the principle of reversal. In reality the husband-wife relationship was the opposite of its portrayal, at least as promulgated by a male-dominated society.

The role of the single male and female was established as early as *The Hall Room Boys* (1910) and *Polly and Her Pals* (1912) and continued by others such as *Tillie the Toiler, Betty*, and *Dixie Dugan*. The bachelor was depicted as the eternal, hapless pursuer subject to the whims of unobtainable, fickle females. The designing female was also stereotyped as forever trying to snare the eligible bachelor from his carefree but deluded existence. In reality, the male viewed himself as the strong hunter and the female as his helpless prey, the pursuit being only an elaborate ritual to be acted out by both sides. The comic strip concept, however, amused the male reader by presenting a lover so inept that his own ego was bolstered by comparison while his fears of the predatory female were confirmed. On the other hand, the female reader found her romantic fantasies played out and saw herself in the comics, if not in society, as equal or even superior to the male.

In *Li'l Abner* (1934) the classic male chauvinist view came to fulfillment. Daisy Mae became the declared pursuer and Abner the pursued. This role reversal was a parody of the typical male-female relationship of the time but gradually became less valid as women took a more forceful role in society during and after World War II. As the participation of women in all aspects of society changed, so did the satire of comic strip romance and marriage. *Blondie* can be seen as a transition strip. While Blondie is still the strong-willed and dominant force, she is less the vixen and Dagwood is more frustrated than fearful.

The classic war between the sexes generally became more subdued as seen in the modern suburban family of *Hi and Lois* where the humor is based less on the husband-wife conflict and focused more on children and the small crises of everyday life.

Joe Palooka weds Anne Howe, 1949.
© McNaught Syndicate, Inc.

Mary Perkins' European ceremony, 1959.
© The Chicago Tribune.

Dick Tracy and his forbearing bride, 1949.
© The Chicago Tribune.

Despite the humor based on the male-female conflict, the comic strip has always continued to reinforce traditional middle-class mores, including marriage. One of the first comic strips to have its major character marry was *Gasoline Alley*. Walt Wallet, who had adopted the baby Skeezix five years before, married widow Phyllis Blossom in June, 1926. Years later, Skeezix, having aged along with his readers, married his childhood sweetheart, Nina Clock. The comic strip nuptial proved to be a successful device used by numerous other strips. When Blondie married Dagwood in 1933 it made a decisive change in the

Mickey Finn at the moment of truth, 1970.
© McNaught Syndicate, Inc.

Smilin' Jack, Jr. marries Sizzle in 1973. © New York News, Inc.

direction of the strip. Joe Palooka was the first adventure hero to wed. After eighteen years of courtship and innumerable obstacles that tantalized his readers, the heavyweight boxing champion of the world married cheese heiress Anne Howe in June, 1949. The social season of 1949 was complete when Dick Tracy took Tess Trueheart to the altar. Much heralded romances led to the marriage of other *Tracy* characters, B. O. Plenty and Gravel Gertie, and Junior and Moonmaid. Mary Perkins, star of *On Stage,* married photo journalist Pete Fletcher in Switzerland in 1959. In the post-World War II years the desire for tranquility and normality of family life led to other marriages in the comic strip world. In 1946 Prince Valiant married Princess Aleta in a ceremony performed in a magnificent sylvan glen. Even the most dedicated misogamist, Li'l Abner, finally succumbed to the charms of Daisy Mae in 1952. Kerry Drake in 1958 and Juliet Jones in 1970 were others wedded on the comic pages. In the wake of the Vietnam War Rick O'Shay was united with Gay Abandon. In 1970 the confirmed bachelor, sixtyish Phil Finn in *Mickey Finn,* after a long time of off-and-on romance, was wed to young Minerva Mutton—after a reader poll indicated its approval thirty-to-one.

The new life-style and sexual morality of the seventies is suggested in such new strips as *Doonesbury* and *Mixed Singles,* which focus on the relationship between the sexes rather than marriage. A more ominous note perhaps for the institution of marriage occurred on March 31, 1973, when Smilin' Jack, Jr. was married and promptly flew off into the sunset . . . on the day before the strip's demise.

Marryin' Sam's $1.35 special unites Li'l Abner and Daisy Mae, the day following the nuptials of his "ideel," Fearless Fosdick, and Prudence Pimpleton, 1952. © United Feature Syndicate, Inc.

Kerry Drake takes a wife in 1958.
© Publishers-Hall Syndicate, Inc.

Steve Canyon's shipboard wedding to Summer Olsen in 1970.
© Field Enterprises, Inc.

Rivets by George Sixta.
© 1974 Field Enterprises, Inc.

Four widely divergent family features were created by four leading magazine cartoonists. Jerry Marcus' *Trudy* (1963) features a harried suburban housewife as the fall gal in delightful low-key humor. George Wolfe's *Pops* (1964) and Bob Weber's *Moose* (1965) are lovable loafers in the slapstick tradition. Bill Hoest's *Lockhorns* (1963) are a quarrelsome couple who make marriage appear a dying institution.

There are other notable humor strips of the modern era. Jack Kent's *King Aroo* (1950) was a delightful fantasy of a kingdom presided over by a pint-sized, benevolent despot. Irving Phillips' *Strange World of Mr. Mum* (1958) was a unique and imaginative pantomime that deserved a longer life. Frank O'Neal's *Short Ribs* (1958) has a mixed historical cast from cavemen to spacemen: zany knights, mad Russians, kooky cowboys, and a comic executioner. Frank Ridgeway and Ralston Jones' *Mr. Abernathy* (1957) is an endearing tycoon and would-be Casanova who prefers to be loved *for* his money. Bill Yates' *Professor Phumble* (1960) is the archetypical absentminded professor and the terror of Hoohah U. Art Sansom's *Born Loser* (1965), a classic fall guy, is a lackey and victim of twentieth-century corporate oppression. Howie Post's *Dropouts* (1968) features Alfie and Sandy, two endearing desert island castaways who create their own world in microcosm. Charles Barsotti's *Sally Bananas* (1970) was a charming zany drawn in a piquant, decorative style.

While *Tippie*, *Napoleon*, and Frank Beck's *Bo* are no longer with us, a new assortment of breeds has maintained the popularity of the canine strip. *Rivets* (1953) by George Sixta is a friendly but pesky mutt. *Marmaduke* (1954), a panel by Brad Anderson, is a great Dane with puppy aspirations. *Fred Basset* (1965) by Alex Graham is a quiet, intellectual basset hound. George Fett's *Sniffy* (1964) has a menagerie of wild and domestic creatures as its stars.

Frank O'Neal's *Short Ribs* gets the point. © 1967 N.E.A., Inc.

Mr. Abernathy, art connoisseur, by Frank Ridgeway and Ralston Jones.
© 1959 King Features Syndicate, Inc.

Benjy by Jim Berry, drawn by Bill Yates. © 1973 NEA, Inc.

Professor Phumble by Bill Yates.
© 1965 King Features Syndicate, Inc.

The Born Loser in the French Connection by Art Sansome. © 1972 NEA, Inc.

The chief weighs in *The Dropouts* by Howie Post. © 1973 United Feature Syndicate, Inc.

Bob Weber's ingenuous *Moose*. © 1965 King Features Syndicate, Inc.

Broom-Hilda in love again, by Russell Myers. © 1971 The Chicago Tribune, Inc.

Broom-Hilda, a green-skinned, cigar-smoking, bachelor-girl witch, cast her first spell in the comics in 1970. She is an unconquerable spirit despite an inordinate lack of beauty (even her junk mail is addressed to "Ugly Occupant"). Beneath her crusty exterior is a passionate woman. The pilots of a jet transport were once startled to see her quivering lips pressed against the window in her most ecstatic kiss. Swooping away on her broom, Hilda admits, "It drives 'em crazy, but I just can't *help* myself." Broom-Hilda's first husband was Attila the Hun, who owes her fifteen hundred years of back alimony. She lives in hope of somehow attracting another mate and never goes out without applying her beauty wart. Irwin, a shaggy sad troll, was shocked at seeing its first adult X-rated movie but later concluded, "You miss out on a lot more than I thought by just being a troll." Another foil for Broom-Hilda is Gaylord, a finicky, bespectacled vulture. They all live in an enchanted, ever-changing world of weird forests, bizarre mountains of wondrous natural arches and winding cliffs, and surrealistic landscapes, in the tradition of Herriman's *Krazy Kat*.

Broom-Hilda's cartoonist, Russell Myers, is a graduate of the University of Tulsa, where his father is a professor. He began his career as a greeting card designer and free-lance artist. Myers is married and lives in California.

The counterculture of the seventies on and off campus is the focus for *Doonesbury*. Started in the Yale *Daily News* in 1968 by then-undergraduate Garry Trudeau, and syndicated in 1970, it deals irreverently with the sexual, social, and political concerns and insecurities of cynical Aquarian-age college students. While much of its unrestrained idiom was curtailed for national syndication, it retains its sarcasm about the establishment and reflects the free life-styles of today's youth.

While the drawing is rudimentary, the characters are well defined. Michael J. Doonesbury is a would-be lover who valiantly struggles to overcome an enormously flawed personality . . . and fails. B.D. is the star quarterback who hates hippies (he once beat up an entire commune to commemorate the Fourth of July) and owing to a computer error is Doonesbury's roommate. Mark Slackmeyer is chairman of the SDS chapter and advocates compulsory euthanasia for anyone over twenty-five. Rufus, a product of the

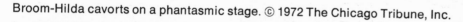

Broom-Hilda cavorts on a phantasmic stage. © 1972 The Chicago Tribune, Inc.

Doonesbury in a matter of semantics by Garry Trudeau.
© 1971 G. B. Trudeau. Distributed by Universal Press Syndicate.

ghetto, plans to be an enlightened slumlord, and Calvin, the resident Black Panther, spent 204 out of 234 days of the last term in jail.

Other new humor strips of the seventies are *Plain Jane* by Frank Baginski, the bittersweet experiences of an unattractive female trying to attract eligible bachelors. Mal Hancock brings special insight into the story of *Polly*, a four-year-old who converses with flowers, stars, and her teddy bear. Tom Batiuk's *Funky Winkerbean* explores the frustrations of living through and surviving high school. Batiuk draws upon his experiences as a junior high school teacher, coping with the new "open" education.

If three strips can indicate a trend, one of "comic history" developed in 1971 with *Pluribus* by Bill Rechin, followed in 1972 by *The Colonials* by Joseph Escourido, and *Sergeant Stripes ... Forever* by Bill Howrilla. Set in colonial times, they can be seen as anticipating the celebration of the two hundredth anniversary of American independence in 1976. Comic histories have been an American tradition and were extremely popular in the late nineteenth century. Livingston Hopkins' *Comic History of the U.S.* in 1877

A typical non sequitur in
Plain Jane by Frank Baginski.
© 1972 McNaught Syndicate, Inc.

Tom Batiuk's *Funky Winkerbean* shows the flag. © 1972 Field Enterprises, Inc.

Dik Browne's *Hägar the Horrible* lacks historical perspective. © 1973 King Features Syndicate, Inc.

The haves and have-nots in *Mixed Singles* by William Brown and Mel Casson. © 1973 United Feature Syndicate, Inc.

was savagely attacked for its irreverence. Snyder's *Comic History of Greece*, published in 1898, included drawings by John Sloan, and Bill Nye's *History of the U.S.* in 1894 was illustrated by Frederick Opper.

An offbeat pair of endearing screwballs—*Frank and Ernest* by Bob Thaves—made their debut in 1972. The Chaplinesque characters live on the fringe of a society they never quite relate to. Told by the doctor to cut his work in half, Frank ponders, "I don't know which half to eliminate . . . thinking about it or talking about it." Another free spirit entered the comic world in 1973 with Jim Berry's *Benjy*, an idealist and dedicated, practicing bum.

Aimed at the 42,000,000 Americans between nineteen and thirty-five, *Mixed Singles*, a unique collaboration, written and drawn by both William F.

Brown and Mel Casson, was launched in 1972. Harvey and Stella Mix run a singles-only apartment house, a new phenomenon coming into vogue, housing a varied cast of young swingers. In a break with comic taboos and reflecting the reality that there is one divorce for every three new marriages, a young divorcée is one of the heroines.

Dik Browne explores the comic possibilities of the Viking era in *Hägar the Horrible* (1973). Hägar is a typical, hard-working barbarian whose trade, looting and sacking, often takes him away, mercifully, from his nagging wife, Helga; son, Hamlet; and daughter, Honi. Hamlet, perhaps the original pacifist hippie, is a "Danish Pastry" and a constant source of disappointment to his father.

Bob Thaves exploits the Horizontal format in *Frank and Ernest*. © 1974 NEA, Inc.

The New Realism

The New Realism permits story lines that are no longer restricted to simple good-versus-evil themes. They can be read at several levels by various age groups, as can the new sophisticated humor strips. There still are heroes, but now they are different; they ponder moral questions, are just as neurotic as real people, and reflect emotional hang-ups and frustrations. The plots are often contemporary and involve such topics as campus radicalism, the drug culture, hijackings, minority rights, and the Peace Movement.

The New Realism in newspaper strips, however, does not approach the freedom of the bitterly satiric and often pornographic underground press and comic magazines (Comix) and their explicit dialogue. They, as well as the campus press, reflect the changing stan-

On Stage by Leonard Starr exemplifies the new photographic realism. © 1957 The Chicago Tribune.

dards in our society: the greater freedom in life-styles and sexual behavior.

There has been, however, a general relaxation in the censorship of the mass media—publishing, film, and, to some extent, television. Newspaper strips, designed for family entertainment, have always exercised self-censorship. They cannot filter their readership according to age level as the motion picture industry does with its rating system or as television attempts to do by program scheduling.

Underground movements and the avant-garde have always exerted a profound influence on the direction of the arts. The Comix, with its freedom to explore inner obsessions and fantasies and its combination of sexual and political satire, has expanded the potential of the comic strip. It remains to be seen if the Comix is a temporary aberration or a harbinger of things to come in the newspaper strip.

A new type of photographic realism in the fifties evolved from the romanticism of Foster's *Prince Valiant* and Caniff's form of impressionist realism. Predating cinéma vérité and the trend of super-hard-focus realism in painting, it is seen in strips like *The Heart of Juliet Jones* by Stan Drake (1953) and *On Stage* by Leonard Starr (1957). This trend continued into the sixties and seventies with *Apartment 3G* by Alex Kotzky (1962) and *Friday Foster* by Jim Lawrence and Jorge Longaron (1970).

Many of the cartoonists of the New Realism were experienced illustrators and commercial artists, who brought their highly polished styles and technical skills to the medium. Most of them adopted the illustrator's *modus operandi* of employing models and taking photographs to give a greater illusion of reality to their figures. Backgrounds and location shots for specific episodes are also photographed. Opaque

Stan Drake brings a subtlety of gesture to *The Heart of Juliet Jones*.
© 1957 King Features Syndicate, Inc.

Drake's photo technique in *Juliet Jones*.
© 1965 King Features Syndicate, Inc.

projectors are frequently employed, which project photographs in any size directly on the drawing paper. The artist then pencils or inks directly over the image. Stan Drake has developed a unique procedure for special effects. When an exceptionally detailed or complicated shot is required, such as a New York City panorama or a vast ocean liner, Drake makes a photocopy of the photograph, which eliminates the half-tones. The result, after strengthening some lines for reproduction, is used as the finished art. Some of the

216

Love and sex in *Apartment 3G* by Alex Kotzky. © 1967 Publishers-Hall Syndicate

effects are startling and give the illusion of a realistic black-and-white rendering.

Drake, a high school dropout who studied under George Bridgman at the Art Students League, started selling illustrations to pulp magazines when he was only seventeen. He nearly followed a theatrical career like his father, a noted radio actor. Before Drake could decide between being an artist and an actor, another request for his services arrived . . . and he entered the U.S. Army. Mustered out a sergeant, he resumed his commercial art career and by 1949 had his own successful art studio. Drake created *The Heart of Juliet Jones* in 1953. A brilliant stylist, he enhances Juliet's romantic adventures with solid draftsmanship and storytelling.

Leonard Starr brings to *On Stage*, created in 1957,

Leonard Starr employs cinematographic techniques to dramatize the theatrical theme of *On Stage*. © 1967 The Chicago Tribune.

all the glitter and excitement of the show business world of his native New York. He studied at the New York High School of Music and Art and at Pratt Institute. Starr was a successful comic book and commercial artist before finding the comic strip the perfect medium of expression for his drawing and writing abilities. *On Stage*, a skillful balance of romance and adventure, faithfully reproduces the backstage atmosphere and current theatrical idiom. The stories are well plotted and taut and the characters believable. Mary Perkins, the heroine, is typical of thousands of star-struck, small-town girls who migrate to New York and struggle for their Broadway Break. For Mary Perkins the dream has come true. She is now a successful actress married to a magazine photographer. The strip concentrates on the emotional, professional, and dramatic conflicts rather than violence as emphasized in many action adventure strips. Starr sees the strip as theater: "It's a lot like writing a play in ten acts, with seven scenes per act and twenty-four hours between each curtain."

It is interesting to note that *The Heart of Juliet Jones, On Stage, Apartment 3G*, and *Friday Foster* all are in the framework of the soap opera and are romantic adventures of young women. The realism of the art records the nuances of gesture and emotion necessary to the genre. Other stylists of the school of realism are Ken Bald (*Dr. Kildare* and *Dark Shadows*) and Neal Adams (*Ben Casey*). John Prentice has gradually developed *Rip Kirby* from Raymond's more decorative and design-conscious style to a powerful naturalistic statement.

Many comic strip artists developed their craft in the comic magazines, where they were called upon to draw everything from science fiction and romance to westerns and superheroes. The volume of work, the discipline of deadlines, and the demands of storytelling and draftsmanship proved invaluable in their later comic strip creations. Among them have been Starr, Kotzky, and Adams, as well as Howie Post (*Dropouts*), Frank Bolle (*Debbie Deere*), Irwin Hasen (*Dondi*), Dan Barry (*Flash Gordon*), John Lehti (*Tales from the Great Book*), Al Williamson (*Secret Agent Corrigan*), Joe Kubert (*The Green Beret*), and Jerry Robinson (*still life* and *Flubs & Fluffs*).

The medium has also developed lettering specialists. Ben Oda, one of the most expert and facile, has performed his specialty for innumerable comic books and dozens of strips, often six or more concurrently. Frank Engli, who has worked on Milton Caniff's strips for forty years, as well as on others, estimates he has lettered 2,000,000 words on more than 17,000 daily and Sunday pages. The cartoon lettering style has become an integral part of comic strip graphics. Many cartoonists tailor the basic style to a more personal expression. Walt Kelly employs various fonts to identify special characters. While caps are the norm, some, such as *Gasoline Alley*, use upper and lower case and a few, like *Barnaby*, have used actual type.

Integrating in the Comics

The changing social structure of American society is no better revealed than in the integration of the comics in the 1960's. While there were leading black characters heretofore, notably Lothar in *Mandrake the Magician*, consideration of the Southern newspaper market prevented the syndication of strips with major black characters, except for stereotypes. This was of course also true in other media: TV, films, and advertising. The civil rights movement and the black revolution forced a reevaluation of the role of blacks in the comics, as it did throughout all of society.

In some cases portrayals of blacks were more sympathetic in the early formative days of the comics at the turn of the century, when ethnic humor was less self-conscious, as seen in Outcault's *Lil' Mose* and Kimble's *Blackberries*. Irish, Jewish, and other ethnic

Outdoor Sports by Tad (Thomas Dorgan).
© 1928 International Features Service.

"A Successful Diagnosis" by A. B. Frost in *Scribner's* magazine, 1889.

The role of the black in early comics, as in life, was largely restricted to menial jobs. *Moon Mullins.* © 1926 The Chicago Tribune.

humor was prevalent in the first decades. But the role of the black until the sixties was mostly confined to stereotypes in graphics and dialogue, as in McManus' *Hambone & Gravy*; Smokey, Joe Palooka's valet; Mushmouth in *Moon Mullins*; and Asbestos, the stableboy, in *Joe and Asbestos*.

After World War II black action groups such as the NAACP protested the crude portrayals of blacks and their relegation to servile roles of maids, bootblacks, and the like. While the black had not yet achieved his full rights of citizenship, he was no longer an acceptable figure for ridicule. The comic strips that retained black roles abandoned extreme caricature for a more realistic representation. Even Lothar, a sympathetic character and a man of great strength and intelligence, became Mandrake's associate rather than his servant.

A stereotyped native chief from an early *Katzenjammer Kids*, the first dialect strip.

"The Kalsomine Family's Glee Club in Full Action" by George Luks in 1897.
A black version of *Down in Hogan's Alley,* also drawn by Luks.

Ironically, African natives were portrayed more accurately in *Tarzan* by Foster and Hogarth at a time when black Americans were still being given stereotyped treatment. Nonetheless, *Tarzan* drew criticism from UN African delegations for projecting an image of Africa as a continent consisting solely of jungles and uneducated natives.

There followed a period of acute racial sensitivity in the comics. While the stereotypes disappeared, the black could still not be treated with equality and a curious double standard evolved. The special problems were explored in Ponchitta Pierce's article, "What's Not So Funny About the Comics," in *Ebony* magazine in November, 1966. Bob Dunn *(They'll Do It Every Time)* was quoted on portraying a black in a

bar; "I'm not sure I could let myself go. I'd have to be sure he's sweet and nice and not offensive."

It was felt that the point was not yet reached where the black could laugh at himself. As Al Capp put it, "The day we can draw a Negro, girl or boy, in caricature, or in a funny situation, the civil rights movement will be over." The immediate result was that blacks became less visible on the comic pages, whereas the blacks themselves wanted to get rid of the stereotype and to replace it with roles that reflected their growing participation in society.

In 1961, when *On Stage* featured a black in a major role as a music coach in one episode, four newspapers canceled the strip, three in the South and one in the North. Black officers began to appear in Steve

Morrie Turner's pioneer integrated strip, *Wee Pals.*
© 1971 Register & Tribune Syndicate.

Two kid strips reflect life in the black ghetto:
(above) *Luther* by Brumsic Brandon, Jr. © 1971 Los Angeles Times Syndicate, reprinted with permission;
(below) *Quincy* by Ted Shearer. © 1970 King Features Syndicate, Inc.

Canyon's Air Force and Kerry Drake's police department.

Until the sixties few black cartoonists achieved national syndication, E. Simms Campbell (*Cuties*) being a notable exception. As did other professions, syndication began to attract the talents of black cartoonists such as Morrie Turner, Brumsic Brandon, Jr., and Ted Shearer.

In 1965 Turner started *Wee Pals*, the first truly integrated strip. The cast includes children of various ethnic backgrounds, and the humor occasionally focuses on race relations. Turner, a former police department clerk in Oakland, California, was inspired by the success of black humorist Dick Gregory. Brumsic Brandon, Jr., introduced *Luther*, another integrated kid strip, in 1968. In 1970 Ted Shearer, a television art director for a major U.S. advertising agency, created *Quincy*, a warmhearted strip (in the *Skippy* tradition) about a nine-year-old black child in a ghetto. To involve the reader with his characters, Shearer includes authentic backgrounds of grimy streets and dilapidated tenements. One poignant strip,

for example, has Quincy carrying a glass of water through the street and carefully watering a tiny weed struggling to grow through the cracked pavement. "Gotta let it know someone cares," he soliloquizes.

Butter & Boop is another strip about a black youngster growing up in the ghetto. Written by Lewis Slaughter and drawn by Ed Carr and Claude Tyler, it began in ten black newspapers in 1969 and was nationally syndicated in 1971. The year 1971 also saw *The Badge Guys* by Chuck Bowen and Ted Schwarz, a humorous police strip with an integrated cast.

In 1968 the first integrated adventure strip with a black co-hero appeared: *Dateline: Danger*, written by John Saunders and illustrated by Alden McWilliams. It featured the reporting team of Danny Raven, a former black football star, and the tall blond Troy Young, who traveled the world pursuing exclusive stories.

The role of blacks in the adventure strip reached its fulfillment with *Friday Foster*, the first black heroine in the strip of the same name. It dealt with the glamorous jet-set world of high fashion and the media

221

The first black heroine, *Friday Foster* by Jim Lawrence and Jorge Longaron.
© 1972 The Chicago Tribune.

jungle. *Foster* was a long-distance collaboration between Jim Lawrence, a veteran adventure strip and science-fiction writer, living in Summit, New Jersey, and Jorge Longaron, an experienced illustrator of juvenile books and comic magazines, who works in Barcelona, Spain. Longaron has a brilliant illustrative style and composed each strip with great technical virtuosity. In spite of his living in Spain, Longaron imbued his strip with a contemporary spirit in his use of authentic New York backgrounds and careful attention to fads and fashions. Integration of the comics suffered a setback in 1973, however, when both *Friday Foster* and *Dateline: Danger* succumbed owing to failing sales.

In the eighty years of comic strips a cycle has almost been completed, where blacks are again featured, although without the earlier stereotypes and the more recent self-consciousness. The comics, along with the rest of the entertainment media, are reaching a greater degree of maturity by appealing to all elements of society and by satirizing and ridiculing the importance of their differences. Of course it would be naïve to ignore the fact that the evolution was greatly assisted by the growing market in the black community.

While some deplored the popularization of bigotry and ethnic humor, others welcomed the fact that real problems were at last being dealt with in the comics and on TV. In fact, it became *de rigueur* for strips without black characters to introduce them. In 1968 Franklin, a black youngster, joined the cast of *Peanuts*. In 1970 Lieutenant Flap, a hip black with an Afro and goatee, made his debut in *Beetle Bailey* with the memorable opening line, "How come there's no blacks in this honky outfit?" Three Southern papers refused to run any Lieutenant Flap episodes. Even *Stars and Stripes* dropped the strip, but after an overwhelmingly favorable reaction by both black and white readers, it was shortly restored. Walker sees the lieutenant as "just another funny character in my lineup, who will get his lumps and his laughs along with the other dopey denizens of Camp Swampy." Lieutenant Flap may be ushering in a new era of unself-conscious treatment of ethnic characters and a greater sophistication in humor strips.

Beetle Bailey deals with black aspirations. © 1971 King Features Syndicate, Inc.

COMIC SUPPLEMENT
OF THE
NEW YORK
AMERICAN
AND JOURNAL
MAY 25th 1902
COPYRIGHT 1902 BY W R HEARST

The Sunday comics section has been an American family tradition since the *Yellow Kid*. Most Sunday newspapers come wrapped in the multicolored comic pages. It has become an integral part of the feel and smell and look of Sunday morning and, for generations of Americans, the most fought-over section of the paper. Children have literally got up in the wee hours to meet the delivery boy to be first with the comics. For them Sunday was the highlight of the week: The glorious, garish colors danced in row after row after row of neatly ruled boxes; the bubbling, floating balloons streamed from the mouths of absurd and grotesque and heroic characters in a panoply of low comedy and high adventure. They brought a bit of entertainment to the Depression home, romance and exotic locales to rural America, and humor and escape to millions of the sick and confined. The Sunday comics have a unique intimacy: leisurely read while sprawled on the floor, relaxing on the couch, or even savored with a special Sunday breakfast in bed. The atmosphere allowed an involvement that the daily strips or, indeed, any other entertainment media could not match. The Sunday comics, week to week, provided a cumulative experience that often lasted a

''Getting in Training'' from *Family Portraits* by J. Norman Lynd. © 1941 King Features Syndicate, Inc.

The pretensions of the privileged class dissected in W. E. Hill's *Among Us Mortals*. © 1920 New York Tribune.

lifetime. Today if the passion is not perhaps as intense, the reading of the comics in most American households is still a Sunday ritual.

From the time of the *Yellow Kid* until the first daily strip, *Mutt and Jeff,* in 1907, comic features were practically all Sunday pages. Since the advent of the daily strip most became either daily strips alone or daily with a Sunday page. However, many features continued to be created solely for the Sunday comics section. Many classic strips of humor and adventure have been exclusively Sunday features, such as *Prince Valiant* and *The Little King*.

Among the early notable Sunday pages was W. E. Hill's *Among Us Mortals* (1916), a page of sharp satirical character sketches in a near-photographic style. J.

Norman Lynd's *Family Portraits* and Russell Cole's *Topical Page* were later features of a similar concept. *Dinny Doodles* by F. C. Collinge was a unique page of pictures, verse, and music in the 1920's.

Another Sunday feature of picture and verse of the time was *We Have with Us Today* by the noted sportswriter Grantland Rice and J. N. (Ding) Darling, a Pulitzer Prizewinning editorial cartoonist. Tony Sarg's *Lazy Larry* also appeared in the twenties.

Tales from the Great Book (1954) were illustrated Biblical stories by John Lehti. Other features drawing on historical, educational, and literary sources are Disney's *Treasury of Classic Tales* (1952) and *Our New Age* (1958) by Athelstan Spilhaus and Gene Fawcette.

Ever since Palmer Cox's *Brownies* was first

Walt Scott's *The Little People*. © 1968 NEA, Inc.

True Classroom Flubs & Fluffs by Jerry Robinson. © 1965 News Syndicate, Inc.

published in *St. Nicholas Magazine* in the late 1800's, tales of fantasies about tiny people have enthralled youngsters. Other worlds in microcosm have been seen in *Teenie Weenies* (1933) by William Donahey, *Tiny Tim* (1936) by Stanley Link, and Walt Scott's *The Little People* (1952).

In the tradition of early comic supplements three features were created for the family Sunday audience: *Flubs & Fluffs* (1964) by Jerry Robinson, a visual parody of true classroom boners; "*Super*" *Duper* (1968) by Rolf Ahlsen and Bill Kresse, the antics of an easily diverted apartment house superintendent; and *Sunday Comics* (1974) a mélange of gags by the noted magazine cartoonist Gahan Wilson.

Panels

If the comic strip is the "film" then the panel (and magazine) cartoon is the "still." The strip is a continuing development of narrative and character; the panel is, for the most part, a single quintessential moment. Whereas the essence of the comic strip is movement, the panel, like the painting, is a frozen event. The ability to capture that exact suspended moment is the art of the panel cartoonist.

While lacking the picture sequence of the strip, many panel cartoons have had a continuity of theme or character giving them an identity beyond the usual anonymous magazine cartoon from which they evolved. While restricted by format in storytelling, the panel's scope of subject material was unlimited. It provided a flexibility in makeup from the strip and could be used throughout the newspaper in addition to the comic pages. The demand for the panel cartoon grew. By the 1930's panels were a well-established staple, and soon practically all newspapers carried them to complement their strips. Syndicates have continuously found a ready pool of talented panel cartoonists who sharpened their techniques in the popular magazines. *The New Yorker*, founded in 1925, refined the traditional "he and she" joke into the succinct and sophisticated "one-liner." The often crude and vulgar graphic humor as seen in *Puck, Life*, and *Judge* of the 1880's and 1890's were the predecessors. From the 1920's on, the panel cartoon became an integral part of virtually every American magazine. Established magazine cartoonists such as Gluyas

225

Judge Rummy's Court by "Tad" Dorgan. © 1919 International Features Service.

Williams, Otto Soglow, Carl Anderson, Rea Irvin, and Mort Walker created strips. Others brought to the panel characters developed in the magazine, such as *Little Lulu, Hazel,* and *Tippie.* Some features, such as *Dennis the Menace* and *Toonerville Trolley,* have been daily panels but continuity strips on their Sunday pages.

Three gifted cartoonists created a social portrait of America with perceptive definition: Thomas Aloysuis "Tad" Dorgan (1877–1929), Clare Briggs (1875–1929), and H. T. Webster (1885–1925). Tad Dorgan, born in San Francisco, was one of the country's great sports cartoonists, as well as a political cartoonist for the New York *Journal,* before creating his first strip, *Judge Rummy's Court.* He also did an early panel of riddles and poems, *Daffydils, Silk Hat Harry* (the characters were dogs in human dress), and *For Better or Worse* (a

Sunday page about a slightly daft couple). But in *Indoor Sports* and *Outdoor Sports* he found the perfect format for his rich comic gifts. In the tradition of T. E. Powers, Tad's humor was lusty and yet capable of sensitivity. His forte was the put-down, and his panels were full of droll characters and fanciful dialogue. The caustic comments of the background players mocked the assorted pomposities of the others. Tad enriched the popular idiom with catchphrases: "applesauce," "ball and chain," "the cat's pajamas," "yes, we have no bananas," "23-skiddoo," "cake eater," "benny" (for hat), "dogs" (for feet), "you said it." His comments included, "You'll find sympathy in the dictionary" and "Half the world are squirrels and the other half are nuts."

Briggs and Webster, both born in Wisconsin, were masters of extracting humor from the mundane. As

Tad's *Indoor Sports* and *Outdoor Sports* were a broad burlesque of human foibles. © 1927 International Features Service, Inc.

Coulton Waugh described Briggs, "It's the idea that gets you: the homeyness, the truth of it, the insight, the looking into so many tiny dramas, the hopes and frustrations, which no one else ever bothered with, and which are utterly real." Briggs was an experienced newspaperman (as were Tad and Webster) before creating his famous panel in 1917. The title changed from day to day according to his subject. Some of them became standard themes, their titles reflecting the flavor of the gentler life and concerns of the early decades of the century: *Ain't It a Grand and Glorious Feeling?*, *In the Days of Real Sport*, *When a Feller Needs a Friend*, *That Guiltiest Feeling*, *Someone Is Always Taking the Joy Out of Life*, and *It Happens in the Best of Regulated Families*. Briggs' classic strip of family life, *Mr. and Mrs.*, featuring the squabbles of Joe and Vi, evolved from the panel. It was continued after Briggs' death by Frank Fogarty, Ellison Hoover, Arthur Folwell, and Kim Platt.

H. T. Webster's panel was also notable for its series of subtitled themes. His genteel style and subtle humor reflected the relatively uncomplicated tempo of the times. Some of the best known included *Life's Darkest Moment*, *The Thrill That Comes Once in a Lifetime*, *How to Torture Your Wife*, *Boyhood Ambitions*, *The Event Leading Up to the Tragedy*, and perhaps the one most quoted of its time, *Bridge*. Webster's first strip in 1923 was *The Man in the Brown Derby* chronicling the petty failures of Egbert Smear and wife. However, it was the character of Caspar Milquetoast in *the Timid Soul*, which evolved from Egbert, that became Webster's most lasting contribution to the American idiom, the epitome of the henpecked, cringing, feeble husband.

Another notable cartoonist of the same school was J. R. Williams. Some of the classic subtitles to his panel, *Out Our Way*, created in 1922, were *Born Fifty*

The Saturday golf cartoon from *That Guiltiest Feeling* by Clare Briggs in 1919. © The New York Tribune, Inc.

Out Our Way by J. R. Williams. © 1963 N.E.A., Inc.

One of H. T. Webster's classic series on *Bridge*. © 1931 New York Tribune, Inc.

227

"Mae's a Joke. Why, it took her three months of trying before she could even be introduced to him, and now she keeps telling him it was fate brought them together."

Metropolitan Movies by Deny s Wortman.
© 1941 New York World-Telegram.

Our Boarding House by Gene Ahern.
Major Hoople in a typical ego trip. © 1927 N.E.A., Inc.

"Supposin' I am late to dinner, if a customer finally shows up and it's before closing time, am I gonna worry your soup's getting cold on the table?"

From the series "In and Out of the Red with Sam" in Wortman's *Metropolitan Movies*.
© 1941 New York World-Telegram.

Years Too Soon, Why Mothers Get Gray, The Worry-Wart, and *Heroes Are Made—Not Born*. Williams, too, did a Sunday family strip of *Out Our Way*, featuring the day-to-day trivia of the Willett family. The Sunday is now done by Ed Sullivan and the daily by Negley Cochran.

A panel of great depth and perception in the tradition of Briggs and Webster was *Everyday Movies* by Denys Wortman. (It was created in 1913 by Roland Kirby, who went on to become a Pulitzer Prizewinning political cartoonist.) Convincingly drawn, it caught the tawdry quality of city life, from Times Square to Coney Island: tenements and cold-water flats, sidewalk peddlers and Seventh Avenue merchants, saucy secretaries and brassy dance hall girls, sailors on leave, as well as the continuing vignettes of two bums, Mopey Dick and the Duke. Wortman's view of urban life wasn't sentimental. He captured its grime and its sadness, along with its poignant humor, in telling detail. Wortman died in 1957.

Gluyas Williams, the noted *New Yorker* cartoonist, also did a panel of distinction that delicately delineated urban-suburban absurdities. Titled *Suburban Heights*, it was a pantomime with text, and Williams often used sequences within the single panel.

One of the most successful panel concepts has been Robert Ripley's *Believe It or Not!*, created in 1918. It is the repository of all oddity, animal, vegetable, or mineral: bizarre freaks and fanatics, fakirs and fakers, uncanny coincidences and unbelievable statistics. Ripley's most controversial cartoons were the Marching Chinese and Lindbergh's Flight. If all the Chinese in the world were to march four abreast past a given point, they would never finish passing though they marched forever and ever. His Lindbergh Believe It or Not was that the Lone Eagle was the sixty-seventh man to make a nonstop flight over the Atlantic Ocean. Paul Frehm, an experienced illustrator, has continued the feature since Ripley's death in 1949. Elsie Hix's *Strange as It Seems* and R. J. Scott's *Did You Know?* were other panels dedicated to the incredible.

Our Boarding House, later to star the bombastic, stuffed-shirt Major Hoople, was created by Gene Ahern in 1921 with the *Squirrel Cage* as the top. NOV SHMOZ KA POP, a nonsense line that was widely parroted, originated in the *Squirrel Cage. Our Boarding House* was continued after Ahern's death by Bill Freyse for many years and recently by Les Carroll and Tom McCormick. Ahern, who previously did *Auto Otto*, left Newspaper Enterprise Association and created *Room and Board* for King Features in 1934 with Judge Puffle taking on the Major Hoople persona.

Jimmy Hatlo created *They'll Do It Every Time* to replace *Indoor Sports* and *Outdoor Sports* when Tad Dorgan died in 1929. *They'll Do It Every Time* celebrates society's obnoxious characters and relishes exposing their hypocrisies. In a split panel it examines the double standard practiced in everyday life. Many of the true-to-life incidents are contributed by readers, who are thanked in the cartoon with a "tip of the Hatlo hat." Little Iodine, first seen as a popular supporting character, was rewarded with her own strip in 1941.

Bob Dunn continues the rich comic tradition of Gross and Hatlo. Dunn, son of a Newark, New Jersey, fire captain, spent three years at the Art Students League, and his first job was for the Newark *Ledger*. In 1933 he joined King Features Syndicate, where he created his first comic page, *Just the Type*. Dunn was Hatlo's assistant for many years. Since Hatlo's death in 1963, he has continued *They'll Do It Every Time* with associate Al Scaduto, and *Little Iodine* with Hy Eisman. Dunn, a warm, gregarious, and genuinely funny man, has contributed his own comic inventions to the burlesque of assorted pests, chiselers, loafers, and braggarts.

The oddities of life by Robert Ripley.
© 1959 King Features Syndicate, Inc.

The vanities of man exposed in Jimmy Hatlo's celebrated panel.
© 1943 King Features Syndicate, Inc.

Bob Dunn adds his own flourish to Hatlo's creation with the aid of Al Scaduto.
© 1971 King Features Syndicate.

"Three girls won contests, wearing our suits—unfortunately, they also were arrested."

Cuties by E. Simms Campbell.
© 1971 King Features Syndicate.

As official toastmaster, Dunn with his irreverent introductions has for years enlivened meetings of the National Cartoonists Society. An accomplished writer of comic skits and an experienced chalk-talk artist, he has been seen on his two TV shows, *Face to Face* and *Quick on the Draw*. Dunn has also authored a number of humor books, including *I'm Gonna Be a Father, One Day in the Army, Hospital Happy*, and *Knock! Knock!*

There Ought to Be a Law, created by Al Fagaly and Harry Shorten in 1944, now done by Whipple and Barth, is a split panel that also explores the basic themes of the lusty put-down pioneered by Tad Dorgan.

The influence of the flapper, as portrayed by Russell Patterson, led to the popularity of the glamor girl. In World War II the flapper became the pin-up girl and the long-stemmed, busty, not-too-bright model-types proliferated. Their principal exponents were leading

"...And the man we pick must not only have the stamina to go into orbit...he must also be able to endure the countless luncheon and banquet meetings, afterwards!"

"I've tried to give them every kind of medical warning, doctor!...Maybe it would help if you told the students that marijuana causes pimples!"

George Lichty's stylish panel *Grin and Bear It.* © 1959 Field Enterprises, Inc. © 1968 Publishers-Hall Syndicate.

magazine cartoonists: Jefferson Machamer (*Gags & Gals*), E. Simms Campbell (*Cuties*), Don Flowers (*Modest Maidens*), and Jay Allan (*Glamour Girls*). The postwar transition to the liberated working woman was epitomized by the attractive secretaries of Gregory d'Alessio's *These Women*. D'Alessio gave up his stylish panel for a distinguished career as a painter and instructor at the Art Students League. Today's working girl can be seen in Phil Interlandi's bright and saucy *Queenie*.

Lichty, né George Lichtenstein, born in Chicago, edited the University of Michigan's *Gargoyle*. He won an Essex Sports Roadster in the 1928 College Humor contest (third prize was won by Milton Caniff). A cartoon career was inevitable. While on the Chicago *Times* he created the strip *Sammy Squirt*. *Grin and Bear It* has consistently been one of the most outrageously funny panels since its creation in 1932. Pompous tycoons, hypocritical politicians, and overbearing wives have been some of the favorite targets systematically destroyed by Lichty's deceptively slapdash burlesque style.

Side Glances, created by George Clark in 1929 and continued by William "Galbraith" Crawford in 1939 and later by Gil Fox, and *The Neighbors* (1939), also by

"Since I read that book on child psychology I understand why Junior acts as he does— but it doesn't make me like it any better!"

The Neighbors by George Clark. © 1963 The Chicago Tribune.

231

"Two degrees in business administration—and all you learned is 'Buy cheap, sell dear'?"

Strictly Richter by Mischa Richter.
© 1962 King Features Syndicate, Inc.

"THE BEAUTY SHOP JUST CALLED. THEY'RE CALLING BACK THIS MORNING'S GROUP."

The Lockhorns by Bill Hoest.
© 1970 King Features Syndicate, Inc.

George Clark, are skillfully executed and lively views of contemporary life. George Clark grew up in Arkansas and Oklahoma where his first art job was for the *Oklahoman* and *Times*. While still a teen-ager he worked on an animation of *The Gumps* along with another aspiring strip artist, Harold Gray (*Little Orphan Annie*). At twenty-one he headed the art department of the Cleveland *Press*. Clark's folksy

view of the office and domestic scene is told in beautifully rhythmic compositions and figures of supple and natural gestures. Typical of Clark's low-key approach is the child pausing to ask the teacher on the way home, "Did I learn anything today, Miss Watts?"

The panels of a number of cartoonists continued to parody a wide range of subjects, without set characters, in one-line gags as they did in the magazines. Among the earliest and longest running have been Fred Nehr's *Life's Like That* and Ed Reed's *Off the Record*, both started in 1934. Others have been Jo Fischer's popular *From Nine to Five* and noted *New Yorker* cartoonist Mischa Richter's *Strictly Richter*, beautifully executed in stark black and white. Of more recent vintage have been *Laughing Matter* by Salo (Roth), *Laughtime* by Bob Schroeder, and *Farriswheel* by Joseph Farris. Roth is a member of a unique cartooning family; his three brothers also became prominent magazine cartoonists: the late Ben Roth; Irving, who signs his work Roir; and Al, who adopted the name of Ross.

Other notable graduates of the magazine field created thematic panels. Ed Nofziger who had become identified with animal humor, drew *Animalogic*. Virgil Partch continued his brand of logical incongruity with *Big George*. Hank Ketcham created *Dennis the Menace*, who has become America's favorite brat. Jack Tippit continues the capers of the precocious moppet *Amy*, created by Harry Mace. Ted Key brought to the comics America's most famous maid, the ubiquitous *Hazel*, whose antics became so familiar in the *Saturday Evening Post* and on TV.

Fontaine Fox first used the bird's-eye view to record graphically a series of interrelated events in *Toonerville Trolley*. The potential of the device was further explored in Dudley Fisher's *Right Around Home* in 1938. It consisted of one crowded shot of frenetic family activity around the home, swarming with kids, pets, neighbors, workmen, and passersby, with simultaneous dialogue scattered throughout the page. Bil Keane in *Family Circus*, created in 1960, successfully continues the tradition each Sunday. It also appears as a daily panel. Keane started his professional career with the Philadelphia *Bulletin* and now resides in Phoenix with his wife, four boys, a girl, and a dog, all of whom were the original models of his cartoon family.

"Wow! I bet he's good at licking pans."

"Which is how YOU'LL sound if you don't practice."

"Don't forget to ask us to turn in our homework
...since I did mine."

still life by Jerry Robinson. © 1971 Chicago-Tribune-New York News Syndicate, Inc.

Political-social satire became the focus for a new genre in the 1960's. While there had been political allegory in such strips as *Pogo* and *Li'l Abner,* these new features comment directly on current issues with sophistication and indulge in undisguised caricature of leading public figures. Space on the editorial, or op-ed, pages, heretofore restricted to the newspaper's regular editorial cartoon, began to open for political satire with *still life* and *Berry's World.* Employing a new type of symbolism, *still life* by Jerry Robinson is the first feature with inanimate objects as its characters. Topical satire is expressed in the counterpoint between the objects and their irreverent dialogue, expressed in balloons rather than in the usual panel convention of captions. *still life* first appeared during the extended New York newspaper strike in February, 1963, on the editorial page of the *Metropolitan Daily* and on

NBC-TV News, and was soon nationally syndicated.

Berry's World, a witty and incisive satire by Jim Berry, also appeared in 1963. Berry employs a novel technique; his pencil drawings are Xeroxed for reproduction, retaining the spirit and spontaneity of the original sketch. Berry captures the essence of politicians with brilliant simplicity.

Others in the modern mold of political satire followed. In Morrie Brickman's *the small society* (1966) miniature political figures cavort against a Washington backdrop in an acid dialogue on political foibles. *Soliloquy* (1966) by Ric Hugo employs sequential monologue in a frameless strip. Ben Wicks has contributed his bright mini-editorial cartoon from Toronto since 1966. *Dunagin's People* (1970) by Ralph Dunagin is a trenchant commentary on the current scene, as, for example, a husband's sudden revelation:

the small society by Morrie Brickman. © 1972 Washington Star Syndicate.

"YOU SHOULD GIVE UP SMOKING!"

"ALBERT, SOMEDAY, LET'S BECOME REAL 'ACTIVISTS' AND WRITE A LETTER TO OUR CONGRESSMEN!"

"LOOK'S AS THOUGH OLE LYNDON HEADED 'EM OFF AT THE 'CREDIBILITY GAP'!"

Berry's World by Jim Berry. © 1968 N.E.A. Syndicate, Inc.

"The TV set was on the blink last night, and I discovered I was married and had two kids."

The eternal fall guy character has not been restricted to the strip. Panel versions are seen in various guises: Ned Riddle's *Mr. Tweedy*, Dave Gerard's *Citizen Smith*, McGowman Miller's *Noah Numbskull*, Dave Eastman's *Carmichael*, and the latest, *Simpkins* by George Crenshaw. Simpkins is not exactly a model of the competent, efficient American workingman but a lovable goof-up who is able to perform equally incompetently in all trades.

The husband-wife relationship is explored with comedic insight in *The Little Woman* by Don Tobin. Franklin Folger's *The Girls* is a loving view of the foibles and idiosyncrasies of the suburban matron, reminiscent of Helen Hokinson's amiable but vague clubwoman in *The New Yorker*.

"THE PRESIDENT SENDS HIS BEST... ME."

Dunagin's People by Ralph Dunagin.
© 1973 Publishers-Hall.

Soliloquy by Ric Hugo. © 1972 Publishers-Hall.

PEOPLE BLAME THE ADMINISTRATION FOR ESCALATING THE WAR BY BOMBING AND MINING HARBORS...

...RIDICULOUS—

...WE'RE MERELY ACCELERATING THE PACIFICATION!

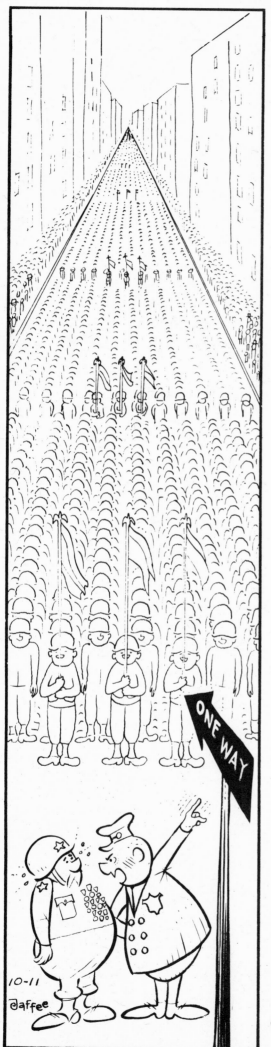

"You're right, Emma—it would be very unpatriotic to skip the Washington cherry-ice-cream dessert."

Franklin Folger's *The Girls.* © 1973 Publishers-Hall.

A unique panel is *Brother Juniper*, probably the first newspaper feature about a clergyman by a clergyman. It is undoubtedly a testament to Father Justin McCarthy's catholic humor that the strip found a mass audience.

A recent innovation has been the special interest panel. Because of their content and flexibility they are not confined to the comic pages but are used throughout the newspaper. Subjects have included: health, as in Michael Petti and Jud Hurd's *Health Capsules*; sports, as in *Looking Back in Sports* by Lenny Hollreiser, *Time Out* by Jeff Keate, *Trim's Arena* by Wayne Stayskal (Trim) and Eddie Germano's *Sporteaser* television, as in *TV Laughs* by Cliff Rogerson, *Channel Chuckles* by Bil Keane, and *TV Tee-Hees* by Henry Scarpelli, and finance, as in Henry Boltinoff's *Stoker the Broker*.

The search for the new ideas and formats have led to the adaptation in the 1970's of current political and social phenomena in such panels as *Graffiti, Bumper Stickers, Campaign Buttons, Button-A-Day*, and *Signs of the Times*. Another interesting experiment in format was Allan Jaffee's imaginative *Tall Tales*, a long, one-column panel.

Tall Tales by Allan Jaffee.
© 1958 New York Herald-Tribune, Inc.

The Imports

American comic strips have been translated into virtually every language. In many countries they have become so much a part of their culture that the fact that they are not indigenous creations is not generally known. On the other hand, few foreign imports have been successful in the United States. In most cases, they were created for a homogeneous population and culture, and their style and humor proved too narrow in appeal for the diverse American society. Some, however, have run for some time with varying degrees of success: an English family strip, *Pop*, by J. Millar Watt (1929); two South American strips, *Patoruzo*, a sort of gaucho *Popeye*, by Dante Quinterno (1949), and a beautifully drawn western, *The Cisco Kid* by José Luis Salinas (1951); three clever pantomimes—*Little Pedro* from Mexico by William de la Torre (1950), *Ferd'nand* by Dahl "Mik" Mikkelsen and *Moco* by Morgensen and Cornelius from Denmark; *Ginger* from Australia by James Bancks; *Fred Basset* from England by Alex Graham; and three English adventures—*Modesty Blaise* by Peter O'Donnell and Jim Holdaway, *Tiffany Jones* by Pat Tourret and Jenny Butterworth, and Ian Fleming's *James Bond* by John McLusky.

Little Pedro by William de la Torre. © 1971 Los Angeles Times, reprinted with permission.

Moco in a variation of the "marooned on a desert island" theme by Morgensen and Cornelius.
© 1972 Los Angeles Times, reprinted with permission.

The comic strip that has traveled best is an English import, *Andy Capp*. Reginald Smythe, a onetime butcher's helper in the English industrial town of Hartlepool, created the squat, potbellied, raffish and raucous limey in 1956. Capp is a lowbrow character in the tradition of Moon Mullins. A cigarette is permanently glued to Capp's lower lip, and he is always in a floppy cap, whether eating, sleeping, taking an infrequent bath, or, most frequently, drinking. Capp's doctor, in fact, once told him to cut down his drinking a shade and he'd have nothing to worry about. After mulling it over, Capp asked plaintively, "Can't yer operate?" He is outrageously arrogant, selfish, and rude, as well as a wife beater, which is a switch from American comic strip dogma, where the reverse has been the norm (as in Maggie clouting Jiggs with the rolling pin). His wife, Flo, regards him with mixed emotions: "Bein' away from 'im is almost as miserable as bein' with 'im." Andy, definitely not a sexist, once remarked about a neighbor, "Second time this week I've seen 'im kiss 'is missus. The man's a sex maniac." Andy's basic appeals, including an aversion to hard work, are seemingly widespread. Once Andy had a job. Returning home after a half hour, he told his wife that he had to quit because the foreman used obscene language. "He kept saying things like, 'Okay, mates, get your backs into it.' "

Reginald Smythe's *Andy Capp* discovers a forgotten virtue.
© 1972 Daily Mirror Newspaper Ltd.

This book makes no attempt to deal in any depth with the development of the comic strip abroad. In the European and South American tradition, comics are published in magazine and book form, as well as in the newspapers, and are worthy of separate study. While the comic strip is an American invention and has exerted a dominant influence throughout the world, Europe and South America have adopted the medium with great enthusiasm. They have developed cartoonists of extraordinary talent who have created significant strips and introduced innovative techniques.

The pictorial narrative has been well established in Europe since the early nineteenth century with the work of Rodolphe Töpffer and later Wilhelm Busch *(Max und Moritz)*, Caran d'Ache, Georges (Christophe) Columb, *(La Famille Fenouillard)*, and others.

Alley Sloper's Half Holiday, a new comic weekly, appeared in England in 1884. Others in the magazine genre begun by *Punch* in 1841 followed, such as *Illustrated Chips* and *Comic Cuts* (1890), and *Dan Leno's Comic Journal* (1898). They introduced a rich collection of characters, among them Alley Sloper, a seedy loafer with sarcastic tongue by W. G. Baxter and

later, W. F. Thomas, and Tom Browne's Weary Willie and Tired Tim, a pair of ne'er-do-well pranksters. Noted music-hall comedians of the time (as was Dan Leno), T. E. Dunville and Charlie Chaplin, were also starred in the comic papers. The comics form was adopted by such pioneer Argentinian artists as Acquarone and Manuel Redondo in the magazine *Carcas y Caretas,* founded in 1898. The "Tokyo Puck," *Kitazawa,* brought the comics tradition to Japan in 1906.

Weary Willie and Tired Tim by Tom Browne, 1918.

1. Our merry adventurers went out and did some early Christmas shopping on the nod last Stewsday. "Get a move on yer, Willie!" twittered Tim. "P.-c. Parker's on our track." Then young Percy Pomeroy rolled up with his hoop.

The first appearance of *Charlie Chaplin* by A. T. (Bertie) Brown from *The Funny Wonder*, 1915.

1. Here he is, readers! Good old Charlie! Absolutely IT! A scream from start to finish. What's he doing now, eh? "'Twas here," says he, standing in a graceful posish, by an artistically designed coal-hole, with the faithful hound attached to his cane: "'Twas here I was to meet Maggie! Phwpsts!" But see! A rival approaches!

"Un Banco Quebrado" by Acquarone, 1901.

Sa grand'mère vient d'arriver à Clocher-les-Bécasses où elle doit passer quelques jours. « — Quelle douillette tu fais ! dit-elle à Bécassine... Enfin, c'est la première dent, j'vas la garder en souvenir. »

Bécassine, pour se remettre de cette grande émotion, a été se promener dans le village. « — Tiens, lui disent ses amies, t'as perdu une dent. — Elle èst pas perdue, répond-elle, puisque grand'mère l'a dans sa poche. »

Jean-Pierre Pinchon's *Bécassine,* excerpt from "La Dent Arranchee."
© Gauthier Languereau.

Les Pied-Nickelès (excerpt) by Louis Forton. © SPE

Le lendemain, Croquignol s'en alla retrouver Filochard et Ribouldingue pour leur dire :
« Notre régiment, la France entière ont les yeux sur nous. Du moment que nous avons commencé à les épater avec nos

exploits, nous ne pouvons plus en rester là... Tiens, v'là justement le sergent. » On demande, annonçait ce dernier, trois « poilus » décidés pour aller reconnaître les tranchées ennemies. « Sergent, gouaillait Ribouldingue, reconnaître les tranchées,

Attilio Mussino's *Bibolbul.* © Corrière dei Piccoli.

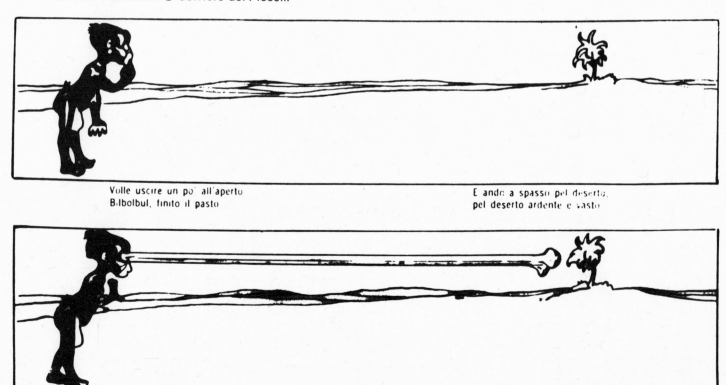

Volle uscire un po' all'aperto
Bibolbul, finito il pasto

E andò a spasso pel deserto,
pel deserto ardente e vasto

Una palma tremar vede
come se qualcun la tocchi

Per saper quel che succede
Bibolbul allunga gli occhi

Bonaventure by Sergio Tofano, 1917.

Jean-Pierre Pinchon, a French painter, drew *Bécassine* (1905), the adventures of a young French girl, with a text below the illustration in the tradition of the *Image d'Epinal*. The integration of the balloon, an American contribution, had not yet been adopted. Louis Forton's *Les Pied-Nickelès* (1908), about the escapades of three underworld characters, was another early comic with a complementary text. An early Italian strip was *Bilbolbul* by Attilio Mussino in 1909, about a little African boy, told in verse. Sergio Tofano's *Bonadventure* in 1917 featured a highly decorative linear style.

The comics form was expanded in Argentina by Arturo Lanteri with *Las Aventuras del Negro Raúl* in 1917 and *Pancho Talero* in 1922.

Zig et Puce by Alain Saint-Ogon in 1925 was the first genuine French comic strip. The world-spanning adventures of the two boys and their pet penguin often employed original pictorial techniques. One of the first daily strips in England was J. Millar Watt's *Pop* in 1921, featuring the low-key humor of a squat, top-hatted, offbeat hero. In .1934 the daily strip was introduced in France with *Les Adventures du Professeur Nimbus* by A. Daix. The first modern adventure strip in Europe was René Pellos' *Futuropolis* in 1937. Perhaps the most famous of European comics is Georges "Hergé" Rémi's *Tintin*, first introduced in 1929. The beautifully delineated adventures of the boy, Tintin, and his dog, Snowy, have since appeared in dozens of books as well as its own magazine. Among other popular features are André Franquin's wild adventures of a hotel page boy *Spirou* (1938) created by Robert Velter, and Maurice (Morris) de Bévère and writer René Goscinny's charming western spoof *Lucky Luke* (1947) in Belgium, and Tove Jansson's *Mumin* (1949) in Finland, a sensitive fantasy of comic trolls in the tradition of European fairy tales.

The foreign comics in the modern era have enjoyed a much greater degree of freedom in content than their American counterparts. One of the earliest to

Les Aventures du Professeur Nimbus by A. Daix. © Opera Mundi.

An innovative page from *Zig et Puce* by Alain Saint-Ogon.
© Alain Saint-Ogon.

Tintin by Hergé (Georges Rémi) from *Flight 714.* © 1973 Casterman.

Linear design in the manner of Aubrey Beardsley by Guido Crepax in *Valentina*.
© 1968 Guido Crepax.

Lucky Luke by Morris (Maurice de Bévère) and René Goscinny.
© 1967 Corriere dei Piccoli. By permission of Dargaud Editeur.

Hugo Pratt's *Captain Cormorant.*
© 1967 Editrice Sergente Kirk-SRL.

reflect the more permissive standards in European newspapers was the English strip *Jane* by Norman Pett in 1932. *Neutron* by Guido Crepax is a starkly drawn, slightly sadomasochistic adventure strip, and *Barbarella* by Jean Claude Forest is a sensuous tongue-in-cheek fantasy, with a lithe, semi-nude heroine. Guy Peellaert adopts pop art iconography in *Jodelle.* Italy's Hugo Pratt *(Sergeant Kirk* and *L'Ombra)* is a superb stylist and storyteller. Philippe Druillet *(Torquedara Varenkor)* of France is a wildly imaginative innovator of science fiction, employing elements from *art nouveau* to pop art in carefully structured architectural and geometric shapes. The American West has inspired some excellent dramatic interpretations by foreign cartoonists, among them France's Joseph "Jijé" Gillain *(Jerry Spring),* and J. "Gir" Girard *(Fort Navajo),* England's Harry Bishop *(Gun Law),*

Randall by Arturo del Castillo.
© 1957 Frontera.

Lt. Blueberry by Gir (J. Girard) and J. M. Charlier. © Dargaud.

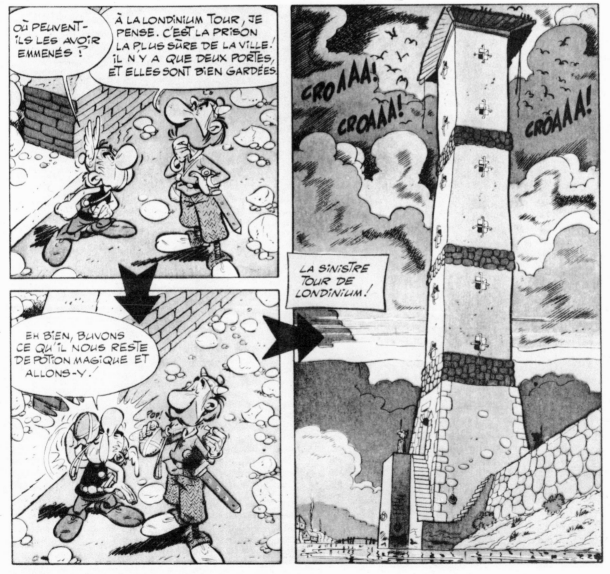

Astérix by Albert Uderzo and and René Goscinny from
Astérix's Chez les Bretons. © 1966 Dargaud.

'*Easy, Easy!*', a modern Japanese folktale
by Eka Nohazima. © 1957 The Bungei-Shunju.

and in Argentina, Arturo del Castillo *(Ralph Kendall)*. Alberto and Enrique Braccia are also South American cartoonists of extraordinary imagination.

Two extremely popular comic fantasies are *Astérix* by Albert Uderzo and René Goscinny, a broad burlesque about a warrior from Gaul in 50 B.C. in the tradition of "comic histories," and *Les Schtroumpfs* by Peyo and Raymond Macherot, a mythical world of gnomes and goblins, reminiscent of *The Brownies.* England also has developed a number of brilliant illustrative stylists, among them Sydney Jordan *(Jeff Hawke)*, Ernest Ratcliff *(Lindy)*, and David Wright *(Carol Day).* Some other noteworthy contributors in Europe have been Jean Ache *(Arabelle)*, Robert Gigi *(Scarlet Dream)*, Paul Gillon *(The Shipwrecked People of time)*, and Maurice Tillieux *(Gil Jourdan)* in France; Fritz Raab and F. W. Richter-Johnson *(Taro)* in Germany, and José Cabrero-Arnal *(Pif le Chien)* in Spain.

Epilogue

America has been habitually slow to recognize its own fertile inventions as "culture." Lasting values have been detected in such American phenomena as jazz, hillbilly, and folk music, the movies, and even television. Ignatius Mattingly, the noted writer and critic, pointed out: "It may almost be set down as a law of cultural history that the vulgar amusements of today are the highbrow art of tomorrow." Italian opera and Elizabethan drama were conceived for the entertainment of the masses, as were the comics. It remained for Gilbert Seldes to include the comics among his *Seven Lively Arts*.

With the birth of the comic strip and the pioneer cartoonist-painters—Luks, Dirks, and Feininger—there has been a continuous interplay with the fine arts. To ignore one form is not fully to understand the other. Picasso, a comics admirer, utilized the comics form in *The Dream and the Life of Franco* in 1937. Jesse was one of the first to recognize the potential of the cartoon idiom for a series of collages, *Tricky Cad*, starting in 1953. Roy Lichtenstein has made extensive use of comic strip iconography for conceptual and structural elements. Andy Warhol (*Nancy*, 1961), Mel Ramos (*Batman*, 1962 and *Phantom*, 1963), Claes Oldenburg (*Mickey Mouse*, 1963), and Ray Yoshida (*Comic Book Specimens*, 1969) are others among those who found the comics a rich source of inspiration, reflecting the deep cultural absorption of its imagery.

The basis of comic art is the visual-verbal statement existing in a single frame forming an imagery that is a totally integrated unit. The flat areas of primary colors, the bold outlines, the border frame that reinforces the two-dimensionality of the picture, the significant use of the balloon that at once separates and yet unites the text and drawing, the concept of multiple repetitive images, the elements of grotesquerie, the reproduction techniques such as Benday—all of these are comic strip devices employed in pop art.

At the time that D. W. Griffith introduced the close-up and the montage in the film, these devices were in wide use in the comic strips. Federico Fellini, Alain Resnais, and Orson Welles have also adapted techniques of the comics in their work.

The comic strip is a singular form of creative expression. Unlike the film or play that requires the coordination of many individual talents, the comic strip is usually the effort of one person. Unlike the novel or painting which normally involves weeks, months, or years of work and many stages of refinement, the comic strip is usually drawn in the space of hours and, moreover, reaches its audience within days or weeks of its conception. This gives the comic its special qualities of immediacy and spontaneity.

Comic art is now being studied throughout the world: Francis Lacassin, noted French critic, conducts a course in comics aesthetics at the Sorbonne; Professor Francisco Araujo holds the chair in Comics at the University of Brasília; and a course in Comparative Comics was held at Brown University. Syracuse, Boston, Kansas, California, and other universities have acquired notable collections of original comic strip art. Cartoon exhibitions have been held at leading museums and galleries, including the Metropolitan, the Smithsonian, and the Louvre. A number of annual exhibitions have been established, notably, The International Salon of Humor in Bordighera, Italy, in 1947; the International Salon of Cartoons at the Pavilion of Humor in Montreal, Canada, 1964; and the International Salon of Comics, sponsored by the University of Rome, known as the Lucca Congress, in Lucca, Italy, 1964. Other exhibitions have been held in Belgium, Sweden, Finland, Germany, England, Brazil, and Japan. The First World Comic Biennial was sponsored by the Escuela Panamerica de Arte in Buenos Aires, Argentina, in 1968, and the First International Comics Congress was held at the Museu de Arte, São Paulo, Brazil, in 1970. The National Cartoonists Society sponsored the First International Congress of Comics in New York in 1972. Founded in 1946, the National Cartoonists Society has a membership of almost five hundred of the leading cartoonists in America and abroad. In 1955 a group of major newspaper publishers and editors, syndicate executives and cartoonists formed The Newspaper Comics Council and, for the first time, the diverse

factions in the industry began to work together for the advancement of the medium. Other organizations for the study and advancement of the comic arts include Socerlid, a society of students of the comics founded in Paris in 1967, and ICON, an international comics organization founded in Brazil in 1970.

In reviewing an exhibition of the development of graphic humor from the fifteenth century to the present at the Bibliothèque Nationale in Paris, David L. Shirley, art critic of the New York *Times*, wrote, "A successful trenchant rebuttal to the long cherished notion that if it makes you laugh, it isn't art." Now that the point has been reached where the comic strip is viewed in museums for its aesthetics, studied in universities as literature, and researched, catalogued, and defined by historians, will the comic strip become too pretentious and lose its essential naïveté? I suspect not. Despite its detractors, imitators, exploiters, and even its ardent disciples, it will go on performing the function for which it was originally intended and what it has been doing with such élan for almost eighty years . . .entertain.

General Subject Index

Index of Cartoonists and Other Artists*

*Numbers in italics refer to illustrations.

252

Index of Cartoon Titles*

*Numbers in italics indicate illustrations.